CHRISTOPHER J. STOCKWELL

The Complete Down and Out in Seattle and Tacoma Series

Sleeping in the Daytime Novella One: Courting Mediocrity Novella Two: Squatting in the Shadow of an Ant Novella Three

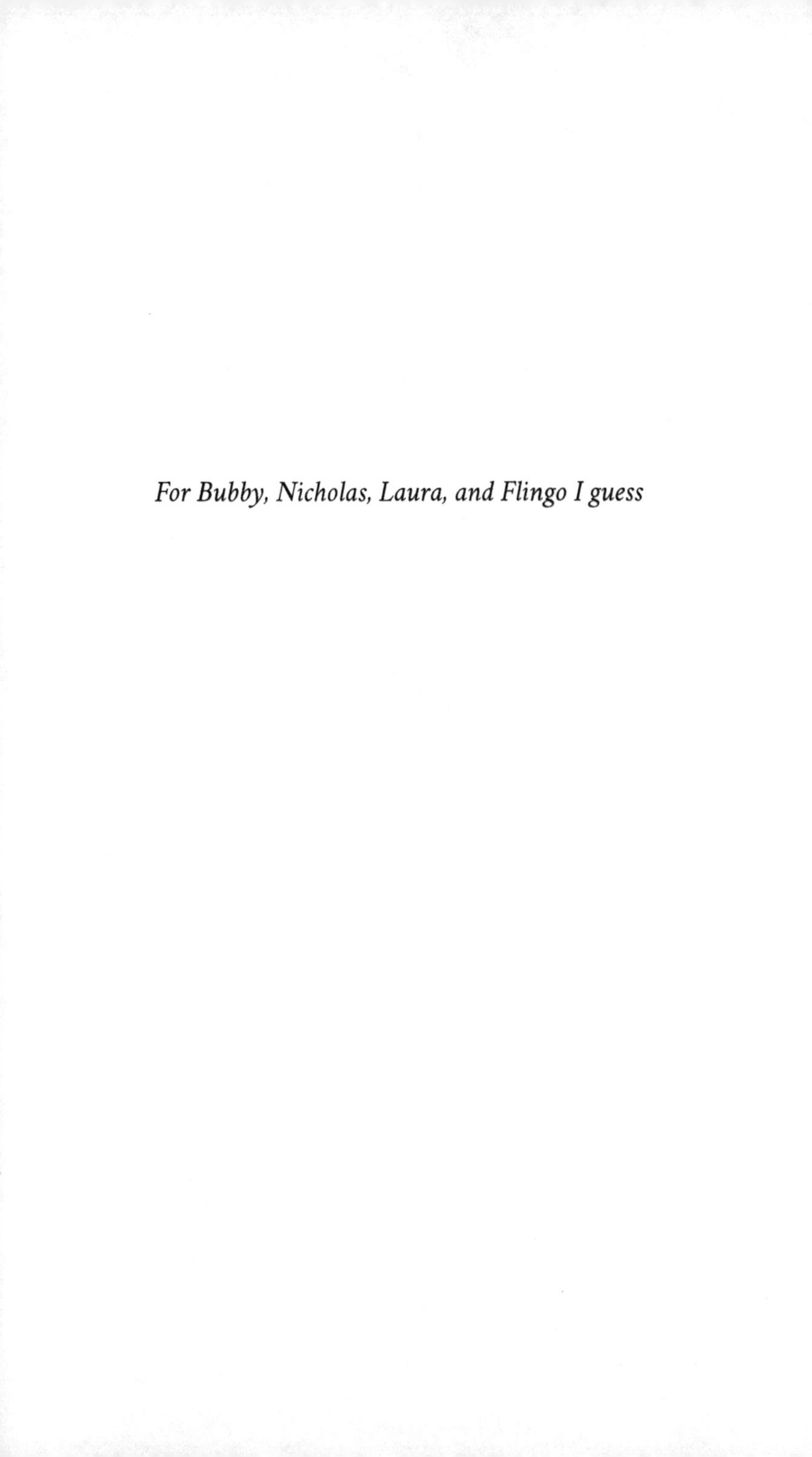

For Bubby, Nicholas, Laura, and Flingo I guess

Preface

"Why do you write?" She asked me during my first press interview for this book. "Why do you fuckin' care," is what my bestie Jack would say. He's always inside me trying to push his way out. When people take a tone, or give me orders, Jack bristles. Chris has a wife, kids, and a mortgage, so most of the time, Chris is charged with keeping Jack in check. Jack is why I write. The world moved on without Jack. His music scene is nothing but burnt ash from the campfire the night before. Jack's city doesn't exist anymore. It might as well be called Seattle 2.0.

I'm a workers' rights attorney, a former prosecutor. When I put on a suit, you can't see me, or should I say you see my mask. Who am I? I'm the counterculture hiding in plain sight. Punk rock gave me a worldview, and I bring that worldview into society every time I speak in a courtroom or you flip the page of one of my books.

Why do I write, because after all these years, Jack and I are still pissed off at the world and everyone in it. And we've still got something to say about it.

Prologue

Was I speaking for Jack, or was Jack speaking for me? I'm the narrator, and while I do most of the speaking in this story, I never get an opportunity to really speak. Jack has got a lot to say, and most of it requires some high-brow interpretation from yours truly. The PNW hoi polloi vernacular takes a little gettin' used to, you know. Fortunately, I'm well versed. So well versed in fact, that it seems like Jack and I used to be the same person. If not the same, then nearly identical, and certainly inseparable.

At some point that changed. I'm not sure when, but it did. He went down the left fork, and I the right. Jack's story became more compelling as he became less salvageable. My story became less interesting as I became more capable. So I became the caretaker of Jack's story just as Beth became the caretaker of his mind. I hope I did it justice.

I

Part One

<u>**Sleeping in the Daytime**</u>

"Living like this is a full-time business."
— Irvine Welsh, Trainspotting

Chapter 1

J ack was addicted to everything: everything he'd ever done, everywhere he'd ever been, and everyone he'd ever met. Painful, pleasurable—it didn't matter; he'd been addicted to it. The only thing he'd never been addicted to was a peaceful, simple life. That life never presented itself to him, but if it had, he might have become addicted to it, too. Probably not, but maybe. Sometimes he had used to wonder about that. Jack had used to daydream that if the sweet plainness of a domestic life ever became a reality for him, it would be the last addiction he'd ever need. That seemed far-fetched, but it gave him something to wonder about.

Jack had never really had a chance. In fact, Jack's *generation* had never really had a chance. He was a microcosm of Generation X and, as such, a perfect representative of the gritty little group. Gen X was like the sinking of the *Titanic*. A whole bunch of people died miserably under terrifying cir- cumstances and for no good reason at all. All of the survivors were traumatized for life, and they lived the remainder of their lives miserable and terrified. They wound up broken toys, shoved in a corner that the world never managed to dispose of. That was Gen X, broken toys occupying space.

There is no happy ending for Jack, but there is a story, and it's a story worth telling. After all, there weren't that many Gen Xers in the first place, there are a lot less of them now, and even fewer of them that would bother to tell the story of a guy like Jack.

Chapter 2

Jack was twenty-eight and was once again inside an institution. Fairfax Psychiatric Hospital, this time. This was actually his second time at Fairfax, but it wouldn't have mattered if it was his first or his fiftieth. It was nothing new to Jack. He'd lived in more institutions in his lifetime than actual residences.

Institutions were his homes, and he'd always felt comfortable in them. That might have been because they always looked the same. The nasty ones had pink tiles in the bathrooms and disgusting ammonia-soaked linoleum on the floor. The smell was always the same, too. Not only did the ammonia fail to cover up the smell, which could only be described as human desperation, but it was actually an integral part of the aroma. The nice ones were simply well-kept wings of nicer hospitals. Jack typically ended up in the nasty ones.

Despite a hundred diagnoses from a hundred different psychiatrists, nobody really knew what was wrong with Jack's brain. Bipolar disorder, obsessive-compulsive disorder, borderline schizophrenia, depression, panic disorder, and post-traumatic stress disorder were some of the most commonly recurring diagnoses. Any or all of those diagnoses could have been accurate. It was safe to say that at least one or more were. What was undisputed was that, on top of whatever else was going on with Jack, he was a bona fide alcoholic, straddling the knife's edge of addiction with every other substance he had ever tried.

At that time, Jack was still in denial. Jack wasn't crazy— not according to Jack. Of course, the more time he spent in places like Fairfax, the crazier he felt. As of that day, he still considered himself a tourist. No, not a tourist; more like a distant relative who was visiting. Jack fit because he had just a touch of mental illness, but those other people were the really crazy ones. He had just flown in for the holidays, and then he'd be back to his glamorous life in the outside world.

Chapter 3

Jack's final meeting with the Fairfax staff psychiatrist went well. In his time, he'd had many final meetings with psychiatrists. To Jack, they were simply a matter of giving canned answers to canned questions. What was his concrete plan for reintegrating into society? Where would he be staying? Was his SSI, GAU, or whatever government program he'd be drawing funds from, in order? Did he have phone numbers for potential therapists? Had his court-appointed social workers set up other services for him? Jack knew what to say to get released: yes, to all of the above.

And not just yes to all: Jack had a song and dance about his plan to join the workforce of this great nation after the successful completion of whatever three-to-six-month vocational program he was pretending to be interested in, and that he was going over to such and such trade school first thing Monday morning to fill out an application for such and such vocational program. Everybody won: the psychiatrist got to sign off on a successful release and rehabilitation of a malfunctioning societal cog, and Jack got to return to the dull roar of insanity he enjoyed when he was out. Most importantly, he got another crack at making it in the normal world.

Really, though, living on the outside never lasted long for Jack. Despite his honest desire to make it work on the outside, he always wound up behind locked doors sooner rather than later. Jack prided himself on being an intellectual loser. He read books that made him appear smart and quoted only the most obvious and memorable portions of the philosophy books he sort of read. At that time Jack's pseudo-intellectual observation was that most people lived their lives behind locked doors, and in that way, Jack reasoned, he wasn't so different from them. Their locked doors were the ones inside of their own brains. Everyone that had ever walked the earth, he pontificated, was behind a locked door of some sort. The sad thing was, they didn't even know it. Normal people had internalized the caged mentality. Normal people, he reasoned, didn't need physical cages anymore. They needed to own things to have security. They needed to make house payments, car payments, and payments into their retirement funds so they could move somewhere warm when they retired. They were imprisoned by their own perceived needs.

Jack's pontifications became more and more elaborate. He imagined that some people knew the truth about the state of things and spent their entire lives rebelling against it. They preached their revolutionary rhetoric to anyone who would listen. In that way, they became slaves of their own ideological angst. None of that changed the fact that Jack always ended up behind an actual, physical locked door. It was a clever false equivalency that allowed Jack to see himself as the same or better than everyone else, but, secretly, he imagined that those metaphorical cages might be the way to go.

Jack admired his father and brother, their gritty tenacity. They knew the world was out to grind them under its heel, and they would always just grind right back. They simply accepted that life was about pain and suffering, and that small glimpses of happiness were all most people ever got. Those types were mostly free. Mostly.

Jack knew all these things but lacked the backbone to do things for the right reasons, or even out of a feeling of responsibility to the people he cared about, or who cared about him. He was a disgusting example of excess, self-centeredness, and a general lack of ability to deal. He used substances, sex, gambling, and anything else he could put his hands on to make his way through the world. That's where Jack fit in. Jack was imprisoned by everything, especially his addictions, because of a helpless inability to meet the world on the world's terms. Jack didn't accept the world, his place in it, or his defective brain, and Jack wasn't free.

Jack's first morning out of Fairfax was actually going pretty well. This time he'd been in for almost a year. A long stay by his standards, but he'd been in fairly rough shape when they'd committed him. Jack's mom had just died, and the remainder of anything that resembled a support system along with her. Jack's father had died a few years before, but that hadn't affected him the same way. His father hadn't offered much in the way of emotional support. It had bothered Jack's father to have a son that, in his mind, refused to toughen up and make his own way in life like he and Jack's big brother Laurence had. Jack was a momma's boy. Jack's mom was the only person who saw more than a lazy, freeloading loser when she looked at him.

After Jack's mom died, things were different for him. When she died, he knew his days were numbered, as his ability to survive had always depended on his mom's support. After she was gone, there was no one to bail Jack out anymore. Jack was really on his own. Jack's mom had been saving his life at least once a year since kindergarten. "Now who'd save me?" Jack wondered. "How would I make it through even one year on my own?" Those had been the thoughts running through his head at his mom's funeral, and Jack was ashamed those had been his thoughts at that moment. While others had wept at the loss of this loving, caring woman, Jack had shaken with fear at the prospect of his own impending doom. After the funeral, it had been all of six days before Jack was committed to Fairfax. Unlike most of Jack's trips, that time, Jack had been in no hurry to leave. "There was nowhere for me to go that time, but after nearly a year inside there, I felt like I was ready to give it a try anyway."

Jack's first stop of the morning after leaving Fairfax was the bank, where he meant to cash his SSI check. His check was wet when he handed it to the bank teller. It was November in the Puget Sound, and the "dark wet" was in full swing. His new residence should have been his first stop, but he was in no hurry to go there. When your new place was a halfway house in downtown Tacoma, you were never in a hurry to get there. The euphoric effect of the medication Jack had been prescribed at the pharmacy before his departure from Fairfax was not enough to get him to walk through the door of that halfway house. Alcohol was a necessary agent to appropriately humble him for that event.

Yes, things were definitely different that time for Jack. No car, no mom, no prospects. That was exactly where Jack's little story should have turned around or ended. It did neither. If Jack had been the protagonist of a feel-good movie, he would have pulled himself up through therapy, tenacity, and hard work. He would have met a girl, found meaning in his existence, and gone antiquing on Sundays. It would be a short movie. But Jack wasn't a simple guy, and his story was complicated. There was a girl, though. There were actually quite a few—and one in particular—but that one definitely wasn't Lisa.

Lisa's place was always a good spot for Jack to crash for a few months while he was in between places. Lisa was also a good one to call up when Jack got off the bus at The Tipperary Tavern, cash from his SSI check in hand. Lisa's bed was also a good place to land when he was in between girls.

Lisa lived right up the street and was also on SSI. Somehow, she managed to keep her rent paid on the small amount of money SSI paid, something Jack had never gotten the hang of. Somehow, she also managed to only ever get high and drunk when it was on somebody else's coin. Another useful skill Jack had never gotten the hang of. After nearly a year in Fairfax Psychiatric Hospital, sex with institutionalized females had worn thin for Jack. Lisa was mentally ill, but not institutionalized. Plus, she was the only date Jack could afford on an SSI check. In days gone by, Jack's release would have been followed by a big welcome home dinner, and his mom would have slipped him the six or seven hundred bucks she'd been saving up for him. After dinner with his mom, it would have been booze, drugs, and whores for however long his mom's cash had held out. This was in stark contrast to Jack's meager little celebration that day. Over five pitchers of Rainer (two of which Lisa finished by herself despite being half Jack's size), Jack wondered if there was cause for celebration at all.

Humping Lisa was neither exciting nor new, but after they staggered out of the Tipperary to her place, Jack did it anyway.

Somehow, Jack purposely missed the eight o'clock curfew at the halfway house. He would therefore have to stay the night at Lisa's. Jack didn't mind. He knew what he was doing, and it already had him concerned, but not concerned enough to make curfew. Where was his resolve, his concrete plan to reintegrate? It was gone, just like his SSI money would be if he stayed at Lisa's for much longer. Actually, that was not the truth at all; his resolve had never really been there, and he knew it. His SSI money evaporating over pitchers with Lisa at the Tipperary would be the truth if he stuck around there much longer, though.

His head felt clear again. It was past ten at night and he'd been passed out for most of the day. Lisa was still out, and she would stay that way all night. Jack's new plan was to watch some TV, try to get a few more hours of sleep, and wake up early.

For maybe the first time in his life, Jack woke up and did what he'd set out to do in the first place. It was just after six in the morning. Before he took off, he left his open pack of smokes on Lisa's nightstand. Lisa never had her own smokes. Lisa never had her own anything, and in Jack's estimation, the smokes and pitchers were payment in full for the night's lodging. He laughed a little. At least she'd have something to be happy about when she finally rolled out of bed.

Jack had spent many a night there and many times had noticed a funny thing about Lisa. She was pretty in a conventional sort of way, and also crazy in a conventional sort of way. Most people looked peaceful when they were sleeping, even crazy people. And, of course, Jack had seen his share of crazy people sleeping. But Lisa never looked peaceful when she was sleeping. Lisa still looked crazy, in her conventionally crazy sort of way. When she woke up, she wouldn't wonder where Jack was, or why he hadn't said goodbye. She'd just answer the phone again in a couple of years when Jack called from the Tipperary at eleven thirty some morning.

Chapter 4

J ack finally had a chance to get into the bathroom at the halfway house. Jack's image in the mirror alarmed him. His poor appearance triggered an anxious twinge in his stomach and heart palpitations in his chest. "I've got ingrown toenails, and psoriasis on my arm, and I'm an insomniac, and I think I got athlete's foot from the showers at Fairfax," he mused. All of that existed on top of his abnormally patchy beard line, slightly receding hairline, and physique that only looked good as long as he was fully clothed.

This sort of anxiety attack was exactly the type that had historically put Jack into a downward spiral about any or all of the conditions he'd come to believe he suffered from. Right then, he became obsessed with a patch of dry skin on his right forearm, and before five minutes had elapsed, he had convinced himself that the dry skin was the beginning of flesh-eating bacteria. He erroneously reasoned that, since he'd shot heroin in that arm about two years before, he must have flesh-eating bacteria. With that, Jack was out the door to the main branch library downtown to research flesh-eating bacteria.

By that time, Jack was certainly living small. Making it to the halfway house with most of his SSI money in his pocket was a huge accomplishment for him. For Jack, an even larger accomplishment was that he was still on his meds. The application for Section Eight housing that Jack had filled out in the hospital, his state-issued identification card, and seventy-five dollars were all he needed to check into the halfway house. Seventy-five a month got you one shared 12x20 room, only slightly larger than a prison cell, but the precise dimensions of Jack's old room at Fairfax. From outside, his room there actually looked like a hospital room, but once Jack was inside, it felt like another prison cell.

The halfway house was one step above a shelter and two steps below the worst public housing. "Oh yeah, public housin', I had to go down to that fuckin' nasty-ass welfare office up on 19th and Sprague that day and check on my Section Eight application." Jack had surmised that it usually took a few months to get approved for assisted housing, but he'd gotten his application going almost two months ago while he had still been in Fairfax. In Jack's mind, that meant that he could be out of the halfway house in as little as a few weeks.

One dingy main hallway linked everything in the halfway house. At one end was the check-in desk, with an office behind it. At the other end was an outdoor, fenced-off smoking area. If a resident checked out after eight in the evening, they were out until the next morning. If a resident showed up to check in after eight, they were out until the next morning. That was a lesson Jack had learned the hard way. "Five after eight isn't before eight. For that matter, one minute before eight isn't before eight, either. As far as that goes, just because my watch says it's seven fifty-five doesn't make it before eight, either." The only clock that mattered for purposes of checkin in or out was the one on the wall behind the desk. "And if you ain't signed in by before eight, accordin' to that clock, you might as well not bother showin' up at all."

In between the front desk and smoking area were all the residents' rooms. They lined both sides of the hallway like a cellblock. Other than the rooms, there was a kitchen, a small game room, and one large bathroom that housed all the showers in that depressing all-male facility. After a couple of weeks, Jack had the place figured out. To Jack, it was a joke. He'd always show up to check in for the night, and when he wanted to go to a party, or the bar, or whatever, he just hopped the fence in the smoking area. The front door was locked after eight and attended by an employee, and the windows in the rooms didn't open at all, but the smoking area door was open all day and night. Jack always signed in before he snuck out. Once he was used to the routine, the halfway house wasn't so bad for him. Because he was able to sneak out almost every night, he even managed to reconnect with his normal party crowd. Better still, all the good drugs and downtown bars were at most a ten or fifteen-minute walk from the halfway house.

Walter never snuck out, and he was always in his bunk before ten. He woke up at six in the morning, when the morning employees came knocking on the residents' doors, and he was always out before eight in the morning, the time when they kicked the residents out for the day. Actually, he woke up half a dozen times before six, but that was just so that he could scream himself awake from his PTSD-induced Vietnam nightmares. Six was when he got his day started.

Walter was Jack's roommate at the halfway house. They didn't choose to be stuck together, and they had very little in common. They both smoked cigarettes, and Walter never had any, so they both liked Jack's cigarettes. They had that in common. Walter was so far out there that Jack wasn't really sure who Walter even was. He was a six-foot-four-inch-tall Native American man with full head of waist-length black hair. Walter's perfect hairline made Jack feel self-conscious about his own mildly receding hairline.

Walter was a Vietnam vet and had become so schizophrenic that any real living person was always the third person in a conversation with him. Eventually, Walter would get around to revealing his entire life story, but he wouldn't tell it to you. He'd tell it to the people that weren't there, and he didn't tell it like he was telling a story. It was more like he was debating whether his past had actually happened with an unseen adversary. "'NO, NO, NO, DON'T FUCKING SHOOT HER! NO!' 'GET ON THE CHOPPER WALTER! GET ON THE FUCKING CHOPPER PRIVATE!' 'FUCK YOU! THIS ISN'T REAL! THIS DIDN'T HAPPPEN! I WASN'T HERE!' "It was all fuckin' night long with Walter's night terrors and screaming, but he always narrated both parts of the conversation, so at least you could follow the story."

Walter never showered, and he smelled like it. In the six weeks Jack had spent there, he had seen Walter shower once, and then only because the halfway house employees threatened to drag him into the shower by force if he wouldn't go willingly. In a place with forty residents and five shower stalls, all of which were located next to each other, and fixed windows of time in which to bathe, everyone knew who didn't shower, and Walter didn't shower.

The reality was that Walter shouldn't have been in the halfway house at all. He should have been committed, and he had been several times. But at the end of the twentieth century in America, if you were like Walter, you fell through the cracks. Walter slept in a cot not six feet from Jack's, but that didn't bother him. The fact that Walter's attire looked like the free clothes bin at the homeless shelter had thrown up on him didn't bother Jack either. Jack single-handedly supporting Walter's smoking habit didn't even really bother him. Buying Walter like sixty cans of Coca Cola from the soda machine in the lobby was fine by Jack, too. What bothered Jack was Walter's fairly normal past, his fucked-up present, and his bleak future.

Like most roommates, Jack and Walter eventually learned to tolerate each other, even like each other. Or, more accurately, Jack learned how to tolerate Walter. Walter seemed to like Jack from the beginning, and Jack suspected that Walter would have liked anyone who tolerated bunking with him. Despite that, Walter's mere existence bothered Jack. This scared Jack like nothing else ever had. Walter had graduated from high school. Walter had been to war overseas. Walter had been married, had children, even had a decent job for many years. All the while, he had been fighting his schizophrenia. For much of his life, Walter had been relatively successful for someone struggling with extreme mental illness. In fact, Walter had held his life together for over thirty years before completely deteriorating.

Jack had never been successful or stable, and he was pushing thirty right then. If this was where Walter, who'd managed an essentially normal life for so many years, had ended up, where would Jack, who had never managed to disguise or disregard his neuroses, find himself? Even if Jack knew he would eventually end up like Walter, he preferred to avoid staring it in the face, and bunking with Walter was staring it in the face every day.

Chapter 5

For Jack, kissing the foul stench of the halfway house goodbye was cause for celebration. Saying hello to the foul stench of his new place was also cause for celebration. Jack scratched his head: dandruff. Jack scratched his eyebrow: dandruff. Even though he had severe dandruff on both his scalp and in his eyebrows, he still felt a cut above the other residents at his new building. Jack caught a glance of his slightly receding hairline in an outside building window at that time of the day when the window was basically a mirror. "Hopefully," he thought, "if my hairline recedes any more, the dandruff will disappear with the hair." However, a bald man whose dandruff persisted despite his lack of hair would fit in perfectly at Jack's new building.

Who else fit in there? The young black woman that had severe brain damage from a catastrophic car accident who used a walker and sat in the foyer all day bumming cigarettes? She fit in. The sweaty, longhaired butt-rocker with the gigantic plasma donation scars on both arms? He fit in, too. All the old people that had no families to take care of them but were not ready for the nursing home? You bet they fit in. The guy with one arm? Oh yeah, that guy definitely fit in. The HIV positive gay dudes that fucked anything they could get their hands on when they were well enough to get out of bed? You had better believe they fit in. How about the screwball alcoholic building management team? Anybody that would work there clearly couldn't get a job anywhere better, so yeah, they fit just like recycled condoms: wet and loose. Everybody there belonged, Jack thought, except him. Whether they were on the last stop of a long, underprivileged life, or just layovers on short, miserable ones, everybody there belonged, and if they didn't when they arrived, they would within a few years. Or, as Jack always said, "You can only slum it there for a while before you become a permanent fixture."

Here, was The Winthrop Apartments. It was one of the most interesting buildings in Tacoma. The Winthrop Apartments were constructed in the twenties as the swanky, high-end Winthrop Hotel. The time period in which they were constructed was made evident by its enormous closets and tiny bathrooms. People used to travel with baggage, lots of baggage.

Before there were transatlantic flights two thousand times a day, traveling could be arduous and time consuming. Just the travel time involved in most early twentieth century long-distance journeys was equivalent or greater to entire vacations these days. Back then, you'd spend a week on a ship crossing the Atlantic or on a train crossing the continent. Today, people started their vacations by getting on the red-eye at two in the morning on a Monday, and they were back on the same flight heading home the following week so that they could be at work Monday morning, not a very relaxing vacation.

Those travelers from the early twentieth century measured their trips in months, sometimes years, never weeks or days.

If you were leaving home for months or years, closet space was preferable to bathroom space, or even sleeping space, for that matter. The building's tenure as the grand lodging of the south sound, however, was short-lived. Tacoma was not much of a tourist attraction, and from the environs, one supposed it never really was.

The Winthrop fell into disrepair almost immediately. It was sold a few times before the Conifer group bought it in the seventies. Finally, someone had found the building's market niche. Over two hundred units in a building with no grounds, or parking, best of all very little upkeep. They realized that the units were not adequate for apartments, not without major remodeling, which would have cut the number of units in half. Nor was the building any longer adequate as a hotel. But as low-income apartments, it was a cash cow.

Poor people on public housing, such as the residents of the Winthrop, didn't expect prompt repair of problems in their apartments, and even if they did, what could they do if they didn't get them? If they were in subsidized housing—and all the residents were—it took months to find another place, so they'd just deal with the habitation issues. For the owners, converting to low-income housing meant they got full market value for each subpar unit. Housing and Urban Development paid the owners the difference for what they didn't receive directly from their tenants. Better yet, there was a steady stream of subsidized housing applicants in Tacoma, so the apartments were always full. The Conifer Group got the full market value for each unit every month and barely put a dime back in for maintenance.

"Sometimes, when I close my eyes, I can read these things, ya know. Like, the things I can read behind my eyes always seem important, or like they should be important to someone, just not important to me. And they're very detailed. Behind my eyes none of it reads simple, though. Detailed directions for building all sorts of things pop into my head. I always see these entire poems, or chapters from what I figure are classic books of literature that I've never read. Sometimes, I can read the entire script to an episode of a television show that won't air till next season. Then I fuckin' see it the next season, and I'm like WTF!

"When this shit comes, I can read as quickly or slowly as I like. I can try to comprehend as much or as little as I like. But once I've moved on to the next line of text, the previous line disappears into the space above. Like at the beginning of *Star Wars*. I guess there's only so much room on the movie screen of my brain. It's free information, information that I'm not bright enough to put to good use, or maybe I just don't understand its significance yet.

"Maybe, just maybe, it's shit I was never meant to receive. Like somethin' got some wires crossed somewhere, and now I can eavesdrop on sensitive material that was en route to someone important. I'm spliced in on some celestial phone line that runs over my apartment on the way to a spiritual or world leader somewhere. Sometimes, when I pick up that phone, I get some fuzz, static backwash, not enough to do any damage with. Maybe someday I'll get somethin' really sensitive, somethin' I can use to extort some rich fucker or the government into givin' me millions of dollars. That'd be fuckin' kewl!"

Jack knew somewhere in the city there was an apartment building with normal people, with normal lives, that he could get into with his HUD application. There were these sorts of mixed, or subsidized and unsubsidized, apartment complexes all over the city. You just had to look for them. Getting into one took a while, but it was a real option for someone like Jack. "Why didn't I never have no premonition tellin' me where to find those elusive buildins'?" The reality was that he had never looked. If he was being honest with himself, he knew that living somewhere with a bunch of normal apartment dwellers wasn't for him. Instead, he chose to live in a studio apartment that was the size of a closet, with a closet that was big enough to fit a bathtub inside, and a bathroom that was too small for the toilet and bathtub that were already in it. It was no wonder the residents in that place were crazy. Just negotiating the dimensions of those units could drive a sane person mad.

Then, of course, there were the roaches, and then there were more roaches, and then there were a few hundred thousand roaches after that. Jack was too tired, though. He didn't even mind the roaches so much, so as long as they stayed out of his sleeping space. They never did. Sometimes, when the lamp Jack had found on the street was on and he was lying on the pee-soaked mattress he had found next to the lamp, he could see them running up and down the walls. Sometimes, they ran across the ceiling, down the TV screen, up the sink drain, and anywhere else they saw fit to run.

During that time, it seemed that Jack had fallen into the trap that many people with little to do fell into. Sleep. "Sleep was my master." When he lived in the halfway house, he knew he had to be out at a certain time, and that sleeping was only allowed during certain hours. At the institution, he had a structured existence as well. Not that the residents at either place did anything important with their time. But the structure was there. Now, Jack had a steady SSI check and a closet-sized apartment with its bedroom-sized closet. Sleep could be done at any point in the day. Any hour was his to sleep, and he slept whenever he didn't feel like sitting upright. The less you had to do, the more you slept. Ask any convict. Jack's idea of paradise became a big comfortable bed with clean sheets. This was also how Jack envisioned heaven, but in heaven the sheets were designer and silk. "Yep, that's right, I saw it in a vision one time."

When getting a comfortable bed so that you could forget your waking hours in style became important, you were done for. You were really done, you had lost, life had beat you like an abused dog, and that bed was just a placeholder for the coffin that would shortly replace it. Jack took too much solace in the fact that he still found the energy to get up to urinate in the toilet instead of his bed. There were times when Jack considered adding a few of his own pee stains to the preexisting ones. "Thus far, I hadn't, but I've been tempted. Other of my bodily fluids that exit the body through the penis had found their way onto that mattress, though." However, not nearly as much of them as one might think. Most of the time, knocking back off for a few hours seemed more interesting to Jack than jerking off. Jack had a new addiction: sleep.

He wasn't drinking. He wasn't gambling. He wasn't doping. He wasn't popping pills. He wasn't soliciting prostitutes. He also wasn't living. Over the past several weeks, his waking time had dwindled down to about eight hours a day. The average workday of a normal person was now the lump sum of consciousness for Jack's entire day.

During the rare interludes where Jack was conscious, he

thought life on the third floor was somewhat nice most of the time. The two ground floors were not numbered, so the third floor was more like the fifth floor, but in the elevator, the button you pushed to get to Jack's place was three.

On the third floor that was actually the fifth floor, Jack was high enough up that the street noise didn't really bother him, but low enough so that he wasn't constantly tempted to take that liberating leap out his window into eternal freedom. From that height, it was just too risky. Jack imagined that, from that height, he was more likely to wind up bouncing off the hood of a car and living the rest of his miserable existence in a wheelchair, unable to even make another jumping attempt.

From the eighth, ninth, or tenth floors, death was pretty much assured. "How do those fuckin' people live up there?" Jack wondered. Jack could ride the elevator up to the tenth floor, walk right out onto the fenced observation area of the roof, hop over the three-foot tall chain link fence, stroll out to the edge, and swan dive for all of downtown to see. At any point, he could do it, and he'd walked to the elevator for that purpose several times, but it took five minutes for the elevator just to get to his floor. By the time the elevator actually got there, some drunk had always stumbled by, or a blue-haired geriatric, buzzed up on her medication rambled by. That was when Jack would always tell himself that if they weren't jumping that day, neither would he. Then, he'd turn around and walk back to his closet apartment and take a nap.

Chapter 6

For a few hours, Jack forgot about Walter at the halfway house. He forgot about the impending doom his mental deterioration would inevitably bring him in the future. For a little while, he didn't even mind his third-floor, closet-sized apartment. For a few hours, he sunk into a shameless remembrance of his days as a juvenile delinquent, all because of a lucky find in the garbage that morning.

It was 1985 again. Jack saw Black Flag at the Community World Theater. BO-soaked leather jackets, second-hand smoke from generic brand cigarettes, and that tangy aluminum smell of cheap beer in a can were the holy trinity of aromas for the punk scene. If punk had a cologne, that was it. He'd been going to punk shows for a couple of years, but most of what he was interested in were local bands like the Fartz or the Wipers. Black Flag was from LA, and they were playing in Tacoma for a crowd of seventy or eighty. Even with the sparse crowd, the room was elbow to elbow. Ninety percent of the hall was completely vacant, all but a piece of floor no larger than 20x20 feet. Every person who was not working the door, selling merchandise at the table in the back, operating the sound board, or performing on stage was squeezed into the tiny plot of land in front of the stage.

Between a fairly significant concussion and his normal alcohol-induced blackout, Jack didn't remember much of the show, but he remembered them playing a song called "Depression." He'd heard it before. He'd heard all their songs before. He had spent the last year listening to all their seven inches, and the last week listening to nothing but Black Flag in anticipation of that Tacoma show. Still, the "Depression" lyrics rang like church bells in his head. They rang so hard it seemed like they rang backwards in time so that, afterward, he could always hear them overlaid on memories of his early childhood. They rang into the future, too. After that night, they were always imprinted somewhere transparent, baked into every experience from then on. Jack thought he'd probably taken some acid that night after he was wasted. He couldn't remember for sure. The acid wore off, but those lyrics ringing in his brain like some time-travelling bell never really stopped. Sometimes they got a little quieter, but that song told him a truth about himself, and he could never unring that bell.

Before that, the Crescent Ballroom was the only place worth putting on an all-ages punk show in Tacoma. A couple of years later, the Community World Theater in south Tacoma would have a short but illustrious career as the punk venue of choice. A very forgettable band named Nirvana played their very first show there, and at the time Jack had assumed it would be their last. A year or two after that, the Crescent Ballroom would become Legends. In the early nineties, there was a place in the basement of a Stihl Chainsaw store called, somewhat unoriginally, The Chainsaw, where several people were nearly killed during an Accused show, which was, notably, the most violent room Jack had ever stepped into, then or now. There were a lot of other venues; most existed for a matter of months, sometimes weeks, but those three or four were on his mind that afternoon.

On a normal day back then, Jack would wake up late, skip school, skate, get stoned, skate, get stoned again, get drunk, masturbate, and pass out. Next day, repeat. And so on and so forth. Sometimes he'd even squeeze a meal in, but whatever was going on, the punk rock soundtrack blared in the background like war drums. Jack was so baked right then that he faded out of consciousness as the Shit Split spun away on his new record player.

Jack's new place was right across the hall from the third-floor garbage room, which had some definite advantages and more than its share of disadvantages. Most of what Jack currently owned came from the garbage room. There was no garbage chute in that building, just a room with galvanized-steel garbage cans. Every floor had a room like that one across from Jack's apartment, and living across from the one on his floor gave Jack the bug, the garbage-digging bug. All he had needed was a taste, and he was hooked.

For once in his life, Jack seemed to have acquired a habit that wasn't harmful to anyone, including himself. One of his few daily activities had become ransacking the garbage rooms of each and every floor in the building. It was tricky; even in a building with only a couple hundred tenants, Jack immediately realized that the competition for the good garbage was fierce.

There was always new garbage because somebody was always moving, getting evicted, or dying. Not surprisingly, the departing tenants routinely left most of their meager possessions behind. Each tenant of the building was an opportunity-motivated dumpster diver. Those dilettantes put no more effort into the practice than simply grabbing anything that looked good when they were dropping off their own garbage. There were also two guys that routinely dumpster-dived the cans. Neither of them went out every day, and neither of them hit all the cans like Jack did. One hit the low floors and the other hit the higher floors. Of course, Jack hit them all, and often.

Those two guys tried a few times to ward Jack off from hitting their cans, but Jack had long ago developed his universal response to all requests from other people he didn't care for. "Get the fuck out my face" was his standard response, and more than that the ever-present mantra of Jack's life. As usual, it worked well enough to spook the dumpster divers in his building. Those two never directly confronted him after receiving the standard response, but they did start going out earlier in the day to get to the good stuff before Jack.

That day Jack hit pay dirt. It was just what he'd been looking for. An old Sanyo stereo with a turntable on it. One look verified that the needle was still attached to it. Jack's rounds for the day were over right then. He knew those other dumpster divers would get some good stuff out of the garbage he missed that day, but he didn't care, because he'd found the jewel. As soon as Jack got back to his place, he plugged in the stereo and checked out the speaker connections. The connectors on the big house speakers he'd found a couple weeks before didn't match the Sanyo, so he just chopped the connectors off the speakers' cables and wired them straight to the back of the Sanyo.

Jack's friend Todd had been babysitting his record collection. Todd was one of the only friends Jack had left. More than that, Jack actually cared about his friendship with Todd. And, even more important than that, Todd had the only possessions that Jack really cared about, Jack's records. Once Jack was confident that the Sanyo was in good working order, he immediately headed downstairs and caught the bus to Todd's.

The back door of Jack's building opened up onto a patch of sidewalk with an rusty-iron pole sticking out of it and a small, covered bus stop with a sign that had the number twenty-five on it. The iron pole stuck up about a foot out of the concrete, and it was jagged all around. Every time Jack walked out the back door, he seriously considered "accidently" slipping and landing right on top of that jagged pole. He knew this guy who had done just that a couple of years ago on a similar hazard the city had failed to take care of, and he got six thousand dollars for what amounted to a bad cut on his butt. "Six-grand for throwin' yourself butt-first onto a pole, that was good fuckin' scratch!"

Normally, Jack was just walking out this door, headed to wherever on foot, but that day he had to sit and wait on the bus for several minutes, which gave him quite a while to ponder the iron pole. Jack's best guess was that the pole had used to be the bus stop, and that some incompetent or lazy city employee had seen the pole was cemented into the sidewalk when they built a new bus stop sign, so he had just sawed it off. "But the dumbfuck sawed it too far off the ground so any fuckin' body could just come along and plop themselves right down onto the fucker." The city never bothered to come grind it down. It was rusted to a dark red color all over, and Jack guessed it had been like that for years. He decided to reserve "accidently" slipping on the pole as a plan b if he ever needed it.

"Cause, you know, if you got evicted or somethin', six grand would be a lot more useful than it is when you already got a place to live."

The twenty-five bus took Jack almost right to Todd's door. He lived right off of Sixth Avenue, about a mile and a half away from Jack's place downtown. Jack could have walked to it in about twenty minutes, but it was raining. That was no real excuse, since it was always raining, but Jack was also characteristically lazy that day. Jack justified spending the sixty-five cents for bus fare by telling himself that the twenty-five's bus stop was right outside his back door, and it would let him off a half block from Todd's house. In this case, it was almost like Jack wasn't going outside at all. Jack hated going outside. That had to be worth spending sixty-five cents and enduring the bus people he tried so hard to avoid. Jack also hated the bus, and he was annoyed that he had to ride a thing he hated to avoid going outside. At the end of the day, Jack hated going outside more than he hated the bus. Back when he had gotten his first car, he had sworn to himself that he'd never again become so familiar with the buses that he knew which bus numbers went where, but there he was, and he knew the twenty-five went to Todd's house.

Todd was a member of the old crew. If he had a role, it would be the archivist. Unfortunately for him, he was the archivist of people and times that lacked any significance to anyone outside a handful of losers. He had artifacts from their youth that every other member of their crew had long since abandoned. His house was a museum, the sole purpose of which was to document their youth. It helped that Todd was also sort of a hoarder. If you couldn't remember the date of a show, Todd knew. He had a ticket stub, or a flyer, or a weekly paper from that week. He owned t-shirts that didn't even fit him, that had never fit him, that he got from friends in trades for no better reason than to stick it in a closet and preserve it for posterity.

Todd was tall and sort of large around the center. In fact, he was sort of large everywhere, and a little unkempt—a lot unkempt. He looked like a hibernating bear would look if you stuck a smoldering cigarette in its mouth and dressed it up in worn-out Levi's and a holey Anti-Nowhere League t-shirt. Actually, he looked more like a bear that had just woken up from hibernating, because although Todd was always awake, he never seemed all the way awake.

There were picture albums full of people Jack had forgotten even existed, people they'd met at a party, or show, and never seen again. One time, he found a letter from one of Jack's ex-girlfriends addressed to him in Todd's kitchen drawer. It was a letter Jack remembered reading, and had probably discarded in Todd's garbage, where Todd no doubt flagged it as something important and preserved it. Or it may have been in some box destined for the garbage one of the times Todd had helped Jack move. Maybe Todd had thought Jack would want it at some point in the future, or maybe he just didn't have much to remember Mandy by. As far as ex-girlfriends went, Mandy was alright, but Todd and her had hung out a lot back then. Just another example of the odds and ends one would find at Todd's house.

Todd and Jack were half of the old crew. People hear crew and think gang, but a crew was not a gang. Gangs were together for protection. Right at their cores, that was what gangs were; that was why they started, and in the end, it was all they had in common. They may pull some jobs, bury a few members, and sell mountains of dope together, but in the end, fear was all that kept them together. A gang could go on and on with new members to replace the dead or incarcerated ones. They routinely went on until no original members even existed, or even to the point where no current members knew who any of the original members even were. In a gang you were disposable, and the ranks needed to stay filled. On a block with a gang, kids were scared to not join, and once they were in, they were certainly too scared to leave.

About the only thing a gang had in common with a crew was that, in both cases, you were in for life. But that was where all similarity ended. Gangs had names, and real crews rarely ever did. You weren't beat into a crew or tattooed with the ritual gang logo. "I met guys at McNeil that had been in so many gangs they had gang tattoos coverin' up older gang tattoos. They'd just simply run out of skin."

A crew was all about love, not fear. Nobody was controlled, and nobody had anything to fear from anyone in their crew. Any real crew only lasted until the second to last member died. There were no replacements members. At some point, everybody involved knew what it was, and who was part of it. That was the moment when it became a crew and the members were linked forever.

When somebody died, the group's number dropped by one, and they were never replaced. Those tragedies were often the things that brought them back together after spanning out into the world of adult life. The strain actually revealed how strong the bonds were, not how much separation had deteriorated them.

It was not something that was put together; it grew together organically, and you couldn't manufacture one intentionally even if you wanted to. Before he was twenty-eight, Jack had done time with, or for, every member of that crew. They all had. It was not the blind bullshit loyalty and devotion required by a gang. They had loyalty based on lifelong bonds, and the lack of expectations upon one another made their devotion to each other implicit. When Ron's ex-girlfriend overdosed on his heroin, her brother had beaten Ron half to death. Jack had caught up with the brother about a week later and used an aluminum baseball bat to put him into the hospital and give him a permanent limp.

Ron had kept his mouth shut, and Jack had never done time for that. The cops had known it was one of them, but nobody had talked, and they couldn't charge them. Ron hadn't asked Jack to do it, and Jack had never asked Ron to keep his mouth shut when the cops came around. As a matter of fact, no words had ever been spoken about it, then or after. It had just happened. That was how it always worked, and when people forged bonds of trust with violence and love, those bonds lasted.

The crew had sort of split in the last few years. They'd gone their separate ways, but Jack and Todd were mostly still around Tacoma. Todd wasn't up to much. Neither was Jack.

Mike had been dead for several years by that time. Before he had died, he'd gotten himself a girlfriend and a job and had been taking his best shot at domesticity before really rapidly deteriorating in the months after that girlfriend had taken off. They spent a lot of time talking about Mike that afternoon, and of course Todd marched out several Mike-inspired relics from his museum of loserdom for them to reminisce over.

Ron had recently done some time at Walla Walla State Penitentiary and left the state when he was released last year.

Todd told Jack that Ron was living in a small city in Northern California called Grass Valley, ironically selling weed. By that time, Ron had done some time at a few Washington State penitentiaries. They'd all done some time, but Ron more so and more recently than the others.

They called Ron that day, but nobody picked up. Jack updated Todd on what he'd been up to as much for his own information as for the next time somebody asked about Jack Todd would know what to tell them. Collecting SSI checks and living in low-income housing downtown wouldn't sound so great in most circles, but considering Jack's peers, it wasn't so bad.

It never ceased to amaze Jack how little things ever changed inside the confines of Todd's tiny house. Even Todd himself seemed frozen in time, same t-shirt and jeans, same half pack of full-flavor GPC kings sitting on the coffee table. Five years earlier that place looked just the same. It would probably look just the same five years from then. Todd broke out the bong as soon as Jack showed up. Within a few minutes, Jack was so stoned that he started to really realize how it was that time stood still in that house. For all he knew he could have been there for ten minutes or ten hours. After the first bong hit, everything had gone fast and gray. In reality, Jack had been there about two hours, and if Todd hadn't asked Jack if he wanted a ride home, he could have been there for two days.

It would have taken a couple of trips to get the records home on the bus. Jack had a lot of records. Even after trading a couple of the gems of his collection to Todd for a quarter ounce of chronic, he still had a lot of records. It didn't matter to Jack; Rodney on the Roq and DOA's Something Better Change for quarter ounce was a good deal. Jack didn't ask for a ride; Todd just offered it.

The weed was good, Jack already knew that. They smoked another bowl while they were loading Jack's records into the back of Todd's Civic hatchback. By the time they'd gotten in the car, Jack was so baked that he had a hard time figuring out how to roll the car window down. Todd didn't seem that stoned to Jack, but Todd never seemed that stoned. Todd was one of those guys that always seemed sort of stoned, never really stoned. That was convenient, since Todd was always sort of stoned. Jack was more than sort of stoned, and to him the world was humming, and he was parched.

It only took about five minutes to get back to Jack's apartment building, and Todd found a loading zone in front of the building so that he could park and help Jack bring his records up. Todd had a look at Jack's place, but he didn't stay long. He could have. He could have moved his car to a regular parking space, come back up, and smoked a while, listened to some records, but he hadn't. It was pretty clear to Jack that his unannounced arrival at Todd's had preempted something that Todd was supposed to be doing, but when one of the crew showed up on your doorstep, everything else got pushed to the back of the line. That was exactly what had happened that day. If Jack had showed up on Todd's doorstep with a bag of his clothes and no money, Todd would have let Jack stay on his couch for as long as needed, no questions asked.

There were times in the past where Todd had come over to Jack's place for a smoke and wound up moving in for six months, and other times where they hadn't seen each other for over a year. That day they hadn't said *let's hang out, or I'll call you.* They never did. They never had to. For the first time in years, they lived pretty close to one another, but proximity wasn't what kept them close. Near or far, Jack and Todd would see each other when they needed to, no words necessary.

Chapter 7

Dolores worked at Grounds for Coffee. Jack tried to stop by every couple of days for a latte. Sometimes she wasn't there. That annoyed Jack. On that day, he'd already ordered a four-dollar latte before he realized she wasn't there. After he put a dollar in the tip jar, Jack was out five bucks. That annoyed Jack even more than the fact that Dolores wasn't there. Jack knew you always tipped at a place where someone you liked worked, even when they were not there, so once he'd bought the latte, he had committed to the dollar tip.

Jack had used to emphasize that point pretty regularly. "Cheap never works with girls. Also, don't haggle with call girls over their prices. It annoys 'em, and that annoyance definitely shows up in their performance. Even if the girl you like works somewhere you can't leave a tip, you still buy somethin'. If she works at a movie theater, buy a movie ticket, or at the very least get some quarters to play video games." Jack knew you needed a girl's friends and coworkers to know you weren't cheap. That approach was the main reason Jack didn't have much luck with real estate agents and girls that worked at BMW dealerships.

Jack imagined he knew Dolores. He mentally framed her as

the girl at her workplace that didn't quite click with the other employees. Tragically unique. She was too cool, too aloof, or too insecure. At a hip coffee shop like that, all the employees hung out together, partied together, and knew each other's boyfriends and girlfriends. She always got invited, but she never went. Then, she went home by herself and wondered why she never hung out with her coworkers. She probably thought that they just asked her out to be nice, but didn't really want her to go. Actually, they wondered what was the matter with them when she didn't show up at all. They wanted her, and she didn't want anything to do with them. It was a John Hughes movie in the making. Regardless, Jack needed some mental framing for his masturbation session later. "Cause jerkin' it feels better when you have some context even if you have to invent that context yourself."

One day while Dolores was making Jack's latte, a thought occurred to him: He'd never seen Dolores out of her apron, and that if they ever went on a date, he'd expect her to be wearing an apron. It was possible that fifteen years of drug and alcohol abuse had damaged Jack's imagination. Jack couldn't even pretend to get to know her unless he was sitting at the coffee shop. Whenever he tried to imagine her when he was sitting in his apartment, he would just get distracted by something or fall asleep. As a way to picture her out of the apron, he started trying to think of her in something else. His problem was that all he could come up with were work uniforms. Jack had never seen her do anything except work. Again, Jack's imagination, as well as much of the remainder of his brain, had likely been significantly and permanently compromised.

What his imagination was able to produce was bizarre at

best. When she handed him his latte, he saw her as a banquet waitress, then a car mechanic, next a pharmacist, then a huge step down to McDonald's shift manager, and, finally, a park ranger. In each incarnation, she was doing something appropriate to the uniform. The waitress was putting a plate of food in front of him. The car mechanic was showing him a broken alternator. The McDonald's shift manager gave him a Big Mac. The park ranger told him, "You can't camp here!" However, the pharmacist was the hottest because she was giving him Vicodin. Who wouldn't want a girlfriend whose job was to give you narcotics?

It was an inconvenient time for an acid flashback, but nonetheless it had snuck up on him, so Jack managed a thank you and quickly made his way to an empty table.

From the relative safety of his favorite table, he could observe Dolores's snug pinstripe slacks. At first, his flashback compelled him to sit down in the first open chair he spotted, but once he'd gotten his bearings, he quietly moved to his preferred table in the back of the elevated part of the dining room. That was the best vantage point for creepy stalker patrons to leer at baristas. Jack wondered if the baristas were wise to that fact.

Dolores wore that pair of pants to work about twice a week, and those were Jack's favorite days. Her hips made the pinstripes bend out and curve just a little bit. That pair was about a size smaller than her other pants, so those stripes bent a little more than they were designed to. Sometimes, when Jack was drunk, he used to like to talk about tight pants. His thoughts on the matter were fairly simple and straightforward. "No one ever said make 'em looser! That's what I'm talkin' 'bout! Right!"

That day, Jack utilized the time he didn't spend staring at Dolores's pinstripes to add to her imaginary life story. He decided she'd started, but not finished, community college, and only worked part time here, because she intended on going back to finish. She's didn't make enough money to go shopping for new clothes nearly enough, so she bought clothes that were flattering and had maximum utility, such as those pinstripe slacks. "Because those pants were built to last." And, clearly, she had great taste in music. Jack would never daydream about and pretend to date a girl who didn't have great taste in music. Of course, she was always reading an interesting book, and had just the right tattoos in just the right places. It went without saying that she would need great balance to stay atop the pedestal Jack had built to keep her on.

A few days after the acid flashback incident, Jack was back at Grounds for Coffee. That was the first day Jack had walked in and sort of wished Dolores wasn't there. Right then, he was so stoned that the best he could do was to not say anything, and the worst he could do was seem like a stoned moron. In years past, Jack could have made stoned moron cute, but he was in his late twenties, and that shit had long since worn thin. It didn't stop him from being a stoned moron. It's just that nobody thought it was cute anymore. That day, he really just wanted a five-dollar coffee, and some water, and a muffin, and a sugar cookie with the pink frosting and sprinkles on top, and a scone, and one of those slices of dried brown bread that they keep in a jar. "What the fuck are those things? I've always wanted to ask. I think they dip 'em in their coffees."

That day, she was laughing. Jack had never imagined her laughing and he'd certainly never seen it. He took a mental picture to add to the imaginary personality he'd built for her in his head. Her laughing actually snapped him out of his stoned euphoria. She had the same short pixie cut, but, though her bangs had been fire engine red earlier that week, that day they were blue. The remainder of her hair was a mix of her natural brown roots and platinum-bleached ends, the remnants of a previous hair incarnation that she'd neglected to update. Jack wanted to compliment her new color, but she was laughing, and then he was drooling at the pastry case again, and before he knew it, the moment had passed. Apparently, pastries were a greater force than love. But, that day, despite Jack's pastry envy and blank stare, fate intervened and saved him from himself. For a moment, Jack wondered if being a stoned moron was having a renaissance.

"Do you want something out of there?"

"Yeah, I want all of it," Jack said.

"Why don't you start with some of it, and if you're still hungry, come back for the rest."

Dolores lingered in that uncomfortable way that people do when an interaction is over but there was nowhere to go. She worked there, and part of her job was waiting on him, and he, well, he was stoned out of his gourd and ravenous. Eventually, she broke the awkward silence. Whether it was ten seconds or ten minutes, Jack couldn't tell.

"You come in here all the time, you might as well tell me your name."

In his head, Jack spoke, but he must not have, because she asked him again.

"Say again. Your mouth moved, but no noise came out," she said.

When Jack did finally speak, he wished he hadn't.

"Sometimes I have to remind myself to speak out loud, but only when I'm really fuckin' stoned. I'm Jack. Did I speak that time?"

Her eyebrows raised. "That, I heard."

She smiled just slightly before walking off to help another customer. Jack assumed that was the last interaction he and Dolores would ever have.

Chapter 8

Jack's most confusing thoughts always dressed up like strange visitors, and they came over to have conversations at the most inconvenient times. "They don't speak straight! It's all garbled and stuff." Those thoughts were just riddles to him. Jack was terrified of his mind and the real people it dressed itself up as. Jack was terrified of most things, but his mind was the scariest place on earth. One thing was certain, strange visitors always meant change was on its way.

Jack was scared that night. He was as scared as he had been that time he had found an old roll of 110 Kodak film crammed in the back of a kitchen cabinet in an apartment he'd just moved into. He had driven around for two hours trying to find a one-hour photo place to develop it. That 110 film had been more or less a dead medium even back then. He eventually had found a one-hour place that still had developing equipment for the 110 film. When he had gone to pick up the prints, the person at the photo place had worn a very strange look on his face. He had handed the developed prints of that film to Jack.

What Jack had seen on those prints was morbid. Jack had only seen those types of postmortem child photographs in documentaries on PBS. Nonetheless, there they had been, like some Victorian death photo album: a little boy, about twelve, wearing a blue suit, lying in a pine box. Based on the décor and the boy's clothes, Jack speculated this boy's funeral had taken place sometime in the mid-seventies. Jack spent enough time wrestling with the ghosts that were already in his mind. He hadn't needed an adolescent boy apparition as well. He had burned the film and prints straight away.

The year before that, Jack's father had come to visit late one night. When he had showed up, Jack had thought he was still asleep because he didn't remember letting his father in. Jack had been sitting in his chair in the living room. The two of them had just sat there watching TV at two-thirty in the morning. If the time wasn't strange enough, the fact that Jack's father had been at his place at all was. Jack's father never came any place where Jack lived, and he certainly didn't hang around and watch TV. It had been a while since he'd seen his father. Jack knew it was because his father had actually been gone for quite a while. As always, they'd parted on bad terms the last time they had seen each other.

Jack's father had appeared physically solid but a little older than the last time Jack had seen him. Jack's father wasn't overly intimidating in appearance; he was more an obvious example of the strong physical specimen that almost all blue-collar middle-aged men became. Jack's father had a head full of salt and pepper hair, calloused skin, and pear-shaped biceps. His shoulders chest and back muscles stretched and contorted the natural shape of his shirt, but his slight paunch signaled that he was just a humble working man. His standard attire was work boots, jeans, and a t-shirt. They resembled each other just slightly but only in the face.

Over the prior several years, it had become impossible for Jack to talk to his father without it turning into a lecture, a row, or, sometimes, an actual fight. For once, it had been nice to just sit and hang out with him, like they had when Jack had been a kid. They had talked like they had used to before the onset of Jack's difficulties, before Jack had become different, before he had become somebody that his father didn't accept as proper offspring of his hard-working gene pool.

They had talked about nothing in particular, but they had done so kindly, and for a long time. After an even longer time, and during one of those seven-minute lulls, Jack's father had told him that he was proud to have him as a son no matter what he did with his life. Jack's father had apologized for not standing by him before. Then he had told Jack it was late, and he needed to go and pick up Jack's mom. When he had left, it had still been two-thirty.

When he had left, Jack had known that had been the last conversation he'd have with his father. Jack was pretty sure that the conversation they'd had years back before he passed away was the last conversation they'd have, but nonetheless there he was that night.

Jack had so many varieties of fear, he rarely bothered trying to categorize, name, or even remember the underlying events attached to those fears. This fear had been different. It had not been self-centered the way most of his fears were. It had been loss for him and others. It had been fear that choked him like a rubber band wound around a finger, cutting off the blood supply. "After he left, I popped open my last 40oz, and lit a smoke. Seein' my pap again made me forget about the horrible feelings of abandonment that I'd been havin' for several months, but just for a minute or two. Like I said, that relief didn't last. It never does. My pap was gone, and we never even got to be friends. I sure hope he came to visit me that night, but it could've just been my twisted mind tellin' me what I been waitin' years to hear. Who fuckin' knows."

At a time when Jack had been legitimately trying to get his life together, it seemed like his support system had crumbled around him. Jack had reached that time in early adulthood when the friends that he had formed bad habits with had stopped being a de facto family and daily fixtures in his life. Instead, they had started becoming people who got jobs, went to prison, or moved away.

It was also at that point in life that siblings had started getting too busy to call each other on birthdays, and information about one another was primarily conveyed through conversations with parents. Worst of all, it had been the time in life when a guy like Jack had peaked and begun the long descent to the place most people had known he was heading the whole time. His bottomed-out loser shtick had worn thin. When he had been younger, Jack had been the guy that the girls in his orbit had talked about amongst themselves. He had been the guy that got punched at the bar because some tipsy girl had told her boyfriend how hot Jack was. Now, those girls had become grown women, and he had still been a boy in an alcoholic man's body. His drinking and pill-popping had soared to new heights, and, of course, he'd just received an eviction notice.

The phone ringing had woken Jack up. It had been about three-thirty in the morning. His brother Laurence's voice had come across the line. Jack had known he wouldn't want to hear what Laurence had to say, mostly because he couldn't remember the last time he'd spoken to Laurence that he *had* wanted to. It hadn't yet become clear what variety of bullshit Laurence was bringing his way, but he had been sure it was bullshit, whatever it was. It had turned out their mom had been driving home after dropping her friend off at the airport for a red-eye flight when a drunk driver had veered into her lane and hit her head-on. She had been pronounced dead at the hospital a few minutes before, but Jack was pretty sure that she'd checked out of her body after the accident about an hour ago, when his father had come to pick her up.

Laurence had told Jack to get down to St. Joseph Hospital, then immediately changed his mind and told Jack he could take care of things there, but that he was coming by Jack's in the morning to start figuring out what to do next. Laurence had been right, of course. Jack would have been useless at the hospital, so he might as well have been useless right where he was. From Jack's apartment, he could have walked to St. Joseph in ten or fifteen minutes. Instead, he had just tilted his head back, and his eyelids had rolled down like window shutters. The abyss of unconsciousness was little refuge from his existence, but as always, he had retreated there to take whatever solace it had to offer him.

They buried her one week later, and Jack had been committed less than a week after the funeral. Playtime was over, and Jack was really on his own. Nobody really grows up until that happens. Regardless of how old you are, you aren't really an adult until your parents are gone.

For some people, growing up happened the day they were born. It was a fact of their birth. Abandoned at birth, or shortly thereafter, they grew up in foster homes, or with relatives that treated them more like lodgers than family. If they survived their adolescence and early adulthood without being killed or incarcerated for the rest of their lives, they could count themselves lucky, and certainly a cut above. Beating the odds did that for a person. Getting a job, wife, and a family of their own meant purpose and love. Those people stuck out. They're black and white, and three-dimensional, in a world full of two-dimensional people splashed with obnoxious coloring. Jack saw them everywhere, and if you were looking for them, they were easy to spot. They walked with their heads held high, and they had good reason. Again, beating the odds did that for a person.

Other people grew up during the natural course of life. Family members and friends passed on, walking in tandem with the tiny successes of life. They graduated from college; a sibling died unexpectedly. Their first child was born; they defaulted on their first home mortgage. They retired; they put their mom in a nursing home. And so on. Life went on for most in this manner. Something like Jack's brother Laurence.

There were others who were coddled throughout their entire lives, and when reality hit, it hit all at once, and it left them bewildered. It was an unexpected slip on the invisible ice that coated the front steps of life. They were upside down and stunned before they actually knew what happened. The trouble with being taken care of was that, eventually, the person in charge of your care left or died. All that while, this person had watched over you out of love. They never imagined the disservice they were doing you by bailing you out at every turn. What they did, they had done out of love, but they had left the object of that affection unable to cope with even the most insignificant happenings of normal life.

Jack had touched his mom's hand for the last time as she lay in the casket. It had been waxy and cold. He hadn't been able to help but think of a bowl of that wax fruit that tacky people used to use to decorate their homes. It hadn't been just her hand; his whole mom had been wax fruit in a bizarre-shaped bowl. He had tried to see the wax corpse as something more than a human fiction. He had tried to see it animated, as his living mom, the way he remembered her, but he hadn't been able to. And right then he had realized he couldn't even see his own memories of her alive. That wax fruit lady had been the only image of his mom he could see, and that wax fraud would permeate all his memories of his mom for the rest of his life. When he reminisced about the Christmas morning when he had gotten an Atari, it hadn't been his mom on the couch, it had been the wax fruit lady. When she had dropped him off for his first day of high school, yep, that had been the wax fruit lady too. And so it went, on and on. He had lost his mom the week before, but he had lost his memories of her to that abomination in the box that day, and forever after.

Jack was no sociopath, and he genuinely loved his mom, but he was also a self-centered and scared child in a man's body. The fact that the mortician had turned his mom into wax fruit bothered him, but not nearly as much as the adrenaline-fueled panic attack that shot through his entire body whenever he really stopped to acknowledge what her death meant for him.

Chapter 9

At eleven years old, Jack really had no idea what the world had in store for him, but the ringing in his left ear left no doubt as to what his seventeen-year-old brother Laurence had in store for him. Eleven years of age was about the last time Jack's life had seemed normal to him. Not perfect, but basically normal.

The therapist running the group session asked questions, and then he asked another question, but in response just said "um-hmm." He did it in much the same manner that a hundred therapists had done to Jack in the past, and likely the same way that a hundred more would do in future—that is, Jack thought, if he lived long enough to see a hundred more group therapists.

Besides the sporadic 911 calls, occasional attempted knifings, and regular baseball bat duels, things had actually been pretty good between Laurence and Jack back then. Actually, occurrences of life-threatening confrontations between Laurence and Jack had been down since the summer before Jack started sixth grade.

Their mom had grown tired of sitting in the emergency room and having strangers stare at her like she was some sort of child beater, so for Christmas, Santa Claus had brought

Laurence and Jack boxing gloves—pretty big ones, too. At least, they had seemed big on Jack's little hands. In retrospect, Jack couldn't tell you if they had been twelve or sixteen-ounce gloves, but Jack's gloves had been like enormous marshmallows on his hands, while Laurence's gloves had seemed like they were just thin strips of leather protecting his fists from injury.

Jack's gloves had actually been quite a bit smaller than Laurence's gloves, and that had been evident when they were sitting side by side. Jack's gloves had been a child size. Laurence's had been an adult size. Even so, Jack's little hands just hadn't filled those big, squishy marshmallows, and it had showed in his lack of punching power. Meanwhile, Laurence's gloves had struck Jack like socks full of pennies being swung at him.

Those Christmas gloves had been supposed to serve one purpose, and that had been to keep Laurence and Jack from doing any damage to each other that would result in scars or hospital visits. In that endeavor, they had achieved only tepid results. Unfortunately for Jack, that had meant semi-regular, undiagnosed mild concussions as direct results of taking too many blows from Laurence's much stronger, larger, and faster hands. The cuts and blood resulting from their brawls had been less frequent, but the intensity and length of time their battles took on had become legendary in scale. One thing had become clear to Jack very quickly: getting hit a couple hundred times in ten minutes several times a week certainly took a toll on a kid, but he could do it again and again.

Except for a white stripe over the front of them, their gloves had been a sort of a dried blood color. Jack had supposed the white strip over the front was the part of the glove that was supposed to connect at the conclusion of a well-thrown punch. The only parts of Laurence's gloves Jack had ever seen were the white stripes. Laurence had never seen the white stripes on Jack's gloves. Sometimes it had been hard for Jack to tell if he was seeing the white because Laurence's right glove was still in Jack's face or because Laurence had rung his bell so hard that he was staring at the white ceiling of their garage. Jack had devised a clever way to figure out which white he was seeing. If he had to get up off the ground it had been the latter. If not, it had been the former.

One day when Jack was sitting in his fifth-grade classroom, he had gotten out his sixty-four pack of Crayola crayons to color something. Fifth grade had been the last year of school in which coloring was still considered schoolwork. Upon seeing a not-quite-brown and not-quite-red crayon, Jack had immediately pulled it out and said to himself: "That's the color of dried blood. The color of dried blood is the exact color of our boxing gloves." The crayon had indicated on its half-torn-off paper sleeve that it was Burnt Sienna.

Along with Jack's inability to connect a punch with Laurence's face, one of the reasons that Laurence had never seen the white stripes on Jack's gloves was that the blood gushing out of Jack's nose and mouth had covered the white stripes and dried there. Jack's gloves had been all Burnt Sienna, no white stripes remaining. Laurence's gloves had stayed clean because he hadn't pressed them into his face constantly in a futile effort to stop his nose and mouth from bleeding. Laurence's gloves had always been near his head, protecting his face. Either that, or they had been punching Jack in his.

Boxing with Laurence was about as close as Jack had ever gotten to a positive life lesson. Jack had actually learned the value of losing during those fights. He had learned the value of perseverance. If Jack could have ever applied what he had learned with those boxing gloves on, he might have been alright. He hadn't.

One day, Jack had snuck a left hook past Laurence's gloves and bloodied his nose. Jack had been too timid to even try hitting Laurence for the longest time. Hitting Laurence had seemed an insurmountable task, and so it had always seemed smarter for Jack to cover his face and mitigate the inevitable damage. That day, Jack had realized that even when he spent all his energy covering his face, he still ended up bruised and bloodied, so he had decided to try to hit Laurence. It had turned out it wasn't really that hard to hit Laurence after all. In fact, Jack had unleashed a flurry of punches culminating in that left hook, slipping by Laurence's block and breaking his nose.

That had been the last fight and the last trip to the emergency room. It had been the summer before Jack started sixth grade, and Laurence had been the one in charge of watching Jack while their mom was at work. Laurence had called their mom's work number. Jack had thought Laurence was crying, but he had run out of the room too fast to see for sure. When she had gotten home, she had almost laughed when she saw Laurence's nose. It was bent so far to the left of his face that it looked like a steamroller had come along and meticulously flattened it. Her and Jack were the only ones that could possibly have found the situation funny. Practically every day that summer, she had come home to find Jack with toilet paper shoved up his nose, or raccoon eyes. The irony that one square blow had managed to do to Laurence's nose what Laurence's fists had failed to do to Jack's nose over those last months caused a little bit of twisted joy in their mom.

The doctor had reset it, but you could still see that Laurence's nose bent off to the left side of his face a little if you were looking for it. To Jack, it was the best trophy on earth, and it would never go away, not as long as Laurence was still around.

The other patients usually just sat there and let Jack talk, even when he was rambling. They were just happy somebody was saying something. It took the focus off of them. In any normal group of people, Jack would be delighted to sit in the background and remain unnoticed, but in there he always felt a little superior, and of course that meant he suddenly had plenty to say.

Jack's anxiety and social phobia typically kept him from speaking in even small groups of normal people, but in there, in that place with all the other throwaways, he was a star. And, just like with his inability to apply those lessons he'd learned during those fights with Laurence all those years ago, he similarly failed to make use of any lessons that place might have had to teach him. Instead, he squandered his time there showboating, showing a crowd of unimpressed staff and patients how he was the best of the malfunctioning cogs.

Jack was good at sinking a few balls—hard shots, too; banks off multiple rails, stuff like that. Ironically, he always missed clear shots at the eight ball, all night long, every time. It was the most frustrating thing for people in Jack's life to watch. Watching a light go on in someone's head for a moment before they proceeded to slightly miss the mark over and over when it was time to apply what had been learned during that momentary epiphany.

Watching someone that might have made it fail was more

heartbreaking than writing off the people who had never had a chance anyway. Jack was a fifty-one-card deck. He was hard to throw out, because he was so close to functional. You always thought that other card would just turn up in a junk drawer or a couch cushion, so you keep that incomplete deck in a cabinet. You kept it forever, and, of course, that missing five of spades never showed up, and looking at that fifty-one-card deck eventually became a point of frustration and resentment.

They ended group before Jack was done talking, but Jack still had a captive audience of one. Beth had been sitting in the corner listening to their group session.

Beth was more than a secondary character occupying a few forgettable pages of Jack's story. Beth was beautiful, and she was genuine, and she probably spent more time looking for that fifty-second card than anyone else in Jack's life.

Beth had heard this story before, but she intently listened as if it were the first time. She'd probably heard all Jack's stories before, but she liked hearing them again. It wasn't even the stories themselves; it was how Jack told them. He was a good storyteller, and he could tell you about sitting at the Department of Licensing for three hours and make it entertaining.

"So, what happened next?" Beth asked.

"Nothin' really, I busted Laurence's nose. I mean, he went to the doctor, and they set it and all that, but that was the last boxin' match. We still argued about petty brother shit, but no more physical altercations. Those gloves went into the closet for good after that. Eventually, they went into the garbage can when I was cleanin' some of my old shit out of my parents' place. For a minute, though, I think even my pap saw a little of himself in me. I'm sure it was just a little bit, and just for a minute, and never again. Nonetheless, it was worth a childhood full of put-downs and a summer filled with beatins'. At least I had a moment, and after that I just became who I became."

"Who did you become?" Beth's expression changed. Her eyebrows twitched upward, but just a little. It was subtle, but Jack had spent so much time by that point studying her face that he noticed any subtle change. That tiny expression meant she hadn't been expecting Jack's last statement.

Beth wasn't just humoring Jack; she really wanted to know what had brought Jack to the place he was in. She felt guilty for devoting so much attention to this one patient as she clearly and simultaneously neglected others. She felt guilty for feeling something more for this one patient than a professional caregiver should have felt. She felt guilty because she felt like she was being emotionally unfaithful to her long-time boyfriend, Tim, who really was a good guy. She felt guilty, but she kept doting, kept listening to the stories, and kept wondering what a repaired Jack could do if given the opportunity.

"You know. Whatever the fuck I am now," Jack said.

Beth was about five years older than Jack, and she'd had some interaction with him during each of his four prior visits to Western State. There may have been one or two other familiar faces amongst the staff from his first visit, but the only one he knew for a fact was there from his first time was Beth.

"I'm fuckin' scared. They're all gone. And not that bullshit momentary scared like when you have to talk in front of the class. It's scared like in my gut, and, like, all the time. It's the scared that's a constant dull ache in my stomach, not just a jolt at a horror movie. Sometimes it goes away when I'm drinkin' or fuckin', or pilled up, but rest of the time it's there. The ache is in my gut, and the thoughts are in my brain. They stick to my brain. They coat it like the way super glue coats your fingertip. The thoughts, they don't go away, they don't get tired out, they don't quit. They just win, and they make my gut ache worse.

"My family's gone, except my brother, who barely spoke to me even when our parents were alive. My only friends are either ekin' out a miserable false façade of normality or circlin' the drain right along with me. If I don't get it together this time, I think I'm done for. Dyin' don't really scare me, and it don't really bother me neither. I kind of wish it would just come already so I can get done with all this, this place, this life, this planet. Fuckers die, they don't even appreciate it. Give it to me, I'd fuckin' appreciate it. The only miserable people I know are alive. The dead ones are at rest and no doubt happy. I don't fuckin' know. I'm scared of bein' scared, and I'm scared of bein' alive. I can't kill myself, but dyin' some other way would be more easy."

"What would make you want to live, she asked."

"I don't have to be a millionaire, or famous, or even financially secure. I don't need a wife, a good job, or a house in the suburbs. I'd just like to have peace in my mind for five minutes. I'd like to live without the terror of existence that taps my brain like fuckin' non-stop war drums. Thump, thump, thump, I can't escape. It's on the move, and it's comin' after me. I'd like to feel safe and secure without the assistance of alcohol or drugs. I want to be Laurence, not Jack. Being Jack is the worst."

Beth and Jack had started at that place, but Jack hadn't known all that yet. All he had known was that the year he had turned eighteen, when he was committed to that place the first time, he'd met the only person he'd ever have a real connection with. She had known it before Jack did. She had even transferred wards and gotten off graveyard shifts to spend more time with him.

Some might call it love at first sight. It was an open question whether Jack could even understand what love between two mature people was. It was just as likely that Jack was lovable in the way that an abused dog was lovable. It was also possible that he would have become devoted to the first person to come along and toss him a bone. Whatever it was, it was certainly a meaningful connection on a level that people didn't typically understand. Some things just stick when they are thrown together, and nothing else matters. Once in your life, you might stick to someone and not be able to disentangle yourself, not that you would ever want to. If that happens, consider yourself one of the lucky ones. Beth and Jack had stuck together. That was just how it was.

Chapter 10

Liberating his mind from Mormon indoctrination might have been the only bold stand Jack had ever taken. Abusing one's body with substances as Jack had done certainly took balls, and suffering mentally as he had done took endurance, but a stand was different. For an eleven-year-old, taking God out of your life was a big step. It was more than that; it was a stand. Liberating your mind from anything encumbering it was a step in the right direction, and a step toward owning the only thing that anyone could truly own, their own mind, couldn't ever be the wrong choice. "That is, you own it right up until the fuckin' moment you don't." Nevertheless, the mind was the last refuge. Whether the refuge held up or not is another story, but for most people, it was a domain they could own absolutely.

For Jack, that first step away from Mormonism had happened at school. Of course, it hadn't happened in a classroom, or the gym, or even the cafeteria. Like most of Jack's revelations back then, it had happened on the playground. On that occasion, school had not even been in session. It had been summer, late summer. Even summer school had been let out a few weeks before. It had probably been August, but nobody could ever know for sure.

When the playground went quiet in the late summer, the truly odd kids came out to play on it. The kids whose parents had let them walk to school in kindergarten. The kids that broke into the abandoned houses in the neighborhood for no better reason than to see what was inside. Those kids were the ones that went to the playground on days like that. Those kids didn't go there to find kids to play with. They went just to haunt an abandoned playground. Jack had been such a kid. "*The Omega Man* and *Dawn of the Dead* changed my whole perspective on shit. A world without all those pesky humans would have been a playground for me. It was my best fantasy. A playground without a bunch of kids was my best reality."

He hadn't been looking for them, but Jack had found people that day at the playground. They hadn't seemed to mind being found, either. As a matter of fact, they had seemed pretty excited at Jack's arrival. Fernando and Angelina had been in the same grade as Jack, and they'd all been in the same class more than once. Fernando had been the only Latino kid at Jack's elementary school. He had been Puerto Rican. He'd moved to the United States a few years earlier. When a new kid from somewhere interesting showed up at school, girls were always immediately interested. The Puerto Rican thing had worn off a long time before, but he had still had an accent that Jack suspected he had embellished to remind everybody that he was from someplace exotic. To eleven-year-old Jack, Puerto Rico had seemed exotic.

Angelina had been what you would call unremarkable in every way imaginable. She hadn't been popular, but she had known a few girls that she had hung around with at school. She'd had a goofy-ass little girl bowl cut which kids had made fun of and had certainly hurt her overall appearance, but she hadn't been ugly. She hadn't worn nice clothes, but the ones she had worn were clean and well-kept. Jack hadn't ever talked to her, so he had assumed she was shy, but for all he knew she could have been a horrendous bitch.

Jack had stared at that bowl cut. He'd never been that close to it. He hadn't been able to not stare at it. She may have been unremarkable, but she had also been the first girl Jack had ever smoked a joint with, and the first girl he had ever made out with. The fact that both things and more had happened on the same day had made Jack a god amongst other eleven-year-olds. That had also made Fernando the first guy Jack had ever smoked a joint with, but nobody really gave a shit about the first guy you had smoked a joint with.

That day had started the same as every other day that Jack had spent at the playground to be by himself that summer. He had liked to go to the ballfields first. They had been the first part of the school grounds that Jack had come across while walking to the school, so they had been an easy place to start. Sometimes, adults had come and played there. Adults and older kids playing on the fields would forget or lose things. Sometimes, they had just left useful things behind. Usually, it had just been sports equipment. There had been those rare occasions when somebody had taken off their watch or a ring, or better yet set a wallet on the bench by home plate.

After combing the ball fields for valuable possessions and useful castoffs Jack would head over to the swings to comb through the grass behind them and see what had shaken out the pants pockets of those who had been swinging. The last stop on his tour of the playground had always been a unique feature that not all playgrounds had. There had been a gigantic gravel pit next to the portables where the kindergarten kids had gone to class. That had been where the big toys were. The gravel pit had always been good for a few things. There had almost always been a couple of *Star Wars* action figures or some Hot Wheels cars that kids had lost. There had never been anything great, but there had always been something worth taking home.

The tire mountain had never had anything worth taking home, but it was always worth looking inside of it. The thing had been unavoidable. It called out to you. A mountain constructed entirely of gigantic tractor tires large enough for grown men to climb inside of and sit down. Judging from the items regularly left behind in the tires, it appeared they had also been large enough inside for grown men to drink Jack Daniels, smoke cigarettes, shoot IV drugs, and pass out in pools of puke. Venturing into the tires was always a trip into the unknown. Normally, Jack would find a dormant, transient body curled around a nearly empty bottle of Night Train or the aforementioned Jack Daniels. That day, all he had found was Fernando and Angelina.

Jack had seen the joint they were holding. They hadn't mustered up the nerve to light it. Jack had been all in the second he saw the thing. They hadn't been expecting Jack to show up. For whatever reason, they had seemed to think that Jack had smoked a joint before and would be able to show them how. Jack had ended up being the one to light it up and take the first hit. It had tasted like he was smoking perfume made from pond scum. He had inhaled the smoke and held it in like he'd seen Cheech do on *Up in Smoke*. Jack had known immediately that he was in love. As he had exhaled, he had felt electric sensations running up the various blood vessels in his head. It had felt like when you stood up too fast, but much more intense.

Fernando had taken a couple of puffs, but Jack didn't think he had really even inhaled it. Angelina and Jack had smoked the rest of the joint, which Fernando had lifted from his older brother's room. After it was gone, they had been really baked. Jack had an even harder time not staring at Angelina's bowl cut. To Jack's stoned mind, it had seemed more like some sort of animal that had taken residence on top of her head than a haircut.

It turned out that Fernando had actually taken the joint from his brother's room because Angelina was his across the street neighbor, and he'd told her that his brother always had joints in his room. She had told him to get one so that they could smoke it. Of course, he had wanted to impress the neighbor girl, and next thing they knew they were sitting in the tire mountain. That was when Jack had showed up.

After they had smoked the joint, Fernando had seemed to go crazy. Contact high, Jack had guessed. Jack doubted he'd had a real hit of the thing at all. Jack had felt crazy too, but he had maintained his composure because there had been a girl there. Just like at home when Lisa, his hot babysitter, would come over. He had always had to take a dump because his mom had made macaroni and cheese with hot dogs in it for dinner whenever she had left him with a babysitter. It had been just like that. He'd had to eat, so he had eaten, then he'd had to shit, so he had shit.

"You got to get to that bathroom and do your thing, but you got to maintain your cool. You can't be poopin' yourself while you're sitting on the couch watchin' the movie with the hot babysitter. You can't even fart into the cushion, too risky. There's always smell leakage. I'd risk it if it was just my mom or Laurence, but not when Lisa was there. Eventually, though, you got to make your move for the bathroom. The best time was like halfway through the movie, right after Lisa went in and peed out the Tab she'd been drinking. Plus, as an added bonus, the bathroom had a faint hint of what girls smell like after they pull down their jeans. It was sweet and sour."

Fernando hadn't maintained his composure. He had just gone bonkers and run away. Fernando had been the kind of kid that pooped at the wrong time when the hot babysitter was over. It had taken about thirty seconds before Jack completely stopped worrying about what had happened to Fernando. It had probably been another full minute before Jack had forgotten that Fernando existed at all, and about five minutes after that he forgot the entire rest of the world had existed at all. Nothing outside of the tire mountain had mattered, and Jack had become convinced that nothing out there was real anyway.

It was very deep introspection, but very insignificant when you realized that every other eleven-year-old kid who had smoked a joint, or taken a hit of acid, had had the exact same experience. While that may have been true, those other eleven-year-olds hadn't had a hot bowl cut girl like Angelina inside a gigantic tractor tire. Or maybe they did, but Angelina had been Jack's hot bowl cut girl.

Being eleven, stoned out of your mind, and stuck in a universe that consisted of the inside of a gigantic tractor tire had a way of breaking down barriers that kept eleven-year-old kids from touching each others' private parts. Angelina had started talking about what it would be like if they touched certain parts of each other's bodies. Jack had begun to feel even stranger than he already had from the weed, so he had just reached out and grabbed one of Angelina's boobs. Or at least, he had grabbed what would someday be a boob. Still, he had known he was getting somewhere, and he had gotten two full fingers full of nipple.

Jack had been content to keep touching nipple over her shirt because she had kept acting like she was enjoying it. Then she had done something unexpected. She had stuck her hand in Jack's jeans and grabbed his hard cock and slid her tongue in his mouth. Jack had kissed her back and immediately stuck his hand inside the waistband of her shorts. He had felt wetness, and he had smelt that sweet and sour smell that his babysitter left in the bathroom, but much stronger. Without even trying, Jack had gotten to third base. He hadn't even known what that meant, but she had seemed content. Jack had cummed a few seconds later, which had immediately answered for him a long-standing question: what exactly was an erection good for? When Jack had been little, he had used to wonder why God had created a body part as useless as a dick. Weren't there a hundred other more efficient ways to move urine out of the body? Jack hadn't known everything, but he had known that girls didn't have dicks, and they seemed to manage peeing just fine. Jack had known this because he'd been in the women's restroom at the Bon Marché numerous times with his mom when he had been much younger. When he had been little, and he needed help going, she had brought him into the women's restroom. All the women in the bathroom seemed like they peed out of their butts just fine. Needless to say, it had been epiphany central in the gigantic tractor tire that afternoon.

After Jack came, the mood in the tire had changed. Jack had still been really high, but Angelina had looked at him like she had done something wrong. Jack hadn't really understood why the mood had changed; he just knew it had. As far as he was concerned it had been a perfect day. He had gotten baked for the first time, and he'd had his first hand job. It had lasted all of ten seconds, but Jack figured endurance would come with more practice. Jack had started to think about heading home. He had figured the afternoon cartoons would be coming on soon and he hadn't wanted to miss Star Blazers. He had told Angelina that he was going to head back to his house, and that she could come watch cartoons if she wanted. She had just shaken her head.All of a sudden, conversation had stopped, physical interaction had stopped, fun had stopped, and weirdness had begun. Jack had asked if she was okay to walk home, and she had nodded.

This is a scenario that would play out again and again with every girl Jack ever had sex with. Except for Beth. There were intimacy problems from the start, but never with Beth. For some reason, Jack immediately got the feeling that he owed Angelina something, but he wasn't sure what was expected of him. He had wanted to leave because he hadn't known what would make things feel normal again. He had wanted to put distance between him and the weirdness. So was born Jack's postcoital routine. For most of Jack's life, he had been more comfortable paying for sex because he knew exactly what the girl wanted: the money. It was a transaction, and everybody walked away with what they bargained for. Jack really believed that. That was one of the reasons he had never tried to lowball working girls. He figured if they were nice enough to bang the guys they were expected to bang to make ends meet, they'd earned every penny of it.

At night, Jack would sneak out of the house and roam the local alleys in his neighborhood. In his house, he could have walked right out the front door, and no one would have even noticed. His dad couldn't have cared less what Jack did, his mom was always asleep on the couch in the evening, and it was doubtful his brother would have even noticed. It was even more doubtful that any of them would have given a crap if they had noticed. Nonetheless, Jack had employed covert tactics.

His room on the second floor had had a laundry chute in it. Basically, it had been a smelly hole where people had dropped dirty clothes into a compartment that looked like a cabinet in the laundry room on the first floor. There had been a flip top lid on the chute that had stanched some of the smell, but a week of a family's dirty clothes sitting just below your bedroom had a sour stench all the same. Where others only recognized the ripe stink of dirty underwear, Jack had recognized opportunity. The chute had gone straight down, and it was only about six or seven feet from top to bottom, so one day Jack had tried lowering himself down it. After that, Jack would turn on his TV, turn out his light, and lock his door before exiting the house through the chute. Since he had always slept with his TV on and his door locked, no one would think anything strange was up if they came by his door.

Jack would brace the rubber soles of his Sauconys on the side walls of the chute, grip the rim of the chute, and lower himself down slowly. From there, popping the chute door open from the inside and lowering himself onto the washing machine had been no problem. The back door to the house had been in the laundry room, and no one ever locked any of the doors at Jack's house, so reentry was guaranteed. Even if it hadn't been, there had been at least five windows on the ground floor that didn't lock at all. Getting back up the chute was a little more time-consuming, as he'd had to brace his shoes against the walls of the chute so he could inch his way back up, but it really hadn't been any more complicated than getting down, just more intensive. This was how young Jack had gained absolute freedom of movement.

Dragging his Radio Flyer red wagon behind him, he would snatch the aluminum cans other families had been collecting for recycling. They'd leave them by their garages, on their back porches; anywhere Jack wouldn't have to breach a lock to get at their cans made them fair game. Jack's covert tactics had cost him a few bite wounds from filthy canine mongrels, but he had always been victorious in the end. Sometimes he had recycled newspapers as well, but they were bulky and hadn't paid out the way cans did. Also, when they got wet, none of the recycling places had wanted them. The recycling places not taking wet newspapers had sort of been a coffin nail to Jack getting seriously involved in the newspaper game, as he had pulled his goods in a little red wagon in Washington where it rained even when the sun was out. Still, if he found a motherload of newspapers under a carport, he would still grab them and gamble that he'd get them to the recycling center mostly dry.

Because of cans, Jack had always had a pocketful of cash, usually six or seven dollars. On that day, he had needed it because he had felt compelled to bring Angelina to the Korean lady's candy store by the school for candy and soda. Jack had gone to that store almost daily for years. He must have dropped a thousand dollars into the Frogger machine at that little store, but he had never known the woman who owned it by anything other than Korean lady, which could be confusing since he had lived in a neighborhood that was about a third Korean.

As a matter of fact, his friend that lived five blocks north of him had gone to a similar store by his house that was owned by a Korean lady, and he had called that store the Korean lady's candy store, too. In Alabama, if you said "the Korean lady," everybody knew who you were talking about, since there were probably all of three Korean ladies in the whole state. In south Tacoma, the Korean lady could have been anyone.

Jack was white, but when he was little, his two best friends had been Korean. Most of the small businesses in his neighborhood were owned and operated by Korean people. There had been Korean writing all over signs and business banners in his neighborhood, all of which seemed perfectly normal to him until that day. Jack had started to wonder if the Korean lady at the store referred to him as the white kid that always played Frogger. He had started to wonder why he called her the Korean lady, instead of just the lady at the candy store. He had figured there was something more there to think on, but his brain had been mushy right then, and he hadn't been able to formulate coherent thoughts anymore.

Still high, but now convinced that the world outside might actually exist, and be safe, they had ventured out. For a while, Jack had really considered never leaving the apparent calm and safety of the tire. Even at that age, Jack figured that if a girl gave him sexual attention, he should buy her something. Walking through the door, Jack had asked Angelina if he should get some quarters for Frogger or Pac-Man. She had declined, but he had offered, and to Jack, as long as he got credit for asking, that was all that mattered. Once they were in the store, Jack had told Angelina that she could get whatever she wanted, and however much she wanted of it. Jack had grabbed two Charleston Chews, a Three Musketeers, and a Coke. She had opted for an ice cream sandwich, and an A&W Root Beer.

Outside the store, Jack had enjoyed the best meal he'd ever had, then or since. Angelina had nibbled at her ice cream sandwich and barely sipped the root beer. Five minutes later, Jack had felt the way he'd felt for the eleven years previous to the joint: bland, normal, shy, bored, depressed, and embarrassed. Even so, he had offered to walk Angelina home, but she had preferred to walk alone. She had lived in the opposite direction, so Jack had been happy to let her go. Plus, he had figured her parents would know what they'd done if he showed up with her. Jack had imagined the events in the tire would play like a movie projecting on his forehead for everyone to see. He had envisioned Angelina's dad as a big burly man, and upon his arrival at her house, he'd scream "did you just fuck around with my daughter" right in Jack's face. That was actually the nice version of what he had envisioned her father would do after seeing the pornographic tire mountain movie on his forehead.

Jack had just said, "see you later," and watched her walk off down Park Avenue. He'd see her from time to time for the next several years, but they had never really talked again. "Hi" or an awkward "how's it going" was about all they were ever able to muster after that. Eventually she grew the bowl cut out, and Jack realized she was more attractive than he'd initially thought. Luckily, they'd had nothing before that joint, so it hadn't been much of a loss that they had nothing after it, either. Right then, it had occurred to Jack that, if he ran home, he could probably catch the last half of Star Blazers.

Chapter 11

I n retrospect, Jack could admit that being committed at eighteen had advantages that being committed at twenty-eight did not. To start, when he was eighteen, he had still been able to remember what being with Angelina in the tire had felt like.

By twenty-eight, the visceral feeling of that experience had disintegrated into a worn-out Betamax tape version of itself. Sure, you could still watch the *Stand by Me* tape you'd watched a thousand times, but all the sharpness was gone. Not only that, but there were entire portions of the tape that were just snow on the screen, eaten, crumpled tape. The experience was nothing that was really real to Jack at the age of twenty-eight. It might as well have been someone else's memory, or for that matter an actual movie on a worn-out Betamax tape.

Jack sat and wondered how many of his real memories were really real at all, or if he'd just told himself a particular lie so many times that his brain had accepted it as the truth. He figured that most of his memories had started out as real events and received some embellishments shortly thereafter to increase the curb appeal to other people who might hear the memory as a story Jack told at some point. However, the pristine, if somewhat embellished, final theatrical release version of the memories were ultimately altered and degraded through the telling and retelling of them. "It's the Betamax tape that got played over and over. By the way I'm the one who came up with that Betamax metaphor thing, not him. I just told him about it one time, and now he uses it all the time like he thought it up."

Jack also figured there was a bit of collective memory that was appropriated to oneself. "Because that reminds me of the time that I was super wasted, and I boned that girl Cherise, but then I ran into that dude Phil like a year later, and it turned out that he boned her. I was just there in the bed half asleep. Man, I was sure I boned her, but it turns out it was Phil." Jack was so upset about it that he had called Cherise after he had found out. They had hooked up shortly after that. Apparently, he felt he'd lost something when he found out he hadn't had sex with her, and just really wanted to get it back. A notch on his bedpost had been subtracted, and he couldn't mentally square it being gone, so he'd had to make it the truth.

None of that had helped him ask Dolores out on a date that day. Stories of pre-teen ejaculation, post-teen institutional commitment, sibling brutality, and an inability to discern his own memories from those of his friends weren't good icebreakers with female baristas. At least, he assumed they weren't. Jack lacked real dating experience. For instance, when he had called up Cherise, he had just asked her if she wanted to watch a movie. He had showed up at her apartment with a case of Schmidt Ice, and a VHS of *Clerks*.

Two hours later, it had been on. Two hours and ten minutes later, he had felt guilty. He had wanted to leave, so he had left the open pack of Camels on her bedside table and the rest of the beer in the fridge. He had taken the *Clerks* tape, since he used it pretty regularly to hook up with girls, but he had figured the beer and smokes were an appropriate illustration of his gratitude for a good time. He had seen her a couple years later at a show. She had been with some guy. She had said "hey" when Jack walked by, but other than that ignored him. At that point, he had figured that the beer and smokes must not have been enough gratitude for Cherise, and wondered if maybe he should have left the *Clerks* VHS at her place, too.

There were plenty of baristas that were into beer and sloppy hook ups, but Dolores didn't seem like one of them. Jack was scared of pretty much everything already. Talking to girls wasn't typically on the list, but it was that day. Since Dolores couldn't be wooed by a case of cheap beer and a movie, he was very far out of his element. He'd spent two months going to Grounds for Coffee almost every day to see Dolores. It certainly wasn't for the overpriced, pretentious coffee. Jack usually went home afterward, where his only window pointed at the coffee shop. Jack could see Dolores inside working for the rest of her shift.

Jack pumped himself up to ask her out. "She was probably insulted that I hadn't asked her out. She probably thought somethin' was wrong with her because even the guy that lived in the low-income apartments that spent all his SSI money on coffee wouldn't even ask her out." As soon as Jack felt the requisite amount of courage to go through with it, his brain would drag him right back down. Jack didn't bring much to the table as a potential mate. Unfortunately for Jack, that was exactly what he said to her the following day.

She was doing a "find your ideal mate" quiz in *Cosmopolitan* when he walked in to order his morning coffee at one in the afternoon.

"What do you bring to a relationship as a potential mate, Jack?" At first, he thought she was being glib, but she looked genuinely interested in getting his response.

"Well, I'd bring my SSI check every month, and make sure the house is clean. I've been with a lot of girls, but I don't have a lot of relationship experience per se—" (he added air quotes when he said "relationship") "—but I have a sincere desire to have a lastin' connection with another human being."

Her mouth hung open like she was about to say "wow" in a get me the fuck out of here sort of way. Jack figured that at any second she was going to start backing away from the counter to put some space between them before realizing she was sort of trapped in a fairly confined coffee shop with him. In reality, she thought he might be the funniest person she'd ever met. She couldn't figure out how he'd come up with such a great response so fast. She was quite impressed with his ability to fabricate such a clever retort to the ridiculousness of a cosmo quiz with an equally ridiculous and contrary response. Dolores had been attracted to him before, but with that one brazen show of wit, he was fifty percent more attractive immediately.

It was unfortunate for Dolores that she couldn't recognize a person who had just dumped too much crazy and too much honesty on her the way a five-year-old sheepishly admits to eating all the cookies.

"Wow, that's a mouthful. All this stupid quiz says is to look for somebody who puts down the toilet seat and has a job," she said.

Jack hadn't seen the magazine until after he was done speaking. He thought she was asking him to apply for the position of her boyfriend, just like that, right there in that coffee shop.

Jack replied as confidently as anyone could in such an embarrassing circumstance. "Well, I have one of those things goin' for me, but it's not the job." Then he frowned.

Jack had employed many strange techniques with the opposite sex, and he'd had many of them work, but he'd never used the crippled angel routine. It wasn't a routine, though. Jack needed somebody right at that moment. He'd just spent Thanksgiving, not two weeks earlier, eating turkey sandwiches made from cold cuts he had bought at the store with his food stamps. They weren't even the good cold cuts from the deli counter. They were the shitty packaged ones in the refrigerated aisle of the store. He needed somebody to give him a chance to start getting somewhere. He'd done the best he could do for himself, without help, and failed pretty miserably. On his own, all he'd been able to manage was a crappy apartment, a monthly check from the state, and endless hours with which to contemplate what to do with the next allotment of endless hours.

He didn't need something; he needed somebody, just like he always had. People had always been the only stability in his life, and all his people were gone. Jack figured that if he could just make a start with someone that was willing to believe that he could be more than he was at that moment, he might be okay. He needed somebody that saw a project, not a lost cause. Jack wondered if Dolores could be that girl. Jack assumed it wouldn't ultimately matter, as he could never overcome his ill-advised disclosures to her. "It's like takin' a dump at a girl's place the first time she invites you over. You just can't come back from one of those!"

"I know you like coffee because I see you in here almost

every day. What else do you like? What do you do when you're not in here drinking coffee" she asked.

Jack almost said, "I sleep eighteen hours a day because I'm broke as a joke and spend all my spare money on this outrageously expensive coffee so that I can talk to you for sixty seconds," but his common sense had finally caught up to his mouth, and he stayed quiet for a minute.

Finally, Jack spoke. "Honestly, I don't do much, but I like you. I like you a lot, and I'm just tryin' to figure out how selfish it is for me to impose myself and my issues on someone else."

"Well, my life is already coasting in neutral, so now's a good time for you to hop on. Do you feel like hopping on, Jack?"

There was some definite innuendo to that last little part. Jack could tell by the way she leaned forward and let him get a good look at her cleavage when she said it.

"All I can do is slow you down, and all you can do is break my heart," Jack said.

"Well, then, why don't we try having a little fun before we start destroying each other's lives?"

Jack figured he had no business going out on a date with a girl, even if said girl was unwise enough to agree to go. Dating was the sort of thing people with jobs, cars, and decent apartments did. All he wanted right then was to take this girl out, but he had a hard time justifying it in his mind. Jack decided to waste his entire month's spending money, which he had rationed so carefully from his government issued SSI check, on one night out with Dolores. He wasn't even trying to get laid. If he was, using all his spending money might actually make sense. He just wanted to take her out on a nice little date; dinner, movie, whatever.

Here he was again, imposing his poor circumstances upon

another. This other didn't even really know what she was in for. She still thought his approach was some shtick or something, and he was about to blow all his spending money for the month keeping up that façade. She had passed on his clear offers to withdraw and leave her in peace, but he knew she couldn't possibly know how bad of shape he was really in. So it didn't seem right from the outset, but Jack wanted it so badly that he forced the quieting of his forebodings.

He knew it was selfish, but he pushed that down anyhow. He needed this. He needed a lifeline. He needed something to leech off of for a while so that he could feel partially human again. Whenever Jack sucked, he had a bad habit of leaving a dried-out husk behind. Most of his husks knew what they were getting into right up front, so he'd always been able to tell himself he wasn't really a bad guy, but Dolores was different. She was about to be sucked dry without proper notification. Jack knew that, and he felt bad about it, but Jack had to look out for Jack first and foremost, so he did it anyway.

In fairness, if you had to judge Jack, you wouldn't call him a bad guy. He was certainly selfish. He was fearful of life, so fearful, in fact, that, to him, his existence seemed more like walking through a real-life horror movie than a real life at all. That also made him extremely paranoid. Outwardly, any casual observer could characterize him as a train wreck simply on the basis of his substance abuse alone. He used people, and in the process often used them up, but his goal was not to destroy them, not even close. Jack was just a germ with feelings, and germs destroyed things. He wasn't a sociopath, and he didn't like it, but germs destroyed things. That's just what they did. That's what he did.

Jack was actually giddy planning out his date with Dolores.

He really had no idea what a "good date" consisted of. Jack always did finger quotes when he said "good date." He knew dinner and a movie, but what restaurant? What was the dress code for a "good date?" How much full-frontal nudity was appropriate for a "good date" movie? The Mecca Theater in downtown Tacoma, which was right next door to his apartment building and across the street from Grounds for Coffee, had movies, but they were of the XXX variety. He supposed the Mecca was not a good choice for a movie on a first date, but the location was convenient. Plus, they sold cigarettes at the counter and you could smoke in the theater. Those were the upsides. The downsides were, again, that all they played were pornographic feature films, the employees were perverts, and the theater smelled like cum. "Not only that, but there was always a fifteen-year-old male prostitute suckin' off some scuzzy seventy-year-old man two rows in front of you."

For all Jack knew about dating, you took a girl to the drive-in movie, then to the malt shop afterward. Everything Jack knew about dating, he had learned from watching *Happy Days*. Fucking, on the other hand—Jack had learned everything he knew about fucking from being a drug-addled, derelict, degenerate piece of shit who hung out at places like the Mecca. As a matter of fact, Jack knew so much about the nastiest kinds of fucking that he knew he could get a five-dollar blow job at the Mecca Theater from a woman with four teeth that night.

He seriously considered heading down to the Mecca right then to get a five-dollar movie ticket and a five-dollar blowjob, but he realized having ten fewer dollars would seriously damage the Dolores date fund, so he just took care of himself. At least he'd made time to watch *Happy Days* when he was a kid or he'd really have been out of his element.

Without *Happy Days*, Jack's vision of a date would be a quick trip over to his dealer's house to suck on the big glass dick, then over to the Ol' Lonesome tavern for a twenty-course meal of one-dollar beers. The girls Jack usually had sex with not only considered that a more than generous use of his money, but also a classy night out, and certainly enough to seal the deal at the end of the night. What was even sadder was that Jack himself had just recently realized why, for normal girls, that did not count as a classy night out.

Jack polished his one pair of Doc Marten boots and tried to make a perfect crease in the cuff of his Levi's by laying several books on them. He didn't have an iron, so he had to be creative. He kept looking for an iron while he was dumpster diving, but had not come across one.

During the three days before his date with Dolores, Jack spent practically every spare moment either planning or thinking about it.

One thing he didn't want to do was go to the coffee shop. It seemed awkward to go in there in the days leading up to the date. "I mean, what was I gonna to say, I can't wait 'til I see you on that date we planned, you remember don't you. That seems a little desperate, even for me." Of course, she remembered the date, and Jack didn't feel like either one of them deserved the additional clumsy conversation that would be the inevitable result of going in there every day.

Plus, he now lacked coffee money, since he was blowing it all on the date. Jack figured she would notice that he wasn't coming in for his normal daily coffee. He assumed she wouldn't think it was strange since they'd just made a serious alteration to their current relationship by agreeing to go on the date at all. On the morning of the date, he planned on showing up for his morning coffee and talking freely about the date. That way, she wouldn't have to wait all day for his confirmation call. For a moment, cold blood ran though Jack's veins when he realized that if the date went poorly, he'd have to find a new place to get coffee. It went away when he realized that anywhere else he went for coffee would cost him about half of what it did at Grounds for Coffee. A silver lining: He'd have to walk further, but he'd save a lot of money in the long run.

In the meantime, he'd been soliciting advice from every person at his disposal, which in totality amounted to very few people. That being the case, Jack decided to widen his pool of advisors. Nearly any living adult had more experience at dating than Jack, so he just started asking people at random, or semi-random.

Stu was the maintenance guy at his building, and he looked like he'd taken a few girls to nice restaurants, so Jack asked him. Todd didn't date much, but he had, somehow along the way, picked up some practical dating tips. Jack even went so far as to ask the guys that dumpster dived his garbage bins. It took some prodding, but Jack discovered that even the dumpster divers had been on a few dates of their own. He still didn't like that they dived the dumpsters that Jack coveted, but they did tell him what they knew about dating.

To the best of his understanding, stemming from this diverse panel of advisors, it appeared that it was not necessary to take a girl to the nicest restaurant in the city for a first date. That much was a relief to Jack. That was exactly what he'd planned to do. It was widely agreed upon by his advisors that he had better spring for a taxi to get around. That one didn't seem negotiable. No car was fine with most girls, especially if you were a city dweller. Lots of people in the city didn't have cars, but that was no excuse to make a girl ride the bus on a first date. For some reason, it appeared that New York City was the only place in America that public transportation was a viable option for car-impaired daters. Jack wished he was a New Yorker for a moment, then realized that getting a taxi once for a date was easier than dealing with a lifetime of smelly, rat-infested subways. Anyhow, it was a problem that might very well remedy itself, seeing as how Dolores had a car of her own and probably preferred driving to riding in a cab anyhow, but Jack had to feel it out.

The next phase of the date was conduct. It was a good general rule to keep conversation on most first dates somewhat light, best to steer clear of possible sore subjects. Molestation, politics, animal rights, abortion, prostitution as a sensible employment option for academically challenged men and women. These were all subjects that Jack figured were possible sore subjects, and best to be avoided altogether.

First dates were all about finding enough common ground that two people decided they were lonely enough to have sex with each other. A relationship might or might not blossom from that first hookup, and if it did, that was the time to find out you hated each other, not before. After that first date with Dolores, Jack really thought he would have dating and relationships figured out.

"It's probably only gonna take 'bout a week for two people to get to know each other. By the time that happens there's a pretty good chance they're gonna hate each other. Or they're gonna dislike each other enough to not want to sleep with each other. Basically, two people have less than a week to have sex, or it probably ain't gonna happen, so they better find a few things they like 'bout each other as soon as possible so that they can start fuckin' immediately. That's how you build a solid fuckin' relationship. Also, if you move in together right away, it's even harder to break up, so you can hate each other even more and still stay together. That's a fuckin' great deal for everyone involved."

Jack was a brave street philosopher. He knew things inherently that others didn't, and he said things that others wouldn't. Jack's learned philosophy that dating was just the pretext and camouflage for fucking was one such example. Nobody says it, but it's what most people are thinking. Or it is what most guys are thinking, at least, and as far as Jack was concerned, the girls should be notified of that fact if they hadn't been already. "It's not cool to keep it a secret, eyes wide open, right."

Before he had dated, he had known how to find girls that understood how it worked. After he dated, he realized that not every girl knew how it worked, and he could never understand how so many of them could have missed such an obvious fact. "How is it that mentally ill, dope fiend prostitutes understand that fuckin' is the linchpin of human interaction, but professional girls with college degrees think it's mutual admiration. God, them bitches is dumb! I guess there's some shit you just don't learn in a book." To Jack, it seemed like pulling the curtain back on something, but in reverse.

Strangely enough, with the smart girls, steering the conversation as far away from the issue of sex as possible was typically Jack's only chance of getting laid. Not talking about it somehow gave it power. The sexual tension it created masked itself as a meaningful connection, and once that threshold requirement had been met, even the smart girls started inviting him up to their apartments. Whether the smart girls realized it or not, Jack simply found a different route for making sex the primary concern on a date.

Later, and for a very brief period of time, Jack was even able to frame his indigency as a bohemian and artistic lifestyle choice, repudiating conformed and assimilated America in favor of a more evolved existence focused on the realization of the self. Jack found a book in the garbage one time that gave him some stellar talking points. He got more ass from smart rich girls with good jobs during a four-month period, after he put all the pieces together, than he got for the remainder of his life combined.

All that was the master class. Planning one date with Dolores was the survey level. Jack's research revealed that it was proper to attempt a peck on the lips at the completion of a successful first date. A successful date included a minimum of weird, awkward pauses, at least two locations i.e., a restaurant and a movie, and a good flow of light conversation that in no way pertained to sex. On that basis, you could expect a positive response to the peck on the lips. "At that point, you will know if you're bein' prompted for somethin' more simply by how her body moves in your arms. If she melts in your arms all smooth like black tar heroin over a flame, you're in. If she's brittle, like puttin a razor through a choppy rock of angel dust, your night is over, my friend."

Jack still didn't know it all right at that moment. Stu the maintenance guy, who Jack added to his list of advisors when he started planning his date with Dolores, provided him with some nuggets of wisdom:

"Look, I go out with bitches all the time, and some of the time I can't match the phone number in my wallet to no face. I gets a lot of digits. But if I gets the digits, I wanted to hit it enough to gets the digits in the first place, and I be trustin' my own good judgment, ya know. I try to write somethin' down next to their name to help me remember 'em, and hopefully to remember what they likes to eat, o' where they likes to go out. That way when I calls 'em, I say somethin' like ha lets go here o' there, o' let's eat here o' there. And, also, when my wife finds them digits in my pockets, I can just tell her it's some ol' lady who lives in the building who I took out to lunch on her eightieth birthday, o' cos she's got no family, o' some other bullshit. But what I'm getting' at is just this. Women want to think that the guyz they goes out with cares enough 'bout them to, ya know, know what they like, even when we just met them at the club o' something. O', that, at the very least we want them to have fun, and that we care 'bout where they want to go o' whatever, whether we do o' don't.

"So, plannin' a date is the easies' thing in the world. Decide on somethin' that you won't hate doin,' and someplace to eat you won't hate eatin'. Then ask, if that's okay with her, and that if she prefers, she can choose the restaurant, o' whatever else you got goin' on. Easy, like that. Trust me, I date several times a week, and I got a wife. Ya know wot I'm saying?"

All adulterous and misogynist motives aside, what Stu had to say made lots of sense to Jack, and it made planning the date much easier. Going on a date was all about entertaining the person you were going out with. Dating was like everything else in the world: just a means to get what you wanted from somebody.

For once, satisfying his own physical urges wasn't what he

had in mind. That was not to say that his aim was entirely altruistic. You could say that Jack's aim was more sinister than using somebody for sex. It was his intention to use this girl for her emotional and mental stability. Jack's was clearly nonexistent and always had been. She worked at a coffee shop, likely for not much more than minimum wage, and probably made no more than twenty bucks in tips a day, but she went to college, maintained an automobile, and had an apartment. It was not Jack's intention to make himself happy at her expense, but if his emotional and mental security had to come at a negative cost to hers, he was willing to make her suffer a little.

Chapter 12

And back to this again. Jack was sure he was shrinking. Somewhere he'd heard that you only stayed your maximum height for seven to ten years, and since he hadn't grown since he was sixteen, he was overdue to start shrinking. Statistics be damned, Jack still felt like he was too young to get short. Maybe he wasn't shrinking, but some asshole had put that seven-to-ten-years statistic out there and Jack had freaked. He wasn't even short. Jack was six-foot-one. At least, he was when he stood up straight, which he almost always did after hearing that shrinking statistic.

Jack couldn't understand why people said things like that, why they didn't just keep their big fat mouths shut. From that time forward, Jack, who was not shrinking, had walked around standing up so straight he had looked like someone had shoved a sign post straight up his butt. The end result was that, because of his hypersensitivity to height and his new overly-erect posture, he now looked taller and crazier. "Man, I fuckin' hate the person who made up statistics. What a fuckin' prick. Why do they have to study things? Why can't we all just be stupid and think we're tall? At least we'd probably be happy."

Sometimes, Jack thought the hardwood floors in Dolores's

apartment were making him shorter, and he knew for a fact that lifting heavy things was making him shorter. One day, Dolores asked Jack to lift up the corner of the couch so that she could adjust the rug and Jack blurted out "no fuckin' way" with such apprehension that she was sure he'd misunderstood the question. She repeated the question and received an identical response. She asked why, but Jack couldn't bring himself to tell her: "It's because liftin' shit compresses your vertebrae, and it makes you shorter. If I'm gonna fuckin' shrink, it better be for a good reason, not liftin' some couch." This much should have been clear to anyone: Jack was addicted to being paranoid.

To Jack, moving in together seemed like the next smart thing to do. Moving in was good for staying together because once everybody was moved in it was harder to just leave. Also, back then, it was just how relationships were done. You met each other, went out a few times, fucked a few times, had a pregnancy scare, and then, since you were already sort of making plans to move in, you just shacked up. Dolores had just done her first morning-after pill, and she was sick to her stomach for two days. Jack couldn't handle a child, and he knew it. They'd never know if there had even been a baby to worry about anyway in the first place, but Jack knew it didn't sit right with Dolores.

Dolores came from lonely circumstances herself. She was an only child, and her parents had split when she was a teenager. Her relationship with her mom was poor, and her relationship with her father was nonexistent. After that, Jack had always gotten the feeling that she'd actually wanted to be pregnant that time. Or not that she really wanted to be pregnant, but that she'd have welcomed some stability in the way of a child. Jack had latched onto her because of what he perceived as her stability, but she really only looked stable to Jack because Jack was so unstable that anyone that was not currently committed to an institution looked stable to him. Even though she'd never get pregnant on purpose, Jack was sure that, if it were solely up to her, and she was in fact pregnant, she'd have had the baby.

Abortion was never an option for Dolores. It wasn't a political thing. She was pro-choice, but she'd been clear that she herself would never get an abortion. For Jack, telling Dolores about the brand-new morning-after pill made it possible to erase the mistake of the previous night. It was abortion lite, if you will, and it was easy enough to convince Dolores to take a pill. It was simple to get a prescription from her doctor and make it physically go away. Making it go away emotionally was a harder slog. What men never took into consideration was that even a possible pregnancy was a big deal to a lot of women. The emotional scars took a lot longer to heal for them, and there was usually resentment directed toward the man in the situation. She never openly showed the resentment, but some things were easy enough to figure out even if no one said them out loud.

Would having a child have made things better? Jack didn't know, but probably not. Things would have been different, but life was already complicated enough without that to worry about. Afterward, they settled into a normal sort of living arrangement.

Dolores's apartment was comfortable, and a radical change from the Winthrop. A one-bedroom in a renovated twenties brick building, it was comfortable and had style. There were even framed posters lining the hallways, noting some of the more important events, movies, or industries of the twenties. The posters were all originals, or at least that's what Jack liked to tell visitors, though in reality, they had to have been well-crafted reproductions of originals. Strange plants also littered the areas near the elevators, and there was a check-in window attached to what had used to be the manager's office just inside the front entrance. Jack told people the building was retro art deco, but Jack didn't really know what that meant. It did sound like what he thought the building was, and nobody ever corrected him, which emboldened his continued use of the phrase.

The elevators had those collapsible pull-across gates. Jack figured they were made out of iron, but were painted a gold color, a gold that had worn or chipped off much of the surface of those gates. The sound of those gates opening or closing caused an ear-piercing screech. It really completed the mood. That is, it would have, if Jack had any idea what a retro art deco mood was supposed to feel like. Walking into those elevators felt like walking straight into an early Joan Crawford movie.

Another noisy feature of Dolores's building was the furnace, which came on sporadically at best. In the summer it would come on all day long. It put out so much heat in the summer that you could see distortions in the steam. They reminded Jack of the distortions you see coming off gasoline when you're filling up your gas tank or off hot concrete. Conversely, in the winter, you could go an entire evening without the telltale clanking that let you know a minimal amount of heat was on its way to your apartment. At those times, during those twenty-five-degree nights, Jack would have killed for the opportunity to try to sleep through the sound of metal grinding on other metal that the furnace made when it ran.

Waiting for it to kick on in the winter was just as futile as waiting for it to kick off in the summer. That summer, Jack would sit, soaked in sweat, trying to enjoy his favorite soap opera, *General Hospital.* Meanwhile, that winter he would have killed to see just a hint of that heat distortion that indicated that the furnace was on. All of this was happening on top of Jack's shrinking; or maybe, he postulated, it was the heat melting him. Multiple daily measurements to ensure his six-foot-one status were not only common but an activity religiously performed. It was all becoming too much, and Jack was getting ready to snap again.

Considering the faulty premise on which Dolores and Jack's relationship was based, it lasted for much longer than one might have expected. Not only that, but they were actually quite content being with one another a good deal of the time. Jack loved Dolores, but more as a caretaker that he was allowed to fuck from time to time. Dolores loved Jack, but more like a beloved classic car that could never do anything but sit in a garage and deteriorate.

They made it work for better than a year, though, and during that time Jack reached the pinnacle of his success as a functioning human being. Dolores was a high point for him, even if it was destined to failure from the start. "Hey, some people never even got a month of stability, much less a year."

The ritualistic swallowing of Jack's Depakote started and ended every one of his days. Just another of his structure-building activities in a regimen of structure-building activities designed to give his life order. Popping that Depakote was an important one, though. Unlike every medication Jack had ever been on, the Depakote worked. Originally, it was developed for epilepsy, and it was an effective anti-seizure medication. Somewhere along the way, somebody figured out that people using the Depakote who also had bipolar disorder were doing a lot better with their mood swings.

As disorganized and scattered as Jack's life had been, it was ironic that everything about his it boiled down to a ritual. Before the first card was dealt, or drink taken, before the needle hit the vein, or even before the ritualistic closing of the locking door in the mental ward, there was the ritual itself. In his mind, he asked forgiveness for what he'd done, and especially what he was about to do. And, of course, he sought forgiveness for crashing and burning that night, or morning, or year, or whatever the case turned out to be. It was the rare occasion that Jack gave any thought as to who or what the ritualistic plea for forgiveness was directed at, but he always went through with it, hoping there was something looking out for him. During that time, Jack started paying a lot more attention to where these pleas might be going, almost as much attention as he'd give to the content of these pleas themselves. Still, for all he knew, they just floated off the top of his head and into the cloudy northwest atmosphere that was always residing right above his head. But at least what happened to them concerned him, and Jack could only call that progress.

The content of these ritual conversations was now un-known. As Jack stared that morning's Depakote in the face, he asked that it continue to give him stability of mind, so that he could use his energy to try to create a good life for Dolores and himself. Even though he'd given her full disclosure of his past in his own words, she really couldn't understand. She was not prone to those mental quirks and physical addictions. For a lot of people, it was hard to feel empathy for someone's plight unless that person had lived through similar experiences, or at least could apply the feeling of a difficult experience to another's plight. It was not that people were all sociopaths—most really want to be empathic across a broad spectrum—but without firsthand experience, it was hard. Jack was no different. He had a hard time understanding the pain of others unless he'd felt something similar under similar circumstances. He sensed that Dolores wanted to be empathetic, but she couldn't really get it because she hadn't lived it.

Even the greatest storyteller could still only tell a story. Some stories could only fall on deaf ears; some things could only be experienced. Painful and powerful experiences could usually only have a limited audience because of their personal nature. That Dolores had not endured these things made Jack thankful, because he loved her, but because she had not lived these experiences, he knew they could never connect on the level required to truly understand each other and be happy. That's what Jack figured whenever he unloaded some sordid detail of his past on Dolores. "But what the fuck do I know. I'm a fucked-up, degenerate, loser, the biggest in the world, so far as I can tell."

But for a while, he pulled the wool over everybody's eyes. Even Laurence started to believe Jack might have clawed his way out of the addicted underbelly of society.

On moving day, Laurence was on inspector duty, like always. When he called Jack, it was the first time they'd spoken since their mom's funeral. Laurence may have been disappointed, disgusted, or disgruntled, but one way or the other he'd kept good tabs on Jack. He had made sure he knew Jack's phone number and address. Jack, of course, had made no such effort to keep track of Laurence. Jack had figured Laurence felt obligated to continue to be the big brother. It was what their mom would've wanted, and they both knew it. Looking after Jack, even if it was from behind the scenes, was Laurence's birthright, and he would fulfill it despite anyone's, including Jack's, objections.

Moving day was Laurence's opportunity to assume his big brother role in the largest way possible, and as noted, neither Jack, nor Dolores, nor Christ himself was going to stand in his way. Jack did need Laurence's help moving, but he did not need the constant, condescending commentary that Laurence also considered to be his birthright and responsibility, and Jack knew it was coming the moment Laurence set foot into that apartment.

Jack, for a moment, actually wondered if Laurence had tapped his phone. The phone was the only place he could recall having talked about moving with anyone. Maybe Todd had told him; maybe Todd gave him my phone number; maybe Todd had been a double agent the entire time. Jack didn't really know. Whatever the truth, the fact remained that when Laurence called one day he knew precisely when Dolores and Jack planned to move, and he showed up to help without Jack ever contacting him whatsoever.

Jack thought that if he and Dolores had never moved, he could have avoided seeing Laurence indefinitely. If he showed up for moving day, Jack figured he would definitely show up for a medical emergency, and Jack decided right then and there that he would have to make sure to never become physically ill again. Being sick was bad enough, but if it meant Laurence would be there, that was so much incentive to stay healthy. Maybe, Jack thought, if they'd stayed put, Laurence never would have called. If he never called, he probably wouldn't have shown up to help them move and criticize everything they had, everything they did, and every way they did it. Similar to a medical emergency, Jack decided that if Laurence was going to show up whenever he moved, that he'd just make sure never to move again. If that kept Laurence away, it was well worth it.

But maybe he would have come out of the woodwork eventually anyhow. And then he would have criticized the woodwork, and complained about the way Jack was moving the woodwork. But he never really had a chance. Dolores wanted a dog, and a garden, and more space than her little one-bedroom apartment afforded them. And Jack wanted to give her all of those things more than anything else. Operating on a selfless plane was not native to Jack, but he thought it felt good.

The phone rang. *Must be fuckin' Laurence*, Jack thought. "Even his ring looks down on me."

"Hello," Jack said.

"So, are you ready to go?"

That was his impolite way of asking Jack to come downstairs to let him in. Without him saying so, Jack already knew that he was talking to him on his cell phone outside the building. He was just waiting for Jack to ask where he was, so that he could say, "Well, I'm standing outside your building ready to move all your crap. Where are you?" Jack wasn't going to give him the pleasure, so he just said:

"Okay, be right down."

"Yeah, okay," Laurence said.

The other pleasure Jack would deprive him of today would be the opportunity to silently judge Dolores. Since Laurence and Todd would both be there to help him, it didn't make sense that Dolores should be there. Since there were three of them to handle the heavy stuff, Jack told her to go have fun with her friends for the day, and that she and Jack would get the light stuff the next day. "And I knew I was goin to shrink like a whole inch on movin day." Dolores didn't have many friends, and the ones she did have she didn't spend a great deal of time with, so Jack was sure it seemed like an odd request. But she was sweet, and so she just said "okay." That way, she wouldn't have to endure meeting and subsequently spending the day with Laurence. A whole day was a lot of Laurence to handle for anybody, even Jack, but at least the long years of his life preceding that day had conditioned him for it. Dolores had no such conditioning to fall back on. There really was no good reason Jack could think of for Dolores to meet Laurence. Laurence was more than capable of making a judgment about somebody he'd never met by simply looking at the photographs and belongings that were all over their apartment. How did two people born from the same gene pool turn out so different? They were born to the same parents. They'd die with the same family name on their respective headstones. But nothing else about them resembled one another in the least. Jack wondered a lot about how that happened. He had never come up with a satisfactory answer, but he assumed their parents would want them to stick together to the greatest extent possible. That was never going to happen, but Jack did begrudgingly make infrequent attempts to tolerate Laurence's presence. He figured moving day ought to satisfy that minimal effort quotient for at least a year or two.

Right around the time that Laurence and Jack had gotten the bed and dressers into the moving van, he started to wonder where the rest of their help was.

The phone rang. *Fuckin' Todd, not showin' up*, Jack thought. "Even his ring feels like he's going to leave me hangin'."

"Ha, dude, I'm way stoned, and I sort of don't want to really see your brother either," Todd said.

"Is that right! Well, that makes two of us, but Laurence won't mind. Laurence never gets sick of his own company. He may not even notice that you didn't show up. By the way, how did Laurence know I was movin' today?"

"Sorry man, I totally gotta go. Later."

At first, Jack was kind of pissed. And, for a moment, he envisioned going over to Todd's place and catching him sleeping off that stone and smacking him in the head with his bong. But, right about then, Jack actually understood his point of view, and if Jack were him, he'd want to sit on his couch and get stoned rather than see Jack's brother, too. And why did Jack want him there anyway? Basically, Jack wanted Todd there so that he didn't have to talk to Laurence himself.

A few minutes later, Dolores walked into the apartment with bags full of meatball subs from MSM Deli on Sixth Avenue. Jack silently wished she had walked in five minutes earlier. If Todd had known they had meatball subs from MSM, he probably would have showed up. People remember the oddest things. One of the only things that Laurence and Jack could unequivocally agree on was that MSM meatball subs were the best meal that could be had for less than ten bucks. And that the sandwiches had to consist only of meatballs, sauce, and cheese. Of course, that was exactly what was on these subs, which were both plentiful and numerous. On the weight of one sentence that Jack had mumbled a few months back that went something like, "Me and my brother love those meatball subs at that place, just meatballs, cheese, and sauce," she'd taken it upon herself to provide Laurence and Jack with their favorite meal for lunch, and in the process, leave Laurence with an impression that would be hard to criticize, even for him.

How could you not be in love with a girl that went out of her way to impress your pretentious brother after she'd been cut loose for the day? And Laurence couldn't help but be impressed. Jack didn't even tell Laurence how she knew about the sandwiches. Jack just let him ponder whether she had great intuition, insider information, or uncannily good taste. Laurence ate his sub with a slightly amused, slightly confused, but completely content look on his face. For about three seconds, Jack saw something he had used to like about Laurence, something that hadn't happened since they were younger. It reminded Jack of when Laurence had first gotten his driver's license and a part-time job. He'd taken Jack to MSM for meatball subs, and then they had gone to a movie and eaten candy and drank pop until they were nauseous. The feeling only lasted for three seconds, no more. Jack counted. But still, it was nice to see that it was in there somewhere. With an ever-diminishing list of reasons for them to stay in contact, Dolores had given them a reason to stay brothers for at least one more day.

Puyallup was a small town outside of Tacoma. Actually, it was a large town. Actually, it was a small city. That was what they called it, anyway. The downtown was filled with turn-of-the-century buildings, and the houses in the old part of town also dated back to that time. Main Street was actually called Main Street. The fact that a railroad ran through town was still a big deal to the citizens, but the annual fair, which took place on fairgrounds that had once housed an internment camp for Japanese citizens during World War II, was its main attraction. Puyallup was a town that was actually a city that was nostalgic about being a town. It even had its own little fire department, and twelve police officers. Was this the municipal apparatus of a town or a city? Who knew.

Puyallup was where Jack and Dolores's new place was. Everything about that city, or town, or whatever, was small, and so was everything about Jack and Dolores's life there. They lived in the littlest house, with the littlest yard, on the littlest street in that little city. And inside the front door of that littlest house lived two people with the littlest lives in that little city—for the time being, anyway. How it was that their new two-bedroom house along with front and back yard could possibly be smaller than Dolores's little one-bedroom apartment was beyond Jack. But they had a yard, and a yard was important to Dolores.

II

Part Two

Courting Mediocrity

"Why do you insist upon destroying yourself?"
— Charles Bukowski, Hollywood

Chapter 13

One day, Beth had told Jack the strangest thing. The peehole belonged right at the tip of the head of the penis, not on the underside of the head. That put Jack's peephole clearly south of the mark. Like he needed something else to be paranoid about.

Jack's first trip to Western State Hospital had happened when he was eighteen. If Western State had taken juveniles, he would have ended up there sooner. Nobody could ever put their finger on exactly what Jack's mental problem had been, likely because he had suffered from so many mental disorders simultaneously. When he had arrived at Western State that first time, he had been transferred in an ambulance from Fairfax. Fairfax had had a juvenile facility for people like him. Nobody had known what was wrong with him at Fairfax, and nobody would figure it out at Western State either.

Among other things, Jack had been suffering a fairly nasty flare-up of his obsessive-compulsive disorder. At that time, it had been considered untreatable, and most had not thought of it as debilitating anyway. To most, even if they had been aware of it, OCD was just a personality quirk, not a severe mental illness. The more severe aspects of it, such as the accompanying anxiety, had been treated as discrete conditions, not symptoms of OCD.

In the ambulance, Jack had discovered a smell he had immediately named sanitized filth. An ambulance looked clean to a casual observer, just like a hospital did. Sanitized. But no place that saw as much filth and gore as an ambulance or hospital room could truly be clean. Every surface had seemed alive with it. It had danced on the defibrillator. It had snoozed in the suction device. It had leapt from one place to another on the net where the EMT's stethoscope had hung. The inside of that ambulance had been the most alive place Jack could ever remember having seen. That would have been entertaining if it hadn't been filth and disease animating the ambulance.

At that early stage of his mental illness, Jack would have found the thought of calling a place like Western State Hospital his home, even for a little while, repugnant. Just looking at the paramedic sitting on the bench seat next to him had put ideas into Jack's head about what he might be able to accomplish when that little stint of committal was over. Jack had thought he could fill that square-jawed EMT's uniform. He just needed to get his mind right, and then he would be off to EMT school.

In Jack's mind, he and the EMT hadn't been that different. They had both been about the same height and build, and they had even had a similar deviant look about them. But something in the EMT's life had steered him that way rather than this. He could just as easily have ended up a career criminal of some sort. In some other reality, he could have been the dope pusher, or even worse, the dope user. He could even have been the one lying on a gurney in an ambulance on his way to the funny farm. All had been possible options for the somewhat twisted-looking young man with the noble profession, but he had ended up there tending to Jack in the back of that ambulance. In Jack's opinion, all he had needed to do was recover a few of his marbles, and he could have had the guy's life within a year. Jack had been able to imagine a different life for himself like a champ. Unfortunately, imagining it had been about as far as he could usually get. Even imagining the different life had typically become boring to him after a few minutes.

Every few years, Jack had looked back over those that had just passed, and every time he had, he had always been left pondering one thought.

"Even with all the other things I could, or perhaps should, be wonderin', or reflectin on, or tryin' to figure out, it's just that one thing that sticks with me. And that one thing is simply this: Whether those past few years have been good or bad didn't matter. What mattered is how I felt 'bout it those past few years. One thing that always comes to mind when I'm thinkin' 'bout those past few years is, if I had known what I'd be in for over the comin' years, if I would've just killed myself back then. Now I'm startin' to catch on. I'm pretty sure that in a few years I'll look back on this moment in time, and the years that came after, and wish that I'd killed myself today." Jack had delivered his message as cogently as he was capable.

"That sounds like bullshit to me, because if you felt good about the past few years, you wouldn't have wanted to kill yourself in retrospect. And whether they were good or bad must have some bearing on how you feel about them. I don't think you've ever had a good few years, and that, if you have no interest in changing, you never will. If the last few years were bad, then you should have plenty of motivation to do something different with the next few," Beth had said.

Beth had not suffered fools, and had tolerated little to no bullshit from Jack. She had always believed she was looking at a broken but fixable human being. This sappy pseudo-introspection had already become her least favorite part of Jack's personality, and she had intended to drum it out of him without delay.

"No, you don't really understand. If they'd been bad but productive, I'd feel differently. If I'd gotten somewhere, it would be different, but I haven't. And it seems like the next few years are going to just be more of the same," he had said.

"Well, maybe you're right, Jack. The next few years will likely be bad if you don't put recovery from your neuroses ahead of everything else. You've said a lot about how you sink into the shit, but I haven't heard anything about how you diligently apply yourself to changing your circumstances. Recovery from anything, whether it's purely a mental affliction or garden variety substance abuse, takes work. Can you work for recovery?"

That was the first time Jack had met Beth, and although he hadn't been sure that he was in love with her, he had been sure that he liked her better than anybody else in that place, and possibly anybody else on planet earth. Her mode of speaking to Jack had been direct and candid. Jack had never totally bought the rationalizations he had spun for the rest of the world. Most of his motivation had been to use the intelligence he was born with to justify his circumstances to others. Intellectualizing his poor circumstances was easier than dealing with them. Jack's ideal solution had been that this intellectualizing of his problems would somehow cause somebody to come along and fix his problems for him in one fell swoop. What Beth had advocated was taking action, and that had sounded like a lot of work to Jack. Jack had, characteristically, not been a huge fan of work.

"None of it really matters. What does matter is that I won't kill myself because I fear that Mormon doctrine on the subject may be true and I'll wind up in Hell, and guilt over what I'd be doing to my family keeps me from following through on it. Do you want to know what really bothers me, though?"

"You don't know how many more times in your life you'll be required to feel this way, and nobody, not even the best educated therapists, can give you any guarantee on your mental health. And you feel like the rest of your life is going to go as it has, just one empty, miserable year after another, like doing time in a penitentiary. Were you going to tell me something like that?" Beth said.

She had said it as though it had been said to her many times before. Jack had hit a bit of a roadblock. Beth hadn't been mean to him, so he hadn't been able to write her off as just some cold bitch. She hadn't bought his narrative, and she had simultaneously challenged him to be better. Normally, this was where Jack would have found some way to put some distance between himself and her. And if you had known Jack, this would have made all the sense in the world. As mentioned, one thing Jack had always despised was work. He had wanted to be around this Beth person, but she had wanted him to attempt to improve his circumstances by doing uncomfortable things. He really hadn't known what to do with that. For whatever reason, at that time, and for that one person, he had wanted to be better.

Beth was twenty-three and just months out of nursing school when they had met. She had been an LPN. LPN was the nursing course of choice for people whose ambitions, funding, or attention spans would only allow a year's schooling. Even the name sounded lame. *Licensed practical nurse.* It was like you were practically a nurse—not actually, but practically.

Beth had been a different story, though. Most bright and ambitious people that wanted to go into nursing found a way to complete an RN program. They then became productive members of the middle class with good jobs. Someday, that would be Beth, but back then she had just been a green LPN recently out of an abusive and short-lived marriage. Jack had imagined that marriage was what kept her from finding a career until then. The truth was more interesting than he had imagined.

Beth had gone just awry of normal and had spent her teens and early twenties developing addictions to a variety of prescription pain medications and alcohol. After the end of a brief and miserable marriage, and a short stint at an inpatient drug and alcohol rehab program, she'd decided that nursing was the career she wanted to pursue. She had been a fuck-up half-breed. Jack, on the other hand, had been a fuck-up pure-breed. So of course, Beth had spoken Jack's language better than some overeducated therapist ever could have. However, unlike all the other fuckups in Jack's life, Beth's words had carried credence. Remember, she had been a fuckup half-breed. She had walked in two worlds simultaneously, so the stories she had brought from the normal world were practical and believable.

Even though he was pretty new at the whole institution circuit, Jack had already begun to notice some similarities they all shared. Actually, he had noticed that most things from institution to institution were very similar. People were different, just as locations were different; even the methods in which various facilities were funded were different. But really, they were all the same. The people at Western State had really just been replicas of their Fairfax counterparts. Just as the interior layout and outside grounds had just been copies of copies of still other copies of some master planned institution conceived in some architect's mind and residing outside a sleepy New England town.

In a future Jack could only imagine, he was a millionaire. He'd developed a PC game that was a simulation of institutional living. Years of institutional living had uniquely qualified him to create such an unquestionably controversial game. It was a true simulation, 3D graphics and all, everything you'd ever need to know to survive in an institutional setting, and more.

Cheeking your meds at the nurse's station so you could trade them or dope up on them later when you'd saved enough to get really high would be a Level One skill. Level One was behavioral and mental institutions.

The Level Two series of simulations would bring you through the gauntlet known as substance abuse institutions, halfway houses, and homeless shelters.

And, finally, there would be the most fearsome of simulations: the criminal justice system that brought you through the journey from arrest right into the county tank or city jail, followed by your trial, and finally the state penitentiary. Of course, your crimes would determine whether you went to a minimum, medium, or maximum-security prison. Upon arrival, your behavior would determine which gangs would be interested in you as a potential member or target.

The caption "Good luck" would be emblazoned on the front

of the game box, along with graphic animations of some of the nastier aspects of institution life, informing the potential buyer of the violent nature of the game. In Jack's mind, he figured it would be so mature and violent in nature that they'd have to invent some parental advisory label for it, sort of like the ones they started putting on all the punk, rap, and metal records a couple of years before. He had laughed to himself. "Like they'd ever put warnin' labels on fuckin' video games! Movies and records, sure, but a video game, no fuckin' way."

Nintendo would buy the game outright and develop a version for their game console. It would look great, like 3D Worldrunner in institutions. The best thing was that it would be a true hybrid between a first-person action and role-playing game.

"Somehow, my poor luck, bent mind, and painful life experiences had paid off to the tune of millions. It seemed too good to be true, and there was just one thing that could make life sweeter. It was finally my opportunity to rub Laurence's face in my fuckin' success, and I'd do it by givin' him a few hundred thousand bucks. There couldn't be anythin' more humiliatin' for Laurence, but he would have no choice but to accept. And every time he looked at whatever he bought with the money he'd re-live that humiliation. Just as ultimate revenge for my wasted life was within my grasp, I awoke to the sound of a ten-pound sledgehammer fist beating on the door to my room. It was Jon, the orderly. He was a huge man, and he was there to hold me down while a nurse administered my Thorazine shot. Good fuckin' times."

The first ones that you noticed were the droolers. They stuck out. When you thought about a ward in a mental hospital, the droolers were the first ones that came to mind.

There was that scene at the end of *One Flew Over the Cuckoo's Nest*, where McMurphy comes back from his lobotomy. Nobody's home. Yeah, they made him a drooler. Droolers didn't like to stay in their rooms, either. Something about drooling all over the common areas really made their worlds go around. You could almost see their tiny, expressionless faces light up when you went to lean on a handrail and your hand landed in a big, gooey pile of saliva. Even more fun than that was when someone fell right down a set of steps because the pool of handrail saliva they'd put their hand in was really slippery. Of course, they were mostly just walking shells of humans, but with a little imagination you could tell a few things were still going on in their blank little minds. Besides, after receiving icepicks to the brain, they deserved a little comedy in their lives. Not that lobotomies had still taken place by the time Jack had made the institution circuit. Still, some of them had been so old, they might have been the recipients of the icepick back in the day. Although Jack imagined most of them had wound up that way naturally, or that it had been brought on by the drugs they received for decades there at Western State.

The wall walkers had stuck out too, and Jack had really had a soft spot for them. By virtue of being in the hallways all the time, they were usually the next ones that you ran into. "It just makes sense, if you think 'bout it. I mean, if you're hangin' around in the common areas, you're going to get seen. It's like a runway at a fashion show. Everybody else is just sitting in a folding chair, but all eyes were on the droolers and wall walkers." By the same Jack logic, they had also been the ones that most commonly stuck their hands in the drool on the handrails. "Come on, I mean, they're literally leanin' on the walls when they're walkin', of course they're going to get the handrail saliva. Watchin' a wall walker take a header after grabbin' handrail saliva, that's good times for everyone involved, except for the wall walkers I guess. When their hands slide off the handrails, and they lose their footin' on the linoleum, a nasty spill was sure to follow. There is no greater joy in the mental ward than an especially active afternoon of watchin' wall walkers givin themselves serious head trauma after slippin' and slidin' in the droolers' saliva pools. If I had a video camera in here, I'd sell the videos on late night TV. I'd be a fuckin' millionaire."

On one such afternoon, Jack had sat at a table in the common room of C-Ward. There had been a checkerboard in front of him with the remnants of a red checker victory still on it. He had wished there was a chess board in the ward, but he had immediately realized even if there was, there probably wouldn't have been anybody on C-Ward with enough of their marbles left to actually play. With all the Thorozine, Jack had doubted he could even play the game worth a shit himself. Right then, he had witnessed a wall walker take an epic header. He had known it was handrail saliva. Jack had just seen Mary, one of the more active droolers, over by that stairwell a few minutes ago. She'd made a quick escape in her wheelchair when she had noticed Jack looking over at her. That had been where the epiphany happened. Wall walkers that took epic headers sometimes suffered severe head trauma, enough head trauma to turn them into droolers. "That's how the fuckin' droolers were reproducin'." Jack had never touched a handrail at Western State again. "I got my fuckin' issues, but I ain't ready to be a fuckin' drooler. I walk up and down them steps with my arms crossed. It looks weird when I do it, but shit, you just do what you got to do to get by, you know."

Jack had also asked for a notebook and a pen. He had spent the next three days obsessively writing a horror movie screenplay about the droolers' slow-moving plan to take over Western State through handrail drool headers. Jack had been the main character, and the genius that ultimately foiled the droolers' plan of taking over Western State. At least he would have been, but Jack had gotten bored of the screenplay right around the time he had developed the hivemind aspect of the droolers' existence. As with most of Jack's great ideas, the screenplay had been better used as a hook that had allowed him to daydream about making it big someday. When Jack had left Western State, he had packed the spiral notebook containing his unfinished screenplay, *The Droolers*, into a box. That box had gone into a storage closet at his mom's house, and years later it had gone right into the garbage when Laurence had cleaned out their mom's house after she had died. Even Jack had to recognize that there was no maliciousness on Laurence's part here. It had been a box labeled "Jack's stuff from Western State." When deciding what to do with all the things in his dead mom's home, Jack's stuff from Western State had seemed like an obvious choice for the dumpster. The sad part was, *The Droolers* had actually been good, and in other circumstances, a guy like Jack probably could have made a living writing screenplays for low-budget horror movies.

Other than walking with the sides of their faces and torsos glued to the walls, the wall walkers had mostly been uninteresting to the people at Western State. All they had really done was walk along walls and moan. Nonetheless, Jack had been endlessly fascinated by them. He had decided that if *The Droolers* got made into a movie, he'd write a sequel and call it *The Wall Walkers*. He had liked the wall walkers so much that he had felt bad they would only get the sequel, but even he'd had to realize that droolers, with their hivemind and unconventional method of reproducing, were pure movie gold, whereas wall walkers were pretty one-dimensional.

It was the difference between vampires and zombies. While Jack had loved zombies, they didn't really do much. Vampires, however, were complex and interesting. Anyway, as far as low-budget horror movies were concerned, droolers had clearly needed to come first, even if Jack had ultimately preferred wall walkers.

On the subject of moaning, there had always been a few of those, too. Moaners hadn't really constituted a class of their own, though. The main reason was that sometimes wall walkers had moaned, and sometimes even droolers had moaned. Even Cliff Clavins had moaned when they were jacked on Thorozine. For that matter, Jack had moaned sometimes for various reasons, including the Thorozine. Sometimes he had thought the employees were going to start moaning. Every once in a while, you would get some weirdo who only lay in their bed and moaned. This rare breed, a pure moaner, had been the exception, and the only kind of person that could really lay claim to the title "moaner." Plus, they had been even simpler than wall walkers. At least wall walkers had roamed around. Pure moaners had just laid in bed. Therefore, Jack had refused to characterize them as a discreet group of their own.

If you made it to the TV room, you'd have been bound to run into a few of the aforementioned Cliff Clavins. The Cliff Clavins had always been in the TV room, always coming up with new conspiracy theories. The local news had been good for getting them going, and the national evening news had been even better, but the good Cliff Clavins had been able to get a conspiracy theory going about a twenty-year-old sitcom. Jack had even heard some good ones during Saturday morning cartoons. Newspapers had also been a rich source of conspiracy material for the overactive, mentally impaired minds. Most of the Cliff Clavins' conspiracies had focused on the government taking control of your mind through media or locking people up for trying to expose their master plans for mind-control of citizens in the name of global domination. Since they had all actually been locked up by the government, some of their conspiracy theories had almost made sense to Jack, but then something like alien overlords had always arrived in the narrative, and Jack had remembered he was in a mental hospital. The particulars of the day's conspiracy theory hadn't really mattered. The themes were always the same, but listening to a Cliff Clavin explain a conspiracy theory in detail had been a good way to kill time. You had at least been able to have a conversation with a Cliff Clavin, unlike most of the residents of C-Ward.

Screamers had been mostly boring and loud. Those screams had cut through Jack's skin the way a sharp knife sliced through your finger when you missed while cutting an onion. Then nothing—no explanation, no context, just screams— then quiet. At least the wall walkers had done interesting things like fondle the walls in inappropriate ways. Between their skin-slicing screams, the mystery stemming from lack of interesting backstories for said screams, and the fact that they could agitate staff as well as patients, they had qualified as a group worthy of an official title. They had definitely been irritating, but they had been a discrete group worthy of an official title, just barely.

The last major category of patient you normally ran into in a mental ward was the impersonator, or helper. The terms were mostly interchangeable. Sometimes, a patient had just been a helper, or had just been an impersonator, but if a person was one, they were probably both. Depending on who was around, you could have been talking to the impersonator, or the helper. When hospital staff was present, you were probably dealing with the helper. This person had kissed the staffs' asses when they are around. When staff hadn't been around, they had pretended to be members of the staff when family members had come to visit or EMS crews had dropped off new patients. They had even tried to fool new patients and hospital staff from other areas of the hospital. Sometimes they had been pretty good at it, too.

"I've seen paramedics give entire reports on incomin' patients to an impersonator. Meds, history, chief complaint, the whole ball of wax, then an LPN walks up and sends the impersonator to the day room. As a professional, that's got to be fuckin' embarrassin'. But it's understandable; most of the staff didn't wear any visible identification. Plus, most of them wore street clothes. The nurses wore scrubs, but impersonators would get into the storage room where the scrubs were kept. They would put them on and walk around the ward all the fuckin' time. It doesn't help that when a patient is brought in off the street, and their clothes needed to be washed, that hospital staff put them in scrubs. Always look down in a mental ward. This is a hard and fast rule that will allow you to always know if you are talkin to an impersonator. Patients don't have shoelaces, ever. Even though I knew everybody that worked on C-Ward, I still looked down before I took my meds from them. Never swallow unless you see the shoelaces of the nurse giving you the meds. Who knows what some of the psychos around there would try to stick in your med cup."

There had been some positive things about the C-Ward, and all the facilities like it. That one in particular had allowed Jack to eat basically however much he liked. The wall walkers and droolers had barely eaten anything, but they had been given full meals just like the rest of the patients. They had never seemed to complain when Jack had grabbed the meal of a patient that was neglecting it. He hadn't just stolen their food. He had always made sure that they weren't going to eat it first. But he had figured, why waste good food? If Jack hadn't eaten their food, it had just gone into the garbage. Sometimes, getting an extra dessert hadn't been worth it, though. Getting food from a drooler second-hand hadn't typically been a great plan. If it had been in their possession for more than about thirty seconds it had gotten drool on it. That was a lesson Jack had learned the hard way more than once. Jack had even tried wiping drool off food he really wanted—or, if it was soup, just stirring the drool in. After doing this ten or twelve times, he had learned that sometimes it was better to just let it go in the garbage can. Wall walker food had been great, though—always nice and dry.

Not only that, but he had been left alone to do his own thing most of the time. "If a guy weren't careful, he might even be able to get his head together in a place like this." Jack had known it wasn't going to happen by going to group, or taking his meds, but by just having time to reflect on what had gone wrong and determine how to rectify the things in the past that pertained to the future. He had imagined driving down avenues of refrain, cruising effortlessly past those things that had brought him down once on the outside. And that was what Jack had done with most of his time.

Following the program had been for losers, or for the lifers that would never leave there. Jack had known it. He wasn't normal, but he had teetered a lot closer to it than the freaks there on C-Ward. In his mind, that had given him the right to skip group or meetings with the psychiatrist. It had given him the right to sit in his room and read or spend time with Beth. When the RN on the ward had made Beth go back to work and stop wasting time with Jack, he had gone to the dayroom and monopolized the TV. He hadn't partially inhabited normalcy like Beth had, but his nearness to normalcy had entitled him to play TV remote dictator and occasionally, when one of the Cliff Clavins wouldn't shut up, boot their ass out of the room all together.

Jack had been young, strong, and, as mentioned, in a proximity to sanity that had made him a mental god compared to the other patients there. Also, he had had a girlfriend, and that girlfriend had access to drugs. So, basically, Jack had been the kingpin of C-Ward, and before long the Cliff Clavins had even made-up conspiracy theories about him. In one of them, Jack hadn't even been a patient; he was an agent of the State of Washington. The place being a state-owned and run facility had made the whole mole-for-the-state theory work for the rat in a maze line of thinking that was the predominate thought process of most of the residents there. That is, the ones capable of thinking at all. The fact that his girlfriend had happened to be one of their nurses had only added fuel to the fire. Soon enough, the Cliff Clavins and everybody else had just left the dayroom when Jack had wanted to watch TV. Nobody would bunk in the same room with him, so he had been moved into a single room. It was smaller, but he'd had it all to himself.

In a strange way, he had stayed off the staff's radar by being the guy nobody wanted to talk to. In any real rehabilitative setting, he wouldn't have been able to intimidate people into letting him do what he pleased whenever he wanted. In a real rehabilitative setting, the staff would have cared about trying to actually help people assimilate back into society. Instead, the staff there had only seemed to truly care about keeping the patients doped up enough that they were docile twenty-four hours a day. There had been no real treatment with medication there. People hadn't been medicated to treat their affliction. They had been medicated for how they acted. Act badly, and you were medicated heavily. Intimidate patients and keep to yourself, you were left to set your own agenda, just so long as you didn't do anything that gave the staff headaches. For Jack, that had included which meds he'd take. Once Jack had been able to dictate what would and wouldn't go into his body the Thorozine had stopped for good. "Too much of that stuff too often will turn you right into a fuckin' drooler, and like I already said, I had zero plans on becomin a drooler."

Dr. Snyder had become interested in Jack's situation right around the time he'd resolved himself to just staying at Western State forever. Much like many inmates and patients that had come before, Jack had embraced making Western State home. The inside had become better than the outside for Jack. Plus, he hadn't even really known how to get along on the outside, anyway, so this seemed like a no-brainer to him. He had been institutionalized. Unlike many inmates and patients in lockdowns and hospitals throughout the world, Jack had had things especially good. What more could he have asked for? He'd had a girl, any variety of drugs at his disposal, and an army of patients who he had been able to dominate. The patients hadn't liked him, but they hadn't challenged him either.

In the good doctor's opinion, anybody who was able to dominate an entire mental ward was more than ready to leave that ward and go live on the outside. It had been a strange position to be in for Jack. After all, in all his life, he'd never been a victim of his own success, and now he'd have to leave his home because of his uncanny ability to thrive in that environment. In the background, the doctor's voice had pedantically rambled on about keeping his weekly appointments with his state-appointed therapist and, of course, staying on the med program that she'd lay out for Jack. Most important, she had said, would be for Jack to find a positive outlet for his otherwise-criminally-minded behavior. In his head, what he had gotten out of this conversation was that his physician had called him gifted, albeit only at corrupt endeavors. Also, that his sharp, self-centered mind was the reason he had been released. The other thing that had become clear to Jack was that no matter how well he'd been able to manipulate the patients of C-Ward, he was a failure when it came to fooling the doctors. And for that reason, Jack had been expelled from his home. The next time, he had resolved to manage better.

Chapter 14

"You know what I had plenty of time to ponder during those months of confinement? Why are there these gill lookin' things on both sides of the head of my cock? These things are right under this weird flap of skin, and there's always this pasty white stuff by them. Wait, don't tell me that's some more abnormal penis shit, too. Whatever."

Jack had spent nine months confined at Western State. Freshly nineteen, and freshly back on the street, he had decided to make a fresh start. Nine months had been plenty of time for Jack's mom to save up some starting-out money for him. His mom had stashed thirty-five hundred dollars away in an account, just waiting to help Jack get back on his feet. That had just been the living expense money. If he had become interested in higher education, there was a college fund at her disposal with his name on it, too.

Although his parents hadn't been rich, they had always been financially capable of taking care of Laurence and Jack. Jack had always believed his mom wanted a couple more children. Jack was sure his father had refused on the grounds that they could really only afford to provide properly for the two they'd already had. Flawed logic, to say the least. Even Jack knew that the more kids you had, the cheaper they got to raise. Bulk meals, hand-me-downs, shared bedrooms. "Shit, if you have enough of 'em, you probably start breakin' even financially. If you have enough of 'em they may even turn into a money-making enterprise at some point. Just look at the Osmonds, or the Jacksons, the fuckin' Partridge Family. I know that last one is just on TV, but still."

Lacking quantity of children had forced Jack's mom to the other extreme. That is, spoiling the two she *had* had. Regrettably for his mom, college hadn't been on Jack's radar screen, and neither had a job.

What *had* been on Jack's radar screen? Debauchery naturally. Debauchery and, of course, any flavor of lawlessness that might have elevated Jack to the stratosphere of leadership and power in the real world that he'd enjoyed at Western State. Those heights of success that he had envisioned for himself had always seemed to elude him. When he thought about it, he could never say for certain what should have happened to make it turn out right.

Sometimes, it seemed to him that his wasted life had been spent in hollow pursuits. Sometimes, it seemed that his wasted life never could have turned out to be anything other than what it had become.

When Jack looked at other people with their seemingly normal lives, Jack wondered if he had ever even possessed the capacity to become educated, employed, and otherwise entrapped into ignorance and middle-class bliss. His conclusion had always been *probably not,* so he figured he should become whatever variety of criminal would allow him to still get normal people's creature comforts. "I think it's the condo. I really want the condo in the city. Those are my favorite daydreams of the future, the ones where I am a heroin-dealin' kingpin. In those daydreams, I always have the condo in the city.

Everybody had to start somewhere. Jack had started in a two-bedroom house in a small neighborhood just outside of Tacoma called Parkland. The biggest thing going on in Parkland in the late eighties had been the college campus. And there had been an old twin theater called The Parkland Theater. "I know, real fuckin' original name. At least the theater was more interestin' than the Walgreens they built there after they demolished it."

The college, Pacific Lutheran University, had been the most expensive, most private, most religious, and most exclusive college in the state. Jack had set up shop two blocks away. College kids needed drugs, that was just common sense, and Jack had been there to provide. Even though he had only been nineteen, and barely that, in life experience he was already light years ahead of those college kids. They had been getting their education. Jack had already had all the education he'd ever need to do what he did.

Jack's clothes, his '81 Volvo, and his rathole two-bedroom house two blocks from the college campus had all been signals to the rest of the world that he was a spoiled college kid whose parents had footed the bill for his life from tuition to toilet paper. Of course, that was what it had all said; that was what it was supposed to say. Jack's backpack had even had textbooks in it. They had sat right on top of the hidden pouch he'd sewn into the bottom of it. The pouch, of course, had held Jack's mobile stash, as well as his easily concealable Walther PPK. Some sophomore kid had needed more blow to get through midterms than he could swing on his allowance. That kid had needed the blow, and Jack had needed a gun. The kid's dad had needed the kid to pass his classes so that he could become some prick lawyer like daddy. His dad certainly hadn't missed that pistol. Besides, a Walther PPK? That was James Bond's gun. how could Jack have passed on that?

Out of his little home, he dealt everything—everything there had been a market for, that is. Jack had a pager before anyone else he had known. He was the only person he had known who had routinely carried hundred-dollar bills in wads that added up to thousands. And he was the only person he knew that had carried a loaded gun. It was Washington State, rainforests as far as the eye could see in every direction, so everybody had owned a hunting rifle. The dealers on Hilltop in Tacoma had carried loaded pistols, but out there in Parkland in the eighties, a dealer with a loaded pistol had been an aberration.

The beauty of the upscale college campus had been that as long you were one of them, and you didn't rock the boat, they had let much slide. In their eyes, Jack had been one of them. At first, he had just hung around campus, gone to parties and sporting events—shit like that. That had been how he first built up his clientele. But, after a while, he had wanted more access to the campus. If you strolled around campus long, and often enough, Campus Safety (which was what PLU called their security people) would eventually start asking you questions. That would have been fine if you happened to be your garden-variety loiterer, but Jack had been packing a Walther, a pager, a couple grand in cash, and an ass-load of illegal substances that could have netted him some real time in the tank. Jack had known it was time to dummy up a fake student ID.

In those days, getting a fake college ID had been pretty easy. At the game room in the student center, people had used their student IDs to rent pool tables. The little rack the game room staff had kept the IDs on was easily reachable from the other side of the counter. One day, Jack had just reached over and grabbed a student ID when the person minding the counter had been tending to something on the other side of the game room. He had taken a razor blade and cut the picture off, taken a picture of himself that matched the gray backdrop of the ID's original photo, glued it on, cut the extra lamination from the margins, and had it re-laminated at Kinkos. In the end, most of it had been double-laminated, but it hadn't looked suspect, and Jack had used it numerous times around campus to prove his enrolled student status.

Jack had had numerous close calls around campus, but they hadn't scared him off. Campus safety had literally caught him in the middle of a deal by the bike rack outside the library on campus. Even though the security guy had known what was going on, he had been too far away to say for sure, and he hadn't even tried to detain Jack and his buyer. He had asked for both of their student IDs and told Jack to stop dealing on campus. Jack hadn't minded close calls. He had just adopted new techniques for dealing with them. That security guy had looked at Jack's fake ID for a little too long for Jack's comfort, and after that Jack had known it was time to step up his game.

Being able to pass as a student had helped out a lot in the beginning, but really being a student, at least on paper, was the next step. One of Jack's best customers had done his work-study in the admissions office. This client had been more than happy to set Jack up as a student in the college system for a few ounces of chronic. "Who knew that becomin' a student was just a matter of shufflin' some papers around and enterin' some crap info into a computer. Crazy, huh!" This customer had had access to a computer platform that had allowed him to make a student file for Jack, and it had even been under his own name. For all intents and purposes, Jack had been a student at PLU. His electronic student file had been pretty spartan, so if anybody had dug too deeply into his file, they'd have noticed that he had no grades, was enrolled in no classes, and had never even filled out a college application. But he was in the system, so he had been able to go get a real college ID card from the office that issued them. For the casual run-ins with Campus Safety, or faculty, it had worked perfectly. His sparse student profile had never been questioned or even looked into, so far as Jack knew.

During that time, Jack actually had gotten a bit of an education. Because he had been on campus all the time, and because he had been constantly trying to expand his customer base, he had started looking at the semester class schedules. He had picked a few classes that sounded interesting to him, things like political science, economics, some history classes. Then he had started actually attending them. He had only gone to classes that had large enrollments, and that met in the big lecture halls. That way, nobody ever called on him, or even inquired as to what he was doing there. He had been just another anonymous face in a freshman course with a hundred other anonymous faces.

Jack had noticed, with some disappointment, that he couldn't really sit in the upper-level classes of the subjects he liked. Those courses had been smaller, and he had not been able to blend into the background so easily. "Sure, a hundred people will sign up to take the freshman level political science course, but only political science majors would enroll for a class called America's Role in Nation Building after World

War II. Oh fuckin' well! Too bad, I really thought that one sounded interestin.'" A few times, he had been able to blend in a class of forty or fifty, but even that had been a stretch. He had even gotten the books and done the readings for those smaller classes so that he could talk in class if he was called on and participate in class activities like small group discussions.

Jack had felt pretty good about himself. Six months out of Western State, and he hadn't been able to see anything horrible on the horizon. His little home had been the roughest-looking thing on the block of 119th Street and Park Avenue South. Jack's house had been such an eyesore that many people on the block had thought it was abandoned. One day, two kids, eleven or twelve-year-old boys, had ridden by when Jack was checking his mail. The bigger one had said, "I didn't know you could get mail at abandoned houses." After some inquiry from Jack, he had learned that this kid's parents, and apparently numerous people on the block, referred to his house as the "abandoned house," so after Jack had told the story to a few people, the name had sort of stuck.

It hadn't been an unfair characterization. The house hadn't had a lawn so much as it had had scattered random patches of brownish grass accompanied by green weeds and dandelions. Jack had never really thought about how the yard looked, and he certainly hadn't given a crap about grass. After talking to those kids, he had taken his first real hard look at the yard, and he had started to see what their parents had. Also, there had been no driveway, just tire tracks through the part of the yard closest to the front door. That was where Jack had parked. He had called it the driveway. Everybody else had parked in the actual yard. Quite to Jack's amusement, he had just noticed for the first time a horribly rusted lawnmower being strangled by interwoven blackberry vines sitting in the corner of the yard next to an equally rusted, prefabbed metal shed. It was not lost on him that the last time someone had bothered to mow the yard, that mower had probably been used to do it.

The yard was a suburbanite's worst nightmare from top to bottom, and there had even been a tire on its side, full of dirt, near the living room window housing the remains of some poorly neglected plant. This had clearly been some prior resident's attempt to grow something using the tire as a planter. Knowing the types of people likely to rent a place like that, Jack had had a pretty good idea of what they had been growing. That said, the house itself had been no better. It had been about four different colors. Jack's best guess was that whoever had built the sad little shack had been trying to save money and decided to only buy a little paint at a time, hoping that the next bucket would finish the job. When it hadn't, he'd run back to the store, and they hadn't been able to mix the paint to an exact match. Voila, a four-color house. There had been cables hanging off it, running to the street or to a box on the side of the house. Jack doubted most of those cables had done anything, and had probably just been remnants of a bygone cable TV installation, or re-routing of a phone line extension. The roof shingles had hung on by single nails and draped themselves over algae-stained gutters like they had been some sort of economically challenged style accent.

As terrible as the outside was, the inside had actually been pretty clean. Nobody would have called it cozy, with its standard white paint throughout and cheap gray carpet. Between the white walls and gray carpet, the house had always seemed a little chilly, sort of like being in the tundra. The appliances had been well past their prime, but at least they had been clean. Jack had supposed the oven was from the fifties. Before he had moved in, cleaners had soaked the bowl-shaped metal things that went under the burners and used some Easy Off on the inside. The refrigerator was similarly ancient, but the landlord had made some effort to clean it out properly. The freezer had even been defrosted when Jack had first gotten there.

The linoleum tiles had looked like kaleidoscopes with oddly colored filigree patterns flanking them. It had been dingy but mostly unnoticeable, unless you moved an appliance. Jack hadn't even known the background on the linoleum was supposed to be white until he had moved the refrigerator one time. Nor had he noticed how spongy that flooring had been until he had seen where the wheels of the refrigerator had sunk a quarter of an inch into that linoleum. When he had rolled the refrigerator back, the wheels had dropped into their little burrows like a revolver's cylinder clicking into place.

Other high points of the house: Jack's room had had a plywood door, like it was some sort of kid's fort, or a kitchen cabinet. There hadn't even been a doorknob, just a janky hook and loop to keep his door closed. The spare room had had no door at all, just a frame with the frame portion of the door hinges still attached. Strangest of all, the bathroom had been carpeted with the same cheap gray carpet that ran throughout the living and bedrooms. This hadn't been a problem at first, but a few months of Jack and Todd drunkenly missing the bowl while peeing had made it a problem. The smell had become overpowering, and their many efforts to mitigate it by spraying carpet cleaner all over it had proven to be futile.

In fact, the mix of the cleaner and urine together had quite possibly been worse than the urine alone.

It was so early on in Jack's story that the core of his crew had been intact, and more or less working together. Todd hadn't really been working, but he was around. He had been around, smoking, slamming, dropping, and swallowing every substance that Jack had managed to sling on a regular basis. Todd had been pulling a paycheck from somewhere for doing nothing, like usual. Mostly he had been living in the spare bedroom at the abandoned house. That had been fine with Jack. That had just meant that Jack hadn't needed to quality-test every shipment of product that he had bought in quantity. Todd had been a more than willing guinea pig. Having to be stoned out of his mind when he was trying to buy drugs was a real hindrance to Jack anyway, and after Todd moved in, he hadn't needed to be. Also, it had meant that there was always somebody around the house to keep an eye on things. Jack had owned a decent Sentry safe, but that wouldn't have stopped somebody from just walking off with it if nobody had been around. Jack was pessimistic and had preferred to err on the side of extreme paranoia, even when it was just for suspicion's sake. Regardless, having Todd sitting there all day while Jack was out about his business had been a pretty huge benefit to him.

Because Todd had been there all the time, Jack had mostly stopped worrying about being robbed. Besides, Parkland had been a small town, and the PLU campus had been even smaller, and Jack had figured that if he ever did get robbed, it wouldn't have taken him long to figure out who had done it. Anyway, with Todd, who seldom left the couch, sitting there lit up all day long, the chances had been good that he'd have blown you away with that .357 Magnum cannon he called a gun. He had almost cut Jack in half with that thing half a dozen times coming through the front door, which was also the back door, or in other words the only door. That was one of the things Jack had liked best about this house: one way in, one way out. That one way out had had two bullet holes in the door jamb. One day, Todd had been doing lines of crank all afternoon and watching *Taxi Driver*. Next thing you know, Jack had come strolling through the door, a day early from a camping trip, and Todd had gone all Travis Bickle. Luckily for Jack, Todd had not been as good a shot as Travis. After that, Jack had told Todd either no more crank for him, or no more loaded .357 Magnum in the house. He had laid off the crank for a while, but the .357 Magnum had stayed loaded.

Mike had been doing the whole having a job and girlfriend thing. It seemed like every few years people had to endure this phase of life. People like Jack were well-versed in this type of relationship. You met a girl, she went out with you despite the fact that you had nothing going on, and after a few months she started to lean on you about getting a job. That started a whole chain of events that wound up with you going to work every day at some terrible low-wage job. The money you did make went to paying the rent for an apartment that you didn't need when you were single and living in your friend's basement, but that was essential in the eyes of your new girlfriend. And if all that wasn't bad enough, your new girlfriend took up so much of your time that you were lucky to spend even one night a week smoking crack with whores up on Aurora Avenue. But they loved Mike nonetheless, and he had come back around when that new girl had gotten sick of him. What could you do? It happened to everybody at some point, and for most people at numerous points over the course of their lives.

Ron had been around, though. He might as well have lived at Jack's place, too. He had been on the couch about half the week. Officially, he had been living with his dad about eight blocks away. Apparently, he'd even had a job as a DJ in a strip club. At least, that's what he had told his dad. In fact, he had just dealt drugs to strippers at the sleazy strip joints on South Tacoma Way. Drugs that Jack had fronted him. Drugs that Jack had fronted him in great abundance due to his chronic lack of funds to make large purchases on his own. Despite being chronically broke, Jack had established a level of trust with Ron. Ron had been part of the inner circle. He might have ripped you off, but he'd never have ripped off Jack, Todd, or Mike. He had always made good when he moved his product. Even on the rare occasions when he had overindulged on his fronted product, and hadn't been able to make good right then, he had owed Jack and made good the next time around. He'd certainly had to step on his supply more than normal to make those ends meet, but he always paid Jack off eventually.

Things had been out of control over there. Jack had pretty well owned PLU and the town's drug trade, but cops had still been a problem. As far as Jack knew, they hadn't known who he was or what he was up to. They hadn't for a while, but eventually they had. Cops were stupid, but even a blind squirrel found the nut eventually. Making money had been the easy part. As long as Jack had had access to suppliers with large quantities, the customers had beat a path to his door. And with the quantities he had moved on a regular basis, he had established an unblemished reputation with most of the manufacturers and suppliers in Pierce County—the ones that counted anyway.

In 1989, the crank had come from the bikers out in the southeast of the county. The bikers had known all the burned-out sixties flower children who kept Jack in psychedelics, and the hippies had known the Mexicans over in Salishan's shack city that dealt the best blow and weed. While those channels were solid, the crack had been the most reliable hookup. It had come from the gangbangers in Tacoma's hilltop neighborhood, good quality too. The bikers had made their own crank, so the quality was always inconsistent, but the supply was always abundant. The hippies had made their own LSD and picked the mushrooms they sold. They'd had some weed too, but not as much as the Mexicans. Who knows where the Mexicans had gotten the blow and weed, but most of the time buying from them was cool. It had been a hodgepodge of suppliers, and it hadn't always been consistent, but most of the time it had worked out.

The crack, on the other hand, had been too easy to acquire. Thanks to the Los Angeles to Tacoma I-5 pipeline, there had always been crack to purchase. Jack had had one hookup with the Mexicans, and two or three with the bikers and hippies, but he had been able to go to a dozen gangbangers he knew on Hilltop for crack in quantity. It was like those heavenly white rocks had just tumbled down off Hilltop into Jack's backyard. He had felt like a lucky prospector who had hit a vein that never stopped producing.

One day, knocking at the door had roused Jack from a mid-afternoon slumber. That was weird. Usually, his afternoon naps had been disturbed by the phone ringing, the other end of the line sure to be an agitated, strung-out college kid. It was always that, or Todd knocking things over in the front room. Strange visitors had always been calling cards of change, and Jack was about to go through the biggest life change to date.

"Stop knockin' already, my fuckin' head hurts. Unless of course you're the cops, in which case, just kick the fuckin' door in already."

"Open the door, Jack," the familiar female voice had said on the other side.

In a moment he'd placed the voice. It was Beth, the LPN that he'd only just begun to fall in love with during his first stay at Western State. It had taken a moment longer than it should have for him to remember to look through the peephole and verify what his mind had just registered. The feeling that it was the S.W.A.T. team outside had still been a little unshakeable. In Jack's mind, the idea that she might have been working with the cops had also been a possibility, but one that he had been willing to overlook, or at least chalk up to meth paranoia. Whatever paranoid suspicions he had harbored, he had still wanted to see her, and he had flung open the door without another thought of arrest.

"Wow, you're a sight for sore beer goggles." Jack had thought that line was clever, but Beth hadn't.

"Try taking the goggles off once in a while and looking through clear eyes, Jack. This place is gross," she'd said.

"You're just jealous that I'm living the dream and you're stuck working at that nuthouse. Don't you know? I'm the king of Parkland. Now that my queen has arrived, my kingdom is complete."

"Great kingdom!" Her sarcasm had not been hidden. "You do grandiosity well, and if your throne wasn't covered in empty 40oz bottles and hamburger wrappers I might consider sitting on it."

"Sorry 'bout that. Let me clean that off for you, madame. The staff are kind of bastards 'bout picking up around the kingdom. The king winds up doing most of the janitorial detail, which as you can see is very little"

"The house isn't the only thing that could use some cleaning up." She had attached no sarcasm to that comment.

"What, I stink or something?"

"Yeah, you kind of do. You're looking sort of rough, boy. The only reason I was able to find you is because you gave this as your new address before you stopped coming to your outpatient group. I hope you appreciate the effort I made to dig you up. They'd fire me if anybody found out I was poking around in your files."

"But you never worried 'bout poking around with me while I was a patient?"

"That was different."

"Why!"

"Because I always had a plan if we got caught."

"Really?"

"Yep, I'd just tell the staff that you were raping me. Then they'd have kept you at the hospital, where I could look after you forever instead of worrying about you being out here on your own."

"But your plan is flawed. What if you lost your job?"

"What flaws? There aren't any, not when a girl is in love. If I lost my job, I could just get committed to the hospital. Either way, we'd be together," she'd said in a sweet tone of voice that had let Jack know that she was sincere.

All this while they'd been inching closer to the front room and toward the couch. The hospitable thing to do would have been to ask her if she'd like a beverage, which Jack had done in a halfhearted tone of voice. She had been there to have a talk, to straighten Jack out, and to put him back on course. Maybe even to rescue him, if she needed to, but that wasn't all that she had been there for. She'd worn that outfit before. Jack had almost never seen her in anything but scrubs. At the hospital, most of the staff had worn jeans and t-shirts, but Beth hadn't liked blending in with the patients, so she had always worn scrubs. Once in a while, she had come in to get something she had forgotten, or just to say hi to everybody on a day off.

The day Jack had seen her wearing that plaid miniskirt with the black button-up sweater and knee-high white stockings, she had been going to a Cramps show. Her makeup had been all-white foundation and black eye makeup, like a China doll. The normally chocolate brown bobbed hair had been turned jet black, and she'd ratted it until it stood out in the shape of a mushroom cap. To top off the ensemble, she had worn John Fluevog creepers with points that stuck out three sizes farther than her actual feet. When she had come in on her day off all dolled up, her excuse had been that she left her makeup bag there. Of course, her face had told the story of a woman who was already makeup bag equipped. Also, Beth had never worn makeup at work, further calling her story into question, but all girls liked to show off a little bit sometimes.

Jack hadn't been able to think about anything but that outfit for a week. Then, there she'd been, identical to that day. The only exceptions had been that the hair and makeup were both toned down a little bit.

She had been trying to make a point, to make Jack see the error of his ways, but her concentration had dropped through the floor. She had been fidgeting and wouldn't look him in the eye. She had licked her lips, and in less than two minutes she'd managed to lick most of her lipstick off. In her mind, she had wrestled with her conscience. She had wanted to do something, but needed to say something. Jack had decided to let her off the hook. After all, he had figured, she'd have plenty of time to talk later. She had finally locked eyes with him when she had felt his hand sliding up her skirt. She had started kissing him, and they had descended onto the couch. Jack's first thought had been, *where is Todd?* Todd was always sitting right where they were making out. Wherever Todd had been that day, he had picked a great time to be absent.

The first time, they hadn't made it off the couch; they hadn't even made it all the way out of their clothes. Beth's thong had been dangling around one of her stocking-covered ankles. Her bra had been unclasped so her breasts could peek out the bottom of it, and other than that she had been fully clothed. Jack's pants and boxers had been around his ankles, and with a shirt and effectively no pants, he had looked like Winnie the Pooh fucking the honey jar. Afterward, Beth had buckled her bra, and then it had been talking time again. Jack still hadn't been ready to have that talk. He had been able to distract her with some post-coital grinding, and then they had been going at it again. That time they had actually ended up in Jack's bed. They had also managed to get all of their clothes off, except for Beth's stockings. The stockings were hot, and Jack had made a point of leaving them right where they were.

Jack had done his best to postpone the conversation she'd come there to have, but after fucking twice, he had been out of energy, out of semen, and out of excuses to not have the conversation.

"So, do you have any little college girlfriends out here?" She had said it like she couldn't care less, but he had known it was a serious question.

"You know how I feel 'bout you," he'd said.

"I thought I did, but then you pulled your disappearing act."

"Me, I don't even know your address!"

"But you knew my phone number, and you were supposed to be at the hospital every week for outpatient group."

"And I went."

"Yeah, for two whole weeks. And if you want to drop out of your outpatient program that's your business, but I said to call when you got settled. You have to understand that being involved with you outside of work is at the very best frowned upon, at worst, I'd get fucking fired. I didn't want to interfere, so I waited. And then I waited some more, even after you stopped group. You made me cry, Jack, and now I figure you're going to do it again."

"And again, and again, and again," he'd said.

"What are you going to do out here, Jack? I mean, I can guess what you're doing, but how long do you think this is going to hold out? How long do you think you can maintain this before you end up right back at Western State, or in prison?"

Jack had said, "What do you want me to tell you?"

"I don't know, but you need to tell me something. You're not the one who drove out here not knowing what sort of reaction you'd get. For all I know, I was just your little nurse fling while you were committed. Just the only girl you could fuck while you were locked up, and then you disappear after you're out. What would you think?"

"I'd think I was a dickhead. That's exactly what I've been. I love you. I think you're the only person I've ever loved for the right reasons. I just forgot 'bout you. That sounds mean, but that's not how I mean it. Everything out here is just so loud, and you're quiet. You got lost in the noise, but I want you more than any of this stuff."

"You have to get out of here. You're not on your meds, there is non-discreet paraphernalia from at least three illegal drugs in plain sight. I don't know what else is going on over here, but if you want me you've got to clean up."

"What can I do? This is my house. I can't just leave. How am I supposed to make money? It's not like I can just walk out, get a newspaper, and find a job making twenty thousand a year."

"Just come, just pack up and leave this place with me. Do what you've got to do, square away what you've got to square away, and get the fuck out of here. We can figure out the details later, but I know you've got to do this now."

Looking at Jack's life from the outside, it probably hadn't seemed like much to leave behind. There hadn't been anything of value that he owned in that house, nothing but his drug stash. He hadn't even owned the house; he had barely owned the Volvo. But it had still been his house, and his life, and his friends, and his lucrative drug dealing business. Despite the illegal nature of his enterprise, he had still felt more in control of his own destiny than at any other time in his life. But, besides that, there had been his friends, the real ones. Good or bad, they had never left Jack in the lurch. How could he have left them behind then? Going with Beth would have meant leaving them, and even though nobody had said it out loud, it had been more obvious than the bullet holes Todd put in his door jamb.

"One week, that's how long it will take me to square things

away here. I think Todd and Ron can take over the lease on this place, and there are some loose ends with people I've got to take care of before I can leave."

Beth had said, "I don't think I want to know anything about what you have to do, do I?"

"I doubt it."

"Just don't do anything stupid, don't get caught. Just do what you have to, and if you make me cry this time, I won't come looking for you again."

Chapter 15

Jack had always wondered if anyone else suffered from chronic nose dehydration. He had figured people had it when it was cold and dry, but not all the time like him. It wasn't some paranoid delusion, either. "My nostrils are never fuckin' clear. There's always snot and boogers, but my nostrils are all dry. These boogers are always hard as rocks, and they're stuck to the walls of my Mojave Desert nostrils like barnacles on a ship's hull."

Jack had been given one week to shed his skin, to become another human being entirely. There had been work to be done, but he had been determined to see it through. As they had been throughout his entire life, the core members of his adopted family, his crew, had been supportive of what he was trying to do. Mike had followed a somewhat similar path with a more domesticated existence away from the action that centered around Jack's place. Todd and Ron, always optimistic, had realized that Jack wouldn't be going away forever. It was just a hiatus from the action. A vacation, or a leave of absence, a sabbatical if you will, and that just like any other cohesive unit they'd always be pulled back together again when circumstances warranted. That was how it always worked. Their bonds were those of family, and families rallied around each other in times of need. Even when the bonds had been strained, they didn't break.

As Jack had expected, Todd and Ron had taken over the rental agreement on the abandoned house. Jack had decided to leave all his furniture, dishes, and TV behind to square things financially with them for his bailing in the middle of the month. Not that things had to be squared with them, since there was plenty of money around that house to go around, but Jack hadn't needed the stuff, and it was what they would have done for him if the situation had been reversed.

"It wasn't like I was goin' to the moon. Parkland was just a suburb of Tacoma, and Beth's apartment was right in the Stadium District of Tacoma, near downtown. It wasn't no more than fifteen minutes' drive from Parkland." Geographically, it had been pretty close, but it was certainly a change of scenery.

Even in a small city like Tacoma, it was very easy to start your life over again. It was amazing, but right on the other side of town, under the assumed shroud of a normal person, you could live somewhat anonymously. Drug kingpin of Parkland, psychotic weirdo in south Tacoma, but up the road in the Stadium District, just some guy living with his girlfriend.

Elements of his previous lives had been around as he prepared his exit, and he had still run into people, but he mostly chose to ignore them, and they tended to ignore him back. People had picked up on that vibe, and mostly respected it. Most of the time, no words had been exchanged at all, and when they had been, they rarely went beyond a simple "hello" or "what you been up to." The only people that had never gotten the brush-off from Jack were the closest of the close. Dealers, fienders, mooches, one-night stands, acquaintances, they could all get fucked, Jack had no loyalty to them. Only Todd, Mike, and Ron had been exempt from this brush-off.

There hadn't turned out to be as much to take care of as he'd originally thought, and he had spent most of the week getting high with Todd and Ron. Some local college upstarts had wanted to get some business of their own going. They'd had plenty of cash, so Jack had agreed to broker a couple of big money deals for them that had netted about forty-five hundred for himself. He'd known that, on top of what he'd saved up, this windfall would keep him luxuriously unemployed for at least six or seven more months.

He had also put together some deals to set up Ron and Todd, from which he had taken no finder's fee. He hadn't wanted to make a profit off of them. He'd wanted them to be comfortable. Before he'd set the college kids up, he had made sure it wouldn't hurt Ron and Todd's business endeavors. If it had, the college boys would have been out of luck. Jack wouldn't have sold out his crew.

Ron had made his money off the strippers at the strip clubs on South Tacoma Way. Todd had been much less ambitious, choosing to stick with a smaller, exclusive clientele that hadn't really consisted of the college students. You had to admire the lack of greediness Todd had exhibited, even if it had been motivated by laziness. His theory of life had been that of the comfortable minimalist, who, even with the tools at his disposal to make a great fortune, was content to work only enough to get by. He had been Buddha with a glass pipe. To Todd, everything had been fine as long as there was food in the fridge, the rent was paid, there was the occasional piece of ass, and, most importantly, the drugs were in the stash box. Todd could exhibit restraint on a level Jack would call otherworldly, except when it came to using drugs. In that respect, his restraint had been nonexistent.

They'd had a party the night before Jack moved out. Jack had already moved everything he had intended to over to Beth's earlier that day. All he had brought was his safe, his records, and his clothes. She had still been on swing shift at the hospital, so she had stopped by the house before work that afternoon. All the people that Jack would henceforth ignore when he saw them had filled the abandoned house by two in the afternoon. Everyone had known that when there was a party at the abandoned house, there'd be plenty of free drugs to go around. Jack couldn't have cared less why they had showed up. He had known he'd be gone before midnight. The original plan had been to head over to Beth's the next afternoon after he'd slept off that night's events, but after she'd stopped by, he had known he wanted to get to her apartment so that they could sleep in the same bed that very night. She hadn't said so, but Jack had been able to tell that she was uneasy about the party.

On the other hand, Jack had been anything but uneasy. All those leeches that had infested the abandoned house at that moment had filled him with anticipation for his new life. He had looked into their hollow eyes, and their rudderless existences, and been grateful to be leaving a similar existence behind. If he hadn't known it before, he had known it that afternoon. He had known he had nothing in common with those people. He had known that everything up until then had just been a terribly low interval in what was going to be a long life. He had known they only liked him because he was the dope man. He'd always done the same thing with everyone except Ron, Todd, Mike, and, now, Beth. When the crank and coke left, so would they.

They were shells of people that had functioned mostly as life support systems for their drug addictions. Other people hadn't mattered to them, not even their own families, and they had been incapable of having real relationships with other people. He had literally prayed that day that he would have the strength to stop being one of them.

Every time someone had asked Jack where he was going away to, he had made up a new story. Jack had told Jill he was going to Tibet to become a monk. He had told Larry that he was getting locked up for a couple of years for selling stolen AK-47's. Bobby had thought Jack was going to Amsterdam with his earnings to become a pimp and hash mogul.

To each plastic person, Jack had spun a different tale, and, oddly enough, not one person at the party had noticed that Jack had told at least twenty different stories about where he was going. He had known they didn't give a shit about him, but all those fienders were so self-absorbed they hadn't even bothered to talk to one another. "Jesus, what do those fuckers even talk about when they're getting' high together?" Not one of those people had actually cared where Jack was going. Without speaking out loud, every one of them had indicated that they really didn't want to know where he was going, and that the only reason they had asked in the first place was because it had been his going away party. On the other hand, if the free crack and booze moved away, Jack suspected everyone would have been genuinely curious about where they moved to.

The only reason Jack had even been there was that his real friends had wanted to give him a party, and he had been there to spend a few last hours with them before setting out on his own. Jack hadn't really even liked parties that much. He'd always viewed a party as a means of getting drunk, high, or laid—all three, preferably. At any given party, if he could convince a girl to leave with him as soon as he arrived while also grabbing a bottle of Jack and scoring some blow, he had been content to ditch the whole affair altogether. Even when he had stayed at parties, he had typically just held court with two or three close confidants. Most importantly, Jack could get drunk, high, and laid without the help of a party at all. Parties were places that mostly just enabled those less skilled at procuring vice in the normal world to get fucked, baked, and smashed. Again, Jack hadn't needed the party; Jack was skilled at hunting for his vice in the wild. He hadn't shot fish in barrels.

That night, even Mike had come out, which had pleased Jack for a variety of reasons. It had reaffirmed that they were still a crew, and always would be. Mike had been scarce since moving in with his girlfriend, and Jack would soon be doing the same thing. Mike had been Jack's closest friend, and at that point, of the four of them, he had become the most distanced from Jack. Jack had known it would most likely stay that way, with the both of them now domesticated. Seeing Todd and Ron wouldn't be too hard when he needed to. They would be there, slinging, sleeping, or partying, and Jack could always make an excuse to come out there once or twice a month for a couple of hours. He had known it wouldn't be the same, but it was something. With Mike, though, it had been different. Todd and Ron hadn't even met Mike's girlfriend, and Jack had only been to their house once. Jack had known it could be the last time he saw Mike for a year. They had rehashed their entire life, adolescent criminal careers to present circumstances, in about three hours.

Mike was the best and worst fighter Jack had ever known. He had excelled at starting fights, and sucked at finishing them. He had also been Jack's best friend, and the best friend to have around when you needed something. His loyalty had often run into conflict with his erratic impulses, which could sometimes simultaneously make him the worst best friend in the world. Mike was a man who was most easily recognizable by his small stature and strange behaviors, but, more than those, he was recognizable by his passion for protecting those closest to him.

When Jack was twelve-years-old, his mom had put him into Keithley Junior High in Parkland because she hadn't wanted him going to his assigned school, the bad school, Baker Junior High, in south Tacoma. It was an ironic choice, since Parkland had in actuality been more blighted than his own neighborhood. The first person he had met at his new school was Mike. Since they had only been twelve, Mike's small stature hadn't been evident yet, but the behavior had been just as strange, and the even stranger look on his face had made Jack wonder about him. He had always seemed like a guy on the brink of doing something stupid. Within a couple of days of their meeting, Mike had proved that it hadn't just been a look, and that he really was always on the brink of doing something stupid.

Jack had met Mike when he was on a two-or-three-day lull from erratic outbursts, but it hadn't taken long before his true colors had begun to shine through. The first noteworthy thing they had ever done together was get the shit kicked out of them. At the time, Jack hadn't even really known Mike at all. He had just been the first guy that Mike talked to at his new school. Those people, the first guys, were like transitional or rebound friends. They never lasted and were really just there so that you had someone to talk to until you made some real friends.

This guy who Jack hadn't really known, and hadn't been convinced that he really wanted to know, had started their friendship by agitating and ultimately punching some kid whose size would have made him a big adult despite the fact that he was in seventh grade. He hadn't been an adult, but instead a gigantic twelve-year-old. Early onset puberty, Jack guessed. The first thing Jack had done as Mike's friend was get his ass handed to him for trying to pull someone off Mike. Jack couldn't say that he'd seen Mike win more fights than he'd lost, but he could say that when Mike had been around, Jack had never had to get his ass kicked alone. Mike had picked fights with opponents like he preferred getting beat down to winning. If true, it would explain why he had picked such big guys to brawl with. Sometimes, he had picked big women to brawl with, but those tended to be prostitutes he had refused to pay.

One way or the other, the beating that the testosterone-infused seventh grader dealt them had bonded them for life, and their crew had been born right then and there. Jack had already been friends with Todd, as Todd's family had been Mormon, too. Ron had actually lived up the street from Mike, so they had already known each other as well. Before long, Ron and Todd had folded into what Mike and Jack had begun that day, and Jack and Mike had become the genesis of what would eventually be an unbreakable crew.

Mike had been the beginning of real disobedience for Jack, and Mike had kept Jack in trouble on a pretty much daily basis until, after many suspensions and trips to the juvenile detention facility, they had both been expelled from Washington High School. Jack had been a misbehaved child before that, but together Mike and Jack had taken it into the realm of incorrigible. It had been the end of both of their scholastic careers, and with Ron and Todd dropping out shortly thereafter, it had been the beginning of an age of realization for all of them. Their families had been forced to put up with them to varying degrees. That they had all been great disappointments to their families was clear. But the four of them had chosen each other to self-destruct with. It had been around that time they had all realized that they had more than just passing friendships.

Jack was a blackout drinker and had been from the start. From that first bottle of Mad Dog 20/20 when he was a kid, booze had always kicked his ass, and he couldn't remember a minute of it. Nothing had been like that night with his first bottle of Orange Jubilee all those years ago. The bottle in Jack's hand always brought the blackout—but nothing brought the newness back—nothing. That had been what always happened, and just to reiterate, it had happened every time Jack drank. Sometimes, if he snorted enough crank, it had taken longer to blackout, but it had always happened eventually.

Why Jack had been sitting outside a mobile home he was familiar with, situated in a small rural town known as Kapowsin, on a wooded piece of property, was beyond him. Coming out of blackouts in strange places was just a part of life if you were a blackout drinker. Missing time and lack of judgment also came along with the territory. The last thing Jack remembered was having shot the shit with Mike at the abandoned house. That had been about six-thirty in the evening. It had been three-thirty, then, according to his watch and the clock on the dash of the Volvo. Considering that it was pitch-black outside, Jack had assumed three-thirty meant three-thirty in the morning.

On rare occasions, Jack had lost entire days in blackouts, but usually it had been like that night. He'd regularly lose eight, maybe twelve, hours. Sometimes Jack had been able to tell he'd been awake the whole time and had snapped out of it, but more often he'd woken up after being passed out somewhere, at which point he'd made his way to his bed or car, whichever was closer. Sometimes it had taken a while for him to find his keys. Sometimes, if he was near his car, he'd driven home right away and slept it off for most of the next day. A lot of times, he hadn't been able to get the key in the ignition, so he'd just slept it off for a few hours in his car. Sometimes, he had been outside the car and unable to get the keys in the door lock, and he'd had to sleep it off next to his car. Sometimes, he hadn't been able to get the key into his door lock at home, and he'd slept it off next to his door. Among other things, this was one of the recurring themes in Jack's life that he had hoped to be saying goodbye to.

Every blackout was different. You wouldn't think so, since alcoholics had little to no recollection of what happened during them. The lack of memory was the same, but the bruises on your body were different. The grass stains on your clothes were different. The dents on your car were different. The looks you got from friends and coworkers were different. Where you woke up was very different. Most of all, that gut feeling when you woke up was always different. Your gut gave you a feel for how things had gone during the blackout. Sometimes, the gut feeling was pretty good, like when you woke up next to an attractive girl in her underwear. Sometimes, the gut feeling was pretty bad, like when you woke up next to an unattractive girl in her underwear.

Good or bad—and for Jack it had usually been bad—you wanted to solve the mystery of the night before. Human beings can't leave a mystery alone. Mysteries beg to be solved; otherwise, why would they leave so many clues around for you to find? Things either felt right, or they didn't. When they didn't was when you started calling your friends and asking what happened the night before. It was those days when you rolled over at two in the afternoon and looked under the bed to make sure there wasn't a dead hooker down there. Jack had used to find cards from the police with incident numbers on them shoved in the cellophane wrapper of his cigarette packs. Had he been the assailant or victim? He had rarely found out, since he had never called the precinct to inquire about the circumstances of the various incidents.

The first thing Jack had always attempted to determine was if he was in his own bed or automobile. If not, he had next determined if he was somewhere he recognized. Often times, he had just been passed out on a friend's couch. After he turned twenty-one it had become routine to find Jack crashed out in a booth at one of his regular bars.

He'd had a lot of bad feelings waking up from blackouts, but he'd never actually woken up next to a dead hooker. He did have blackouts where he seriously thought he might. Sitting outside of that mobile home that night had given Jack the eeriest feeling he'd ever had. Ever. Normally, when he came to and felt anything remotely disturbing, he'd get the fuck out of there that very second and figure it all out later. Jack loved solving the mystery as much as anyone, but he valued staying alive and out of jail even more. For whatever reason, on that night, he had needed to sit there in that driveway and take in the scene. There had been lights on in the mobile home, a truck in the driveway, and motorcycles under the carport. The bikers that lived there had dealt crank. He was quite familiar with that place.

There had been no light to see by, just the one on in the mobile home. "We call 'em trailers." Waking up hadn't necessarily sobered Jack up. He had still been quite drunk, and lighting a smoke had seemed like the thing to do. There was no way he would have gone up to the trailer door and asked what happened, not the way he had felt. For all he knew, someone inside would have just stuck a shotgun in his face. Maybe he had slept with one of the nasty crank whores who regularly congregated around that mobile home. He hadn't known. They had come for the free tweak, and the bikers had let them stay because they put out.

Maybe they had kicked the shit out of him and then shoved him in his car. He was terrified and hadn't wanted to go up to the house, but he had also felt strongly compelled to stay put for the time being. After a few minutes, Jack had started building a likely narrative in his head. He had probably pissed someone inside off. It just happened like that. Jack drank, and people around him got pissed at him. He hadn't been in pain, which meant nobody had actually kicked the shit out of him, and they'd let him pass out in his car. Or they'd put him in his car when he passed out. Either way, they'd let him be out there for who knew how many hours, so he had felt safe as long as he stayed quiet. He had killed his smoke and dusted off the last swig of the 40oz that he'd woken up with between his legs before taking a leak in the driveway. "Warm malt liquor might as well be piss, but still if that's all there is to drink." There hadn't been any more beer in the car, and Jack had almost been out of smokes, but he had been able to get the key in the ignition. It was definitely time to go.

If it hadn't been for the drastic changes about to happen in his life, he may have dwelled on what might have happened with those bikers in the trailer. After all, they'd been one of his main connections for meth, but, driving to Beth's, he had tried to tell himself that he didn't give a shit. Really, he had given a shit. He had known that something bad had happened in there, and that it could have been anything from a dead hooker to unprotected sex with the HIV-positive girl Cheryl that hung around that place.

He wasn't going to be buying from them anymore, and he had tried to put that trailer in the rearview literally and figuratively that night. If he could have shaken that sick feeling in the pit of his stomach, he'd never have given those fuckhead bikers another thought, but he hadn't been able to.

Jack never stopped thinking about what happened in that trailer that night, not for the rest of his life. It was one of those things that had taken a piece of his soul permanently. He had never lived another carefree day after that. The idea that whatever had happened in that trailer that night would creep up on him from behind someday had loomed large as he drove.

Chapter 16

"This seems like a good place to start a new chapter. Pause for dramatic effect. One of the most annoyin' things 'bout listenin' to a story is when the storyteller butchers an otherwise interestin' tale by not knowin' when to take a breath and pivot. My friend Robert—who was a great drinkin' buddy—always did that. Robert wasn't never part of the crew, but he was a reliable alcoholic who you could always count on for smokes, jokes, and beers. Plus, he really did have a crazy story for just about any occasion. It was just his delivery that killed them stories of his.

"Knowin' when to pause is a gift, and since that trailer was the end of one chapter, it makes sense that the drive away from it was the beginnin' of the next. It didn't take no brains to start this chapter exactly where it belonged. Even Robert could have managed this transition without butcherin' it."

The drive to Beth's had only half existed to Jack. He had been foggy, but no longer blacked out. Still, the inability to track events during that drive had persisted. Most of the time, his green Volvo rambled along the streets like a little tank. Jack's blackouts had always ensured that a certain amount of property damage was done while he was driving. Mailboxes beware. Garbage cans and parked cars hadn't fared much better. Curbs, unfortunately, didn't move when you hit them, and the Volvo's rims and steering alignment told the tale of many such impacts. But this hadn't been a blackout. He was fairly sober by then, certainly no longer in a blackout. He had felt more like something had highjacked his mind, leaving him only enough brainpower to successfully pilot the Volvo. He simply hadn't been able to put one single thought together. Nothing had stuck, no matter how hard he concentrated.

Beth had lived in the Stadium District north of downtown Tacoma. The building was an oddity. In a very old part of town where most of the apartment buildings were built in the twenties, Beth's building had looked like something Mike Brady had designed in the seventies, complete with a hideous sandstone masonry facade. It had those flat, non-uniform bricks that sandwiched in three floors of apartments with railed-in outdoor walkways. Jack had been puzzled by this, and the thousands of other apartment buildings like this. Somewhere, somebody in the seventies had thought apartment buildings should look like cheap motels in the desert. The really surprising thing to Jack was that the idea had caught on.

The seventies was a lost decade, overshadowed by the sixties, and quaint in the shadow of the big eighties. Like a middle child stuck in-between the relative flamboyance and success of its more successful siblings, it tried to stand out by dressing itself up in ridiculous getups. Beth's building was a prime example of goofy seventies getups. Those cars, that architecture—what the fuck were those people thinking? Even the seventies would look at some of the stuff it had worn and say, "What the fuck was I thinking?" The cars had finally started to disappear, but places like Beth's apartment hadn't yet become shabby enough for people to start knocking them down, so they were still living with the legacy of that architecture for the moment. And living with Beth meant Jack would be living with it wall to wall.

The other structures in Beth's neighborhood had been huge Victorian houses, mostly converted to multi-family units, or the aforementioned apartment buildings from the twenties. They had been in a state between disrepair and renovation. It was a time well before those sorts of neighborhoods and homes had become sought after by the droves of tech migrants that would flood Puget Sound in the decades to come. They hadn't even yet been appreciated for their sturdiness, or workmanship. The huge maples canopying the cobblestone streets in these neighborhoods north of downtown had always made Jack feel like he was in a Norman Rockwell painting. It was in the city, but not in the shit. Just like those paintings, the mischievousness had been there, but it had been cloaked by the serenity that patriotic normality brought

Driving across Washington State was an interesting experience. If you were headed to Puget Sound, which let's face it, if you're coming to Washington, you're definitely coming to Puget Sound, and you entered the state in the southeast you would find yourself in a desert.

You were also in the breadbasket of the state. More precisely, you were in the applecart of the state. Everything grew in southeast Washington. Apples grew there, sure, but do you like beer? If so, there's a pretty good chance the hops used to brew that beer came from there.How about grapes, yeah seriously grapes—and more than a few wine operations. Cherries, grapes, strawberries, blueberries—all there. In fact, Washington's fruit game was beyond reproach.

But you couldn't stop there; you had to see the Columbia River, too. If you were west of the Rockies, it was very possible that your power came from there. Eventually, you had to cross the Cascade Mountains. People in the east didn't know what a mountain was supposed to look like. The ones in Washington were covered in snow and trees. Their angled rocks looked like they could cut diamond.

After that, you were almost to Puget Sound, which had a nautical culture in the purest sense of the word. If you made it that far, you'd have come a long way across the state, and you still wouldn't have seen the peninsula, the San Juans, the coast, or the Olympic Mountains, to name only a few.

In the future, transplants would flock in droves to this nirvana. They would dress up in garments that said Columbia Sportswear, Patagonia, Land's End, REI, and The North Face. They would have kayaks and snowboards mounted to the racks atop their Subarus. Sometimes, they would have the kayaks and snowboards on top of the Subarus at the same time, tempting locals like Jack to wonder what the hell was going on. "Cause that guy can't use the kayak on the mountain, and he can't use the snowboard on the sound. Where's that fuckin' guy goin' today? Why is he wearin' a windbreaker and a beanie? It's July!"

That was the future, but the present had been Maple pitch all over the cars parked by Jack's Volvo. Under those Maples was the best view of Commencement Bay in the city. Jack had liked to sit in the Volvo and look at the bay. Jack hadn't intuited it at the time, but at some point, in the future, he'd be sitting in that very spot on the road and there'd be a condo building obstructing his view of the bay. Based on how things had been going in the late eighties, he could have told you then that the future condo building would probably have a kayak and snowboard strapped to the top of it.

What only occurred to him many years later as he again sat in that spot, this time with the condominium towering over him, was that his home town didn't wait on his permission to do anything just because he had been born there. The city changed, and, yes, people from other places moved in, built things, got married, drove Subarus, and made lives for themselves right there. Jack had no ownership or veto power over who could live there, or what they might build or drive when they came. That condo would be built to house the new northwest.

Soon, the professional class of the new technology revolution would be there in force. That future condo building would tower like some new stylish company town housing the laborers of the new economy. Jack would just be a victim of progress, that was all—him and a million other unhappy sots that had come before him. The northwest would leave him behind.

Seventy years ago, some guy on the next block up the hill had probably sat on the porch of his Victorian home as the first bricks had been laid for the new, but now retro, apartment building next to Beth's. He had probably said to himself, "An apartment building, now, that's definitely going to wreck my view of Commencement Bay." And that guy had been right; his view of the bay had been wrecked, and the city had gone on in spite of his feelings about it. Jack had just never realized it until that condo showed up in the mid-nineties. That was Jack's future. Enjoying the bay for a few more minutes from the lumpy driver's seat of the Volvo before he went into Beth's place had been Jack's present. It seemed cliché, but he had watched the sun rise anyway.

When Jack had crawled into bed next to Beth, he had imagined that the sunrise was the cleansing dawn of his new life, or some spiritual-sounding bullshit like that. Jack could be sentimental about things like new dawns, clean sheets, and dropped charges. For the first time in a long time, maybe the first time ever, he had daydreamed about what life could be like with another person. Drool had run out of the corner of his mouth and onto to Beth's soft, clean pillowcase, and he had felt himself starting to snore as he dropped off into a chemical-induced coma.

While he slept, he had dreamed about this show at the OK Hotel a few nights prior. It was a dream that seemed realistic both during sleep and after he had woken up. It hadn't been bizarre. It hadn't had weird imagery that only made sense while the dream was happening but then turned into incomprehensible nonsense the moment you woke up. It had been a dream about the other night. Everything had happened just the way it had really happened that night. That had been the weird part—no dream-state weirdness. It had basically just been reliving the night.

Portland was Seattle's violent little brother. Olympia was its bratty little sister. Vancouver B.C. was the cousin that you always wanted to come to parties because he brought beer and field hockey equipment. Tacoma was the uncle that you grudgingly let in because he had good drugs. The other night at the OK Hotel had been Portland's night, and he had come looking for a fight.

It had been three days before, and it had been the one date Beth and Jack had gone on during his week of preparation for moving in with her. Just getting to the OK Hotel had been an adventure. It was under the Alaskan Way Viaduct, right next to the piers. The space under the viaduct wasn't good for anything except parking, and it was the shabbiest parking area in the city. Violent crack-addicted homeless people had haunted that place. You were bound to get jumped and robbed eventually if you were around there long enough, but if you weren't paying attention, it was likely to happen sooner rather than later.

Outside the gig there had been some goofy-looking kid spare changing, even though he was wearing brand new Doc Martens and a two-hundred-dollar leather jacket. The Poison Idea t-shirt he had worn looked like he'd just bought it at Fallout Records and put it on before the show. He had probably only been a year or two younger than Jack, but those years that each had lived could not have been more different. Jack had grown up thirsty and miserable; this guy had been some rich kid on LSD. Jack had given him a dollar because he felt sorry for him. Jack had felt like the kid was definitely going to get killed inside the show, and begging for money, money he didn't need, outside the show, would not endear him to anyone inside.

Jack had spent most of the show trying to sit at the coffee bar in the front of the place. Trying being the key word. If he had moved one cheek off his stool, there'd have been someone else's cheek trying to squeeze in, but it had still been roomier than standing next to the stage. When he had finally been forced to give up his stool, he had gone outside and drank the beers he'd stashed under the viaduct before the show. Jack had seen Nausea several times—Date Rape, too—but he'd only seen Poison Idea once. Jack had been trying to build up his liquid courage for the PI set.

Back inside, people had gotten bloody, and the guitarist, Pig Champion, had sat on a little wooden chair that looked like the sort you found in kindergarten classrooms. Maybe it was a normal size chair, but his mass had dwarfed it. Jack really didn't know. Pig Champion wasn't just a name; the man had to have been six-hundred pounds. Jack's brain had been just the right amount of distorted for this. He had been full of beers, but not blacked out. Squeezing into the mass of sweaty flesh had ensured that he didn't get bloated or have to piss. It had been a like a sauna, sapping any excess moisture from him.

The band had played a song called "Say Goodbye" for the sweaty masses. The air in that damp dark space had been so humid that Jack could have sworn he wasn't breathing air at all, but instead moisture, literally inhaling the beverages, cigarettes, and life forces of those around him encapsulated in airborne water vapor.

It had all been background noise to him, though. Swimming their way through the beer his brain was floating in all his fears of how his life would be with Beth. Every time he had looked across the hall at Beth, he had been amazed how she stood out in that crowd, as if she was three dimensions of full, vibrant color, and everything else was two dimensions in black and white. Then it had happened.

Punk rock shows and the northwest in general had suffered from a terrible affliction. That had been neo-Nazi skinheads. The bands hadn't been racist, the punks hadn't been racist—shit even most of the skinheads hadn't been racist—but those wannabe Nazi fuckers had still come to the shows. They had come to cause trouble at shows, record stores, parks, coffee shops, and bars.

This particular skinhead, Adam, had been well-known in their local scene for the troublemaker he was. On his way to the front of the stage, he had slammed into Beth so hard she had disappeared from Jack's view momentarily. It turned out he'd slammed into her so hard she had been knocked onto her hands and knees. This happened constantly at punk shows. In front, where people were slam dancing, it was expected. It wasn't the fact that it had happened. It wasn't even the fact that he had failed to help her up. It was the fact that the neo-Nazi piece of shit had laughed as he did it. His presence at every show was always an omnipresent insult to everybody, but his arrogance and disregard had been too much for Jack. Jack was a broken person, and his mental deterioration by that point had already been clear evidence of the fact, but he was no pussy.

Jack had closed the distance between him and Adam in a couple of seconds, and he had grabbed Adam's green flight jacket by the collar. Adam had turned around and spit in Jack's eye and shoved him back hard. Jack had had a half-full 40oz of Olde English 800 he'd snuck into the show, and he had smashed it on Adam's bald-ass head. Adam had gone down hard. When he had, his upper body had landed on a corner of the stage. He had managed to turn around, but it had been too late. Jack had already swung his left fist. It had been on its way before Adam had turned around, so by the time Adam had faced Jack it had already practically been buried in his nose. The next three had gone straight into Adam's teeth, which had looked like they were disappearing one by one down his throat. Then Jack had buried a few elbows into Adam's temple.

It was enough already, and everybody had known it, but

Jack had been in a mental frenzy. He had turned Adam around and started slamming him face-first into the stage. First, the bridge of his nose had hit the corner angle of the stage; then, it had been the forehead, opening up a disgusting gash; then it had been the mouth, wide open, being slammed into that wooden stage. People had eventually pulled him off, and Adam had left unconscious in an ambulance. It was the last anybody in the local scene had ever heard from Adam. Friendly punks had dragged Jack outside and strongly suggested he flee the scene before the cops showed up. Jack and Beth had gone back to her place. "Like he said, it wasn't much like a dream, more just a replay of that night at the show."

When Jack had woken up Beth was crying. Actually, Jack had woken up *because* Beth was crying. That had been the day that playtime had really ended. You could say that Jack had become an adult that day. You could say that if he'd learned anything, but he really hadn't. He had still been a mentally ill teenager in a man's body.

Chapter 17

J ack thought it was almost as if he had a receding leg hairline. There were strange hair patterns all over his body, and this was another example to him that God had a sense of humor. How else could you explain leg hair that refused to grow where the sock started? A practical joke worthy of humankind's creator—nothing malicious, just a reminder that's he was floating by on a cloud somewhere, pondering ways to demean lowly humans. The absence of leg hair there cast a sock-like silhouette over Jack's lower legs. God seemed to antagonize humans in much the same way that Jack had used to antagonize his G.I. Joe figures as a kid. Jack had mutilated his toys instead of cleaning his room. To Jack, God appeared to have a similar agenda for humans and planet earth.

When he was a kid, he had owned a set of tiny tools that he had saved up and bought with his allowance money. Those tools had allowed Jack to dismantle every one of his little plastic G.I. Joes and turn them into something new by swapping their body parts. He'd had a real Dr. Frankenstein's lab going in his room back then. There had been a Raleigh Tobacco can that he had taken from his grandparents' house that had stored hundreds of pieces of legs, heads, torsos, heavy-duty rubber bands from the action figures' midsections, and hundreds upon hundreds of two standard-size screws used for keeping the figures together.

In the backyard there had been a small but dignified graveyard for the fallen figures. Jack had liked blowing them up with firecrackers almost as much as he had liked playing Dr. Frankenstein. Many of his experiments had truly been Frankenstein monsters. Jack had rarely bothered matching skin tones, or even genders. Such had been the case of one poor chap with Baroness' breasted torso, Gung Ho's brawny white arms, and Roadblock's shaved black head. Sometimes, when he had run low on body parts, he'd decimated the dignity of the graveyard and picked through the fallen soldiers' graves for usable body parts. Sometimes, all he had needed was half a thigh or a lower leg piece that had survived a firecracker explosion to complete a new creation. Dr. Frankenstein would have been proud.

Jack thought it was a shame that he didn't still have G.I. Joes, considering that he had finally learned how to keep their environment clean. Jack was laughing on the inside, still looking at his weird leg hair. Maybe, he thought, God would finally learn how to clean up after his human toys. Unfortunately for the poor little toys, by the time that happens, God will have outgrown us. Jack's inside laughter turned into an actual laughing fit as he wondered what God would be into when he grew up. After Jack outgrew G.I. Joe, Jack had liked porn, alcohol, drugs, girls, and records. Jack didn't know if God had a gender, and he certainly didn't know whether God liked fucking girls or guys. Drugs and alcohol were pretty problematic, so he could see God passing on those, but records and porn were harmless. "Did God like porn and records? Of course, everybody likes porn and records."

Jack was thirty right then, it was a new millennium, and he was beyond exhausted. He'd been exhausted for years, and every day he wondered how long a person could make it like that. When it got really bad for him, he figured his mind would have to go back to its status quo level of insanity within a month or two, or else it would simply burn out. Somehow, his mind would shut down, or he'd die from a panic attack, or a heart attack. That was years ago, and Jack had lived his life in that emotional torment overdrive every single day since. He hadn't dropped dead as he'd assumed he would, and it had been like that for so long, he had actually started to believe he might just live a long life in that state. In a world full of terrifying thoughts, that one made his blood run cold.

Before Dolores had come along, he'd resolved himself to sleeping as many of the hours of the day away as he could manage. It was his solution to life; it was his escape, it was his lover, and it was his addiction. Sleeping didn't revive Jack's soul, though; it barely recharged his body. Jack had always found ways to artificially fill the hole that existed in his soul. Jack could never figure out how to do it without substances. He didn't even know if it was possible for someone like him.

Jack wondered if he'd ever even found purpose in his life with Dolores. To him, at that time, it felt like it, and right then, it felt like it was good enough for him. Jack had no models for how it was supposed to work, his life with someone. Even if he had a model, it's unlikely he would have figured it out. Jack's life was organized, on a large scale, like someone trying to assemble a jigsaw puzzle without doing the border first. That was Jack, putting together Charles Wysocki's little villages, streams, and trees with no idea where they fit in the larger picture. Dolores made Jack very happy, and by happiness he meant contentment. Maybe being content was the best Jack could ever do, but being content didn't fulfill him. Six months after Dolores and Jack moved into the new house in Puyallup, he realized two things. First, Dolores wasn't Beth. Second, there was someplace else he was supposed to be.

After that, Jack's body and mind just couldn't quit buzzing. Day after day, and week after week, it wouldn't go away. It had never been that bad before. Jack's mind became a wall of televisions with picture in picture, every channel all at once. His brain put itself into information overload. Every fear, every thought, occurred simultaneously. Terrifying thoughts flew past fifty to a hundred times an hour. The massive overload of terror occupying his mind was maddening enough, and there was no way to control or mute it. Sleep didn't do it, nor did drugs or alcohol. Dolores, sweet Dolores, try as she might, couldn't fix it, either. Before long, Jack's terror was mostly fear at the prospect of having more terrifying thoughts in the future. Jack was literally afraid of fears he might have in at some point—not the consequences of those fears coming true, but the thought of being afraid at some point in the near future.

Sometimes, after that, he had money in his pocket, but mostly he didn't. Sometimes he woke up in a motel room; most of the time it was a doorway, or a box, a newspaper bin, or under a bridge. Sometimes, he woke up in four-point restraints in a rubber room.

He fell out of the world. He got lost, and he stayed lost to everyone for years. During lucid interludes in the bipolar, obsessive compulsive, anxious, depressed madness that had finally overwhelmed Jack's life, he was struck with the feeling that he was completely alone. He could have found someone to help him. He could have found a psychiatric facility, a girlfriend, or even just a friend. But his particular blend of afflictions ensured that anyone that might help could never do more than misdiagnose, misunderstand, or pity his plight. That was what really hurt Jack, those years. He was certifiably nuts, and he hated but accepted that fact, but not having one other human being that could really understand his torment was unbearable.

Prior to that period, Jack had given up on himself time and time again, but there had always been some sustaining force keeping him afloat. Sometimes, it had been Jack's crew, or Dolores, or Beth, or his mom. Sometimes, it had just been simple spite, and an ingrained need to prove all those people who had looked down their nose at him wrong. In every instance, the will to survive was simply a distraction from the real problem, the problem of being Jack.

Conversely, self-destructing was just a distraction as well. Neither distraction made his mind quiet or his body stop working. Nothing did. Jack's mind was wired to go bad right away, but his body was wired to keep living for a long time. The end result was always the same: every day, Jack kept waking up. His mind wouldn't give him a moment's peace, no matter how hard he beat it with substances, and his body wouldn't stop living, no matter how hard he beat it with substances. He was stuck, alive, and alone.

Nobody likes self-pity in a character; people want drama and somebody to root for. Sad stories could leave a lasting impression, though. *1984* gives one the bleakest, dystopian views imaginable, but the last line punched you in the gut like a real fist punching you in the gut. An actual punch to the gut went away after a few minutes, but the end of *1984* hurt years later. Sad could work, but self-pity never played well, never.

Jack gave up during that time. He never loved Big Brother, but he was defeated just the same. No human could've remained intact under that strain he was under, and he never pitied himself. He hated his circumstances, was resentful and angry at the hand life had dealt him, but never really stopped trying to get up again. It was futile, of course, and the older he got, the more he realized that he was a fly trying to escape from a closed window. How many flies have you found lying in the crook of a sliding window? There they lie, crusty and dry, only the slightest pressure from a human finger needed to turn those little bodies into a thousand tiny twigs of exoskeleton. The window was solid. That simplest observation of any person was completely lost on the fly. The fly would smash its head against the glass, searching for an open spot you knew didn't exist, until it died. It was cruel to watch the fly without opening the window; it was sadistic to enjoy watching the fly without opening the window. The futility of the fly's situation was obvious and tragic. You might as well have asked a child to flip a fire engine.

Jack was in a bad state then, but he didn't pity himself. He just kept banging his head into the glass, looking, against all odds, for the open spot in the window. Eventually, I learned to pity him, but he didn't pity himself. In any case, for those of us watching his life, it went from unwatchable to unbearable.

Seeing it was unbearable, but living it must have been excruciating. It was four years, give or take, and most people who knew Jack secretly hoped he would find the courage to end his own life, or overdose, or get hit by a bus. Most were ashamed to say it, but Jack's death would have alleviated the guilt of many that cared about him. People are allowed to feel like that. Caring for an ill person takes its toll on the loved ones, too. Everybody suffers. Of course, there's shame attached to any such thought, but it exists nonetheless.

Chapter 18

When a person starts off his mental break by stealing his girlfriend's Volkswagen bug and driving it to Utah for some fresh air, the story probably doesn't get better from there. That's how Jack got started. Sounds ridiculous, doesn't it? It had always been something ridiculous, but it never seemed so to him. It had seemed like the logical next step in a sequence of events, or an imperative. That time, it had been nothing less than that, an imperative. There was a city in the mountains where thousands of unspoiled Mormon college girls resided, a place where there was clean mountain air.

Provo, Utah, that was the destination. As he pulled out of the 7-11 parking lot, forty ounces of Olde English 800 in hand, cigarette in mouth, and prescribed medications nowhere to be found, Jack imagined his future life. That clean air, and pure-minded Mormon college girls, that was the ticket. It was the thing that was finally going to lead him to the clean living. In Provo, he'd find work chopping wood or cleaning mountain cabins. He wasn't really sure, but chopping wood and cleaning mountain cabins were the only occupations his somewhat ignorant brain could come up with.

He figured that, in his free time, he'd ski for free, since

he'd work at one of the ski resorts. In the spring, he'd come down from the resort into the college town. Those college girls would love him. He'd be in great shape from all the wood chopping and cabin cleaning. He wouldn't smoke or drink. Plus, he'd have a great 4x4. It was fall again, which, in Washington, just meant nine straight months of rain and early sunsets, the dark wet. But in Utah, it meant nine months of skiing and cabin parties.

Dolores' car always smelled both abandoned and lived in at the same time. Jack wondered if Volkswagen was thinking about a rainy climate when they had designed it, because, whenever it rained, it seemed like every surface on the inside of the car was constantly wet. In western Washington, that was a bad thing. Everything outside was already constantly wet at that time of year, and importing that to the inside of a tiny tin can of a car made existing in it miserable. Those fake leather seats, wet. The tiny little dashboard, wet. The gross little gearshift boot popping out of the floor, wet. The inside of that flat-as-a-board little windshield, wet. The mushy, carpeted floorboard mats, squishy and wet. The whole car smelled wet, like mildew and old sweat simultaneously. Sometimes it smelled like an old coat. Most of the time, it smelled like exhaust and gas.

Jack's spit was starting to take on the consistency of the malt liquor he was drinking. The taste was rank, but Jack barely noticed it anymore. Sometimes he caught a hint of it when he opened the first one and took a drink, and when that happened, he couldn't help but think he was drinking someone's distilled body odor. It was worth it, though. Soon, Jack's lips would start tingling, and he'd get butterflies in his stomach that let him know the booze was starting to have an effect. He hadn't drunk in a while, and he got that feeling in his stomach, that feeling like he had a fart that wouldn't come out. It was that bloated, gaseous feeling that just made you laugh instead of fart. If you didn't know it was just alcohol pooling and expanding in your stomach, you might be inclined to go sit on a toilet somewhere and wait for the fart to come out.

Jack was a well-orientated drunk, and had great balance, too. One time, at a DOA show, he was standing next to the stage all of two feet from the pit, and this guy had torpedoed out at him like someone had shot him out of a slingshot. Jack had done one of those falls, like in a Looney Tunes episode, where he was completely horizontal in the air before he slammed straight down on his back, but he had turned the beer cup in his hand ninety degrees into an upright position to keep it from spilling. After that, some people in the crowd had picked him up and put him on his feet, and as they had, he had turned the cup ninety degrees back again so the beer didn't spill. One of them had said, "How'd you do that?" Jack had said, "Do what?" "You didn't spill your beer." Jack hadn't even been aware he'd done it.

It was all just some reflex and reaction superpower. Jack was all reflex and reaction, and he needed it. God gave the reflex and reaction superpower to the Irish and house cats. Jack was one of those things. Anyhow, neither the Irish nor house cats could survive without it, and no one was sure why cats had it at all. After all, nobody liked cats anyway. Irish people were another story. Everybody loved the Irish. The English were so in love with the Irish they'd been trying to fuck them for thousands of years. One way or the other, that reflex and reaction superpower ensured that house cats and Irish people survived situations that would otherwise be fatal.

It was true; you could watch a cat fall out of a window and somehow land safely on the limb of a nearby tree.

One time, a guy had hit Jack so hard he was literally out cold on his feet. Instead of collapsing, Jack had lurched toward the guy, fish hooked him, and then fallen down. On the way down, the guy had hit his temple on the hood of the car that was behind him. Jack had hit the ground, but the impact had actually woken him up. The other guy had been concussed and hadn't gotten up for several minutes. Jack had never landed a single punch, but he had been up on his feet, and the other guy had been out cold on the pavement.

Whenever he was driving, the superpower worked double. Jack woke up at the steering wheel a lot. Usually, the car was in motion, and often Jack was only a few seconds from certain death. It was rarely two tons of steel a hundred miles an hour, but scary nonetheless. At no point did Jack wear a seatbelt, ever. On that occasion, in Dolores' bug, Jack woke up to see a large tree coming at him. Jack had passed out, and he was actually coming at the tree doing about sixty. The road ahead curved sharp to the left. It was too late for the brakes, and bracing for impact seemed like his only choice. Instead, Jack somehow managed to clip a raised center median strip with the left front wheel, and it spun the bug one hundred and eighty degrees.

He'd put the bug in neutral, so he was still traveling about twenty miles per hour, only backwards, when the rear bumper hit the tree, slamming Jack rearward into his seat. Jack began cursing his luck until he realized that, without his seatbelt on, and doing sixty, he likely would have been ejected from the bug and died on the ground shortly thereafter. Even if he'd had his seatbelt on, the bug would have been totaled, and he would have been in the middle of nowhere with no transportation whatsoever. As it was, he had some minor discomfort, and a dented rear bumper. "Thank you very fuckin' much, reflex and reaction superpower gods."

He figured the alignment wouldn't be totally right after that, but it hadn't been totally right before that. The bug had stalled during the collision, so Jack pushed the clutch in and tried the ignition. The engine started back up, and after piloting it out of the brush and back onto the dark forest road, the steering seemed no worse for the wear. Jack couldn't remember anything for at least two hours preceding the tree collision. It was definitely time to check the map and compass.

All Jack needed to go anywhere in the world was a map and a compass. It was a handy skill to have before anyone could go anywhere simply because they had navigation on a smartphone. Laurence and Jack had both been in the Boy Scouts. Jack's dad had been their scoutmaster. He had taught Laurence and Jack how to read maps and use a compass when they were kids. Their dad was a Vietnam vet, and he had run their Boy Scout troop like it was his platoon in the jungles outside of Huế City. Jack was sure his dad had thought he was a flake, undisciplined and weak-willed. Jack actually appreciated skills like the ability to navigate from one place to another. In reality, Jack's dad had taught Laurence things, and Jack had just happened to be around. Jack hadn't realized that he was an afterthought to his dad when he was young, but he was fully aware of the fact by the time he was grown.

It took about fifteen or twenty minutes, but Jack finally found an ampm near Caldwell, Idaho. In his blackout, it appeared that Jack had meandered his way down I-84 through at least a couple hundred miles of rural Oregon and into Idaho.

Sometime after he'd crossed into Idaho, he'd gotten off the interstate and onto Idaho State Route 95. Out there was where he had hit the tree. Once he'd gotten back on I-84, finding more beer and gas was pretty simple. There were no hunger pangs, but Jack suspected he should eat anyway. He didn't. Jack actually liked the rubbery ampm hamburgers, but this was not an eating day. He figured he'd eat the next day, after he'd made it to Provo.

Caldwell was by no means a metropolis, but it was big enough to support one or two twenty-four-hour gas stations. It was quiet at night, and, based on the quaint nature of Main Street, Jack supposed the city was pretty quiet during the day, too. There was probably a rager on Saturday night down under the bridge that crossed Indian Creek, but most of the automobiles around there were 1970s GMC, Ford, or Chevy pickups, all equipped with rifle racks. Most of those racks had at least one rifle on them; some had two or three. The Fords seemed the most heavily armed, the Chevys the least, and the GMCs had plenty of rifles, just not as many as the Fords. One rack Jack saw had a compound bow. It was in a GMC. Odd bunch the GMC crowd, he mumbled out loud. He didn't know why, but when he went to new places, Jack always tried to imagine living there. Caldwell seemed like a fine place. It seemed like a place where you could shoot holes in the empty keg after the party down by the river. It was definitely a place where you could hear country music at the bar and hook up with a Treasure Valley farmgirl in a barn later that night. All of that actually sounded pretty fun, and for a moment Jack considered sticking around for a day or two. He didn't. He knew that once he stopped, he'd probably be stopped for a while. No farmgirls for Jack. Caldwell was only going to be a pit stop. Besides, he didn't have a trucker hat or a Stetson, and if he was going to hang around Caldwell, he'd need one or the other. The truck and rifle rack were negotiable, but the hat was mandatory.

It had been a while since he had peed. It had been a while since he had stood up. When you sat and drove for a long time, you could develop some serious bladder control. As long as you didn't move much, you could drive a hundred miles on a full bladder. At least, Jack could. Unfortunately, not stopping to pee meant not standing up. Jack had been drinking the whole drive, or at least he assumed he had. Blackouts had never stopped him from drinking in the past, so why would they now? Jack had it on good authority from practically every person he'd ever been close to that not only did Jack continue to drink in blackouts, but he would get up, go to the store or a bar, purchase more alcohol, and keep drinking.

Jack stepped out of the bug, stood up straight to stretch, and immediately grabbed the open car door. The tunnel vision had come over him quick. The combination of alcohol and whiplash from his earlier accident almost put him on the pavement. In typical Jack fashion, he grabbed the door handle and reclaimed control of one leg on the way down. For a second, he balanced on that one leg while the other pointed straight out behind him. His left hand held the door handle for dear life, and his nose was no more than three inches from the ground. He didn't know how to stand up from that position, but he looked like a figure skater in the camel position. Eventually, he just bent the knee of the leg he was balancing on and slowly lowered himself onto the pavement.

Jack was already out of sorts, even for him, and the inside

of the ampm didn't help. ampms are the emergency rooms of convenience stores. Everything is bright white, or some hideous neon orange or purple. There are bright lines painted on the gleaming white tiles, pointing you to where things are. Ten seconds of exposure to the harsh fluorescent lights alone made Jack's eyes hurt. The hamburgers and hot dogs were all sterile in their aluminum foil packaging. Sterile convenience was a thing.

All ampms were ten percent too much of everything. Ten percent too much light. Ten percent too much bright white walls. Ten percent too glossy floor tiles. It was like it was designed by someone who'd read books about Americans but had never been to America. Even the human behind the counter was ten percent too much.

This particular human was in his early twenties. Somehow, his creator had crammed all the worst things about being an adolescent and young man into this one sad creature. He had terrible acne and a patchy beard. Instead of shaving, he had just let the whiskers grow over the pimples. He was too skinny and too short. Usually, people were one or the other. His glasses were too small, but his lenses were way too thick. Was he human? Was he a facsimile of a human? Jack didn't want to stick around to find out. He asked for a pack of Marlboro Reds in a box, paid for his beer and smokes, and got the fuck out of there. When he walked in there, Jack had been worried the guy would sweat him about almost falling outside. By the time he left, he was just glad the guy hadn't beamed him up to his mothership.

Jack already had that new 40oz of 8 ball a third empty as the gas filled the bug. He was staring at the map and smoking a Marlboro Red when he started thinking about his dad again.

The Cockney Rejects' cassette was playing "Beginning of the End" for at least the twelfth time on this trip.

Jack may have been an afterthought to his dad, but he had never realized that, despite outward appearances, Jack had easily absorbed and utilized more of what his dad had taught them than Laurence ever had. Jack saw the front passenger tire sagging and decided to fill it up before he left. Jack doubted Laurence could have even changed that tire, much less taken apart the front suspension and replaced the shocks that had just taken a beating when he had hit that median back there. Jack could. He had watched his dad do it one time. After that, Jack had started taking everything apart just to see if he could put it back together. Once he had started driving, the cars he could afford to own had routinely been in such poor shape that he had become a fairly skilled backyard mechanic. As for navigation, Laurence had gotten lost in the woods by their house growing up; he would certainly have been no help on a rural state route highway.

Chapter 19

Jack felt sorry for people that should have felt sorry for him. That is, Jack felt sad when he looked at people with low-paying jobs, crappy apartments, and shitty cars. Jack had no job, a cheap motel room, and a stolen car. When Jack made it to Provo, he immediately started feeling sorry for all the locals.

Jack turned thirty during his first week in Utah, and in a few more weeks the millennium would end. The prophetic Cockney Rejects tape was still playing, the beginning of the end indeed. People had been talking about all the computers crashing when their clocks rolled over to the new millennium. Y2K was the buzzword of the season. Jack didn't worry much about it. In reality, he thought a world without an electronic infrastructure could be good for him. He'd failed to excel in the world up to that point, but a chaotic mind, he thought, might thrive in a chaotic world. He was probably right. The ambitions of the insane always seemed to thrive in a vacuum of order. Jack's problem was that he kept trying to assimilate into polite society. He'd bottom out, then eventually try to assimilate again. If he rejected a rules-based structure altogether, he'd probably be much happier.

Provo didn't live up to the wood-chopping, clean living

paradise, he'd made it out to be in his head. He settled into a place ironically named the Six Star Motel. It was ironic because of the reality of the place, but also because there was no such thing as a five-star motel, much less a six-star one. After driving around for three hours, it was the only motel he could find with a weekly rate. One hundred and ten dollars a week. He had about five hundred in his bank account, so he figured he could survive for about a month if he quit eating food altogether and only drank cheap beer on the weekends. Cigarettes, however, were a daily necessity. The plan sounded solid; plenty of time to find a job and apartment.

It turned out that living in a garbage motel was actually not very cheap. In fact, on a day-to-day basis, it was a lot more expensive than an apartment. After he'd been in town for a couple of days, he started buying the Daily Herald at the 7-Eleven up the street. There really wasn't much to do at the Six Star Motel most of the time, and reading the paper killed a large portion of the afternoon. It turned out that Jack could have rented a studio apartment for less than two hundred and fifty dollars a month. Jack intended to stop drinking during the week, but instead he just started buying cases of Rainier at the 7-Eleven. The convenience stores couldn't sell strong beer, wine, or booze, so he had to resort to drinking more beer.

Jack didn't know it when he arrived, but the strongest beer convenience stores could sell were only 3.2% alcohol. The 7-Eleven clerk tried to explain something about the difference between alcohol by weight and alcohol by volume, but Jack didn't really track it. All he knew was that his Olde English 40s still tasted like shit but barely got him drunk. He loved Olde English, but mainly because of its effect. It had always tasted like shit, and now the State of Utah had taken away its main redeeming quality. That was why Jack switched to Rainier. Like Olde English, Rainier was cheap, but at least it tasted alright. It was less portable, since you had to buy a case of it to get drunk, but Jack adjusted. There was a state-run liquor store within walking distance where he could get real booze, but the 7-Eleven clerk told Jack that off-duty cops worked at those places, so he steered clear.

There was no motel lobby at the Six Star, just a rusted dumpster out front that was full of old beer bottles. Jack knew it was full of beer bottles because he could see them in the blinding Provo daylight, and because when he threw his beer bottles in, all he heard was glass breaking. The manager's office window was practically on the city sidewalk, and it had a great view of the street, but effectively no view of what was going on in, or immediately outside, the motel rooms. And there was a lot going on both in and outside those rooms.

Every room had an exterior entrance and a bathroom equipped with an ample-sized window located at the rear of the room. The entrance to the parking lot was tight, as the motel sat on the south side of the lot, and a Chinese restaurant butted up against the Six Star's lot to the north. The whole place seemed designed to shield the anonymity of those inside the rooms while allowing the front office plenty of time to see problems like inbound cops. The position of the office also gave plausible deniability to the manager, as he or she could see very little of what was going on inside. Even the bathroom windows seemed intentionally placed to allow people to smuggle their friends in for parties.

The rooms themselves were adequate. The brown shag carpet masked what was surely years of beer and blood stains and who knew what else. The walls were off-white enough not to completely give away their actual level of dinginess. There were sheets on the bed—just sheets, no comforter, which didn't bother Jack. They seemed clean enough, and to Jack "clean enough" just meant they didn't smell like the cooch of the last prostitute to have slept or worked in the room. There were roaches, though. He noticed a few behind the TV, and some more under the minifridge where he kept the Rainier.

The bathroom was nice, though. It was turf-green Formica on the countertops. It was actually turf-green throughout: the sink, the shower, and the floor. When Jack took a dump, he had a great view of the exposed particle board beneath the chipped veneer of the Formica. The first time he noticed this, he also noticed that the particle board beneath the veneer was waterlogged, and he wondered what varieties of mold must have spawned in a near-completely encased piece of waterlogged particle board. He assumed he would see a roach crawl out of the open space between that waterlogged particle board and warped Formica, but it never happened. Then Jack got up, flushed, and looked in the bathroom sink, where he immediately saw a roach crawling into the drain. "I fuckin' knew there had to be one in here! Now shit makes sense again."

It was miraculous to Jack that he'd found the one place in that hive of Mormonism where vice flourished unencumbered. "As far as I can tell, this motel is hooker central, and the only place in Provo to score any blow at all." Nothing about the Six Star was helping Jack realize his goal of good, clean living. The Rockies literally surrounded the city. If Jack had to guess, he'd have said the base of some of them started three blocks west of the Six Star, but sitting and drinking in the lawn chair in the vacant lot behind the Six Star was the closest he ever got to the mountains.

In addition, there were two prostitutes, Rosa and Simone, that both lived and worked out of the Six Star, and Jack had blown large portions of the little money he had fucking them.

Rosa was a voluptuous Mexican woman, about thirty: big breasts, wide hips, full lips, really sexy. She drank a lot as well, so Jack liked hanging around with her. Plus, she only charged him for actual sheet time; drinking and hanging out was free. Sometimes, free was too high a price even for Jack. Rosa blacked out more easily than Jack when she drank, and when she did, she would either start crying uncontrollably or scream and throw things.

If you looked closely, it was apparent that most things in Rosa's room had been the target of her drunken rage at one time or another. The glass of the TV screen was cracked. The blinds were destroyed and discarded on the floor beneath the window. The shower curtain rod had obviously been torn down and rehung poorly. There were holes in all the walls, and if you walked around her room in bare feet you were sure to step on tiny shards of glass, the too-small-to-pick-up, remnants of unlucky beer bottles. They were embedded everywhere, and Jack learned to keep his shoes on in Rosa's room. That is, unless it was sheet time. Rosa was a good time, and she had a good time. She always had friends and customers coming by. Jack had to clear the room in favor of paying customers many times during the few weeks he was there.

Simone, which he doubted was her real name, was less sexy, and more tragic. She was blond and skinny, heroin chic. She had dark circles under her eyes, dried-out lips, and a generally unhealthy appearance. Jack was sure the thigh-high stockings she wore while she was working only stayed up because they were attached to those straps on the garter belt. Rosa's legs needed no straps; her shapely legs were all that she needed to keep her stockings up.

Simone was a cokehead; he knew that much because whenever he came to her room, she was snorting it, and because Jack scored blow off her a few times. She was also probably a junkie, because Jack could see collapsed veins on both arms, and when she took her stockings off, she had what appeared to be fresh track marks on the tops of both feet. If she was a junkie, she didn't like talking about it. Worst of all, once you entered her room, she was on the clock. She didn't like to hang out and drink, and Jack almost never saw other customers come to her room. Jack certainly never saw anyone that looked like a friend come by. They found her dead in her room a week before Jack left town. He never found out for sure, but he knew it was a heroin overdose.

Jack doubted it was an accident.Simone seemed like the sort of girl that either used the last of her money to overdose on purpose, or slammed a hit she suspected was too much for her to handle with careless disregard for the consequences.

Nobody came for her things. Jack and Rosa heard of no memorial. Jack suspected Simone had just been cremated, and after that her ashes had just been placed on a shelf somewhere in a county coroner's office. Jack had never seen one, but he knew there was a shelf like that where Jane and Jack Doe sat alongside all the people with real names but no friends or family to claim them. It was ironic, Simone spent her life all alone, and now she was surrounded by the remains of others, and those others were people who likely spent their lives all alone. Loners that they were, they probably would have preferred separate shelves, but Jack just knew they were all crammed together on one shelf.

Jack parked the bug down the street from the Six Star. About a week after he started staying there, it was towed. It was stolen, so he didn't want it at the motel or associated with him at all. He essentially abandoned it, but he kept an eye on it, hoping it would make its way back to Dolores. He never found out if it did, but he left a note in the glovebox that read:

"Hey Dolores, if you never got this bug back, I'm sorry and I owe you one 1972 Volkswagen Beetle, color orange. If that's the case, I'll have to apologize again, because if you never get it back, you will not have seen this note. If you did get it back, I assume I owe you some towing and inconvenience fees. Plus, there's a new dent on the back bumper and the alignment might be a little out. I'll settle up with you about those later when I have some cash. Anyway, like I said, I'm sorry about all this, and I'm sorry about a lot of other things too. Love Jack."

During a period where he was more or less sane for a couple of days, Jack applied for and, amazingly, got a job at the Taco Bell across the 189 highway from the BYU campus. It was maybe two miles from the Six Star, but Jack didn't mind the walk. Walking was the only exercise he'd gotten since arriving in Utah. All that walking was probably the only thing that kept him physically functional during that period. His Utah experience had consisted of walking to and from the 7-Eleven, which was not quite a mile from the Six Star. Now, working at the Taco Bell, he would more than double that.

In addition, he was eating every day again. He was able to eat at work for free, and that became his daily sustenance. Technically, he was supposed to pay for food he took home, but the night shift manager let him take whatever he wanted. Jack never ate after work, because if he filled his stomach up with food, he couldn't get drunk. He still took food back to the Six Star, though. Sometimes, it would just sit on the table in his room until the next morning, when he would throw it out. Most of the time, he'd go over to Rosa's room with his beers and the food from work.

Pretty much every night after Simone died up until Jack left town, he headed over to Rosa's room with a bag full of burritos and tacos. There were only four channels on the TV, so they would usually watch documentaries on PBS. At the beginning of that last week, Rosa started cuddling with Jack on the bed for no apparent reason. Before long, they were fucking like normal people instead of fucking for money. Jack still had to split when her pager went off. The pager meant a paying customer, and a girl had to make a living, after all, but even Jack had to admit that, for all intents and purposes, Rosa was his girlfriend at that point.

Taco Bell was actually a good place for a mentally ill alcoholic to work. All fast-food places have a strong odor about them, but that seemed especially so at Taco Bell. The smell of refried beans and odd-smelling meats covered up much of the booze aroma that permeated from Jack's pores. Plus, since there were always a couple of other employees that were clearly losing at the game of life, Jack's constant hangover-induced, diminished work performance seemed almost quaint by comparison. It didn't go unnoticed, but almost.

One of his fellow employees was a girl named Megan. Megan's husband got drunk nightly. She worked the drive-thru, mostly, but when she had a fat lip, Thomas, the shift manager, would put her on the back food line making orders. Megan's husband typically used her for a punching bag for ten minutes before using her as a fuck doll. The punching bag part was obvious to anybody that saw her face. Jack found out about the rapes one especially bad day when he was out by the dumpster smoking. Megan and her husband were sitting in his exhausted-looking Honda Civic. It sounded like he was trying to apologize for the previous night's violence when Megan screamed: "But it doesn't matter when you fucking rape me, does it?" She apologized to Jack that he'd had to hear that, but he was pretty sure that she had wanted him to.

Megan was a Pomeranian with glasses—cute, but stupid. She'd worked at that Taco Bell for over two years but struggled with aspects of the job that Jack mastered on his second day. The fact that she was going nowhere and never would made her life sad. The fact that she had two kids that almost surely glued her to that abusive husband for life made her life a tragedy.

Peter, the methhead, actually trained Jack. Peter missed work three times in the two-and-a-half weeks Jack worked at that Taco Bell, yet he was still somehow considered a model employee. Usually, the most exciting part of Jack's morning was seeing what had happened to Peter the night before. Peter only slept once or twice a week, so what had happened the night before, to Peter, was really just what he had done before work.

The manager, Jeff, was a compulsive sex addict and pedophile, and despite being married, he attempted to fuck all the underage girls that worked there. In that endeavor, he was rarely successful, but Jack had certainly seen him coming out of Simone's room at the Six Star. That is, before Simone had died.

The assistant manager, Hannah, on the other hand, fucked all the sixteen-year-old guys that worked there, so Jack guessed she was sort of a pedophile, too. She was probably in her late twenties, but she seemed a lot older. She had pale, freckled skin and curly red hair. She really wasn't much to look at, but her jiggly tits were always spilling out of her balconette bra, which was always spilling out of her work shirt because she didn't button the top three buttons of it. In any other context, she wouldn't have gotten a second look from Jack, but standing next to her tits all day on the food line had broken Jack down, and he'd started wishing he was sixteen. Once, Jack asked her if he could put the meat in her taco. "No, that's not how I said it. I asked if I could stuff her taco. She gave me a blank stare, and I was like, you know what I'm talkin' 'bout. She was like, 'No, I got it.' Anyway, then she just went on foldin' burritos. Clearly, she only liked teenage boys."

This seventeen-year-old kid named Randy worked there, too. He was the only normal one in the whole place. Well, he was normal by Provo standards. He went to church, got good grades at school, and was going to college in the fall. He didn't smoke or get high, and only got drunk with his friends at the occasional party. He was the only underage guy there that hadn't let Hannah bust his cherry.

It wasn't much of a fresh start, but Jack had a job and a roof over his head. Even in a crowd of addicts, molesters, and battered women, Jack sunk to the lowest common denominator. It lasted for about two and a half weeks before it all came crashing down on him again.

Taco Bell was keeping him nourished. Prior to working at Taco Bell, he had only eaten a few times a week. At least when he worked around food, he ate every day. Jack could only get four-hour shifts, but he figured out that what he made at Taco Bell would just barely pay for his room, beer, and smokes.

Knowing that he'd be able to cover the necessities should have been a great relief to him, but he just couldn't keep from fucking up. Jack's cash register was always short, and not just because he was stealing. It was mostly just sloppy cash handling. He only stole a few bucks a day, and that was just when he pocketed orders where a person paid with exact change. Everything else he did was wrong too, though. He was constantly late, not only for his shifts but also coming back from breaks and lunch. His hygiene was an issue, too. He washed his uniform in the bathroom sink of his room, but not very often. In addition, Jack rarely shaved more than once a week, and he smelled like a brewery even on the rare occasions when he showered. The writing was on the wall, so on payday, Jack took his check to the bank during his lunch and never went back. He never went back to drop off his uniform. He never went back to say goodbye to anyone.

He was nearly a week back on rent at the Six Star when he bolted. It surprised Jack that the manager didn't stop Jack and ask him about rent every time she saw him walk by the office. Jack knew the manager couldn't possibly be so blissfully ignorant to believe that he was going to pay that back rent. Did she even think Jack was capable of making good on that rent? Jack figured the manager must be used to derelicts trying to welch on the rent. Maybe she knew Jack wasn't going to pay, or maybe she just didn't care. It annoyed Jack that he couldn't figure out what that motel manager intended to do to get the rent from him, but whatever the case was, it was surely no surprise when Jack just wasn't there one day.

It may have come as a surprise to Rosa that he wasn't there, but he'd never know. He never said goodbye. He didn't even slip a letter under her door. He felt bad, but convinced himself she wouldn't even miss him. "She's so wasted most of the time, she probably don't even notice I ain't there. Just like everythin' else in life, Utah ain't shit to me. Rosa was nice, but oh well. She was a big girl. I'm sure she was fine. It was all just a big fuckin' joke, and I couldn't care less about any of it. Lost some shitty job, no place to go, no semblance of sanity left, and then I just move along leavin' nothin' good behind. Same old shit, different fuckin' day."

If life was that simple to Jack, he'd have been a happier person, but it wasn't. Jack was no desperado, humping and pillaging his way through the old west. Jack incurred invisible scars on his soul every time this happened. His mental illnesses, and the reactionary impulsive actions they caused, ensured he would leave people in the cold, and the innate humanity he lacked the ability to discard ensured he would suffer as a result of those very actions.

Jack's last paycheck didn't buy much, but it didn't need to. What it did get him was a Greyhound ticket back to T-town, a decent meal, a couple fifths of whiskey, and five packs of cigarettes. That was it, almost down to the penny. Generally, he didn't care much for whiskey. Jack was a beer drinker, and more specifically malt liquor drinker, but under the circumstances he had to make do. Drinking on the bus without somebody saying something to the bus driver was hard enough with a bottle of whiskey. It was almost impossible with a paper sack full of 40oz bottles of Olde English 800 crammed in under the seat, or a few cases of Rainier stuffed into the overhead compartment. His alcohol for this trip had to be compact, so whiskey it was. Besides, the bus didn't make a lot of stops at the corner store on the way back to Tacoma, so purchasing more alcohol on the way was not really an option. And drinking whiskey instead of beer meant fewer trips to that rank little pisser in the back of the bus.

On top of all that, if he hadn't spent all his money on alcohol and cigarettes right away, he might have been tempted to buy something foolish, like food. To him, it was beyond debate that booze and cigarettes were much more important than food. Alcohol would continue to hold its lead in Jack's hierarchy of priorities for some time to come.

Chapter 20

Interlude. People really do have a good side and a bad one most of the time. You hear it all the time. "Photograph my good side." All the scars Jack had were on the right side of his body. Even the patchy part of his beard was on the right side. He couldn't even grow a decent sideburn on the right side. He didn't like people lingering around his right side.

Jack lingered around the Greyhound station in downtown Tacoma for a couple of hours. He wasn't sure of his next move. Somehow, he had figured his next move would become clear once he stepped off the bus. It didn't, so he sat in the bus station lobby staring blankly into the powerless screens of one of those little TVs they used to attach to the arms of the lobby chairs. He had no money to turn it on, so he just stared intently into it, hoping the employees would conclude that he was waiting for a departing bus. They didn't. They knew he was just loitering.

Nobody was there to meet him. Nobody knew he was there. He hadn't bothered to inform anyone of his impending arrival. Of course, nobody was there. Jack was still disappointed, as though people should have intuited his early morning arrival. "At least nobody had missed me," Jack muttered to himself.

Right then, there was a knock on the station's front window. The knocker was Walter, his old roommate from the halfway house where Jack had stayed briefly before he met Dolores.

Walter wanted to know why Jack hadn't been home lately. Jack told him that he hadn't lived at the halfway house for a couple of years. Walter had some smokes and five dollars. Jack couldn't remember Walter ever having cigarettes of his own or even one dollar, much less five. He took the cigarette Walter offered him and asked him if he could borrow a quarter for the phone. Walter asked Jack if he was hungry, and since he'd only been out of booze for about eight hours, Jack was both in early withdrawal and, oddly enough, sort of hungry. They trudged up the 9th Street hill in the pissing rain to the McDonald's by the county jail, where Walter bought him two cheeseburgers and asked him again why he hadn't been home lately. Jack was barely able to keep one cheeseburger down, so Walter finished off the other one.

He hadn't seen Walter in two years, but Walter's life story of descent into lunacy was an intrusive thought that had never really left Jack. Sometimes, it went to sleep for a while, but it always woke up, and when it did, Jack's heart palpitated and beads of sweat emerged from the pores of his body with amazing efficiency. Jack's terror was pure and potent, one hundred and eighty proof, and each occurrence of it constituted a discrete PTSD event for him. Jack wondered for a minute how his PTSD compared to Walter's, and that thought triggered another PTSD event for him.

Back when he had lived at the halfway house, Jack was scared he would someday turn into Walter. Sitting at the McDonald's, he started to wonder if turning into Walter was actually preferrable. Walter was right where he had been two years ago and seemingly no worse for wear. As far as Jack could tell, Walter was barely aware of the passage of time at all. Jack was acutely aware of every little thing that had ever transpired. Every single day was a year to him, and every one of those yearlong days was a walk up a muddy mountain trail. Now, Jack cursed God for not turning him into Walter more quickly.

Jack called Todd to see about crashing on his couch for a little while. The next morning, he made a trip to the DSHS office to get emergency food stamps. While he was there, he filled out the forms to get back on GAU.

He framed it to people as a life reboot, but it was just another defeat. Every couple of years, it happened to him. Jack had been dancing dangerously close to involuntary commitment since that night he had left for Utah, and now he experienced the foreboding that preceded the actual commitment. He knew that within a short period, the fear and apprehension would all but melt away, and that by the time it happened, he'd almost welcome it. He always did. Eventually, his minute-to-minute existence would scare him into a desire for the structure that only the removal of personal autonomy could guarantee. He wondered if Beth would still be there all these years later. He wasn't ready to go quite yet, but soon.

Chapter 21

Something had happened at those bikers' place the night of Jack's going-away party. He hadn't known it at the time, but it really had been his going-away party. To that day, Jack couldn't tell you what had happened for sure. Like much of his life, it had happened in a blackout. As with any other blackout, Jack never fully or even partially recollected what had happened that night. He didn't remember what had happened, but he did know a couple of things. He had woken up in Beth's bed covered in blood. He knew that. Also, he hadn't been cut anywhere, so the blood hadn't been his. He knew that, too.

This would be a great pivot point. The part in the story where Jack put all the pieces of the puzzle together and began to live a meaningful life. The part where he faced the music, and ultimately became a better person for it. I, your narrator, and Jack's greatest fan, would like to tell you that story, but that's not Jack's story. Your narrator owes Jack, not the reader, and Jack deserves to have his story told the way it happened. Jack's is a cautionary tale, yes, but Jack is a human being, not a device to make the reader feel better.

Waking up like that was a hard feeling to describe. Jack had woken up covered in blood a hundred times, but when it had happened before it had always been his blood. He'd lumbered into the bathroom, and upon closer examination had always found something like a laceration on his hand, arm, or foot. He'd certainly found broken, bloody 40oz bottles around after waking up with blood on him, and so there had never been much of a mystery to solve. He had fallen with a bottle and sliced his hand or arm. He had walked on a broken bottle he'd forgotten about and sliced up his foot. Going to bed with a wound gushing rather than dressing it was a very Jack thing to do. In any case, in the past, bloody sheets had always been pretty easily explained, but not then. And Beth had certainly never woken up in a blood-drenched bed before.

Beth had been pretty freaked out, obviously. Her reaction had been that of a person who had never woken up with the soft sole of her foot sliced through to the big toe's tendon. She certainly had not been happy about the state of the sheets. She hadn't screamed, though. She was a nurse, after all, but she had been pretty scared and confused. Of course, her first reaction had been that Jack had bled to death in bed, so she had woken him up immediately.

Jack had had a pretty clear mind, which in and of itself had surprised him. He had felt pretty banged up, but he had been able to tell, even without a self-examination, that he wasn't cut. Beth's sheets had blue and white zig-zag stripes, and Jack had thought the pools of red blood actually gave the sheets a bit of a patriotic appeal. With the backdrop of Beth's antique iron-frame bed, the scene had been a nice little slice of Americana. Jack imagined that a painting of the two of them staring at the bloody bed would have made a handsome addition to some art gallery or museum. It could be titled something like *Patriotism and Valor at Home.*

Beth had begun questioning Jack about what had happened. Jack had been as polite as possible under the circumstances, but also annoyed. She had to know that he had been blacked out. Asking him what had happened wasn't going to make an answer magically appear. He was used to blackout mysteries, and he had periodically had some luck solving them. He was more interested in beginning the process of retracing his steps.

Waking up not knowing what happened was always scary, but that day it had been terrifying. This was different. Most of the time, he had woken afraid something bad happened, even though there was really no indication that anything had. That day, he knew something bad had happened because there was every indication that it had. If that wasn't bad enough, he had felt shame, because he could tell that Beth had been scared of him. She had tried to conceal it, but she had been genuinely scared of him for the first time since he'd known her, and that bothered him to no end.

Good or bad, Jack had wanted to know what had happened. He hadn't wanted Beth looking at him like that anymore, and the sooner he could find an innocent reason for the blood, he had figured, the sooner she'd go back to looking at him like she had used to. He had just prayed, literally prayed to God, that it wasn't as bad as he suspected it was. But it had been.

They hadn't had to wait long to find out. Todd and Ron had started calling within an hour of Jack and Beth waking up. The cops had been looking for Jack, and they were asking about those bikers. That was all they had known, but they had known from the officers' demeanor that Jack needed to leave town if he didn't want to spend a great deal of his near future in a jail cell. Of course, they had covered for him. Ron and Todd had told the officers Jack had taken off the night before, and they had no idea where he was.

Ron and Todd would lie to the cops for Jack; that had never been in question. But it wouldn't take the cops long to track Jack down all the same. Plenty of other people had known Jack was with Beth, most of whom wouldn't be shy about pointing the cops in the right direction. Despite the ridiculous stories he'd told many at the party of where he was going, he'd told more than a few of his regular buyers over that past week that he was moving in with his girlfriend Beth who worked at Western State. Jack had figured a hard knock on the door could happen any time They had sacked all the bloody sheets and clothes before remaking the bed and taking showers. Jack and Beth hadn't spoken as they worked, they had just jointly and intuitively carried out their tasks. Cleaning up had taken them ten silent minutes.

Pondering any decision for too long was poison to Jack. It was just like that, like the pondering really was poison. His stomach made terrible sounds, like the creaking a sinking ship makes when water pressure begins to implode it. His head throbbed. He shook all over. He sweated buckets and buckets and buckets. It was the anticipation he couldn't handle. Jack had no avoidance mechanism, and no ability to stop his ruminations. He always felt as though anything that *might* happen was currently happening to him. Making a decision, and taking physical steps to ensure he couldn't change his mind later, gave him certainty and alleviated the illness of pondering. Even when the decision turned out to be stupid or impulsive, he felt better. In reality, it was just his OCD compelling him to seek certainty about a situation that he did not accept and could not control, and those assurances that were bought through rash actions were always fleeting.

It had seemed clear to Jack that either running or staying meant being separated from Beth, but that staying and dealing with whatever happened meant that he might have a chance to be with her someday. Running would likely have meant leaving her for good. After his shower, he had asked her to go away with him for a few days. Packing some clothes had taken five more minutes, and with that, they were off.

Traveling and traveling, more driving to places that didn't even matter. It had seemed to Jack this was the totality of his life, even though Jack really didn't go that many places. "How can somebody spend as much time travelin' as I do, and still go nowhere interestin'?" He'd go places to get to things, and to get away from things and people, but no place ever sufficed. On that day they had traveled in Beth's Volkswagen Jetta. Everybody had owned a Volkswagen in the nineties. Nobody had driven anything else. Jack had thought, when he got back from wherever they were going to send him that time, that he was going to get himself a Volkswagen; not a Volvo, a Volkswagen. He had arrived back in Tacoma, and a little vacation was all Jack had needed to get his head straight about what he had to do next. His life had been about to hit the skids again when it had never really gotten off them from the last time. He had laughed to himself. "I fuckin' suppose 'the skids' are a multileveled journey. Man, what I wouldn't give to just be on the skids that I'd just been on a few days ago instead of the fucked-up skids I'm on now." Jack still hadn't even known what the new skids were, since he still hadn't known what had happened the night before. He had just known the present skids were worse than the previous ones.

Instead of a lifetime with Beth, he'd gotten three days in Long Beach Washington.

Beth had said, "What do you want to do first?"

"Find a time machine. If we go back about thirty-six hours, that ought to do it," had been Jack's response.

"Seriously! Your negative sarcasm is pretty funny when there's nothing at stake. Right now, it's less funny, and more desperate. Desperate isn't a good look on you, so if you're going be funny like that, be funny about something that's worth laughing about. Okay?"

Jack had felt like an asshole. She had been sweet and acted positive about a situation that negatively affected her, too, a situation that scared her and that she had done nothing to bring on herself. Meanwhile, Jack had sulked during what was likely to be the last days they'd spend together, at least for a while. He knew he'd had no right to. His actions, whatever they turned out to be, had caused the situation.

"How 'bout the motel," had been Jack's tardy response to the initial question.

It was funny how people appeared to you in everyday life, and at certain times became other people. They literally became different people—not different personality traits, but entirely different people. On many occasions, Jack became a different person. It happened when he was drunk and high, or in the ugly depths of one of his many mental illnesses.

Sometimes he was taller. Sometimes his eyes would change color and shape. His whole face, his whole complexion, would change. His voice, tone, inflection, vernacular—they'd change. Just like he was a different person altogether. The change in his body language was especially eerie. In order to notice the changes to his voice, eyes, shape of his mouth, or complexion, you had to be close to him.

His radically different body language and unexplained drastic height gain were noticeable from afar. Body language and height didn't change; they were hardwired. Mannerisms came out whether you liked it or not. In poker, it was called a tell. Body language let people know who was coming. The hand signals, posture, and facial twitches were huge neon signs as big as the ones on the Vegas strip telling all that were paying attention who was showing up in that body. Law enforcement agencies used them to identify people. It must have been some primitive safety mechanism protecting him. It was urban camouflage. It was effective, and he probably never even knew he had it.

Maybe it was possession. Maybe there was really somebody else residing inside certain people's bodies, or perhaps spirits just stopped by to visit the city and utilize bodies with personalities that were vacant enough for them to slide into unnoticed. A spirit periodically inhabiting Jack would have explained a lot, but more likely it was just urban camouflage. It was just one more of those latent Darwinian advantages buried in Jack that he had never learned how to utilize, but that had served to keep him alive nonetheless.

That different person syndrome happened mostly in times of extreme emotion. Jack never seemed to notice it in himself, but he had noticed it in Beth when he was fucking her. Jack had never fucked the Beth that he knew from the hospital. The nurse. That was the Beth he loved, but she had never showed up for sex. The other girl had always showed up. That other girl had been the one with the jet-black hair that reflected light the way skyscraper windows did when the sun hit them in the middle of the day, so black it was blue like a Crow feather. That one's face had been sharper, more carved, with pointed features. The straight, narrow nose had become more like a ski-jump. The cheeks had been raised in an impossibly high and unnatural fashion. The chin had pulled the same trick, only in a downward motion, while the normally soft shade of her pink skin had turned ivory. Her body had turned stiff and rigid, not supple like nurse Beth's body.

All in all, the appearance of this more intense-looking individual had rattled Jack quite a bit at first, and one time in the hospital he had asked her about her shocking transformation. The look in her darkening eyes, eyes that reminded Jack of huge pools of spent motor oil, had told him what he needed to know without her even moving the sharp, dark lips that were not her own. With body language that was also not her own, and a deep voice that resembled her sweet mousy one but little, she had attempted to explain Jack's reaction but had succeeded only in piquing his interest in this most strange of human phenomena. The fact that she had turned into the other girl while she explained it to him had scared Jack quite a bit.

That other sharp Beth had told Jack:

"You see, it's probably just your perception of me that's changed because of the strange circumstance that we've found ourselves in. You're just seeing me differently based on the highly emotional state that sex brings on. Sometimes, you appear to be another person, too. Have you ever met yourself in a mental episode, or during a bender? That's all it is. We're all somebody else sometimes."

Jack hadn't understood her, but he had nodded as though he had. "She was fuckin' right 'bout somethin'. I was seein' her differently, but it was because she'd taken a back seat in her own body, not because of the BS that doppelganger spun at me. She wasn't the one in charge, but she was there. Sometimes it used to feel like cheatin' to me, but after while it just felt like a threesome. Maybe sometimes when I'm loaded it's a foursome. Maybe sometimes it's two total strangers using our bodies to have indiscriminate sex. Who fuckin' knows."

In Washington State, just because the beach was right outside didn't mean you wanted to go there every day. Washingtonians understood this. To people in Washington, the beach was only a semi-event. Not all coastal areas were white sand and blue water. Here, it was clouds and rain most of the year. In southern California, the beach was nice year-round.

The beaches looked different around there. There were rocks and driftwood everywhere. Crusty clumps of sand crunched under your feet like dirt clods, and waves of ice-cold green water battered those hard beaches all day long. Seaweed washed up during low tide. It looked like some giant drying his homemade green spinach pasta on the beach. Algae-covered rocks that looked like sea monsters dotted the landscape and were serious trip hazards.

Even in the summer, when it was nice there, Washington beaches were a hard sell. In LA, the sand was white, and the water was that fake-ass aqua blue you saw in colored contact lenses. You half expected Pam Anderson to come running down the beach with her flotation devices bouncing in slow motion.

Running barefoot on the beach in Washington was more likely to result in slipping on a dead crab or cutting your foot on a broken seashell, than a lifeguard in a bathing suit rushing to your aid. As a matter of fact, the lifeguard presence at most Washington beaches was pretty sparse. But if you drowned, there would certainly be some volunteer firefighters from the local station waiting for your body to wash up at high tide. "Washington's coast is actually a couple hours' drive from the big cities in the Puget Sound, so Bobby and Jim from the local volunteer fire station is most likely who you're puttin' your life in the hands of if somethin' goes wrong on your visit to a Washington beach. Good luck with that, you fucker tourists."

Jack and Beth had spent three days at Long Beach sleeping in a motel room that he hadn't been able to remember the décor of a month later. They had eaten meals that he hadn't tasted. They had walked on the town's boardwalk, but Jack hardly remembered arriving or leaving the town at all. Morning had been afternoon, and afternoon had, in turn, become bedtime at blinding speed. A few times, Jack had forgotten about his situation, but only for a few minutes here and there. Jack's mind had refused to allow him to be present, and as such, the three days with Beth at the beach had felt like three hours at best, and while he hadn't known it yet, a three-year sentence awaited him.

III

Part Three

Squatting in the Shadow of an Ant

"It would have been so pointless to kill himself that, even if he had wanted to, the pointlessness would have made him unable."
— *Franz Kafka, The Trial*

Chapter 22

Jack had gotten numb after that. He'd had to. He had surrendered himself to the Pierce County Sheriff's Department and was incarcerated at the Pierce County Jail for several weeks. Most of that time in county was a blur. Jack had attended several court hearings in his orange jumpsuit, where he had barely understood the proceedings. He had eaten food off a plastic tray. He had worn the county-issued slip-on shoes twenty-four hours a day because the concrete floor in his unit had been colder than an ice rink. He had asked for, and had never received, extra blankets, because those welded green steel bunks in his unit hadn't been much warmer than the floor.

To pass the time, Jack had read books and played cards with his cellmates, of which he'd had about sixty-three. Jack was guessing, but 4C had had sixteen bunk beds in the top cell, and it had had sixteen bunk beds in the bottom cell, and they had always seemed full. There had been movie nights, too, which Jack had loved whether he liked the movie or not. Breakfast had been at four in the morning, and lights out had been at ten, but other than the terrible hours, jail had sort of been like a non-stop slumber party for grown men with very little to no drugs or booze. Plus, the hours hadn't been too bad after all. Once you had eaten breakfast, you could just go back and sleep for a few more hours in your bunk. Nobody at county gave a shit if you were using your time productively.

Jack had preferred to sleep until lunch and then read after lights out by the halo of a streetlight that had shone through to his bunk. He'd had a top bunk, so it had been difficult for the corrections officers to tell what he was doing on their rounds, assuming they even cared. The windows had been that distorted shatter-proof glass they used, which made it impossible to see outside. The jail was in downtown Tacoma, and the windows had kept Jack, and everybody else, from seeing what was going on outside, but they hadn't filtered out the sounds of the city. Jack knew the corner of the city his cell had pointed out at. It had pointed toward Hilltop from 9th and Yakima. He had been able to hear people late on Friday and Saturday nights stumbling home from the bar, mentally ill homeless people screaming, fender benders, and more than a few fights.

The books had kept his mind mostly occupied, but in truth, Jack had looked forward to being transferred to a prison. Jail had been like drowning twenty yards from shore. Jack had been so close to where he wanted to be, but just hadn't been able to get there. Prison was like being stranded in a lifeboat in the middle of the ocean: no reason to struggle, just get comfortable and hope someone came along to rescue you at some point.

He had read three Stephen King novels while he sat in the county jail: *The Stand, The Shining,* and *Misery.* He had liked *The Stand* best, but had identified most with Paul Sheldon's plight in *Misery.* Halfway through *The Shining,* Jack had gotten a new bunkmate who didn't play cards, and by the time *The*

Stand was finished, he'd accepted a plea bargain and was off to McNeil Island to do a stretch of three years and two months.

Three years was a long time, but it wasn't life. McNeil had been the last island prison operating in the United States when Jack was there. Walking off the prison bus down the catwalk at Steilacoom Dock had felt like living a Johnny Cash song. The feeling had faded by the time he was on the full little ferry to the island. By the time Jack had arrived, the old cell houses at McNeil had no longer been in operation. Instead, Jack had arrived at a nearly new facility. He had been told by the corrections officer escorting him across the water on the prison's ferry tug that the facility was dormitory style. Inside the processing center, Jack had seen pictures of the old cell house at McNeil, and it had given him the willies. It looked just like the rusty old cell house at another island prison in the middle of the San Francisco Bay: Alcatraz. Jack had visited it with his family when he was a kid, and he had never forgotten it. Mental institutions were not nice places, but those old cell houses looked like hen sheds, with rows of cages stacked on top of each other, wide open to the elements.

The new McNeil was more like Jack imagined reform school was like, and he had taken to it pretty quickly. The worst part, for him, had been the five-thirty wake up time. It hadn't been like county jail, either, where you just went back to sleep after breakfast. At McNeil, you ate breakfast, and then you went to your prison job, but even that had gotten to be routine after a couple of weeks.

Because McNeil housed only minimum and medium security prisoners, its air hadn't quite been ripe with the sheer terror that the constant threat of violence brought. Based on his offense, he knew he was lucky to have been classified as medium security, and lucky to have been sent to McNeil at all. Jack had been arrested dozens of times. He'd been committed several times. Fortunately for him, he hadn't been convicted of a crime until then. That was all that had kept him out of a maximum-security facility. He could have ended up someplace like Walla Walla where the threat of daily violence is a welcome reprieve from the reality of actual daily violence. That, and a tenacious public defender. His public defender had gone to Harvard Law School, and despite trying to hide it, was clearly from money. "His preppy ass was just out there slummin' it as a public defender in Tacoma for a couple years until he went and started his real life, probably at daddy's big Manhattan law firm." All this was grand, but to say that McNeil was violence-free, or that there hadn't been serious animosity and drama amongst the prisoner population would be erroneous. But again, McNeil had been more like *Reform School Girls*, less like *American Me*.

Jack had gotten a lot of visitors at first. You were actually allowed three visits per week, and McNeil was right outside Tacoma, so most people he knew had lived well within an hour's drive. After a while, they had tapered off. After a few months, it had mostly just been Beth and Jack's mom. Jack's mom had come once a month religiously, and Beth about every other weekend. Of course, he had been allowed to make phone calls, and he had talked to Beth a few times a week. That had held true for about a year, but eventually he had stopped calling Beth altogether.

It hadn't been a principled stance on his part, or another guy on hers, not so far as Jack knew, anyway. One day, he had called and gotten her machine. He had gotten her machine at a time that she was always around. The next day had been

Friday, and he hadn't called. She hadn't showed up during visiting hours Saturday, and then she hadn't showed up for visiting hours on Sunday. He had gotten her on the phone on Tuesday, and she said had she had a present for him, and would bring it on Saturday.

That Saturday she had brought Jack a book called *You Can't Win*. It was the autobiography of a career criminal in the early twentieth century who had ultimately worked at a newspaper in San Francisco, lectured on prison reform, written his autobiography, and apparently committed suicide rather than become a burden on his friends. Beth had brought Jack a Bible of sorts for the down and out. The author's name was Jack, Jack Black. Jack admired Mr. Black, especially his conviction and character. Jack Black had had a code and stuck to it. Even his seeming choice to die on his own terms rather than become a burden on his friends had complied with that personal code. To some commentators, his ostensible suicide may have seemed self-righteous or selfish, or even the last attempt of an old man to garner attention, but not to Jack. Not at that point in his life.

Jack had spent all week reading and then rereading *You Can't Win*. Calling Beth hadn't occurred to him. Beth hadn't shown up on Saturday, and then she hadn't shown up on Sunday. That wasn't strange. She had been coming about once every other week, and she had just visited the week prior. She hadn't come that next weekend either, but Jack's mom had and as he'd requested, she had brought him a copy of *Junkie* by William S. Burroughs, which he was now obsessed with. Calling Beth hadn't seemed important. Understanding that there were other people like himself had. After two weeks without a call, Beth hadn't felt very important, and she had intended to tell him so when she came that weekend. The guard at the front office where visitors were allowed in, who openly disliked Jack and was secretly obsessed with Beth, had told her that Saturday that Jack hadn't wanted to see her.

It took about a month, but she had finally written Jack a letter. Beth had written that she still loved Jack, but that she was devastated by how he'd treated her. She, however, had made no reference to his refusal to see her that Saturday. Her intent had been reconciliation, and the continuation of their relationship as it had been. Jack had understood it as a request for separation from him, which had not shocked him, as he had severely neglected Beth over the past several weeks. After he had gotten her letter, he had called at a time he knew she'd be at work. He hadn't wanted to talk. He had wanted to leave a message. He hadn't. When her machine had come on, he had just hung the receiver up. They had not communicated again until some time after Jack's release from prison.

Jack had kept the letter on one of this two shelves in his cell. At McNeil, you had an actual room that was rarely locked down, and in it you and your cellmate had a bunk, a desk, and two shelves to keep personal items. Jack's bottom shelf had housed his clothes and toiletries. His top shelf had held his books, a couple photographs of Beth, and letters from his friends, mom, and Beth.

Jack's roommate had been a middle-aged black man named Frank. Frank had kept very few personal items on his shelves, just clothes, toiletries, a bible, and a book called *Alcoholics Anonymous*. Frank had had a medium-length, unkempt, salt-and-pepper afro and a powerful little frame. He couldn't have been more than five-foot-seven, but he had probably weighed in at two hundred pounds. On Jack's first day, Frank had told him, "I sleep on the bottom bunk, I always sleep on the bottom bunk, don't ask if we can switch. Ever!" Jack wasn't even sure Frank could have climbed the ladder to the top bunk. He had been about as wide as he was tall.

Frank had reminded Jack of one of those yellow barrels full of sand they put at freeway exits to absorb kinetic energy from crashing cars. They were actually called impact attenuators, and Frank had certainly been an impact attenuator. Hitting him could only realistically have resulted in you injuring yourself . A few months into Jack's sentence, he had been walking with his breakfast tray full of food when he had run into what appeared to be a ten-foot-tall Native American inmate. Jack had tried to apologize and hadn't noticed the giant's right fist was already in transit toward his face. Frank had magically appeared between Jack and the giant, harmlessly absorbing the punch on his ample shoulder while simultaneously defusing the situation.

Jack had only been a few months in when the mess hall incident with Running Cloud, the giant Native American, had happened. At the time, Jack hadn't understood how he had missed seeing Running Cloud's haymaker coming but Frank had known what was going to happen from across the mess hall. Jack had been a newb. After he'd been in for a while, Jack could see the Matrix, but at that time, Frank had been Morpheus, and Jack had just been Neo falling off a building.

Jack and Frank had both worked in the facilities department. Frank had been in the electrical shop, and Jack had been in the paint shop. They hadn't seen each other much during the day, but their unit had walked to the mess hall together for breakfast, and both their shops had been in the same building, so they had walked to work together. They had always seen each other at dinner, and sometimes, when their workdays had ended at the same time, they'd walked back to the unit together. Plus, they had shared a dorm room. "They don't call 'em cells in McNeil. It's like they want you to think it's college or some shit! When people ask me if I went to college, I tell 'em, yeah, I went to McNeil University, and I learned how to paint concrete prison walls." Frank had gone to church on Sunday mornings, and Alcoholics Anonymous meetings on Tuesday and Thursday evenings, neither of which Jack had attended. "I didn't go to no AA meetin' at first, but I did start readin' that Big Book of his when he wasn't around. Fuck the church, though! I never fuckin' went there!"

Jack didn't really think there was a solution in the book, and he certainly hadn't understood how it worked, but he had liked the stories a lot, and eventually he had started going to the AA meetings with Frank. The first meeting Jack had gone to was the Tuesday night meeting. It had been called "Free as a Jailbird Now." AA meetings always had ironic names that were supposed to be funny, and most of them just sounded like some bad dad joke. "That said, Lynyrd Skynyrd was pretty fuckin' cool for seventies rock." The meetings had been held in the prison. Frank hadn't told Jack that he was the secretary of the Tuesday night meeting. Frank also hadn't told Jack that he was going to be the speaker at his first meeting until he announced it in the meeting ten seconds before Jack was supposed to speak. Frank had also become Jack's AA sponsor, a fact that Frank had only informed Jack of after the meeting.

Frank had been convicted of a vehicular homicide. He had been in a blackout when it happened. He had woken up in the King County Jail and had never been home since. He'd done nearly seven years of a ten-year sentence, which on its face seemed unfair, because Jack's homicide had happened in a blackout and he had only received three years and a couple of months. Plus, Jack's sentence had already been reduced several weeks for time served in county, and he assumed he would get out early for good behavior. To Jack, it had seemed like either his sentence was too easy, or Frank's was too harsh. Neither conclusion had sat right with him.

Nothing said is meant to minimize that Frank was an alcoholic, or that he'd ended somebody's life with an automobile, but he hadn't been a lifelong criminal, either. He had worked in the electric shop at McNeil because he had been a commercial electrician before he came to McNeil. He had been thirty-nine years old when he was sentenced, and his vehicular homicide conviction had been a first offense. He had a son and daughter that had been teenagers when he went in. They were grown by then, and they had visited sometimes. His son had actually gotten married and had a daughter of his own. Frank had a wife too, but she had divorced him a couple years into his sentence.

Frank hadn't kept pictures or any personal belongings from his life because his life no longer existed. He had been denied bail pending trial. He was never allowed to go back to his life after that blackout, not even to put his affairs in order. His family had become different people. His wife had remarried, and the kids he was raising had become adults with lives of their own. The house he had raised those kids in had been sold by his ex-wife and was somebody else's home. The kids' lunchboxes on the counter and coats thrown haphazardly on the floor of the closet had only been seven years ago, but that life could never exist again. Being reminded he had missed the last few years of it had been too much for Frank. Alcoholism had robbed him of his life, and it robbed his family of its father.

Frank had gotten out about a year before Jack, having done about eight years of a ten-year sentence. Jack did just over two for essentially the same offense. At the end of the day, in Frank, society had lost a contributing member, capable of rehabilitation for the better part of a decade. Simultaneously, in Jack, society had returned a hopelessly broken cog back to the streets in just over two years. Jack lacked the vocabulary and education to articulate the situation in academic terms, but based on his experiences at McNeil, he clearly understood the implications of what we now call institutional racism and white privilege. "In other words, it was pretty fucked up!"

For a while after Frank was gone, and Beth hadn't come around anymore, Jack had mostly served his sentence in his head. By that time, it seemed that visitors had started coming around again. The members of the original crew had showed up sporadically, but often. One member of the original crew, at that time, was about to serve a sentence of his own at McNeil.

Jack's mom had showed up like clockwork once a month: second Saturday, two in the afternoon. Jack assumed her visiting time had been a well-grooved habit. She had been used to supporting Jack financially, and the second Saturday was the day after her first payday of the month. She had always put money on his commissary account and brought him whatever book he'd been asking for and some takeout food for them to eat for lunch. She picked her first payday for a reason. She'd put money on Jack's commissary account even if she needed it for rent, so she had come the day after her first payday of the month, well before the next month's rent was due.

Other than that, he had done his best to isolate himself from the outside world completely, but engaged pretty heavily within the prison itself. The Frank Model, he called it. During that time, he'd actually started serving as secretary of the Tuesday AA meeting at McNeil. Running Cloud had been the secretary of the Thursday meeting at the same time as Jack was secretary for Tuesday.

Also, during that time, Jack had read *Ham on Rye* by Charles Bukowski. The prison counselor had suggested he read *Catcher in the Rye* by J.D. Salinger. Somehow, Jack's mom had turned up with *Ham on Rye* instead. "That turned out to be a blessin' in disguise. I read *Catcher in the Rye* after *Ham on Rye*. It was about some rich kid who keeps getting' expelled from prep schools. I mean, it's probably a pretty good book if you're a rebellious teenager in Chappaqua, but it didn't do shit for me. Bukowski is all about LA, skid row, old man hotels, dive bars full of alcoholics. He speaks my language." *Catcher in the Rye* was the first and last Salinger book Jack ever read, but he had spent the remainder of his sentence reading everything Charles Bukowski ever wrote.

The books Jack had read in there were timeless. They hadn't existed in his time. They hadn't even existed in their own time. Philosophers and craftsmen of great fiction rarely used their surroundings or time to make their works interesting. They used their unique minds and experiences to drive their writing. A spattering of worldly reference here and there, maybe, but just for flavor, the way a great chef sparingly sprinkles spices to create something pleasing to the palette. Other than punk rock music, it was the only true art and culture Jack had ever absorbed. Jack's mom had brought at least one book a month, but Jack had read one or two books a week. The library at McNeil had filled that donut hole. It hadn't had anything very current or provocative, but it had been chock-full of classics, so Jack had read a lot of Hemingway, Melville, and Kafka, each of which had offered different and interesting merits.

Other than that, time had mostly just rolled by just like it always did. People say doing time, and that's exactly what it was. There was no vacation to look forward to. There was no big date on Saturday night. Just one day after another. After a while, Jack hadn't even counted days, or even months. He hadn't even meant to stop counting. It had just happened. One day he had been in the yard during rec time and he wished he'd brought his jacket. That had been it, no jacket. Right then, he had realized it was the middle of November. The last time he'd thought about what time of the year it was, it had been August. He hadn't thought about the days or even the weeks, not in terms of his sentence, anyway. AA had been on Tuesday and Thursday, he had worked Monday through Saturday, and his mom had showed up on Saturdays, but only once a month. That said, other than a vague cognizance of a couple days of the week, he hadn't really given his sentence much thought, not in a long time.

As he had walked the fence line in the yard that November morning, he'd had to really think about how much time he had left. "There was no way to know for sure. Shit like time off for good behavior—whatever the fuck that meant—made it hard to work out, but at that time, I think I'd done about fourteen months." Jack *had* gotten time off for good behavior: two and a half months. How does someone with six physical altercations, two with corrections officers, and no less than twenty contraband violations get credited time off for good behavior? "It's because mostly everybody else in there was a bigger fuck up than I was, so I looked well-behaved by comparison." Even Jack had understood that "good behavior" in prison didn't even rise to the level of acceptable behavior in the rest of society.

For Jack, prison had been boot camp, an orientation to life mostly free of substances and that ever-steady drum beat of mental illness. There had been too much structure and not enough time for his mental illnesses to severely torment him. Every day, he had known exactly where and when he was going to be waking up, when he was going to sleep at night, and at what time meals would be. And, thanks to the meal calendar in the mess hall, Jack had even known what he'd be eating at every meal for the remainder of the month. His OCD had loved the perfection of the meal calendar, but had also caused terror and trauma in him when the kitchen unexpectedly changed the meal plan, which had happened with all too much frequency.

After Frank left, Jack had bunked with nobody in particular, even though it was someone very specific. He name was Barry, but he was so uninteresting that Jack had referred to him as nobody in particular as though it was his name. "Who is your new cellmate?" Jack's mom had asked at a visiting hour. "No fuckin' body in particular," Jack had responded.

Jack had taken pride in his immaculate cell and his new muscles, courtesy of the gym equipment in the yard, that swelled the way water balloons did when you attached them to a garden hose. When he flexed, they had bulged the way those same water balloons did when you squeeze them. Jack's mind had woken up, and it had jackhammered routes through sludge that had been blocking pathways that had never properly developed. Where no roadways existed, his mind had built them. If Jack had spent another twenty years at McNeil, he could have truly made something out of his life. Or, at least, he could have had some serenity and peace in his mind, a steep price to pay for mental wellness.

That's not to say that Jack's alcoholism, drug addiction, and mental illnesses hadn't continued to plague him to some extent. There had been drugs and alcohol at McNeil, but they had been hard to get, and there had been no steady supply of either. Jack drank exactly five times in prison, and not once had he been able to acquire enough hooch to get properly drunk. The drugs that had been available were, again, only available in limited quantities. "What's a balloon of coke going to do except make one afternoon of work fly by. It's like gettin' a six pack of beer, you can't get drunk, you can't even barely get a buzz off six. This one guy would give you a balloon for a list of commissary items that was 'bout a hundred fuckin' bucks, why fuckin' bother at those prices, right." Without enough booze or drugs to get properly high or drunk, he had lost interest in even trying to get fucked up.

For several months after he arrived, his PTSD, OCD, depression, anxiety, borderline schizophrenia, and bipolar disorder had kept him climbing the walls, scared of every sideways glance another inmate threw his way, but eventually he had got the hang of being in prison without prescription medications, illicit drugs, or even his undisputed bestie, alcohol.

Jack's overwhelming life problems had been pushed into the background, and his focus had shifted to what was directly in front of him. In much the same way that a man stranded on a deserted island ceased to worry about his rent and instead became interested in how to kill a small animal for his next meal, things like not being stabbed with a fork in the mess hall had become imperative. All those things that were very bothersome in the real world had seemed to be of little consequence in McNeil. Surviving his sentence, both mentally and physically, had become the big thing in his life. At McNeil, the equivalent of no money for rent had been avoiding a beating during rec time, or filling seventeen hours a day without going crazy.

Chapter 23

Anything you do for long enough becomes normal. It's called habituation. One year was all it took for Jack to become totally habituated into prison life. For Jack, one solid year of doing the same thing day in and day out was quite an achievement, even if he'd had little choice in the matter, but doing it without prescription medication, drugs, or alcohol was unprecedented. That whole time had been spent just figuring out how to get by in there. When Jack looked back on it, he imagined what it would have been like if he hadn't met Frank. Then his mind would immediately begin creating every worst-case scenario. To him, the thought of the first year at McNeil without Frank was too scary to think about, but once that trap in his obsessive mind was sprung, it would usually cause hours, if not days, of rumination on those could-have-been-terrible outcomes.

Several months after Frank was released, Ron had arrived on his unit. The abandoned house had really been abandoned then. Todd and Ron had finally gotten pinched. The house had been raided after an extensive sting operation. Ron had taken a plea bargain and gotten eighteen months at McNeil. Todd had refused a deal and was convicted at trial. He'd gotten two and a half years at Monroe. It was likely the first and only time Todd hadn't chosen the path of least resistance. He had chosen poorly and did more time in a harder prison for his poor choice.

Ron had been a perfect fit for prison. He was industrious and motivated. His life, from a very early age, had consisted of scheming to improve his lot in life. His goal over every summer break when they were kids had been to trade or sell enough of his old beat-up, worn-out shit to get new shit for the next school year. When he fell short of the mark, he had resorted to stealing shit he could sell like bikes and car stereos. If he still hadn't had what he wanted for school by late August, he had just started going to the shops at the mall and taking what he wanted. His method had been to just put on whatever clothes he wanted, snip the security tag, and walk out. When someone figured out what he was doing, he had run.

Ron had done pretty well at this, too, much better than his siblings. Food had been a luxury around their house, while drugs were abundant. Sometimes, he'd just sold the weed and pills he had stolen from his mom. Sometimes, when she ran out of weed and pills, he'd sold her cheap wine and cigarettes. There had always been kids in the neighborhood in the market for Ron's mom's drugs, cigs, and hooch. Ron had lived and died by his wits. He was the first kid that Jack had personally known who came from a truly broken home.

He had run away from home dozens of times, beginning when he was fourteen. When he was lucky, he had lived with one of three older siblings. When he wasn't lucky, he had slept in an abandoned car, newspaper bin, or even his own backyard. There had been an old pickup truck canopy by the detached garage back there. All told, between the ages of fourteen to eighteen, he had probably spent seven or eight months sleeping under that canopy without his mom ever suspecting he was there.

Even in the midst of all this confusion, Ron had been able to graduate from high school. Jack had never understood why he bothered. It wasn't as though Ron had showed any interest in going to college. Jack had come by that canopy to find Ron under it in his sleeping bag, reading textbooks with a flashlight. Apparently, doing schoolwork had been a great time killer and distraction from the rest of his life. Also, he may not have intended to go to college, but he had figured that a high school diploma would secure him at least enough of an education to get some semi-skilled blue-collar job. Since getting away from his mom's house had been his primary purpose in life, finishing high school had seemed like the most expedient way to move away from there and not return.

Through scheming, Ron had survived, and that hadn't changed because he was locked down in a prison. If anything, prison made Ron even more crafty than he had been when he went in.

Chapter 24

During the last six months of his sentence, Jack had started to loosen up and even enjoy his life. Ron had worked in the paint shop with him during the day. It was the most time they'd spent together since they were in junior high school.

Ron had become a reliable merchant of contraband items. He'd sold drugs. His drug mules had mostly been the teenagers that dealt for him on the outside. When it came to drugs in prison, the smaller the better. Also, things that could be snorted or swallowed had been preferred. It made sense. Sneaking in an ounce of weed would have been hard. It was big, and it smelled, and people had mainly wanted to smoke it. Nothing about any of that had been fine-tuned for prison. Coke, meth, and pills had been the bulk of the trade in there.

Other than occasionally holding some of Ron's stash, Jack had avoided the contraband trade. Ron had offered to cut him in numerous times, and of course had offered him free drugs often. For the first, and only, time in Jack's life, he had avoided substances. He had kept going to the AA meetings. He had actually enjoyed them by that point. Jack had always shared in meetings and had normally held a service position. Ron had attended, too, but mostly because it was the best place at McNeil to deal drugs.

For some time, Jack had been trying to keep the outside world from coming into McNeil, and he had become quite comfortable in his isolation. Ron's arrival had brought his old life right into the prison walls. Two years earlier, that might have been a problem for Jack. He'd been quite successful at adopting the "Frank Method" of doing time. That is, keep your outside life on the outside, and keep your inside life on the inside. It had served its purpose well. It had gotten Jack through his sentence, but things had changed. Frank had no longer been around to give him advice. Even if he had been there, he'd only been out a short time anyway, so what could Frank tell him about the outside. He likely had forgotten how to be on the outside himself. Jack just hoped he hadn't carved "Frank was here" into a halfway house wall. In a short time, Jack would, once again, be on his own, without a guide.

Between Ron's presence and the handful of months remaining on his sentence, Jack had felt like the prison was melting away right in front of him. There were times where he had doubted anyone would even stop him if he'd decided to just walk out of the prison down to the dock and catch the ferry back to the mainland. The prison counselor had met with him often about his reintegration plan. These meetings had terrified Jack. Jack would be free to go when his sentence was served, but there were resources for him to utilize if he so chose. There were halfway houses, lists of employers that hired ex-convicts, etc.

During one of those meetings, it had occurred to Jack that, thanks to his newly acquired prison muscles, he could snap that prison counselor's neck before anyone in the office complex could stop him. Then, they would have had to keep him in prison. It had been a comforting thought for a minute. Then it had been an intrusive and scary obsessive thought. He would have been in prison for years to come, that much was true. But he would certainly not have stayed at McNeil. Jack would have been relocated to some terrible maximum-security prison somewhere in the state, probably Walla Walla. Twenty or thirty years locked down twenty-three hours a day with the most violent criminals in the state was not what Jack had in mind. Right then, Jack had decided to accept that he would once again be a free man.

Chapter 25

As expected, when the day had come to actually go home, Jack was ambivalent about it. Jack assumed he must have become institutionalized quicker than anyone in history. In just over two years, he'd become reliant on prison life, so much so that, for several months leading up to his release, the thought of leaving had given him awful panic attacks. In the past, being released from confinement had always been an occasion to celebrate with debauchery. This had not been like those other times. Jack had thought about all the hard days he'd lived in his life, and how, late into any given hard day, he had inevitably thought to himself that if he'd known what the day had in store for him when he'd woken up, he would have just stayed in bed. He had figured his whole life was about to become one long, never-ending hard day, and there would be no bed to hide in.

At the same time, it had been impossible to ignore that he was literally being released from prison. Even if he crashed and burned in spectacular fashion, he'd been away for so long that, for a while, everything would seem new again. His mom had been scheduled to meet him at the ferry dock on the mainland. The ferry was underway, and that boat rocking back and forth under his feet had felt strange. Seeing his mom hadn't seemed so weird. He'd seen her dozens of times while he was at McNeil. But the gravel under his feet on the walk from the ferry dock to the car had felt alien.

Jack had been twenty-two. He was a killer, and an ex-convict. He had been going home to live with his mommy. Jack's ability to process stimuli had been overloaded. He hadn't even started drinking right away. Nor had he found drugs, fast girls, or trouble of any kind. Just processing his situation had left him exhausted. He'd felt high, but not the good kind of high. He'd felt too high, crazy high. He'd slept a minimum of twelve hours a day for the next week. Most of the time he had been awake, but he had stayed in his bed pretending to sleep so his mom wouldn't try talking to him.

After his mom went to bed, he'd gotten up to watch TV and try to eat. He had mostly eaten Ritz crackers with little slices of cheddar cheese on them. He'd had a glass of milk to wash them down, but that had only been on "good" days. Many days, he had eaten nothing at all. Eating had been something that he could control, and he had realized that after sixteen or seventeen hours of fasting he stopped being hungry altogether. He hadn't even controlled sleep. He could lie in bed all day long, but he hadn't been able to control whether he actually fell asleep. Whether he ate or not was completely within his control, and he had clung to that sliver of control because there had been no other ropes to cling to.

Unfortunately, that control had eventually become the basis of a new addiction and led to more lack of control. "I know, an anorexic dude! It's a little lame, but it totally happened." In combination with the general appetite-suppressing effects of the drugs he had routinely used and the alcohol he had consumed, not eating became a problem that would plague him for the remainder of his life.

Eventually, Jack had risen from his bed and joined the living. The novelty of the world outside McNeil had worn off, and he had been hungry for booze, ass, and dope. Happiness was trying to simultaneously satisfy as many of your physical, and mental cravings as humanly possible. That had been Jack's motto for as long as he could remember.

It wasn't that he had woken up, because he hadn't really been asleep. Two years at McNeil had made him forget what it felt like to come out of a blackout suddenly.

His head had been hyper-extended over the headrest of the passenger's seat of his mom's car. Jack's dad had never come to visit him in prison, so he had figured asking him to borrow his truck was a non-starter. His mom, on the other hand, had been more than happy to offer up her car keys even though Jack didn't have a valid license. "I'm back on the streets behind the wheel, the paper's gone but I still got the feel." As he'd sat, half-conscious, taking sips of a warm 40oz of malt liquor, he had caught a glimpse of himself in the rearview mirror and realized there was a rolled-up dollar bill sticking out of one of his nostrils. He hadn't been able to remember snorting any meth that night, but, seeing the dollar bill jammed up his nose, he had figured the meth he didn't remember snorting had been the only thing keeping him awake. He had peeked inside the little hole at the top of the 40oz bottle for a minute, but it had given him vertigo.

The girl blowing him hadn't realized, or hadn't cared, that Jack had whiskey dick. He hadn't recognized the top of her head, but he had recognized the parking lot of the roofing company he had been parked in. It was on South Tacoma Way, and he had inferred that the unrecognized bobbing head was a prostitute he had picked up in his blackout. Jack had immediately started hoping that the bill rolled up in his nose was a twenty. He had assumed the hundred bucks his mom had given him earlier was long gone, and he had been right. "That was a one-dollar bill crammed up my nose, not a twenty. That was one angry prostitute. She punched my cock so fuckin' hard when she realized I couldn't pay her, but I had the whiskey dick, so I didn't really feel it. She should have punched for my fuckin' balls."

Jack was back, but Jack's motto had been broken. He suspected his motto had never worked that well in the first place. Sometimes, he felt like debauchery had kept him from sinking lower into the abyss of his soul, but when he was honest with himself, he knew it had just distracted him from a sinking that never really abated. There was no happiness, not in the bottle, not in that line, certainly not in the angry prostitute's warm mouth, and definitely not in his own existence. "I don't think happiness is really a thing. It's like God. People made up God because they're afraid of not existin', and to people, existin' is all. People made up happiness because they can't deal with sadness, and to people, lack of sadness is all. That's all there is to it."

And what exactly had he done two years for? Jack had never thought about it in prison, but after his release, it had come back to him a lot. He hadn't meant to kill that biker. The way Jack figured it, that guy hadn't really left him any choice. That hadn't made it righteous, but it had made it self-defense. He believed he had done time for a killing that a prosecutor wouldn't even have charged him for if he had been someone with status, money, or a decent defense lawyer. Worst of all, it had been a disagreement over half a gram of crank; that was it. Just a couple of sped-up, drunk dopers arguing over a little bit of meth. That biker had tried to screw Jack, that was true. Jack had felt blood rush to his face, and his hands had started trembling. He knew he should have forgotten it. He knew that had been the moment to walk out. But he hadn't been able to. Jack had showed that biker the handle of his PPK. In return, that biker had swung the heavy end of the axe handle he had kept under the kitchen table at Jack's head.

In her police statement, the biker's girlfriend had stated that if Jack had left then, that would have been the end of it. Instead, Jack had smashed a half-full 40oz bottle into the biker's skull. The glass had shattered and the skull had popped simultaneously, and when it had, it made a mostly indescribable disgusting wet noise. Not that Jack remembered, but the girlfriend's statement had been graphic. She had run away. She had gotten in her car and gone to her sister's house for the night. That dope fiend biker had collapsed right there in his kitchen nook. Jack had done like any smart addict; he had kept his money, grabbed that biker's meth, and hit the road. The driveway was as far as he had made it before he had blacked out and then proceeded to pass out in his car. By the time the girlfriend came home the next day, it had been much too late for that biker.

The bottle being half full had made a significant impact. It had been like a hitter warming up with weights on his bat. The beer in the 40oz bottle had increased the velocity and impact of the bottle when it had hit his skull. It had shattered his temple, and the resulting sub-cranial bleeding had done him in while he lay there alone for the next twelve or so hours.

That was it; that was the story. It had cost him years of his life, this one moment of self-justified rage. He couldn't remember much of it, not when it happened, and honestly not years later, either. His brain had, over the years, filled in the gaps to construct a fairly likely chronology of events. This was based mostly on what the girlfriend had said in her statement, and the little Jack himself recollected.

He had stared across the parking lot at that dick-punching hooker sauntering away and decided to run her down. He had revved the engine up and dropped it into drive. The look on her face as his mom's shabby Corolla had begun to bear down on her had actually broken his tunnel vision for an instant.

That biker, Jim, hadn't really been a bad guy, and neither had his girlfriend. Her name was Stacy. Jack had actually spent quite a bit of time at that trailer talking to both of them when he was buying meth. Jim had been as fucked up that night as Jack had, and Jim had made a mistake in trying to cheat Jack, but Jack had made a worse mistake by not walking away. Now Jim was dead. Jim wasn't coming back, no matter what. Death was final.

Jack had veered the Corolla hard to the right and onto South Tacoma Way. He had missed that hooker by a couple of feet. It had felt like a couple of inches. Jack hadn't learned much in his life, but for at least one moment that night, another person's life had been more important to him than his pride. "And that's not nothin'!"

Chapter 26

Going to prison had begun with a going-away party, so a welcome-home party had seemed like an appropriate way to bookend that chapter of Jack's life. The timing had been a little off, since Jack had been released almost two months earlier. There had, of course, been a coming-home dinner hosted by Jack's mom and grudgingly attended by his brother and father. That had been the day after he was released. A coming-home dinner with the family a couple of months prior was a far cry from what had been planned at Mike's house that night.

Lots of people used drugs that made them feel good. Shit like molly, shrooms, or acid. Jack was from Tacoma, and he liked his drugs dirty, not designer. Meth and PCP didn't feel good. They felt like a flesh-mutilating nightmare that you couldn't wake up from. Alcohol was no better. As a matter of fact, it was poison to the human body. Disorientation and vomit were the first side effects of alcohol. Complete blackouts, loss of consciousness, and a depressed nervous system came next. Keep drinking, and death was the final side effect. Death from alcohol could happen just like that from one night of drinking, but if it didn't get you like that, eventually it would get you with Cirrhosis. Jack felt that bottles of booze should have Mr. Yuck stickers on them just like the cleaning products under the sink did. Even though Jack drank every day, he still suffered from crippling hangovers. At many points, and for extended periods of time, Jack's life was really just a hangover spilling over into drunkenness, and then back into a hangover.

What a body will endure is quite amazing. What it will endure and keep functioning through is even more amazing. Sitting with his family during his welcome home dinner had felt nice, for once. Laurence hadn't been a bastard, and Jack's father hadn't been completely cold. They had sat in a wood-paneled booth overlooking Commencement Bay. As usual, Jack's mom had sat next to him, her on the aisle and Jack against the window. She had always sat next to him like that. He wondered if she had realized she was literally shielding him with her body. She had sat as a physical blockade, like she could keep the world from getting to him if she put herself in the way. Laurence and his father had sat next to each other stoically on the opposite side of the booth.

His mom, naïve as usual, had been hopeful. This was regrettable—not because of her hopefulness for her beloved son, but because she'd already lost the debate about what he'd do with his life. This was the case despite the fact that the discussion had not even taken place. Everybody had just known. Jack loved her for having faith in him, even to the last, and he felt guilt over what he continually put her through, but the pity he had for her was the strongest emotion of all. He could feel all the guilt in the world, but at the end of the day, when he looked at her, he felt pity. She was hopelessly deluded about Jack. All she saw was the sweet kid she'd raised. She refused to see, or wasn't capable of seeing, the lout he'd become.

Jack thought a lot about that family dinner on the night of his party at Mike's house. Mike's house hadn't really been a house so much as a studio apartment downtown. After him and his last girlfriend had broken up, he'd downsized considerably. That place had been similar in many ways to the studio apartments Jack and his friends had found themselves inhabiting at various points over the course of their lives. Similarly, Mike's building had been exactly the type of place you liked to party at, or live at for two months before being evicted. Mike had been there about a year.

It had mostly been filled with residents that couldn't live anywhere else, and the pores of the building had reeked from depravity of every persuasion. Four stories of the biggest losers, prostitutes, crack dealers, speed dealers, fienders, beggars, punkers, stoners, actually crazy people, sort of crazy people, criminally insane people, criminally cutthroat people who were surprisingly sane, and any other square peg that the dirty little city had failed to jam into a round hole. On any given night, half the apartments in the building had been having a raucous party. The other half had just had a few friends over to smoke some rocks.

The building had been dangerous during its calmest moments, but after the sun went down, it had become downright terrifying. The bare brick walls on the inside had oozed anxiety and tension. There hadn't even been carpet in the hallways, just concrete floors, like the ones at McNeil. Jack had just done two years in prison, and walking into Mike's building had been more terrifying that anything he could remember ever doing. At least in prison, the corrections officers had broken up fights eventually. "At Mike's buildin', nobody was likely to break up shit." You could die in that building, and Jack found out later that the building had actually averaged about one homicide a month. At that building, the police hadn't shown up unless there was a body.

The fact that nothing short of a corpse ever brought out law enforcement meant it was equally unsurprising that the fire marshal never showed up to issue citations for fire code violations, either. On the night of the party, there had been no less than thirty people, many of them Jack and Mike's friends, literally crammed into Mike studio apartment like sardines. For the first time ever, Jack had noticed the fascinating aroma that three people's breaths made when you smelled them simultaneously. He had also realized that not only would he not be able to sit down at his own party, but even getting a beer seemed out of reach from where Jack was standing.

The people at the party had mostly been people that Jack knew—at least, they had been at ten o'clock. The faces had been just like the ones at the abandoned house the night Jack had killed Jim the biker. Other than Mike, they had consisted of a few people Jack would have called friends, a bunch he would have called acquaintances, and a handful that he either hadn't known, or hadn't cared for at all. "Today they call those ones you don't really like but are nice to nonetheless frenemies. By midnight, most of the friendly faces had cleared out, even the frenemies. They'd been replaced by the faces of people Jack had assumed just roamed from apartment to apartment in search of a free high.

Mike's big, round, vacant eyes had stared out from the chair where he was sitting. Other than the stained and sheetless twin mattress on the floor, Mike's chair had been the only place to sit in the entire apartment. Jack hadn't noticed it before, but the more he had looked around, the more he had started to realize that Mike's apartment actually resembled a crack den. Normally, by midnight, Jack would have been well into a blackout, but he'd been smoking meth with this guy Brett earlier, so he had been quite aware of his surroundings. The meth always kept the blackout from happening, at least for a couple of hours. Jack wasn't addicted to meth, but it was always around, and he had infrequently smoked and snorted it order to keep the party going.

Jack didn't like crack and had only smoked it a handful of times. Tacoma was on the back end of its part in the crack epidemic of the eighties. Tacoma's part in that epidemic had been a significant one. Despite the epidemic being mostly in the rearview, it had still been pretty prevalent in Tacoma in the nineties. Most drugs hadn't scared Jack, but crack did. The few times he'd smoked it, he had immediately felt a sort of euphoria that made every problem in the universe so small it could fit on the head of a pin. Those problems had become so miniscule, one could say they just simply hadn't mattered. Of course, there was one problem that crack didn't make smaller; in fact, crack made this problem gigantic. That problem was, how does one get more crack?

The last time Jack had seen Mike had probably been a year previous, during visiting hours at McNeil. That was before Mike and his last girlfriend had split. At that time, Mike still had his normal, husky build. He wasn't tall, but he normally carried a little extra weight. His cheeks had that cherub appearance, and his features were full. That night at the party, Jack hadn't really looked at Mike, until he had. Mike had been sitting in his chair, literally staring at the wall. There hadn't even been a TV in his place anymore. All his records had been gone. Jack hadn't even thought he had any clothes in the apartment, except what he was wearing, and what he was wearing was pretty drab. He'd had on two different shoes, filthy sweatpants, and an undershirt that had been white at one time. His eyes had been sunken and dark, and Jack estimated he had weighed no more than one hundred twenty-five pounds. He hadn't shaved in days, maybe weeks, and his hair had been thin and wiry.

Mike's crack-smoking "friends" had continued to crowd in, which had made Jack want to slip out. Jack had squeezed through the crowd to Mike. He'd had a glass pipe in his hand. Jack had hugged Mike and said he needed to get some air, and that he'd catch up with him later.

Jack had taken the stairs up to the roof. From the ledge facing straight west, Jack had been able to see the heart of downtown. If you looked straight east, you could see crack dealers at the Lucky 7 and the entrance to People's Park on 9th and MLK. Jack hadn't realized it at that moment, but four months later, Mike would be shot to death on that corner. Sickly, slender, and hollow, sitting in his chair, was how Jack had last seen Mike alive. Pale, puffy, and waxy, lying in his coffin, was how Jack had last seen Mike dead. Todd and Ron had still been locked up when it happened, so the mourners had consisted mostly of Jack, Mike's parents, and Mike's little brother. There had been ten times as many people crammed into his little apartment the night of Jack's party, none of whom had seen fit to show up at his funeral.

Jack had hopped into his mom's Corolla and headed up to the Lucky 7. The outside window ledge had been decorated with bottles of Cisco and King Cobra. Jack couldn't understand why someone would drink King Cobra on purpose.

"For a quarter more you could get a bottle of Olde English. Why bother with that other garbage?" The guy at the cash register hadn't seemed to care who bought booze or cigarettes as long as they had money. Everybody in line had bought beer, and nobody had gotten carded. Jack hadn't even had a valid I.D. His driver's license had expired while he was in prison, and he hadn't bothered to get it renewed. It had made sense to Jack. When your parking lot was the biggest open-air crack market until Oakland, the cops weren't worried about teenagers getting wasted on beers.

Right before Jack had headed up to the roof, Mike had offered him the glass pipe, one big rock sitting in the blackened bowl. Jack had declined. Mike had said: "Suit yourself man, you've already experienced everythin'. You're not missin' anythin' at this point. You're just relivin' it. Most people don't even get to try it all once, much less live long enough to abuse it until it's borin'." The best Jack could do was to keep writing the same chapter over and over again. Best-case scenario, it would continue to be fun; worst-case, it would get harder and harder. The past few years had not been fun, and Jack had thought he could see which way the wind was blowing. That was the last thing Mike had ever said to Jack, and it had stuck to him like gum on the sole of your Vans.

Mike's crack problem hadn't magically transformed Jack into a choir boy, and the night had still been relatively young. Nobody had hassled him at the Lucky 7, which was a change of pace. Usually, he would have been offered crack by at least two dealers before he even had gotten in the door. He had gotten two forties of Olde English, bought two packs of Marlboro Reds, and filled the Corolla's gas tank. He had cracked the first 40oz. It had been cold going down his throat.

He had enjoyed it because those forties only stayed cold for about two minutes, tops. He had reached into his pocket for a smoke and found a quarter of crank he'd bought from that guy Brett earlier and forgotten about. Earlier that night, he'd actually thought he might meet a girl at Mike's, maybe get to fuck. "That didn't happen!" He had still been in the mood for some action, and he had known where he could purchase some. South Tacoma Way had beckoned, and Jack had answered.

Chapter 27

In any lifetime, there were ups and downs. There were times that Jack was legitimately content with being a fuck-up. He knew what he was. He didn't hide from it. Sometimes, he wore it on his sleeve like some badge of honor. He was never happy, but nobody was ever really happy. Some people were just better at deceiving themselves than others. If Jack had deception in him, he'd have told himself he was happy too.

"Maybe Paxil-poppin' soccer moms were happy. That must be a great drug. People in *Brave New World* seemed happy, with their Soma. Most of them were happy anyway. It was just a couple of them that realized their happiness was a drug-induced psychosis. That's no more of a solution than being in a coma, but who am I to talk! Nobody would accuse somebody in a coma of being happy. I don't fuckin' know. Sometimes, though, in my early twenties, I was alright."

Alright was hard to maintain. Misery was easier to maintain. Jack knew how to keep misery around. You just kept doing whatever your current impulse or compulsion told you to do. That was it, easy! Bleakness offered comfort. Misery was both attainable and sustainable. Once you accepted misery, it immediately ceased to be such a scary proposition. Misery was normality, alright was the aberration.

Having half of a life was much scarier. "When you had somethin', you had somethin' to lose." When you had something to lose and lacked the ability to maintain it, that became a hard existence to be in. That's what alright was. Alright couldn't ever be happiness. It couldn't be happiness because the moment you realized you were alright, you also realized that you couldn't be alright for long. Pain would be along soon, and there was nothing you could do to stop it.

Nobody Jack ever knew could maintain alright, but Jack liked remembering the alright times just the same. He was nostalgic. He really didn't know why. "Yes I fuckin' do! You fuckin' idiot. Why are you the one tellin' my story anyways! I mean, I'm right fuckin' here. Why ain't I the one tellin' it? Anyway, nostalgia for the alright times happens because nobody can take the alright times that happened in the past away from you. You don't have to worry about when pain is going to start because it already happened. You already know when the pain started. You never have to relive the pain and misery when you're rememberin' the alright times. You just live in the alright times, and never go to the pain and misery times. That's why. Duh!"

Jack couldn't remember exactly what had happened with Beth while he was in prison. She had been around, then she hadn't. He knew being with her had been the most alright time of his life. He figured he bore some of the blame for what he assumed was a breakup, maybe even most of it, but he just really didn't understand what had happened there.

The day after the party at Mike's place, Jack had picked up the handset to the phone in his mom's kitchen and dialed a number from memory. The last time he had dialed that number, she hadn't picked up, so he had just stopped calling. That day, she had picked up.

"Hello." She'd sounded a little annoyed.

"Ha, what's up," he'd said.

"Jack! Oh my fucking God! Where are you!"

"I'm out. I'm at my mom's. I wasn't sure if I should call."

"Don't go anywhere. I'll be there in twenty minutes."

Chapter 28

She had worn old Levi's, a plain white t-shirt, and her black hair tied up in a handkerchief. She hadn't bothered to look in her bathroom vanity before she had run out the door. She had slid on the loosely tied Pumas she ran errands in and grabbed her wallet and keys. On the way out of her apartment, she had ignored a hello from an annoying neighbor, and on the drive, she had ignored most of the traffic laws designed to keep people safe. It wasn't that Jack had called and she had come running. She hadn't known if she was running to a fight or a reunion. He'd blown her off, and for a long time she'd avoided confronting him about it, but then she had buzzed with anticipation, and her brain had raced with possible scenarios.

That day, Beth and Jack had never really figured out who was to blame for their breakup. They had never really been able to determine if there even *had* been a breakup. As such, they had just tried to pick up where they'd left off.

Jack's cigarettes had almost been gone again, and he hadn't had much luck locating a job. Jobs had never really been something Jack did well. He hadn't been drinking, and he hadn't been using any recreational drugs, but he was pretty sure that he should have been back on his Lithium. Getting money to go to the community clinic hadn't really seemed to be a priority right at that moment, though. Beth would have bought his prescription for him if he'd asked, but he' had already been living for months in an apartment that she had paid for and eating food that she had bought. He had figured the least he could do was take care of his own nicotine and medication needs. That was what he had told himself, but the cost of his Lithium prescription had been much cheaper than food or rent, so he had to concede that his reason had just been a deceptive self-justification.

In reality, being non-compliant with his medication had been a passive-aggressive way to sabotage himself. He'd been diagnosed with bipolar disorder, but he had never believed that diagnosis, and not filling his Lithium was his way of rejecting it. Somehow, he had found money for cigarettes every day, but failed to come up with five bucks for a month's supply of Lithium.

Whether he was compliant with his medication hadn't mattered much longer anyway. Whether he believed his bipolar diagnosis had similarly ceased to matter much. Within six months of being released from McNeil, he had walked away from Beth and toward desolation. She'd said something that had hurt his pride. No, it was more than that; she'd genuinely emasculated him, and when she had, his brain had started buzzing. No matter what he had tried, it wouldn't be quiet. Wounded or not, he had been too sensitive, and she had done everything within reason to amend the situation, but it hadn't mattered to Jack.

His mind had clung so obsessively to her words that seeing her brought a strange fusion of hurt pride, resentment, and anger. Eventually, just the thought that they both occupied planet earth had become aggravating to him. He hadn't chosen not to forgive her; he had been genuinely incapable of forgiving her. Within days, he'd become so resentful toward her that he simply hadn't been able to stick around. The thought to disappear had begun as a juvenile fantasy to get back at Beth. He had been incapable of feeling better, but he was confident he could make her feel worse. Over several weeks of planning, it had grown into a full-blown plan to cut and run. The plan itself had developed a life of its own and became a quest for self-reliance. Once his obsessive, impulsive brain had started buzzing about it, there had been no stopping him. Beth had no longer mattered to him. She had just become the lady who said the thing no woman was allowed to say to a man. With that, he had been off again.

Chapter 29

He had left when she was at work, on foot, with just a backpack of clothes and essentials like his toothbrush and deodorant. He'd had his wallet, his expired driver's license, and about two hundred bucks he'd squirreled away. Enough of his things were gone that Beth had known he'd left on purpose, but so much had been left behind that she had assumed he'd be back within a few days. Beth had been concerned, even worried, but most of all sad and betrayed. It had only been a few weeks since Mike's funeral, and she had guessed Jack was off on a planned bender. Beyond her own hurt feelings, her main concern had been that Jack would once again wind up in prison, or dead.

For a few days, she had kept her hopes up. She had still been angry—of course she had been—but she had been in love with him. She had understood that he was selfish and juvenile, and that to be with him, she'd always have to accept the hurt he did her and apologize for any she inflicted on him, no matter how slight. By day four, her growing worry for Jack's wellbeing had largely replaced her hurt feelings, and she had sufficiently subjugated that rational part of her mind that screamed at her to let him go.

That time, Beth had spent months haunting the local

shelters and missions looking for him. His two remaining best friends had still been in prison, so she had sought out people that were no more than casual acquaintances of his to no avail. Of course, she had called his mom, who had been just as baffled and distraught. She had called local jails, local hospitals, and, finally, local morgues. That time, it hadn't been so easy for her, or anyone else, to find him.

Chapter 30

J ack had sought out the company of others like himself. It hadn't taken long. It hadn't taken long for him to start drinking again either. Beth had been on graves, which had worked out pretty well for Jack. They had both slept in every day. Beth because she was tired from work, and Jack because he was too hung over to drag himself out of bed. Jack had thought she didn't know that he was drinking every night she went to work. He had normally passed out an hour or so before she came home from her shift. Despite being blacked out, he'd been pretty successful in disposing of his empty bottles before she came home. Jack hadn't realized that a person who drinks all night sweats it out in their sleep. He hadn't realized that a person who drinks all night exhales it into the air as they sleep. So, he hadn't realized she knew, but she had.

Mostly, they had only seen each other before she went to work, or on her days off. Before she went to work, they'd played cards, or board games. Sometimes, they'd watched prime time TV. All the time he had sat, almost annoyed, waiting for Beth to grab her keys and purse, and head out the door to work. Then he had been off to the convenience store for a few forties of his favorite malt liquor, which at that point was whatever was $1.99 a bottle and strong.

Some of the homeless crusty punks who hung out at Wright Park came over on nights like that. Sometimes he'd gotten too drunk and there had been fights. Sometimes he'd gotten too drunk, and they'd ripped off a bunch of Beth's shit. At no time had he gotten too drunk to fuck Kristy, the crusty punk girl that had routinely came over with the crusty punk guys. No one had called her Kristy; they had all just called her Krusty, sometimes Krusty the Clown. She hadn't been ugly or fat, but she hadn't been beautiful or thin, either. Jack had come out of more than one blackout to find his pants down and her on his lap, grinding him. Usually, her tongue had already been shoved into his mouth. Always, her black jeans and bullet belt had dangled around one of her ankles. All Jack had been able to taste was the PBR she had been drinking and the GPCs she'd been smoking. All Jack had been able to feel was a huge thick bush on his hard cock. Jack had never fucked Krusty, but after Beth had called him an unemployed loser, he had seriously considered it.

Krusty the Clown and her huge thick bush had never persuaded Jack to fuck, but her lifestyle had convinced him that he needed a change of scenery.

Chapter 31

It was funny how well a homeless person could live. There were a variety of homeless people. There were, of course, the gimmies, who were constantly out for handouts. They sat on the side of the road begging for change and standing in line outside of the homeless shelters for hours just to sleep on a shitty cot in a room with a hundred other smelly guys. On nights Jack spent in shelters, he had been able to hear twenty other guys jerking off at any given time. Anyone who thought prison was scary had never spent the night in a homeless shelter. There were the crazy people, who just roamed the streets without any purpose whatsoever. Then, there were the working homeless. If they were named appropriately, they'd be the thieving homeless, but Jack just called them The Johnson Family. Their signs would say, "will work for food," but their motive was always to get into your house, your car, or anywhere they could rip something off. If they couldn't get into your house or your car, a tool shed was also a treasure trove. Even a good plant, repotted and transported correctly, had a street value if you knew where to sell it.

The working homeless had drinking and drug problems to support, and while they were habitually dirty, they rarely slept in the mud. As a matter of fact, most of these people could make rent at a motel with weekly rates if they didn't smoke, slam, and drink the proceeds of all their hard work. Staying drunk and high most hours of the day required sacrifices to be made. The main sacrifices were a normal standard of life, and bathing. Jack had fit right in.

"After the lifestyle chose me, I sometimes found myself wonderin' why people pay for things that can regularly be acquired for free. Things that could not be obtained for free were fairly easy to steal, and a covered place to crash was never more than a broken window or half-full newspaper bin away." Jack's Johnson Family lifestyle had been part pioneering, part piracy, and all lunacy.

The story of the west was the story of pioneering. The people who settled the west were the offspring of the original European colonists of North America. Nobody claimed those pioneering Europeans were the first people to inhabit the continent, nor that they had rightful claim to much of the land they had taken; only that wanderlust and lunacy, along with whiskey and laudanum, had fueled their hairbrained, ill-conceived westward expansion. Later immigrants to the United States had clung to the eastern cities like life preservers, but psychotic, intoxicated American pioneers had set off into the wilderness with only what they could carry on their wagons. Walking into the Rocky Mountains with your spouse, children, and everything you owned on a rolling wooden shoe box took a certain sort of person.

When humans move out into the solar system, and settle Mars, descendants of pioneers will be at the helms of the first ships to hit Martian soil. Jack was such a descendant, and if he'd been born in 2170 instead of 1970, he might have been at one of those helms. It's more likely that he'd be pushing a mop or washing the dishes in the galley, but he'd have been on that ship somewhere.

His pioneer ancestors had pushed into country they'd never seen that was foreign to them. Since then, the world had shrunk. There was no more west to explore, just a huge ocean. Nevertheless, Jack had survived on nothing but intoxicants and balls. Instead of living off the land, the way his ancestors had, he had lived off the underside of society in country that was new and foreign indeed. Cities were his wilderness, and resources in his wilderness had been plentiful, and ripe for the picking. All that had been required of him were the guts to go out there and grab what he wanted. And at the end of the day, instead of building a fire next to his horses and wagon, he'd built it in an empty freight car or an apartment complex still under construction. Hardship had become a sort of salvation. He had felt kinship with his own ancestry, as well as the punks that he had shared his food, drugs, and sometimes even his sleeping bag with.

Right around October, it had started to get a little too chilly to be comfortable living outside in Seattle, and so, they had done like the birds do. They had migrated south for the winter.

Chapter 32

This migration south hadn't been a product of Jack's genius, regardless of how much he'd like to take credit for it. It was a time-honored tradition of the homeless punks. Seattle was the place to be in the summer. Its climate was mild, and there was plenty of free food. There were lots of upper middle-class people to rob. Also, those same people wore their liberal socioeconomic guilt on their sleeves like badges of honor, so most of the time they just gave you money. Winter in Seattle, however, was just a little too cold and wet for outdoor living. Even for somebody from the northwest, like Jack was, living outside in the winter was a non-starter.

Jack's new girlfriend had been suited perfectly for outside living. Marie had had an Antischism tattoo on her chest, waist-length black dreadlocks, and a Doom back patch on her sleeveless black denim jacket. She'd had gorgeous brown eyes. Despite her Latino ancestry, an entire summer outdoors, and the inevitable thin layer of dirt and sweat covering her, she'd still had extremely pale skin.

She had been low-maintenance in every way without being a tomboy. As a matter of fact, for a homeless, crusty punk girl, she had been quite feminine. She'd had a pretty face, which Jack later realized was inexplicably a cross between Salma Hayek and a valley girl. Jack hadn't known it, largely because Jack and Marie had never talked about themselves or backgrounds, but Marie's mom had been a white, blond lady who was a cheerleader in high school. But again, Jack had never known one thing about Marie's family, past, or whatever else there was to know about her. She'd been from Eastern Washington—Pasco in the Tri-Cities, to be exact. He knew that much. She hadn't known where he was from. She had assumed Seattle, since that was where they had met. The past was the past, and you couldn't change it, so why bother talking about it? That had been their rule, and it had worked for them.

Pretty as it was, almost nobody ever saw Marie's face because her dreadlocks had constantly hung in front of it. She'd had nice tits too—big, but not too big—and a round ass. Almost nobody ever saw those either, because, again, her dreadlocks had hung down over all that, too. The oversized jeans and Anti Cimex t-shirt she'd always worn also didn't properly frame an otherwise great body.

Living outside had worked for Marie. She had never looked emaciated. Quite the opposite; she had looked like someone who worked outside all day. That is, she'd been tan, dirty, weather beaten, and muscular. She had been thick in the right spots and thin in the right spots, too. And she hadn't just looked tough; she was legitimately potent. During their time together, Jack had been forced to pull her off three different girls that had made the mistake of mouthing off to her. One time, in the parking lot of a shopping mall, Jack had watched Marie dismantle two preppy girls with Nordstrom bags at the same time.

Marie had fucked on her period, smoked while you went down on her, and stolen her tampons from Walgreens. Having a bottle and a pack of cigarettes had made her happy. If she was able to get to a punk show, so much the better, and if she was able to squeeze a cock into the equation, it was a magical night in Marie's world. In a lot of ways, she had been the perfect woman, all the stuff guys loved about girls and none of the bullshit.

When a homeless man was alone in a nasty sleeping bag, the stench could be pungent, but when a homeless man and woman fucked in a nasty sleeping bag, the smell could be unbearable. Amazingly, you did get used to that, too, and that was the life. Right then, Jack hadn't even been able to tell how bad their sleeping bag stunk. They hadn't washed it in weeks, and neither of them had showered in days. He'd hated thinking about the gross things living in it, but none of that had stopped him from fucking Marie in it. Besides, the friction of a cock repeatedly slamming into a pussy had produced a smell that was more pleasant than any smell the two of them could have produced alone.

Hopping train cars had been the preferred way to migrate from place to place, and Jack and Marie had found themselves in a mostly empty freight car travelling through the part of the thick Oregon wilderness where you started to see the occasional palm tree. "A fuckin' palm tree in Oregon! But seriously, there it was. Then there were a handful more, and then we were definitely in California."

Jack had thought that maybe, when they got off that train, they'd splurge for a motel room and do a load of laundry at the local cleaners. He had started trying to work out where they were on his gas station map. It was a roadmap with very few landmarks, and they had been on a train, not an interstate. Working out where they were had seemed next to impossible, so Jack had just asked Marie if she wanted to hop off at the next town they passed. Jack had thought that, every couple of weeks, it was nice to knock some of the loose dirt off with a shower. He wasn't entirely sure what Marie had thought about his suggestion, but she liked drinking and fucking in the shower. Plus, a warm room from time to time wasn't bad, either.

It was a different life than the one he'd been living, and he'd felt self-sufficient for the first time since being in prison. At the same time, Jack recognized it hadn't just been about a change of scenery or self-sufficiency. He'd been running from himself, plain and simple. He'd been hiding, too. He'd been hiding from everyone he had ever known. That is, everyone except Todd.

One day, Jack had picked up a phone, punched in the stolen calling card number he'd been using, and dialed Todd's old number. To Jack's surprise, Todd had picked up. He must have had someone pay his phone bill while he was locked up. Jack hadn't bothered to ask. There had been so much else to catch up on that how Todd had kept his old phone number hadn't seemed important.

Since being released, he'd been doing what he had always done: keeping tabs on people, relaying messages, and most importantly, keeping up connections with the crew. He had told Jack that Beth thought he was dead, and that she'd been searching for him for months. Todd was the only one Jack had had the balls to call, but he'd been running from him, too. Todd was a link to Jack's previous codependent life. He was a link to Jack's parents, his friends, and Beth. Jack knew that if he had let those people bail him out, he'd have been right back behind institution walls, telling some headshrinker about his plans for creating a normal life when he got out.

Jack had still been angry at Beth, but all the shenanigans he had pulled at her apartment before he had bailed hadn't made him feel better. Nor had his new life living outside. His new life had given him a sense of self-sufficiency that he'd never felt, not even at McNeil, but it hadn't fixed the wound Beth had inflicted on him. He knew that, if confronted, she'd have claimed he'd done worse to her, and she would have probably been right. Jack was used to feeling anger, but when she'd emasculated him, she'd created a whole new emotion in him. It had been anger fused with wounded pride. Jack had continued to lack the ability to forgive Beth, and mention of her name had still produced a dull ache of emotional pain that had manifested physically in his chest. Jack had given Todd explicit instructions to tell his mom that he was alive and well, but that he was forbidden from telling Beth that he was alive.

Jack had been in love with Beth, but as far as he could tell, people could fool themselves into loving just about anyone. Was love a magical force, something that conquered all? Was it just the name we assigned to a group of biochemical processes that happened in every human? Either way, Jack had continued to hurt; he had thought it only fair that she continued to hurt as well. Other than that, he'd had no feelings about her one way or the other at that time.

After that, Jack hadn't even been able to bring himself to call Todd again. It had been easier for him avoid his old life altogether.

Inches away from him, the aroma of fortified wine had been

unmistakable.

"Do you want a pull off this?" Marie had said as her arm extended toward him.

One thing that tasted worse than Orange-Jubilee-flavored Mad Dog was warm Orange-Jubilee-flavored Mad Dog, and the only thing that tasted worse than warm Orange-Jubilee-flavored Mad Dog was warm Orange-Jubilee-flavored Mad Dog full of your homeless girlfriend's backwash, but you even got used to that.

They'd hopped a train outside of Oakland after a few weeks in San Francisco. San Fran was a nice place to stop for a few weeks. It stayed warm a little longer than Seattle, and it got warm earlier in the spring, so the routine was to come into town again on the way back to Seattle for a few weeks. The ultimate destination for the migrating gutter punks was, of course, Los Angeles. It was a good place to lay low. People there were so self-absorbed that anybody else's existence barely registered on their radar.

It wasn't just self-absorbed entertainment industry types that helped make you largely invisible. LA was legitimately dangerous. Even in the early nineties, after the peak of the crack epidemic, Compton and Watts, similar to Tacoma, had remained hives of the crack trade and gang wars of the eighties. LA was also very segregated, and full of invisible borders. You could practically spit into El Sereno from the sundown town of South Pasadena, but no white people ever went south of Alhambra Road, and no Mexicans went north of it. The only exceptions were middle-class whites purchasing drugs from Mexican gang members during daylight hours and Mexican women cleaning rich white people's houses. White people bought heroin, meth, coke, and anything else that came out of LA ghettos, and then scurried back to their white sanctuaries. In simultaneous contrast, Mexican women caught their buses, cleaning supplies in hand, back home before Mr. Important Esq. returned from a long day of being a senior partner at his prestigious law firm.

Dirty, middle-aged alcoholics who all bore a striking resemblance to Charles Bukowski roamed back and forth from the dive bars down by skid row to the old man hotels with weekly rates in Hollywood. Any place with a liquor store on the block and low weekly rates was fair game. The inebriated old man herd had migrated in twos and threes and engaged in casual violence at nearly every intersection. All this just scratched the surface of the underside of LA, and that was just the street crime that happened in full view of the world. What happened in the residences of LA was, without a doubt, just as, if not more, sordid as what happened out in the open. The LAPD had bigger problems than small bands of homeless punks stealing beer and peanut butter from the Vons. Indeed, they had barely even taken notice of them.

Jack and Marie had settled into Hollywood. The irony of Hollywood was that it happened to be the most anonymous location on earth. Nobody noticed you there, ever, not even if you levitated six feet off the ground with your hair on fire and flew back and forth between Vine and Sycamore on Hollywood Boulevard. It was the perfect place to be lost. It was also the perfect place to repetitively commit low-level crime. A tourist's stolen purse was forgotten before the bag snatcher was off the block. You often found the offender literally on the next block pilfering the thing for anything of value and discarding whatever remained. Jack had used to wonder how many tourists found their own stolen bags empty and abandoned a hundred feet from where they had been snatched.

Out in the beach towns like Santa Monica, homeless punks drew too much attention. Those beach cops always hassled them, except in Venice. People at Venice Beach couldn't have cared less if homeless punks slept on the beach in the middle of the day, but robbing tourists was not quite as simple, or tolerated. Still, when Jack had gone out there, he had almost been able to see an opportunity. He'd been convinced that he could sell clam shells on Venice Beach. His plan had been to collect clam shells on the beach, buy a cheap set of craft paints at the dollar store, and paint little pictures on the smooth inside part of the shells. Finding a card table with collapsible legs would be fairly easy, and then he would just sell each one for five bucks. Jack had some talent for drawing and, based on the other garbage that people bought on Venice Beach, he had figured he could clear fifty or sixty bucks a day. That was more than enough to rent a room in a house, as well as cover the cost of beer and smokes. Sadly, Jack's epiphany had never been realized, as Marie had hated the beach, and urged their return to Hollywood every time they were there for more than an hour.

Marie hadn't loved it, but going to the beach once or twice a week was nice. During those weeks, before they moved on to the valley, when a night at an old man hotel was out of the question for lack of funds, the beach had been the only place to get a shower. Plus, you could head out there in the morning, go to a Target on the way, steal some swimming trunks, drop off your nasty clothes at the laundromat, put on your beach gear, and hang out at the beach all day.

Again, Marie had sort of hated the beach, and she really

hadn't liked getting ocean water in her dreadlocks, but she had looked great in the bikinis they stole for her. Since they'd had no use for swimming trunks and bikinis the rest of the time, and nowhere to store them, they had just thrown them out at the laundromat when they went back for their clothes. Sometimes, Marie had kept wearing the bikini bottoms as underwear, but the tops had served no purpose except on the beach. Marie's tits had been too big to be properly supported by a bikini top.

Because they had constantly disposed of swimwear, Marie had gotten a new bikini every time they went to the beach. One time, they had gotten her a low-waisted two-piece with yellow polka dots that tied in the front—very retro. She had looked like Raquel Welch in the sixties. That is, if Raquel Welch had been covered in tattoos and had waist-length black dreadlocks and a bottle of Night Train. Another time, it had been a more of a classic fit one. The bottoms had had side-ties and little pictures of ice cream cones on a turquoise background. The color and print had been ridiculous. It was something a fourteen-year-old would have worn. They had actually gotten it in the girl's section. Marie, a fully-developed woman, had managed to get into the largest girl's size they carried. There had been a plainclothes security guard near the women's section, so Marie had been forced to make do in the girl's section. Her ass had barely fit into the bottoms, even when she tied it loose, and her tits hadn't fit into the top in any meaningful way. Jack had seen her nipples peeking out of the top all day long.

She may not have excelled at actually going in the water, but she had been great at drawing attention while she lay on stolen beach towels with a bottle of whatever fortified wine they had stolen from the liquor store. Something about the tattoos and black dreadlocks as the backdrop for those brightly colored bikinis had really gotten guys' attention. The day with the ice cream cone bikini had been the worst. In that little girl's bikini, with a cigarette hanging of her mouth and a bottle in her hand, Marie had looked like the baddest high school girl in the world, and it had really brought out the pedophile in the male beachgoers.

All in all, those beach days had been the best times Jack could remember. Sometimes, he had even forgotten who they were altogether. He had imagined those short interludes were something like what normal people experienced most of the time. Those days had always had to end though. Sometime near dusk, they'd needed to make their way back to the laundromat, and then get a bus back to Hollywood.

The people at the laundromat had hated them—not just the employees, but the customers, too. They had stayed long enough to run fast wash cycles in the morning before putting all their stuff in one dryer, setting it, and leaving. One of two things always happened during their absence. Either customers had complained, and one of the employees had removed their stuff from the dryer, or somebody had just taken their stuff out and thrown it on a table or on top of a front-loading machine. Either way, Jack couldn't have cared less. Nobody was going to steal their clothes, and the laundromat employees had probably been too scared of them to throw them out.

The main problem with LA at that time for Jack and Marie had been that there was very little in the way of squats. Anything inside of the city had almost always been occupied, and when you found somewhere decent, somebody always ruined it by vandalizing a neighbor's car or throwing a bottle through somebody's living room window. That had always brought LAPD prematurely, and the squat would be blown for everyone. Even if they kept to themselves, the cops had come along within a week or two, booting them back onto the street. "Fuck, man, the homeless punks in Pittsburgh and Detroit must have it made. Half the houses in them cities are abandoned. I could raise kids in a squattin' environment like that."

The condemned house at the corner of Fountain and Lodi, the one with the fire hydrant out front, had been blown for them. It had been perfect. It had been walking distance to a grocery store and several liquor stores. Getting up to Hollywood Boulevard for your daily tourist hunting had been similarly easy.

Best of all, it had only been about a fifteen-minute walk from the old Raji's. The one in the Hastings Hotel. They'd had punk bands all the time, and any night that they could afford it, they had drank at Raji's. Their best days in LA had been at Venice Beach, but their best nights in LA had been at Raji's, specifically when GG Allin had played there. They'd smoked some meth with a random guy in the alley behind the club. He'd had a mohawk and a Discharge t-shirt. They had never gotten his name.

Jack had noticed Marie grinding up on the mohawk guy during the show, so while GG Allin had played "Die When You Die", he had taken Marie to the men's toilet, and waived the mohawk guy over. The toilet stall was covered in band stickers and graffiti, and it had smelled exactly how every other men's toilet in a punk rock club smelled. She had gone down on Jack almost immediately. The mohawk guy had pulled Marie's jeans down. Jack had been able to see she was wearing the ice cream cone bikini bottoms. Jack had seen the mohawk guy start fucking her from the back, while he had watched his cock sliding in and out of her mouth. He'd loved watching her face and looking her right in the eye while she was fucking. Everyone had cummed in about sixty-seconds or less. That was the happiest he had ever seen Marie.

Later that night, one of the punk kids at the squat had thought it would be cool to throw a Molotov cocktail he'd made out of an old pair of boxers and a half-empty vodka bottle at the neighbor's house. The bushes and the side of the house had lit up pretty fast, but the fire had died down on its own almost immediately. LAFD hadn't even needed to use the fire hydrant out in front of the squat. Nevertheless, the Hollywood squat at Fountain and Lodi was over. After that Jack and Marie had moved to the valley.

Jack and Marie had never talked about the past, and they had certainly never talked about the future. He hadn't wondered where Marie came from, and he had been wholly unconcerned with where she'd be after they parted company. Marie was like somebody that you hit it off with during a three-day meth binge and then went on a two-month crime spree with. Their personalities had fit, hand in glove. He'd had more fun with her than any other human before or after. She had been the insane person you spent every second of an entire summer with and then never saw again. She'd been the guy you sucked off just to see what it would be like. She had existed in Jack's then present, but was ultimately a memory to be hidden away in a secret place of his mind for all time and eternity. Jack loved what she was, what they had shared, and he'd tried not to pollute that by wondering about her past or future. She had done the same.

While Jack had never wondered if Marie would be alright in the future, he had often wondered what the future held for some of the other people in the squat. Even if Jack had concerned himself with Marie's future, there would have been no need. Marie was made of tougher stuff. Her insides were as tough as her tanned weather-beaten skin. In sixty years, Marie would still be Marie, doing Marie things, just like she had been that day. During the time Jack spent in LA that first summer, he had realized that most of the other punks in that squat were actually still just kids. That is, most of them were still minors, just runaways.

Jack had had no business worrying about them. After all, he had been perhaps the least functional human being among them. Nonetheless, he had played out sad possible scenarios in his head for each of them. One time, in that abandoned stucco piece of shit that they found in Van Nuys, Jack had taken a head count of fourteen, including Marie and himself. He had noticed that only three other people in that squat were over the age of eighteen. Some had come from legitimately poor circumstances, and if one of them had ever managed to find a job washing dishes somewhere and paying rent in some studio apartment somewhere they'd have been one of the lucky few. That would have been a success story of sorts, but that certainly wasn't what the future had in store for all of these kids. The remainder would eventually be locked up somewhere or dead prematurely. Jack was fucked up, but he knew how to get by. Those kids, he had surmised, were doomed.

At twenty-three, Jack had been the second oldest one there. Jack was a Sagittarius and it was December, which had meant that in a few days he'd be twenty-four. Marie was twenty-three and a Pisces. Obviously, they had gotten along great. Beth had been an Aries, and Jack had loved her even when he hadn't gotten along with her. But Marie hadn't really been someone you fell in love with; she had been a companion and a buddy. Your buddy that you fucked and who kept you company until one of you got locked up for a month of two. If and when that happened, she'd be gone. She'd find the next guy. There had been no illusions about what sort of relationship they had. It was the type of relationship that street people had with each other. Out there, you just needed something to cling on to, and so you grabbed the best-looking thing in the squat. And when they disappeared, nobody waited too long before grabbing something else to keep them company. It was understood.

Jack had had aspirations for the near future, but only the near future. He always did. Marie had had no aspirations for the future, near or far, and she never had. She probably never would. She'd been one of those broken-home types. Abuse, addiction, and molestation had not been taboo subjects in her home, not that her and Jack ever talked about it. Hardship was what she had expected from life, and it had never occurred to her that things could be better for her. She had floated into alcoholism, desolation, and homelessness almost like it was the natural progression of all human life, just the same way that someone else might finish high school, get a job, and go to college. In contrast, Jack's upbringing had been functional, if a little coddled. Marie had stayed right about where she started and had no plans beyond that point. Jack had lost ground from where he'd started, but he was always formulating a plan for the near future to claw his way from pathetic back to mediocre.

Chapter 33

The Van Nuys squat had actually been sort of cozy. The pack they were travelling with had actually stayed there several times. The first time it had been good for a couple of weeks. Then the cops had come along and booted them, but what Jack had realized about that place was that it was in the wastelands of Los Angeles. Nobody really cared what happened out there. If a cop showed up to investigate a neighbor's complaint about squatters, it was just so they could check a box on a report. Even the neighbors that complained probably did so as a mechanical and conditioned response, just a simple exercise of societal norms. Their hearts just weren't in it. Jack had been able to tell that much.

The neighborhood was the remnants of some sprawling postwar subdivision of tract houses, little boxes on the hillside made of ticky-tacky.Needless to say, they all looked just the same. Most had moved on, leaving the neighborhood for the earth to reclaim. A few had stuck around, probably because their houses had effectively become unsellable. It must have been one of the swankier suburban subdivisions, because postwar tract houses were notoriously cheap and small. Every house in their subdivision was one of those midcentury modern, split-level ranch houses. The outsides hadn't looked like much, but they had been shockingly large on the inside with high ceilings and all.

The one they had settled into must have been the jewel of the neighborhood once upon a time. It was a four-bedroom, two-bathroom place. Nobody had been able to tell what color it had been. Any surviving paint that had managed to stay attached to the exterior of the house had peeled badly, and the sun had long since baked any identifiable color off. Sometimes, when Jack had looked at it, he thought it had been blue with white trim, but other times, he thought it had been yellow all over. Whatever color it had been, by that time it had simply become the color of some redneck's stained wife-beater.

It was also the only one Jack had seen in the neighborhood with an inground pool. It was small, but it was an inground pool nonetheless. All the yards there were small, and their house was no exception. Jack assumed some hard-working middle-class suburbanite had saved and saved until he could afford to put that pool in. It had probably been the crowning achievement of his life. How sad that it had ended up just a concrete hole lined with dirt, bottom covered with broken bricks and random castoff garbage.

It had taken several complaints from the few neighbors that did still live there before the cops had even bothered dispatching a cruiser to send them packing. Jack had actually realized it by mistake. In Hollywood, they had lived on the streets a lot of the time, literally on the streets. They'd had the Fountain and Lodi squat for a while, but a lot of the time you found them sleeping anywhere from under an overpass to inside of newspaper bins. Sometimes, they had just slept under the sheltered parts of doorways in alleys. There was one time Jack and Marie had broken into someone's tool shed and slept there. Often times, they'd gotten too drunk and just passed out in a parking lot somewhere. If a car stayed in one secluded spot for more than a day or two, to them it had been an open invitation to not only vandalize and rob it but to fuck and get some sleep in it.

They had towed their sleeping bags around with them because they hadn't known where they were going to be crashing on any given night. Also, on the rare occasions they had left their few belongings hidden somewhere, it had been pretty normal for those belongings to be gone when they came back. Why their things had disappeared, Jack never really understood. To any normal person, their ragged backpacks and ratty sleeping bags would have been garbage. The garbage was likely where they had ended up when they disappeared. Jack suspected that those disappearances had been mean-spirited and not just people innocently disposing of what they had assumed was garbage. When their things disappeared, they had never turned up in a nearby dumpster. Any normal person would have disposed of such items at their earliest convenience if they were just innocently disposing of roadside crap.

Jack understood a lot of things in this world. He understood why people hadn't wanted them sleeping in the abandoned house on their block. He understood why the cashier at the liquor store had stared at them from the time they walked in until they left the parking lot. But he never understood how their presence on planet earth could be so offensive to some people that they would maliciously hide their few meager possessions in an attempt to further deprive them of any comfort whatsoever. Anyway, anything you really didn't want to lose, or that you couldn't live without, had to be kept on your person at all times.

One beautifully smoggy Los Angeles afternoon that was accentuated by a belly full of fortified wine, Marie and Jack had decided to head up north to Sherman Oaks and catch a Dead and Gone show at a punk house up there. After the show, Marie and Jack had started walking back toward the city even though they had both known it would be an all-night walk at best, so Jack had asked Marie if she wanted to rip off a couple of bottles of Wild Irish Rose at the liquor store and go by the old squat instead.

They had stayed there that night, and then they had stayed for another couple weeks after that. The cops hadn't even bothered to remove any of the stuff they'd left at the house from the last time they had been there. At some point, they had gone back to Hollywood to see who was still hanging around. A couple of stragglers from the old Fountain and Lodi squat came up from Hollywood to live in the Van Nuys squat. It was about two weeks before the cops had come to clear them out that time, and the time after that it had taken them eleven days. They'd spent the rest of the winter and spring popping in and out of that place. They'd stay a week or so, then clear out for a few days, only to come back again. In about mid-February, Jack had stolen one of those big coolers that people kept beer in at summer parties. It had been easy enough to find one; he had just roamed around the neighborhood until he'd seen an open garage with one inside. They'd also found an old charcoal barbeque with a sign that read "FREE" on it in front of a nearby house. Jack had put the barbeque down into the back yard's empty pool.

With the cooler, as long as they had ice, they had been able to keep perishables cold. As long as they had charcoal, they had been able to cook food, and nobody had been able to see them down there in the bottom of the pool cooking. After they had put a few lawn chairs in the pool, it also became a good place to just hang out and drink. Someone stole a little boom box from somewhere, and when they had batteries, they'd listen to the same five cassettes the four of them had between them over and over.

The barbeque and cooler meant their food stamps had finally become good for something other than trading for beer and cigarettes. Jack had made hamburgers nearly every night, and that time they had stayed there for the rest of the winter. Even better, there had never been more people than there were bedrooms after Marie and Jack reclaimed it that time. They'd kept it quiet for the most part, and the people that came through did the same. To the world, it was the frowning remnants of some idealized postwar suburbia, but to Jack and Marie, it had been a home. Nobody was getting "TR" branded on them, but if Penelope Spheeris had showed up with a camera crew it wouldn't have surprised Jack.

Whoever had owned the place apparently hadn't given a shit about it, because they had never come down and cleaned it out. Probably nobody had owned it. It had probably been abandoned. They had been close to Van Nuys, but Jack hadn't even known whether they were in a city at all or just some unincorporated part of Los Angeles County. Whatever the case, some local government most likely owned the house and just hadn't gotten around to condemning and demolishing it. "Point bein,' when we got the boot from the pigs, we just left tons of shit behind, and it was always there when we came back. At the beginnin' of the summer, when it was time to head back toward Seattle, I found myself actually movin' out of the place like it was my actual house. I toiled over what I could realistically bring with me in my backpack and what had to be left to the next group of squatters to find that jewel in suburbia. Whoever they were, they were sure getting' a bargain. I left two good blankets, three t-shirts, and a pair of jeans. That, and a really fuckin' kewl Youth Brigade poster that I got free at a show. Oh yeah, we also had to leave the barbeque and cooler. Oh well, and then we were off, back to the great PNW."

Heading back north had been mostly uneventful, mostly. They were in a freight car travelling through northern California when Jack had woken up to the sound of skin slapping skin. Not three feet away from him he had seen this guy Peter, who had hopped the freight train with them, fucking Marie. Jack couldn't have cared less who Marie fucked, but the fact that they were fucking behind his back had rubbed him the wrong way.

The plan had been to get off in the Bay Area and check out a squat they'd heard about there, maybe stay a couple of weeks before they headed back to Seattle. Marie was passed out when they stopped, so Jack had gotten off the train with Peter, and they had shared a bottle of Thunderbird in some bushes near the tracks. After Jack emptied the last of the bottle, he had cracked it over Peter's unsuspecting skull, given his limp body a few swift kicks about the head and torso, and hopped back on the train. For Jack, it had begun to appear that, when he needed to club someone, a bottle was always close at hand. As soon as he had done it, he had sincerely hoped that it was the last time this behavior, that was now becoming a pattern, would occur.

The train wasn't leaving for several minutes, and Jack had watched Peter for what seemed like a long time. Peter hadn't moved. Blood had still run from his head wound onto the ground, so Jack had assumed he was still alive. "If he was fuckin' dead, the blood would stop right?" If he ever woke up, he might come looking for Jack. Peter knew they'd planned to head to Seattle over the summer. Jack knew he'd have to watch his back for the foreseeable future, but he hadn't really cared. The community in Seattle was too small to not run into people. LA was much larger than Seattle, and even there the crusty punks all knew each other. Avoiding travelling punks in Seattle was unrealistic. At a minimum, somebody coming north would bring the story with them, and Jack would have to confront any friends Peter had in Seattle—but he figured fuck them, anyway. Besides, that was all contingent on Peter waking up at all, and based on how he had looked when Jack left him, Peter being alive was a maybe proposition at best.

Death was a harsh punishment for fucking a girl that Jack had just been wasting time with, but he hadn't really cared anymore. He hadn't cared about that guy; he hadn't cared if he was dead, and he hadn't really given a shit about Marie. If he hadn't just left some guy for dead in the train yard, he would have waited a few hours to hop a different train heading east and done some exploring. He would have left Marie far behind. Instead, he had gotten back on the northbound train with Marie. It had been the only one departing at that moment, and Jack certainly couldn't hang around there any longer than he had to. About an hour out of the Bay Area, Marie had woken up from her drunken stupor.

She'd asked, "Where's Peter?"

Jack had vindictively replied, "He said your pussy was nasty and got off the train."

They hadn't done a lot of talking after that. Some time later, while the train was traveling through Oregon and the Palm trees gave way to Douglas Firs and Maples, she had told Jack that fucking Peter was a stupid drunken mistake. Jack had told her that she was his stupid drunken mistake.

What he hadn't said was that Peter was most likely lying in some bushes bleeding to death. Timing had gotten Jack back on the northbound train, but after thinking about it, it was actually a lucky turn for him. He figured that if he stayed with Marie for the time being, he could dissuade her from going back there if she was so inclined. It turned out she wasn't interested in going back to the Bay Area at that point, which was what Jack had hoped for. If he'd abandoned her and gotten on a train headed east, she might have gone back to the Bay Area. She might have found Peter. She might have figured out that Jack had done it. Right then, she had just wanted to go to Seattle and see what things would be like for the summer, and Jack had been happy to stick around with her for a little while.

Chapter 34

By the time they'd been back in Seattle for a few weeks Jack had been beyond bored with the life. Their new squat had been an early century craftsman, and no less than twenty squatters had inhabited it at any given time. There'd been five bedrooms, and everybody had slept wherever they felt like. Leaving your sleeping bag in a spot in one of the bedrooms had been no better insurance of keeping that spot than throwing your coat on a barstool in a crowded pub in downtown Seattle.

All the houses in central Seattle were built in the teens and twenties, and nobody had bothered to update them. They were cramped houses on cramped plots of land, and even their five-bedroom squat was likely only around fifteen hundred square feet. Perched on the crest of Madison, at the crossroads between Madison Valley, Capitol Hill, the Central District, and pill hill, Jack had been able to see most of central Seattle from the attic crawlspace windows. That crawlspace had been about the only spot that Jack could consistently sleep without disturbance.

Even the residents of that place had been scared of the rats in the crawlspace. Jack had been less scared of rats than he was of a shitty night's sleep. Who could have predicted that in a couple short decades, the downtown skyline would grow fivefold, and every house within his view would be worth over a million dollars, including the house he was in?

That place had never gotten busted, and he had been able to stay there for months, but it hadn't been home either. That place had been continuously occupied by squatters for years. Jack had been there before when he had lived at Beth's. Some of the people that Jack had drank with lived there. Marie had been cut from a different cloth than Jack. It seemed to him that she could, and likely would, live the rest of her life on the streets. There was no reason for her to move on when she was so content with her current situation. Squatting wasn't a phase for her, but it had been for Jack.

In the game of loserdom, Jack had been ready to level up. Some of the people he had left behind at that juncture in his life were lazy or stupid, and some of them had just been doing the best they could under fucked-up circumstances. Jack hadn't thought he was better than any of them, but he'd lost the kinship he'd felt with those people for a number of reasons. The ones that were just slumming it for the summer hadn't had his respect, and the ones that just couldn't manage any better for themselves had scared him into a future-tripping state of mind. In his mind, he could see a future where he became like them. Jack didn't like that space in his mind and had tried to keep it closed as much as possible.

Right at that time, Jack hadn't known exactly how he was going to change his circumstances, but he had known it needed to happen soon. Sleeping off his hangovers had become very dull to him anyway, so he had started waking up right when the sun came up at around six in the morning and going to an AA meeting that met in this church basement every morning at seven. Coming in every morning reeking like a brewery had sent mixed messages to the AA people. Some of them had thought he was serious about getting sober but lacked initiative, and others hadn't known what to make of his presence since he had never made a spectacle of himself like so many others that routinely came into those meetings under the influence.

He hadn't been under the influence at all, and he had preferred to just sit in the corner and mind his own business. He had just been nursing his daily hangover, and he hadn't gone there for recovery or their fellowship, either. He had gone there because he could get a couple of free doughnuts or cookies and a few cups of coffee. The sugar and caffeine had helped with the hangovers and given him enough energy to go down to the Capitol Hill Branch library, where he'd spent the mornings reading newspapers and the occasional instructional book pertaining to something he thought he might need to know how to do some day.

Shop manuals about cars had always been interesting to Jack. He also liked books about psychological warfare, manipulating people, and how to tell when people were lying, to name a few. One day, he'd found a book about lockpicking, and he had spent three days reading it cover to cover. For a small investment, a person could obtain a set of lock picks that would get them into practically any house that didn't have a dog or an alarm system. He guessed, based on his own observations, that about ninety percent of houses in central Seattle had fallen into those categories back then.

None of the information he got from those books had put any money in his pocket, though. At that time, he had still relied on his old mainstays. For food, it had been soup kitchens, free church meals, and scrounging the pastries out of the grocery store dumpsters. Nothing else had really been safe to eat out of the dumpsters, but sometimes he'd tried it anyway.

For booze and cigarettes, he had mainly employed his time-tested technique of walking down Broadway and using a one-dollar food stamp to buy a ten-cent piece of candy or a twenty-five-cent pack of gum. If the change from a food stamp transaction was less than a dollar, the store had to give you that change back in actual coins. In other words, you got the change just like if you'd paid with real money. After about ten stops, you had enough for booze and cigarettes for the day. The little convenience store owners hadn't cared, and they had been more than happy to go along with the scam. After all, the state government reimbursed them in real dollars. Sometimes, a cool owner would let you pull the same transaction several times in a day. Even better was the rare store owner who just didn't give a fuck, and would sell Jack beer and smokes for the food stamps straight across. There had been a store like that a couple miles away in the University District, but it was a pretty long walk, so Jack had mostly just stayed close and done the store-to-store method. When he'd been too lazy to go through all that, there had always been people that would buy his stamps at half their dollar value. Marie, meanwhile, had been lazy all the time. She had always sold her food stamps at the beginning of the month, but she'd drink up all the money in a couple of days. Jack went out and did his legwork every day. Even so, the stamps usually only bought beer and smokes for a week and a half, maybe two weeks if you were frugal. That had left Jack broke for at least a couple weeks a month. Plus, Marie hadn't been able to hold onto her money for more than three days, so Jack had always ended up having to come up with another plan to support her habits as well as his.

Stealing from the local stores that let you cash in your stamps was bad public relations. Also, Jack had been trying to secretly squirrel some cash away. That meant Jack had been forced to leave the neighborhood to steal booze, which was a serious pain in the ass. It had needed to be done, though. He'd needed to keep Marie intoxicated. By that time, the thought of Marie touching him had made his skin crawl, but she hadn't seemed to notice. She hadn't really missed sex as long as she was drunk. He hadn't missed sex with her drunk or sober. She had probably been fucking somebody else in the house, anyway. She had been so plowed most of the time she could have been doing it with some other guy and thought it was Jack. She wouldn't even have known the difference.

None of it had mattered to him anymore. In the near future, he was going to be leaving all the fun of the punk rock squat behind. The sound and smell of sex happening between two intoxicated unwashed individuals had been a constant. People had not only pissed but shit in the two bathrooms, which had had no running water, an ever-present reminder of the squalor that they lived in. That was to say nothing of the lice, crabs, ants, flies, and maggots, all of which seemed to prefer to living on you instead of around the house itself.

Outside had actually been a much cleaner environment to live in because crawly things that sought out filth ran indoors to places like that squat. Jack often reflected on how filthy he had used to think Western State and Fairfax had been, but compared to the Capitol Hill squat, they had been the pinnacle of cleanliness. That whole squat was a biohazard, and everybody had caught whatever everybody else in the place had. Everybody there had been ill, but they were all just too drunk and high to notice it.

Stagnant water dripping from the ceiling onto his sleeping bag while he was trying to put it all together in his head had driven him crazy, and he'd decided then and there that living in the mental ward or behind bars was better than living in that squat. It was time for him to go back to work and get the fuck out of there. "And if I got pinched in the process, oh fuckin' well."

Chapter 35

There had been an immediate avenue open to an individual such as Jack that would bring revenue right away. And there was a reason that it was such easy money. Being a daytime burglar was a good way to end up back in the pen for a long stretch, especially for a second-time felon. There he was, barely in his mid-twenties, and if he had gotten caught once doing what he was planning on doing every day for the foreseeable future it would have cost him a few years in prison. Jack was also aware that Washington State had a "three strikes and you're out" law, and he had already had one strike. He had figured that burglary in and of itself wasn't a violent felony that would get him a second strike, but he could easily have committed a violent felony if he came into contact with someone while burglarizing a house, which would get him a second strike. Honestly, he wasn't a lawyer, so he really had no idea what might or might not get him a second strike. Considering that he may have killed that guy Peter, he had figured he was on borrowed time anyway, so he might as well go for broke.

That very next day, he had kicked in the back door of a random three-bedroom house with an attached garage. That sort of residence would be his bread and butter for a little while. That place had been in Madison Valley, a pretty average middle-class neighborhood adjacent to Capitol Hill. Everybody had been at work during the day. Nobody had owned home security systems, and there were very few dog owners. All of those factors had made the neighborhood a prime place to hit.

Dogs were the biggest deterrents, even bigger than home security systems. Security systems didn't sink their fangs into your ankle when you were already retreating. Security systems were for scaring burglars off, but there was always plenty of time to run. The alarm first sounded through the call center of the company that owned the system, and they placed a call to police dispatch. There were too many relays, and even if there was a cruiser right in the neighborhood, you still had five minutes to hide. Cops never looked too hard for people either. More than once, Jack had spent the afternoon in a local dumpster after setting off a home alarm. He probably could have popped his head up after ten minutes, but he had always stayed for extended periods of time, just to be safe.

Most criminals fucked up. They thought they could outrun the cops. Jack had known it wasn't about outrunning them. It was about staying out of sight. It was being the guy that won at hide and seek, and every neighborhood had more than enough places to hide. They couldn't look everywhere, and again, they really didn't try that hard, anyway. One time, Jack had hidden out on the roof of a convenience store. He'd jumped up onto a dumpster and climbed an exterior pipe the rest of the way up. It was right on a main street, and he had watched this cop circle the neighborhood for ten minutes, tops, looking for the prowler. "That fat fuckin' cop never even got out of his fuckin' cruiser. I could have been hidin' in the front yard of the house I was breakin' in to, and he still wouldn't have found me."

Again, though, dogs were the most problematic part of being a burglar. Cops were certainly to be avoided, but avoiding them was pretty easy. You could run from a tripped alarm. A dog, on the other hand, could injure you so you couldn't run at all. You might even have to go to the hospital, and the cops might have already alerted the ER staff to be looking for dog bites.

In fact, Jack hadn't even considered breaking into houses that had dogs at all. Most of the time, if they weren't sitting right in the yard or peeking through the front window, there were good clues that a dog might live at a given house. The lawns would be torn up or patchy. There would be chew toys in the yard. Usually, you could smell dog piss all around the house. Even if the dog that lived in a house didn't pee in the yard, other dogs would pee in front of houses where dogs lived. Jack wasn't sure why they did that. It seemed patently aggressive to mark some other dog's front yard, but they did it anyway. Either way, it had helped Jack flag houses where dogs lived. Even if you missed all the other signs, chucking a rock at the front door of a house would rouse any dog into a barking frenzy. It was also a good way to get any people that might be home to answer the front door without being seen.

The first house Jack had broken into had none of those pitfalls and a bunch of good shit to steal. Rich people's shit was too hard to move. Selling someone's expensive fine china to a pawn shop was a fool's errand. What burglar was going to sit in a house for an hour packing up dishes? Normal people's shit, on the other hand, was easy to find, easy to steal, and easy to sell. Handguns, semi-expensive jewelry, VCRs, TVs, knives, and tools were all good things to steal and sell. Normal people had an abundance of all of those sorts of items.

Those items were all relatively easy things to sell, that was true, but they were also good things to trade. Drug dealers were almost always open to trading tools and home electronics for blow, crank, junk, or whatever. The other bonus of trading those items to drug dealers was that Jack hadn't needed to risk selling them to pawn shops. There were cops whose job was to call pawn shops and look for stolen items. It was the reason pawn shops got your ID when you sell them things. Good thieves, like Jack, had found pawn shops that bought stolen items, no ID, no questions asked, but they'd gouge the thief on the price.

Sometimes, Jack had gotten desperate and sold to a straight pawn shop. There was a huge risk when it came to selling to pawn shops that did things the right way. When one of those detectives whose job it was to prowl the pawn shops looking for stolen items found one, he'd get the seller's information from the pawn shop owner, and then you were being investigated for burglary and selling stolen goods. It was always a risk, but sometimes it couldn't be avoided.

One way or the other, trading things to drug dealers meant that Jack had gotten close to market price for the items, just in illicit drugs instead of cash. He had been able to sell those drugs himself for cash on Broadway, or he had used them to get high. Better yet, he had used use them to get Marie high so that he hadn't had to talk to her. Dealing drugs on Broadway had been less risky than burglarizing homes. Seattle police didn't really care about drug commerce on Broadway, but they cared a lot about homes being burglarized.

Jack hadn't traded firearms to drug dealers, though. They always wanted firearms, but Jack had refrained from trading guns to dickhead drug dealers that he didn't like in the first place. Confrontation with drug dealers was an omnipresent threat. They were always edgy and paranoid. To Jack, it hadn't made sense to trade a gun to a local drug dealer that might very well point that gun at him a day or two later. Jack had saved the firearms for the crooked pawn shop owners.

Jack had filed the serial numbers off before he'd let anyone, especially the crooked pawn shop guys, touch them, and those crooked pawn shop guys had never known his real name. Buying defiled, stolen firearms was a big risk for them, but also for Jack. They could have lost their businesses, or even done a little time, but Jack had already had a violent felony conviction. He would have done years for selling stolen guns. Plus, picking up a second strike had scared the shit out of him. Either way, those crooked pawn shops had probably just sold those guns to the drug dealers that Jack refused to, but at least Jack hadn't done it himself.

Every time Jack had caught himself standing at a pawn shop counter when an SPD detective strolled in and started asking about stolen merchandise, he'd broken out in a cold sweat. It had happened a handful of times during his burglarizing days. Every time he'd promised himself that he'd get a job washing dishes somewhere and just accept being a poor loser like everybody else. He had just needed enough to get a place of his own and some new clothes first.

Jack had recognized the same detective at least twice. How many times had that detective seen him? From a nondescript car, that detective could have seen Jack walking in and out of the local pawn shops on an almost daily basis for months.

How many times had he noticed Jack in different pawn shops around town? How much heroin had been in Jack's pocket? Had the pistols and power tools he had just sold that guy been hidden behind the counter, or were they just sitting out for the detective to see? In a mental frenzy which came on suddenly, like the first hallucination from a few hits of LSD, all those questions and more had flashed through Jack's mind on each of those occasions. All this had happened while he tried his best to keep his outward composure and appear as a casual browser looking for a good deal on a weed whacker.

Jack knew each time it happened that if the pawn shot guy had gotten pinched right then and there, he'd have rolled over on Jack in a second, and since he hadn't known Jack's name or where he lived, he'd have needed to do it while he was in the store. Every time one of those detectives hit the road, leaving Jack be, he'd promised himself: "Just until you have enough to get a place and get settled." In Jack's estimation, he was getting close to either quitting that business altogether or getting pinched. One day, a very close call had prompted Jack to get out of that game while he still had his freedom.

Chapter 36

And so, one day, Jack had just left the squat. At least, that was how it had appeared to anyone that was paying attention, including Marie. In reality, it had been about two and a half months of non-stop running, scheming, and saving when he had decided to leave. He'd managed to save a little more than two thousand dollars. He'd gotten a new state ID while he was burglarizing houses. He'd needed the ID for selling to law-abiding pawn shops.

Establishing your identity from scratch was no easy task. Jack had spent days going downtown to the county records building and filling out papers so he could get a birth certificate, then days more at the Department of Licensing getting a new ID. He had known he'd be looking for work soon, and so he had spent days more at the Social Security Administration office applying for a new Social Security Card. The Social Security card had needed to be mailed, so he had gone to the Capitol Hill post office and got a P.O. Box. He'd had more than enough money for first and last months' rent and security deposit at an apartment, but it hadn't been easy to find someone who felt like renting to an unemployed single male, especially one who had tried to pay with a stack of folded up twenty-dollar bills. Jack had needed a bank account, a checkbook, and a bank card. Jack's next stop had been the Seafirst Bank on Broadway, where he had spent another long day opening a bank account.

He had left the squat without any place to go. It hadn't mattered. He'd figured he had enough to stay at a motel until something came through. It was easier to look for an apartment living in a motel than living in a squat. For starters, there was a phone, so he had been able to get call backs from apartment managers and prospective employers. Plus, there was a shower, so he had been able to look presentable when he did show up to meet an apartment manager or prospective employer.

This was not to be one of his great disappearing acts. It was nothing in the realm of what he had pulled on Beth, his crew, or his family on several occasions. When he had left them, he had done it because he hadn't been able to bear looking them in the face. At the squat, he hadn't told anybody he was leaving because he didn't give a shit about any of them, and none of them had cared about him, either. Nobody there had needed or deserved an explanation from him, not even Marie, and so he had just gone away without informing anyone.

What Marie had deserved was a little something that he could manage. In the pocket of her patch-covered sleeveless black denim jacket, he had left her two hundred dollars. Even more valuable than that was about two grams of good heroin. If she was miserable enough, she could slam all the heroin at once and just check out for good, but Marie was never miserable, so he had been sure she'd shoot the smack safely and drink up the cash in about a week or so. That had been all the goodbye he owed her, and he was pretty sure it was all the goodbye she would have wanted anyway. "God bless her,

I don't believe in no God, but what the fuck ever."

The heroin had been the last of a stash he'd failed to sell before he left. Having the proceeds that selling it on the street would have brought could have been a nice chunk of change in his pocket, but the prior day's events had drastically changed his plans.

It had been a bad day that had nearly become catastrophic. He hadn't even bothered to retrieve his stash of stolen goods, which he had kept in the trunk of a broken-down Honda in an alley behind some empty house two blocks away. The heroin and two hundred bucks he had left Marie just happened to be in his pocket when he had decided to leave the squat. If they'd been with the rest of his stolen shit in the Honda, he'd have abandoned them, too.

The motel Jack had gone to was right on Aurora in the north end of the city, otherwise known as Highway 99. It was the strip where all the street hookers and pimps operated. There were also no less than a dozen rub and tug massage parlors between 80th and 125th streets. There were plenty of drugs up there, too, but mainly it was the part of the city where sex was for sale.

Jack hadn't planned on being there for more than a couple of days. The apartments he had been looking at were right back on Capitol Hill. A couple were no more than a handful of blocks away from the squat. He had wondered how conversations would go when he inevitably ran into punks from the squat. He'd even run into Marie sooner rather than later, but that would probably be more awkward for him than for her anyway. He'd had a pretty clear memory of their time together, not to mention some legitimate feelings for her. From her perspective, Jack had just been a guy she spent half of 1994 and the majority of 1995 with, mostly just a foggy blur.

At the Klose Inn, where he had decided to hole up until he found an apartment, he had been given access to fifty-seven TV channels, a phone, a shower, a bed, and lots of beer. A couple of days at the Klose Inn had turned into a couple of weeks, and Jack had started to become one of the fixtures around the place. Somehow, finding work and an apartment had kept getting pushed out another couple of days, a week, and so on and so forth. As was his pattern, he'd worked vigilantly and socked away some money just to watch it dwindle as he became more and more sedentary and idle after achieving some level of temporary comfort. Drinking, smoking, eating, and a couple of trips to Aurora prostitutes, along with the weekly rates of the motel, had taken a serious negative toll on the balance of his newly established bank account. His savings had gone down to about thirteen hundred dollars. It was still more than enough to get a place, but he needed to find something soon if he was going to get a real apartment. If he waited much longer, his only option would be finding a room in a house with a bunch of roommates. It was true that he had been spending most of every day drinking and watching TV, but nearly every day for almost two weeks he'd also been applying for work at every greasy spoon and coffee shop on Broadway, and then following up, but nobody was offering him work. Nothing.

The day before he forked out another one hundred and fifty bucks for one more week at the Klose Inn things had just sort of fallen into place. That day, he had woken up to the phone ringing at about ten-thirty in the morning. That was early for Jack. Since leaving the squat, he had readjusted to his normal, alcoholically-inspired noon wake-up time, but he had known he needed to sound awake on the phone. The worst thing you could do when you were waiting to hear about a job or place to live was to sound like you were hung over and sleeping when you answered the phone, especially at ten thirty in the morning.

Employers had this strange notion that unemployed people woke up at six in the morning, went to Starbucks for their morning coffee, and then waited by the phone all day for someone to call and offer them a job. Jack only woke up at six in the morning for work, like burglarizing homes. Anyone that had ever been an unemployed alcoholic knew that you drank all night and slept all morning. Afternoons were the time for filling out applications. It was just common sense.

Jack had slapped himself about ten times in the face and practiced saying hello out loud for a few seconds to get that sleepy tone out of his voice before he had picked up the phone. It had been the manager of a little coffee stand called Vivace that was on Broadway just north of Thomas Street. The guy on the phone had asked if Jack was free for an interview that afternoon. Jack had always thought that was an odd question that prospective employers asked. He hadn't had a job. It stood to reason that his afternoon was free. Of course, Jack recognized it was just a nicety that people engage in, but the truth was, if Jack hadn't been available that afternoon, the guy on the phone would have just called the person on the next application for an interview. Jack, of course, had agreed to an interview that afternoon.

As he hung up the phone it had rang again before he could remove his hand from the receiver. Now mostly awake, he hadn't hesitated to pick it right up. The apartment manager of a building called The Gayle on Thomas Street, no more than three blocks away from the coffee shop where he had an interview, had been on the other end of the line. She'd reviewed his application and was wondering if he could come by the building that afternoon to meet with her in person. Jack had laughed at the question a little before eagerly agreeing. Being homeless was similar to being jobless, in that, when you had nowhere to live, what else could be more important than getting to an interview with somebody that might rent you an apartment?

Chapter 37

The nineties were coming to a premature close in Seattle, in what could only be described as their natural conclusion. It was the end of 1995, but the chapter on that decade had already been written. The music scene around Seattle that had been so fresh in 1990 had by then become nothing much more than a corporate grunge fusion and mutual masturbation session for the players involved. Luckily, it was about to end. Major labels, record companies, and MTV had grown tired of Seattle. Nobody cared about flannel shirts, beanies, and long hair anymore.

Without the record industry overlords pulling its strings, Seattle would soon reseed itself with a specific crop of punk bands that closed down the remainder of the decade and millennium. Seattle returned to its independent roots with the primitive and primal noises that crept in from the dark PNW forests, and for a few years, it drown-out the waning sounds of the pseudo cock rock that grunge had become. How about a Zeke record. Death Wish Kids anyone? Queue up the Murder City Devils, please!

The music industry had picked the carcass of Seattle's early nineties music scene clean to the bone. The rock stars that the grunge scene had created mostly imploded over the next several years. And at the end of it all, they didn't leave much more than a footnote on popular culture.

Before they were even done with Seattle, MTV and the record industry in general were already looking for the next big thing. By 1994, they'd found a type of punk was easily digestible by throngs of middle-class suburban white kids. Fortunately for everyone in Seattle, the dangerous war drum appeal of the new Seattle punk scene was not so easy to swallow, so that time MTV and the record executives stayed away. Once the world heard "Longview" by Green Day, the feeding frenzy was on in the Bay Area. Other than Green Day, there were certainly fewer mainstream successes among the Bay Area punk bands then there had been in Seattle, but even bands like Jawbreaker had their day in the sun.

Every year, Jack had seen less and less of the crusty punks and street kids in the U-district until eventually he had barely seen them at all. That little squat he had recently vacated seemed like the last outpost of another dying subculture.

Seattle was becoming the mecca for what would be known as tech bro culture. Back then, Jack hadn't been sure who all these people that wore collared shirts with fleece vests over them were. He had just known there were a bunch of them all of a sudden, and they all had these ID badges clipped to their belts or hanging around their necks on lanyards. All sanctimony aside, the nerds were on the march, and they were about to gentrify Jack and his ilk right out of Capitol Hill, and eventually out of Seattle altogether.

About four years later, a four-day war on the streets of Capitol Hill and Westlake Center between cops and protestors would take place. Symbolically, the nineties had, at that point, been over for years in Seattle, at least as far as the rest of the world was concerned. The WTO protests signaled the actual end of the decade, the end of the century, the end of the millennium, and the end of Seattle as a culturally relevant destination. Those last few years of the nineties were an in-between place in a city that had not come to grips with its quaint, working-class, liberal past and the role it was about to play in the new information economy.

The end of 1999 was still a ways off for Jack. While he had spent those short few days of employment at Vivace, companies like Microsoft, Amazon, and a hundred others people would soon know the names of had already been busy importing an upper-middle-class workforce from top-tier cities all over the country and bringing people from abroad on work visas.

New money, new economy, new people: they descended on Seattle like locusts on a grain field. They had signing bonuses, and were itching to spend them. Nobody local stood a chance. They were a tidal wave. They displaced everything they encountered. Unlike a tidal wave, they didn't recede and disappear. They stayed. "I didn't like what the record industry did to the Seattle music scene, but at least they had the decency to leave after they fucked it up. You can rebuild after MTV rapes your culture, but these technology fuckers ain't goin' nowhere. They're here for the duration. Seattle was over then. It's super over now."

Like so many invaders before, they claimed they brought prosperity. They claimed that their way of life was going to make things better. Just like Spanish invaders in Central America, or Roman invaders in England, they brought their culture but destroyed a way of life that the native inhabitants cherished. To native Seattleites, it seemed like all they brought were glass towers, million-dollar condo listings, and a declining quality of life for everybody not in the millionaires' club. "Right then, I started to appreciate the plight of the Duwamish, the original native Seattleites."

To Jack, it had seemed like the money and prosperity they had brought to Seattle only ever benefitted themselves. What, he often wondered, was the point of having a top-tier city that only a top tier of citizens can enjoy? Jack wasn't necessarily smart—or educated, for that matter—but he had good instincts in great abundance. Jack's instincts on that matter couldn't have been more right. All the information economy's money and talent hadn't been able to see what Jack saw from a sidewalk coffee stand in 1995. That was that Seattle would simultaneously become the richest and poorest place imaginable. By 2022, it seemed like half the city had lived in luxury condos on the fiftieth floor, and the other half lived in tents on the sidewalk, smoking blue Fentanyl pills out of tin foil with plastic straws, outside those same luxury condo buildings. "Progress brings problems, money brings poverty, homogeneity brings its dagger right to the heart of creativity. Oh fuckin' well. Seattle.'What a pity, they've fucked up, this city where I grew up. Now, it's grown too big, and there's no room left for me.'"

From the coffee stand, for the few days he worked there, Jack had really realized how much change was actually happening in the neighborhood and Seattle in general. He hadn't noticed it as much when he was living in squat, but at Vivace he had actually interacted directly with this new Seattle for the first time. What Jack had found even stranger was that the handful of pre-existing residents that did hang on to their place in the city were evolving to conform to the new Seattle. The gay guys that Jack had used to see hanging around at Neighbours and R Place were going to work in suits and buying apartments in the neighborhood. They'd wanted so badly to try to keep some of the neighborhood's soul intact by staying, but in so doing became what they had priorly railed against.

The neighborhood itself had become what it railed against. Bohemian, artistic, and collective became homogenized, bland, and self-centered. It was nothing new; money and the people attached to money spoiled everything. They lacked a genuine viewpoint, taste, or artistic talent. Their talent was in the acquisition of things. Somehow, they thought that if they bought fine art, they had developed taste. Or if they read a piece of philosophy, they had an opinion. In Seattle, they thought if they acquired a unique social ecosystem, they would become members of a unique social ecosystem. In reality, they just let salt water into a freshwater lake. Eventually, the city as a whole, and the entire Puget Sound to some extent, became a more watered-down version of what happened to Capitol Hill.

The coffee stand had been no place for Jack, though. Making coffee for these picky new Seattleites had been too difficult. They had always wanted skim milk in their lattes. Jack had never understood that. "Half the fuckers that wanted skim milk were already fat as shit! In which case, one whole milk latte made zero difference anyway. The other half were skinny fuckin' girls with no asses. In which case, some whole milk might have helped them grow some much-needed curves. I just don't get it. All the normal-sized people just drank their lattes with whatever we put in there." Needless to say, they hadn't liked Jack at Vivace. The customers hadn't liked him, and the employees hadn't liked him much either. Certainly, the manager that had serendipitously called Jack that fateful day at the Klose Inn hadn't liked him. Nobody there had wanted to tell him that he was fired, but after the first week he wasn't on the schedule. Jack hadn't even asked; he had just left.

His paycheck for a week of work at Vivace hadn't gone far, but it had bought him a little more time. After he had gotten some liquor and groceries for his place, his savings was down to a couple hundred bucks. The first and last month's rent had been paid, so he had at least seven weeks before he had to come up with rent. Between the Vivace paycheck and what he had in his bank account he'd had enough to pay another month's rent, and he had decided he would do that with the money. Best not to go to the manager after being there one month and tell her that he already had to use his last month's rent. Besides, there had been food at the apartment, and the power was on. He'd had a TV that he'd stolen on one of his last home prowls. He could always spare change for booze and cigarettes if he needed to, or just steal them. He hadn't been concerned about that at present. Not having a job had been concerning, but it was a concern that he wouldn't have to worry about for long.

"Dumb luck is the luxury afforded to fools, the Irish, and drunks, or some such similar shit." Luckily for Jack, he fit into all three categories. He was certainly foolish, and a drunk. Two of his grandparents were Irish, so he figured that got him into the final category. "My paraphrasin' is pretty fuckin' bad, but it's the truth and a constant fact of life for me." The downside of dumb luck was that it only kept you alive so that you were around to make even bigger mistakes than the ones that you'd needed the dumb-luck to bail you out of in the first place. It was a viscous circle that seemed to have no end, which was also a constant in Jack's life.

One day, not so long after leaving Vivace, Jack had walked down the street and seen a sign hanging in the window of a Taco Del Mar downtown that read: "HELP WANTED." In other words, slackers welcome. When a business didn't even go to the trouble to list a job opening in the newspaper, it meant a couple of things. First, the job required zero brain cells to perform. Second, as long as you weren't smoking your crack pipe while you filled out the application, they were going to hire you. That sign had been a beacon to Jack. It had been a flower in a sea of shit.

"You couldn't buy a better job than that one." It hadn't paid enough to really live on, so nobody with any aspirations in life hung around for long. "But it was also pretty gravy as far as workload." It had also been fairly simple, and the people had been pretty cool. The employees had all been burnouts, and the ones that weren't had been complete flakes. Because showing up for work seemed to be optional, the employees had always left an abundance of shifts to be filled. Compared to the other burnouts at a place like that, Jack had appeared to be an exemplary employee, and he had been able to keep a job like that as long as he wanted it. All that was required was to show up most of the time, and put in minimal effort. Jack had definitely been able to handle that.

The benefits had been pretty great too. Free food, daily tips averaging ten to fifteen bucks, otherwise known as beer and cigarette money, and, again, lenient work hours. Nobody had cared if you showed up hungover, and more often than not the manager and everybody else had been stoned out of their minds anyway. That said, there hadn't been any of the things that people normally associated with the word "benefits" in the employment context. There hadn't been any dental, medical, retirement, paid sick leave, vacation, etc.

Jack had never had any of those things before, so he hadn't given it much thought. He always saw a doctor when he was committed or locked up. One of those things, he had figured, would happen in the near future, at which time he'd see a doctor, so no problem there. He was young and had all his teeth. His nighttime grinding had flattened them out to the point that they looked like little off-white bricks instead of teeth, but he had all of them. "As far as retirement, paid sick leave, and vacation, normal people didn't get those things. Only the bourgeois fuckers got that shit."

The fall had started to feel like winter again, and with it had come that little bit of chill that made the morning bearable. Jack had preferred to work his normal night shift, but a couple times a month, he was scheduled for a morning shift. To Jack, the worst thing in the world was waking up with a nasty hangover, but he had kept drinking, and he had kept waking up, so he had kept waking up with hangovers. If the misery of a hangover had to be exacerbated by waking up in the morning, getting outside into the cool air and pissing rain, which always seemed to fall in a manner more constant and deliberate than overwhelming and sporadic, had been medicine to his hungover mind and body.

As he walked to work on one of those morning shift days, he had pondered that Taco Del Mar was a pretty perfect job for a guy like Jack, but what he hated about it was that he was starting to feel his age. He was starting to become that guy that had never really gotten it together. Lots of people spun their wheels for a few years in their young adulthood, but most of them, even most of the real trainwrecks, usually managed to move into some sort of career and normality in life. They accomplished what Jack had never been able to. They seemed to assimilate into the fabric of society. They didn't work the night shift at Taco Del Mar when they were nearly twenty-five. It didn't take one of his coworkers to tell him that he was like five years older than everybody there, but when they did, Jack's brain had been forced to confront the implications of that. In a couple of months, he'd be twenty-five, and he hadn't accomplished much, unless you counted fostering a festering addictive personality that had left him prone to any and all things addictive. That, and his career background as a monetarily disappointing small-time burglar and drug dealer. "Don't forget commitment, prison, and homelessness."

He wasn't anybody, and he was becoming less of anybody every single hour of his life. It really had bothered him. That is, what had bothered him was that he had the ability to recognize how poorly his life had gone. It had bothered him because it had also meant that he was capable of wanting things that his limited abilities could never provide.

He wasn't climbing. He wasn't even maintaining the ground he had. His wheels were spinning, but the painful downward slide of his life had commenced nonetheless. In reality, he'd been sliding down that slope for years, but in your early twenties you were sort of given a free pass to be a loser. Jack's pass had been punched, then it had been turned over and stamped on the backside despite its expiration date, and then he'd borrowed somebody else's pass. Then he had gotten that one punched too.

He hadn't had any opinion on what he should do about

his situation. It had seemed even sadder that he was now depressed about being a loser amongst burnouts. Even his stoner manager had been going to night school. Jack hated the melodrama, but if somebody had told him what he was in for before he was born, he would have refused to go.

Life seemed to him to be a series of shitty and painful situations with occasional and momentary pleasure. It was like sitting in a park on a fall morning after drinking all night, the only time Jack actually liked being awake in the morning. There was always a couple of hours between the time you ran out of beer at four, and when it went back on sale at six. When that first morning 40oz got cracked open, the smell of the brown bag always mixed with that pungent malt liquor smell. Holding the neck of the bottle as you walked to your destination always conformed the brown bag into the shape of the 40oz bottle inside. It always looked like a little missile, warhead, or torpedo wrapped like a parcel, ready for the mail. Those moments were perfect, but that wasn't life. That was respite from life.

Punishment was life. Humans adapted, and eventually they thrived on what they were fed, regardless of what it was. Jack's life was about failure, and hardship. Jack had been forced to hurt and fail to thrive, and by thrive he meant slow down his inevitable decline. He couldn't be nourished on anything else. Whenever he had been, he had shut down. Clearly, this was ironic and sad for him, but necessary and true nonetheless. "I fuckin' bet it's pretty common, too. I bet a lot of fuckers are stuck in the same shitty boat as me. Well, maybe a little better boat than mine, but still a pretty fucked-up boat"

Jack probably knew things weren't ever going to get better for him. Actually, he always figured they'd get worse, or stay equally shitty. Making it on time to his next metaphorical beating was his purpose. "Crappy food, shitty booze, nasty cigarettes, miserable job, uninhabitable livin' conditions, these are my joy!" He had enjoyed his occasional respite, but, like a Spartan warrior, he had sought only more hardship. Unlike a Spartan warrior, he had done it because life had never handed him another option. Maybe he had sought it out all along; maybe there was another option. But likely not.

Even the one with the greatest stamina for pain and failure eventually tires. Jack believed his next trip to Western State was right around the corner. It would provide some respite, but he had started to seriously desire his ultimate respite. Jack had been running for years, but hungover on that cool wet fall morning, he had known all he'd accomplished was to run in a circle right back to a locked mental ward, right back to where his story had begun.

Chapter 38

But that was when Jack was twenty-five. When he was thirty, he stole Dolores's Volkswagen, and drove to Utah to get some fresh air. That four-year period after Jack's trip to Utah wasn't kind to him. The saddest part of Jack's story is still to come, and the saddest part of his story you'll have.

The final time Jack was committed to Western State Hospital, he was thirty-four. The new millennium was an old story, and the world had accepted the Internet as an indispensable staple of life on planet Earth. Every time Jack had been there, or somewhere similar to there, he'd come at the discretion of the court system or doctor's authority, but on that last occasion, he'd all but come to the front door and begged to be let in.

That time, he'd lost a couple more friends, and a few more years of a remarkably wasted life. In his mind, he'd had the illusion that Beth would somehow not remember him or that she'd moved on. It had been years since he'd quietly left her apartment. Somehow, during all those years, he'd managed to not get committed to Western State. Deinstitutionalization had firmly taken root in the United States, and people like Jack didn't necessarily end up in the state mental hospitals with the frequency they used to. That wasn't to say he'd been living as normal people did.

Since leaving Beth's apartment that day, he'd lived as a crusty punk street migrant, a successful burglar for the first time, a successful drug dealer for the second time, and done that stretch at Fairfax before meeting Dolores. He'd lived in county jails, halfway houses, subsidized government housing, and on the streets again at least a dozen times in some seemingly unending cycle.

Since turning thirty, he'd mostly transitioned from a sporadically transient young man, who the system found resources for, into a hardened adult vagrant and criminal, who the system opted to lock up in county jails for weeks or months at a time awaiting trial on petty offenses. Typically, he wound up sentenced to weeks or months in the same county jails over and over again after being convicted of the same petty offenses over and over again.

By thirty-four, his list of misdemeanor convictions had risen to thirty or more, but Jack had long since lost count. There were no more second chances for Jack, and he'd passed the age where his antics were still cute. He'd also passed the age where his appearance still endeared him to the sort of women that had used to take pity on him.

He could never be locked up for long, because his offenses were always the petty crimes that accompanied indigency. He was never committed anymore because of deinstitutionaliz ation, and because he'd been so mentally ill for so long his mental illness appeared to be his baseline. It was so much his baseline, and so well did he wear it by that point, that his competency to stand trial was never even raised in at least ten misdemeanor cases against him during the course of those hardest four years.

He did his time in whatever county jail he found himself, at which point he was always released onto a downtown sidewalk somewhere to resume his depressing survival hustle. The world was essentially just waiting for him to die so that, in so doing, he would solve the problem that his existence created for the people in it.

One morning, when he was thirty-four, he was roused by a corrections officer. He was in King County Jail. It took him a moment to realize that. When you woke up in different places often enough, that lackadaisical state of reassurance that most people experienced when waking up eventually disappeared. It was replaced with a skipped heartbeat and ice-cold blood shooting through one's veins, the trauma of a fight or flight response. He was put out on Fifth Avenue in downtown Seattle on a frozen February day, wearing clean but ugly clothes that had come from the jail's clothing donation room, which the jail maintained for prisoners being released without the clothes they arrived in. The clothes Jack had arrived in a few weeks earlier had been severely soiled, and were disposed of in a biohazard bin. Jack couldn't count the number of times he'd been shooed out the front door of King County Jail onto that same spot on Fifth Avenue, no direction about what to do next, no lawyer, social worker, or probation officer to point him in the direction of services he might utilize.

He'd just been released on the theft charge he'd been held on. The convenience store where he'd stolen a bag of Cheetos and 40oz of Olde English 800 had lacked functional tapes in their surveillance cameras, and they had lacked a now in-the-wind employee to come and testify to Jack committing the theft. The city had dismissed the case, but Jack didn't even know that. He had probably been informed by the jail staff or his public defender. They had probably given him court papers when he was discharged, but Jack wouldn't have bothered to read them at that point.

They were just another stack of papers to him. Sometimes, they said he'd completed his sentence following conviction. Sometimes, they said your bail had been posted by such and such nonprofit bail fund and you were required to appear in court on such and such date. Sometimes, they said the case you were being held on had been dismissed by the city for lack of evidence. What they said didn't matter. That day, he was out. On any random day before that, he was incarcerated. Inevitably, on some day in the near future, he'd be incarcerated again. Jack had learned something about present-sense awareness and living in the now, something most supposedly successful people never figured out.

Jack had one task at that moment, and he got about it right away. He walked down to Pioneer Square, where he began rifling through the recycling bins of large downtown buildings. Truth be told, he was rifling through recycling bins during the entire walk down to Pioneer Square. He was looking for something specific. He didn't find it along the way, but after six or seven recycling bins near Pioneer Square he found what he was looking for. It was a relatively intact refrigerator box. Some office suite in the high floors above must have had to replace the refrigerator in their office's kitchenette. He carted it over to the Yesler overpass.

From past experience, Jack knew that getting a spot under Yesler could be difficult. It was a prime spot, and people who had spots down there didn't like giving them up. That day he was lucky, and there was just enough space for his Maytag box right on the south side of the overpass. He saw some friendly familiar faces amongst the other tramps, and one or two that he actually knew fairly well. He knew as people currently camped down there disappeared, which they always did on account of being arrested or hospitalized, that he'd be able to move closer to the warmer, dryer center of the overpass within a few days. The center was where they'd get the barrel fire going at night.

Once someone staked out a spot, it was hands-off for at least a few hours at a time. The hobo code. With his new home secure, he began to prowl for anything that he could trade for a hit. It didn't take long. Jack was looking for unlocked car doors when he saw some guy at a bus stop set his backpack down next to him on the bench. Jack got a running start and was around the corner at Fourth and Washington before the guy even realized what had just happened. Within ten minutes, Jack was around the corner of the same block at City Hall Park trading the Sony Discman and a handful of CDs to the dope man for a hit of heroin. He kept the backpack.

Years back, Beth had extensively searched Pioneer Square for Jack. She had quite unwisely walked through City Hall Park and through the Yesler overpass looking for him. He just hadn't made it there yet. She had searched almost daily for over a year, and sporadically after that. She had never really stopped looking, but after a few years, she had resigned herself to accepting that Jack might not ever resurface. One thing was for sure, she was certainly not searching the Yesler overpass all those years later.

One morning Jack woke up back in Tacoma at the Vagabond Motel. "The Vagabond was actually in Lakewood, but close enough." Was it morning? Afternoon? It really didn't matter.

He remembered coming there when he was fifteen to party with some people. It was the first time he had ever gotten blackout drunk. He had drunk a whole bottle of Orange Jubilee Mad Dog and some beer. That night, another guy had fucked his girlfriend. "Man, I woke up with a hangover, and a slut for a girlfriend. But whatever, I guess. I mean I went to bed with a slut for a girlfriend, I just didn't know it yet. But I definitely didn't go to bed with the hangover. I'd have noticed that!"

It didn't seem like nineteen years ago to Jack, but it had been. To Jack, memories never seemed like they had happened a long time ago. He assumed, since he spent most of the hours of the day in alcoholic blackouts, that the memories must have seemed closer in time because there was so much missing time in the interim. There was that, and the fact that nothing ever changed in Tacoma.

Things changed in Seattle. Everything changed in Seattle, but in Tacoma, nothing changed. Even the buildings were never torn down, not even the ones that should have been torn down. The run-down Taco Bell building became a check-cashing place. The Safeway that was literally falling over turned into a Goodwill. The gas station somehow transformed into a teriyaki restaurant even though the decommissioned pumps were still outside.

"Seriously, it's the fuckin' weirdest thing you ever seen. They got fuckin' outdoor tables right next to the old decommissioned pumps that still have the fuckin' Arco logo on 'em. And ain't no fuckin' place to sit inside neither cos it's a fuckin' gas station, right! They don't even have those shitty table umbrellas out there for you. Christ's sake, it's Western fuckin' Washington. Didn't those people that opened the teriyaki place think puttin' up some fuckin' umbrellas for their customers would be nice? It rains all the goddamn time here. You want to sit down and eat, and you're, like, gettin' soaked by the pissin' fuckin' rain! Good spicy chicken teriyaki though, seriously, check it out."

Certainly, the Vagabond never changed. Why would it? As long as the rooms had four walls and working lights, teenagers would come to drink and get high with their friends. In nineteen years, it hadn't changed one iota. And it probably hadn't changed in the fifty years prior to that. Tacoma had the unique ability to remain the same no matter what happened elsewhere. That motel had remained consistently dirty, and dirty in the same fashion, for all those years.

Even the cars in Tacoma never got any newer; they'd had the same era of cars Jack's whole life, the same old shitty economy models with no options, in the same disrepair as the night that guy Lee had fucked his girlfriend all those years ago. The Vagabond had the same old lady owner sitting at the front counter renting rooms, just sitting there smoking cigarettes for nineteen years, and she hadn't aged a day. Of course, she hadn't gotten any younger, either. "That bitch was old and ugly when I was fifteen, and she was old and ugly when I was thirty-four. She'll probably be old and ugly fifty years from now when I'm in a fuckin' box of abandoned ash sitting' on a shelf at the county crematorium. God, that bitch is ugly as puke, old as shit too!"

Just when Jack thought he was the only one that had changed around there, he realized he was wrong. The cars weren't actually the same, they were just new shitty old cars. Fifteen-year-old Jack was still at the Vagabond, it's just that he was now some fifteen-year-old named Chad or Jerry. Jack was the thirty-four-year-old homeless alcoholic guy that fifteen-year-old Jack had used to laugh at.

Nobody tore the buildings down, that much was true, but, just like people, they all entered the next sad phase of their existence and fulfilled their depressing purposes while eagerly awaiting a wrecking ball that never came. Even the ugly bitch who owned the Vagabond had changed. The old ugly bitch at the counter was actually the daughter of the owner who was the old ugly bitch who had always been at the manager's office when he was a teenager. Back then, the daughter had been in her early thirties. She had worked the grave shift after her mom's shift was over. Her perfect ass had always stretched the seams of a worn-in pair of Levi's, and her cleavage had always been half out of a low-cut t-shirt. Back then, Jack had been in love. Somewhere along the line, she had become her ugly old mom.

Jack couldn't see it in himself when he looked in the mirror in his room at the Vagabond; Jack still saw twenty-one-year-old Jack. He saw the Jack that girls had lined up to fix, but it was a fact that while a mirror might cast an accurate reflection of a person, an accurate reflection was not what a person looking in it perceived. It didn't matter if he could see it himself; he realized what other people saw, and he was all of a sudden envious of that old bitch's daughter. When he started to think about how he'd look at her age, she all of a sudden seemed a lot more vibrant and attractive than he'd given her credit for.

Jack's room at the Vagabond looked out over Pacific High-way to an ampm. A windfall of funds from a lucky encounter with a very careless heroin dealer had provided him the cash he was using to rent the room and buy the beer. He and another junkie hobo had rolled this particular heroin dealer when he was stupid enough to come down through City Hall Park after he'd been drinking at a downtown bar. Jack and his hobo partner had recognized the dealer right away. They had also recognized his intoxicated state. They both assumed he was holding, and their decision to roll him hadn't even been discussed, just acted on. They had been two predators closing on prey and instinct alone had guided their actions. Jack had picked up a club-sized downed branch and closed on the dealer. Within ten seconds, Jack had clubbed him like a baby seal, and his predator partner had grabbed the bag that dealer always had his stash in.

They split the stash, but Jack hadn't even stuck around the Yesler overpass for the rest of the night. Everybody under that overpass would know what Jack was holding within an hour, and then he'd be the prey before morning came. He had walked south, past the stadiums. Down by the SoDo train tracks, he'd found a comfy little loading dock to catch some sleep in. He had gotten out his kit, lit up the spoon, drawn up a hit, and zonked out until morning. When he had woken up, he'd known he had to get out of Seattle for a while. He no longer knew anyone in Seattle to sell a significant stash of heroin to, not anyone he trusted. It had been a few years since he'd actually dealt drugs. He still had friends in Tacoma that he could safely unload the stash to, albeit at a discount of what it was worth. He had needed to sell it. If he hadn't sold it, he'd have shot it in a couple of days. Then he'd have been right back under the Yesler overpass chasing his next hit while simultaneously suffering withdrawal. He had been on a bus headed south before it was completely light out.

It seemed like a long walk to the ampm for another bottle of

Night Train or a 40oz of Olde English 800. The walk seemed to get longer every few hours when the need for smokes or another bottle arose in him. He thought it might be because every trip down there might be the one where he didn't come back to the motel at all. Jack had been trying to work up the nerve to commit himself for days, but every time he got down to the payphone, he lost his nerve. For some reason he wouldn't call from his room. Inside Room 311 everything seemed safe as long as the booze and smokes held out. There was a bed, a TV, and somewhere to piss and shit. It was also someplace to puke, something Jack was doing with more and more frequency on account of his liver being effectively shot and the heroin withdrawal he had been enduring. In his state, there was no longer any need for food. Jack managed his nutritional needs between microwave burritos at the ampm and the candy vending machine that was over by the icemaker at the Vagabond.

Every trip, he intended to make the call from the payphone. Most of the time, he got his backpack together and gathered any personal items he still planned on keeping and headed out the door toward the payphone, but every time he just ended up standing there in the store with a bottle in his hand. There was always a good excuse to put it off for another day, a few more hours, or for another bottle. Maybe there was a movie coming on that would make him nostalgic for other times. Since he used very little of the heroin before selling it, there was enough cash to survive at the Vagabond for a little while longer. Since he'd switched from heroin back to alcohol, he wouldn't run out of money buying more heroin. Drinking a few hundred dollars takes a lot longer than shooting it, and Jack needed that extra time to follow through on what he had come there to do. Sometimes he even lost his nerve before he left the room. If he didn't grab his backpack before he headed out, he knew he wasn't making the call that time. Those trips were actually better than the ones where he went through the whole dog and pony show of bringing his stuff with him. At least there were no expectations on him to follow through on those trips. The other times were harder.

One afternoon he got himself together in a hurry. He must have been thirsty the night before, because he'd drunk his eye-opener before he went to bed. After an entire day's sleep without any alcohol, he was in sad shape. Shaking all over, with a cigarette clinched between his lips, he started the walk toward the store. Regardless of whether he made the call this time or not, he'd still need that eye-opener just to get the shakes off him. It would be easy enough to grab a bottle, sit by the phone, and wait for the cops to show up. When they pulled up, he'd dust off the bottle and butt out his last smoke before they took them away from him, then off to the ward. He hadn't come to the Vagabond to commit himself, but at some point, Jack's plan to commit suicide had morphed into a last-ditch attempt to get back into Western State. He figured, if he played it right this time, he could stay there forever.

Walking down that row of rooms at the Vagabond always reminded him of walking down the wing of a single-floor prison. Shitty motels always reminded Jack a little bit of incarceration. The ones with second floors and covered walkways just reminded him of the types of prison wings with second floors and catwalks. They had the same type of layout, and they had the same type of desperation about them.

As he was crossing the street, he had that now-familiar feeling of being somewhere completely foreign despite coming out that way several times a day. Deterioration of his mind secondary to substance abuse could explain it. After all, with everything that had been done to Jack's mind by that point, it would be odd if anything ever seemed normal. But he figured it had more to do with the foreign nature of the action he was about to take. Jack had been committed many times, but he couldn't remember ever affirmatively requesting it, though maybe he had. His mind was so shot that he genuinely couldn't remember. It was the way an Alzheimer's patient or baby must have felt: complete unfamiliarity with the familiar.

Jack's heart was beating out of his chest at the proposition of getting himself committed. He then recognized that it was really going to happen that time. He was finally willing to go through with it. For a few minutes, he stared across the street at his destination, at the payphone that he'd walked away from at least forty times over the last couple of weeks. Cars whizzed in front of him, occluding his view momentarily. "It was Tacoma, so of course they were old shitty economy models with no options, but when they passed, that payphone was there again." During a break in the traffic, he spit out his smoke and walked with a purpose toward it.

Chapter 39

Sometimes, Jack started off being very deliberate with the way he went about doing a thing because he needed it to seem perfect. Jack, of course, had OCD. Sometimes, though, he did it because he wanted to remember every detail of what he perceived to be a pivotal event in his life. Earlier had been one of those times. There he was, taking little mental snapshots of his own stride, flicking his smoke into the street, on his way to take back control of his life once and for all. He viewed it in his mind from a third-person perspective, like there was a camera crew filming him. It was all very dramatic. Sometime during that dramatic event, Jack's resolve faltered again. Then, he was right back in Room 311, sucking down beers and smoking cigarettes. It was later in the afternoon by that point. Jack's stomach was pretty upset, so he was drinking some weak Miller High Life. The malt liquor he normally drank was straight gut rot. The Mad Dog, Thunderbird, and Night Train were no better.

The next afternoon, Jack sat by that payphone for over an hour, and he took note of everything that happened. He decided to switch it up so he drank Wild Irish Rose and ate a hot dog while people came and went. No more than a handful ever bothered to notice him sitting on the curb. Over and over again, he told himself that he was just going to eat something to settle his stomach before making that three-digit phone call. For a while after that, he tried to keep track of the black ants that navigated the asphalt desert of the ampm parking lot. For about half an hour, it was an interesting glance into ant culture. Watching them pick up objects bigger than their own bodies and then set off for some unseen home base back in the bushes behind the phones somewhere was fascinating. They would dodge broken shards of glass, pebbles, and cigarette butts with a twig that weighed the equivalent of a fully-loaded pickup truck. All Jack could think was that if ants were humans, they would never have to go to the gym, and they'd still kick all the humans' asses. Thank God, he thought, ants weren't humans. But ants only seemed interesting until Jack needed more booze, and before he could even consider that he was supposed to be getting himself committed, he had another bottle in his hand and a smoke hanging out of his mouth. By the time he was halfway done with that bottle, he was too buzzed to go to Western State, so he just grabbed an armload of Olde English 40oz's and two packs of Camels before going back to shitty Room 311.

A couple days after that, Jack hadn't made any further attempts to commit himself when he decided he'd head over to Todd's place for a visit. His cowardly behavior the other day was already scrubbed from his squeaky-clean mind. Alcohol had been a good cleanser for him, always had. It left everything spotless, even minds.

None of it really mattered right then, since, within a few days the money he'd gotten from the heroin would run out. When that happened, he'd be out of a room and out of money for booze. There was no other easy payday around the corner. That heroin dealer in City Hall Park was a gift and an aberration, nothing more. When the money from that dealer's heroin was gone, he'd either be back under an overpass or committed to Western State. Jack had had enough of the former; the latter needed to happen.

Something else was becoming an issue for Jack. By that time, it was getting harder and harder to keep his mind focused. Even when he wasn't drunk, he was confused all the time. One of those days, sitting by the payphone, he got up to get a bottle from the ampm, and when he came out, he found a full bottle sitting on the curb where he'd been sitting just a few minutes earlier. He'd just woken up, and wasn't even drunk, but he still had no recollection of buying the bottle. A few days before that, while he was buying a bottle, his total had come up on the cash register and he hadn't been able to make sense of the numbers. It was the same bottle he had bought a hundred times before, and the total was the same as it had always been, but he hadn't been able to make sense of the numbers on the cash register screen. It had been as though he'd never seen numbers before. Also, he hadn't been able to count the dollar bills in his wallet. He was stone-cold sober, it was first thing in the morning, and the cashier had needed to count Jack's money for him. "Well, it wasn't really first thing in the mornin,' more like my mornin,' which was like one thirty in the afternoon." A few days later, he had realized he couldn't read any of the words on a page in the newspaper. The confusion was bad enough, but by that time Jack also shook all over, whether he was drunk or not.

The day Jack went to visit Todd, he started walking to his house. He still liked walking, and it wasn't like he had anything he was going to be late for. Todd's apartment was pretty far, and it was raining pretty hard, but it always rained. Jack stopped at a bus stop after he'd walked about a mile nonetheless. It wasn't the rain—again, it rained all the time. He was afraid that if he walked all the way to Todd's he'd get too drunk on the way and black out.

Jack was soaked, and the bus was a greenhouse. That's what happened when you put twenty-five wet people in a metal box and turned the heat on. Instant greenhouse. Jack couldn't tell how much of the dampness he felt was rain or sweat. As he sat in the little hard plastic tandem bus seat, he hoped Todd's car was running so that he could give Jack a ride back to the motel. That was Jack's last trip anywhere before he took the big trip to Western State. He didn't have enough money to go anywhere else, and he was pretty sure he only had enough money for three more days of rent and booze.

Chapter 40

"Have I mentioned that I'd been having a hard time keepin' my mind focused around that time? Well, I had, and it was fuckin' infuriatin.' Back then, I considered findin' some hyperactive kid and stealin' his Ritalin."

Jack's visit with Todd didn't happen. During the last few years, Todd had let Jack crash at his place often and given him money here and there. He could have lived there, and Todd had offered, but at that juncture Jack preferred to only impose on Todd when he was really hard up. At that point in life, Jack chose to self-destruct on his own. Todd never expected to be paid back, and, as always, he held onto Jack's record collection for him.

When Jack finally got off the bus at Todd's place, it didn't look right. His car was gone. That was strange, because, even if his car was running, Todd never left home for more than an hour at a time, mostly just to get weed, cigarettes, and food. When Jack got up to Todd's apartment, he could see in through the window. Everything was different. Jack didn't know who lived there, but based on the décor, he knew it wasn't Todd's place anymore.

It turned out some girl lived there now. She started beating on the window and threatening to call 911 when she saw Jack peering through her window. For a minute Jack had some hope that she was just some girl that had moved in with Todd, but when he inquired, she just yelled "This is my apartment. I don't know any Todd."

It shouldn't have surprised him. People moved, and Jack had been in the wind for a long time. He could have found Todd if he'd looked around a little. He could have called the last phone number he had for Ron. For that matter, he could have called the last number he had for Todd. He could have called Todd's number from his motel room before he went over there in the first place, but he had just wanted to show up. Todd may have moved, but he had probably kept his phone number. Todd had moved before, but he'd always kept that same number. If he'd looked, he could have found Todd. If he'd looked, he could have found any of them, Beth, Ron, even his brother Laurence. He just didn't want to anymore. It was still raining, but it had let up a bit. He decided to walk back to the Vagabond, and by that time it really didn't matter if he blacked out on the way, so he stopped and got a bottle of Thunderbird.

Right then, he knew he wasn't even really trying to find Todd that day at all. If he had been, he would have found him. It was just the last of the last excuses he could indulge before the inevitable. There was a payphone in an ampm parking lot waiting for him to make a three-digit phone call, and he'd avoided it long enough.

Chapter 41

If there was one thing Jack had an abundance of in his life, it was time to ponder his situation and reflect on his actions. Not that it had given him any insight into himself. None that had helped him to understand or navigate the world any better, anyway. Whether it was time well-spent on someone that reflected and made adjustments to better meet life on life's terms, or time completely wasted on someone that would never understand how to get by, it was time that existed. Jack couldn't do shit with it. He never could, and he would never be able to. It was a flaw. He had a thousand of them, but Jack was actually a pretty lovable guy. How could someone be so fatalistically miserable but also be the person that you had the best time with? How could someone be so fucked up, but seem so close to savable. Who knows, but it was true. How it was true is simply a question without an answer.

Jack was a Thorozine zombie after that. He routinely took comfort in that fact that he wasn't a drooler or wall walker, just a garden variety Thorozine zombie. Since everyone was on Thorozine at Western State, he never gave it a designation like the other groups around there, the Cliff Claven, droolers, etc. He'd also never been as snowed as he was at Western

State that time.They kept him zombified twenty-four hours a day. Those poor wall walkers and droolers didn't have a sense of themselves left. Even pumped full of Thorozine, Jack still periodically remembered himself, who he was, what he was about. For better or worse, there was still some Jack left inside Jack's skull, but not much. Those poor wall walkers and droolers, their foreheads might as well have had neon signs affixed to them, flashing the word "VACANT." "Shit, you could nail the fuckin' signs to those fuckers' foreheads. They wouldn't even know the difference. No-fuckin'-body home! Trust me when I fuckin' tell you that."

After he settled in, he started spending most of his time just roaming around the ward. That is, he would roam when he wasn't too comatose to get out of bed. There was no way to tell how many hours of the day he spent in bed wide awake but too doped up to realize he was conscious. When his head was clear enough to think about it, mostly while he was roaming around, he figured it was a lot of the hours of the day. If he were being honest with himself, he'd have said most of the hours of the day were likely spent in that state. For Jack, the number of hours of the day where he was able to form these somewhat coherent thoughts and inquiries was pretty limited. The remainder of his thoughts were distorted and bizarre. He figured he'd been at Western State for several months. It was sunny outside, and inside his ward it was unbearably hot every day. When he got there, it was definitely cold and wet every day. When he wasn't comatose, he had an extremely restless feeling emanating from inside him. It forced him to roam constantly. He had been sure the feeling was a side effect of one of the medications he was on. He wondered why Beth wasn't there too, but during those hours he mostly roamed.

Chapter 42

Jack was fading into the mosaic of that place fast. Then, one day, he wasn't. One day, he was in a warm bed in a small two-bedroom house in the Hawthorne District of Portland Oregon. There was money on the table in the kitchen, so he took it and walked to the Plaid Pantry and got some Tim's Cascade Jalapeño potato chips and a Coke. It all seemed very normal and familiar, but he had no idea why. He knew his way there, and he knew his way back to the house he'd woken up in. It felt like a routine, even though he couldn't remember doing it before. He went back to the house where he'd woken up. He went inside and turned on the TV. The news was on, and it was about a war in Iraq or Afghanistan. Both? Jack wasn't really listening, but he couldn't have told you where the war was even if he had been, but probably Iraq or Afghanistan. A car pulled up in the driveway. A minute later, Beth walked in wearing turquoise scrubs.

She'd been in Portland for a about six years. She was an RN working in the ER at OHSU Hospital now. Her old boss at Western State had called her when she saw Jack was a patient on one of the wards. Beth had spent several months and a great deal of time and money arranging for Jack to be released to her care, which he ultimately was.

Jack had actually been living with her for about two years. Sometimes he knew that. Sometimes he didn't. Sometimes he knew that he lived there with Beth but didn't know for how long. Sometimes he knew everything and was pretty normal. Those were the days when they'd go for a drive and have a picnic.

Beth deserved something better, and she could have had it. She wouldn't have taken it, though. She wouldn't have taken that something better if it had been delivered to her door wrapped in a million dollars. Her something better was Jack. Most people would agree that her something better was something much worse, but she would've spent every cent in the world to get it. Getting him there did cost her nearly every cent she had in the world, but he was there. They were both there. That was all.

Afterword

After much nudging from friends, editors, and random readers I have grudgingly agreed to write this Afterword. I will not, however, write an epilogue. When I finish a book, the end is the end. If I wanted the reader to know every single little thing that happened to the characters after the book ended, I would have just written a longer book. Besides, wondering what might have happened after a story is over is one of my favorite parts of reading a book. All my favorite books have always given me a framework for conjecture and speculation about the characters and their motives without over explaining. Also, epilogues always remind me of those lame where are they now epilogue scenes in movies like Animal House.

My endings are abrupt, and with this book, I've had several people ask me, "Are you going to write another down and out book?" The answer is no. There isn't much left for Jack to do at this point, and I think he's earned a rest to be perfectly honest. Despite the fact that many readers think the end of down and out is sort of a bummer, I've always thought of it as Jack's happy ending. If you disagree, you should see the original manuscript's ending. I dug it up the other day, and I'd forgotten how truly dark it was.

In any case, Jack does make his presence known across my other work. He has at least one short story in the collection I intend to publish next year, and he makes a cameo in *Professional Camouflage* and *A Lack of Intradimenesional Sync* (which is about half done). I love Jack, and I loved bringing him to life, but he's a handful. While it's true that he's fictional, it's also true there's a lot of parts of real people stuffed into him. Also, Jack exists in a drug and music scene that I really wanted to accurately memorialize out of respect to all my friends that aren't around anymore, but that I really haven't felt a part of in decades. Basically, getting into the mindset to tell a Jack story can be emotionally draining on me because much of it hits so close to home. Plus, I like to create new characters and stories, so I'm pretty confident there will be no more full-on Jack books. Sorry.

If you're still not satisfied, I'd suggest you imagine a present-day Jack—it's 2025, so he's in his mid-fifties—smoking Camels and drinking coffee. He's sitting in his living room watching TV and waiting for Beth to get home from work.

About the Author

I was a homeless teenager. Now I own a home. I was a high school dropout. Now I'm an attorney. I was an alcoholic. Now I'm sober. I was a kid well into adulthood. Now I'm the adult parent of kids. I was alone. Now I have people. I was a punk rock teenager. Now I'm a punk rock middleager. I was Jack. Now I'm Chris.

Also by Christopher J. Stockwell

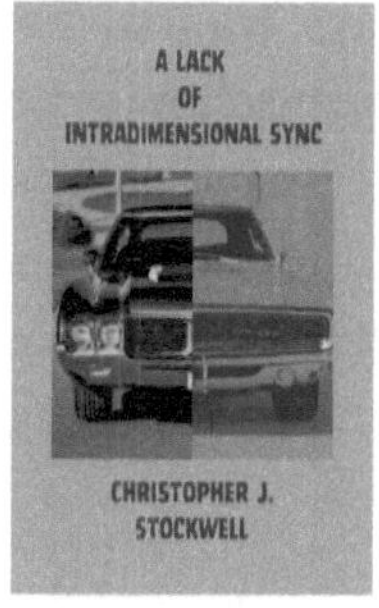

A Lack of Intradimensional Sync
What's real if you don't know if you're awake?   What if you are awake, but everything is unreal? Jon slips in and out of what most people accept to be their reality. he slips in and out of his own dimension, and onto the road.

Planned Release January 2026

City Attorney's Office: Book One: Professional Camouflage
Above the down and out city, attorneys toil away. Maria's Working-class roots keep her humble. A one-ton chip on his shoulder keeps Ben discontent. Erin's Blue-blooded pedigree creates for her unattainable expectations. They're not the lawyers Seattle deserves, but they're the ones it's got.

City Attorney's Office Book Two: The-Land of Lollipops and Suckers

Now that Ben understands how to wield the power of the prosecutor's office, how will he use it. He's always wanted for someone to let him inside the machine so he can mess around with the gears and pulleys. Will that government machine make him a good little cog, or will he throw ideological money wrenches into it. We sort of already know the answer, but watching how he gets there is usually entertaining.

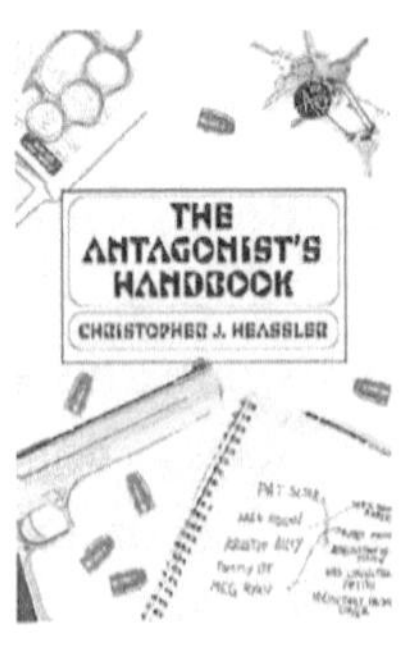

The Antagonist's Handbook

A pair of losers from the PNW start out for stardom by moving to Los Angeles. After becoming paparazzi, they soon figure out that they can blackmail celebrities into posing for their photos. Eventually, they launch their own tabloid. This is out of print.I don't even have a copy, and I can't find the contract with the publishing house, so I don't know if I own the rights. That's what happens when you drink too much whiskey and snort too much coke. If you find a copy,let me know. I'll buy it off you.

www.ingramcontent.com/pod-product-compliance
Lightning Source LLC
Chambersburg PA
CBHW020240010826
48973CB00006B/1586